the Last Place
YOU LOOK

One

"OH DEAR, I think you might be too qualified."

Sophie Tindall adjusted her smile at Warren, the seemingly sweet octogenarian with faded blue eyes and a grin that turned his paper-thin skin into a concertina.

"I hope not." Her attention skittered around the packed common room at Roseford Aged Care Facility. Maybe Warren was right. Maybe her decision to volunteer here *was* an odd choice. "I might have a medical degree, but I still have six years of psychiatry training to complete when I return home to the UK. There's always more to learn."

"Oh, don't get me wrong, dear, I'm glad you've been matched with me." He gestured to the other elderly residents and their volunteer visitors seated at the gray Formica tables around him, then shot her a wink, along with a chuckle. His rough-but-cheery demeanor reminded her of her late father. "I'm the envy of every other codger in here. I'm not complaining."

She returned his laughter and sent her gaze once more across the room. The hum of chatter ricocheted off the cream-colored walls, and the musky scent of people mixed with the light burn of antiseptic floor cleaner. She opened her mouth, about to thank Warren for the compliment, when her stare slammed into a set of deep, espresso eyes.

Her heart stammered, but she turned back to Warren, ignoring the rugged, younger man appraising her from across the room.

"You're doing me a favor, really." She widened her smile, the expression a strain against her hammering pulse. "I plan to use some of my free time in Australia to meet people from your demographic. You see, I want to specialize in geriatric psychiatry."

He clapped his hands in exaggerated delight, leaning back in his seat, oblivious to the beautiful stranger staring her down from behind him. "Ahh. So, I'm your guinea pig then?"

She nodded and chanced another look at *the starer*, a man perhaps in his mid-thirties, sitting next to a woman who appeared to be in her late sixties. She was a little on the younger side for an aged care resident, but it wasn't unheard of.

Sophie refocused on Warren, vowing to set *the starer* aside for now. "I hope you don't mind."

"Of course not." Warren interlaced his fingers over his generous belly. "I could listen to your lovely accent all day. Tell me, what part of the UK do you come from?"

"I live in London, but I'm Scarborough born and raised, sir."

The muscles behind her eyes hurt from fighting the compulsion to watch the man behind Warren again. The heat and mystery in the stranger's dark gaze called straight to the core of why she'd come to Australia. To live a little. To embark on an adventure.

Oh, stop sugar coating this. I want to get laid!

Electricity zipped up her spine, and she shivered at the blunt self-confession.

"Sir?" Warren huffed out a laugh, kindly eyes glittering anew. "Oh, you are a dear, but plain old Warren will serve just fine. We're soon-to-be-friends, aren't we?"

The tension dropped from her shoulders. He had a point; she was here to befriend him, and despite Mr. Dark and Mysterious staring her down—despite her inclination toward staunch professionalism—she could afford to relax a little.

She jutted her chin toward the self-serve tea station. "Say, how about I get us a cup of tea, and then we can get to know each other better?"

He gave a quick nod of approval. "I'll have a white with two sugars. Thanks."

She wrapped her fingers around the rough, crimson fabric on her chair's armrests and pushed herself to standing. "Coming right up."

Even as she walked, she sensed the sexy stranger's glare burn into her back. Or maybe it was more a *hope* than a *sense*. That those alluring, chocolate-noir eyes hadn't left her. That he followed her with as much intrigue as she had for him.

She approached the tea station, and her stomach clenched. She was a bonafide-nerd, someone who preferred books over booty calls. She had no place feeling excitement over this guy's notice. Nothing in her past prepared her for how to connect with a man as rugged and handsome as the one who'd wrenched her attention just minutes earlier.

His warm, olive skin and enigmatic gaze alone demanded notice, much less that coarse-but-still-sexy, indented scar along the top left of his forehead. She hadn't yet found the nerve to appraise his lips, though she figured when she did that they, too, would offer a promise of easy confidence and great sex.

A shiver worked up her spine at the word *sex*.

Okay sure, she was overanalyzing what were a couple of split-second glances, but overanalyzing was ingrained into her personality. Besides, her body recognized his intensity and hoped he'd maybe share a small degree of attraction toward her, too.

She filled two paper cups with boiled water and held one in her hand to warm her palm, leaving the other to sit on the table while the tea steeped. For so long, her life had consisted of one safe choice after another—anything to keep from rocking the foundations of trust she'd decimated amongst her family so many years ago.

But she'd tossed aside *safe choices* the day she decided to come to Australia.

Her thoughts looped over her reasons for being here. Those reasons were two-pronged. First, she'd wanted to embark on informal volunteer work while she had some rare time to do so. Second, she'd ended a four-year relationship with Hector Winthrop in order to escape the mundane life she'd built back at home. A life of predictable relationships and musty text books—a life now dedicated to playing catch-up on a great deal of personal discovery.

Any decent psychiatrist worth their salt needed life experience. And just like any decent psychiatrist, she also needed to make peace with her hang-ups—to do away with caution and find some freedom.

She would let life rough her up a little—or perhaps, again—but with a lot less carnage this time.

Maybe the sleepy town of Roseford wasn't the most daring place to start. But Luke, her tech CEO brother, had been kind enough to offer her free use of his country cabin. As a cash-strapped student, she'd jumped at the chance. From there, she'd been lucky to scrape together enough funds for plane tickets, a hire car, and a bit of spending money.

She already lived in a major city back home, so drew the line at residing under Luke's nose at his Melbourne home. And Roseford's big, community aged care facility, with its volunteer program, meant she could work on her people skills. So maybe living in the sticks would be a welcome change after all.

"Want to grab a drink?"

She jolted, stilling just in time to not pour hot tea on her black leggings.

Burnt umber eyes glinted mere inches from her own. Mr. Dark and Mysterious's gaze did a slow glide over her body. Like a man full of devious, delicious secrets. *Like a man imagining her naked.* Though whatever he imagined probably didn't match the reality of what hid beneath her olive-green tunic—a pair of sensible, beige-cotton underwear with a stupidly high waist.

She lowered her teacup to the table. "I. Ah. You're asking me out?"

Full lips curved higher. "I mean, not now. After the old timers clear off."

His soft rumble wafted over her like smooth butterscotch, and he stood a little too close. But even his close proximity added an air of natural intimacy.

This guy. With his dark scent of incense and sandalwood. He smelled like an ancient church. Sacred and arcane. Or maybe just a really manly soap. And even though his thick, inky curls sat a little scruffy, and his loose, gray sweat pants were a tad on the overly casual side, he still managed to resemble a sexy version of Lucifer—tall, with imposing physicality—minus the horns and gnashing teeth.

This guy probably enjoyed women clad in red lace and hot times, not a med student in high-waisted underwear and a bad case of repressed sexuality.

She took a sharp swallow at the lump in her throat and searched for her ability to reply. This would be her first, and maybe only, chance at exploring her wild-and-sexy side... *Do I even have a wild-and-sexy side?*

Then again, she'd taken risks on men in the past. Long ago. Before Hector—who'd been a whole other mistake unto himself...

"Are you sure?" Her brow tightened with the counterproductive question, but she couldn't stop from voicing her doubt. "You don't know the first thing about me."

Why am I killing this exchange? I should throw myself at him. Just take whatever is on offer and say yes.

"I thought the whole point of grabbing a drink was to get to know each other." He dipped his chin, and those deep brown eyes set forth a challenge—as if he knew more about her than she knew of herself. "But I'm happy to skip the drink and get straight to taking each other's clothes off, if that's what you'd prefer..."

His lip crept up on one side. She glanced away, face hot, heart thundering. Why hadn't she thought to splash out on some serious red lace lingerie *before* embarking on this trip?

"Um..." She cleared her throat, attempting to play cool. "Maybe let's start with that drink."

His eyes glinted, and he gave a quick nod, then turned away, calling over his shoulder, "Catch you later."

He spoke loud enough for everyone to hear. The older woman he'd been sitting beside glared at Sophie.

Sophie loaded herself with cups of tea and scampered over to Warren. His kindly eyes narrowed as she handed him his cup. "That boy is pure trouble. You'd be wise to stay away from him."

Sure, maybe Warren's heart was in the right place, and going on a date with a fellow volunteer held the potential to complicate things should they not get along, but Sophie was a beggar and couldn't afford to be choosey. Not when she'd found an incredibly attractive opportunity for adventure right here in Roseford. And if this opportunity worked out, she wouldn't have to bother with long trips to Melbourne just to get some action.

She waved a dismissive hand, a wave that said a strait-laced woman like her knew better than to engage in any trouble with a man like the one she'd just met. Gosh, she'd accepted a date from someone and hadn't even grabbed his name... Oh well, Warren had to be wrong; no one who was "pure trouble" would spend their time volunteering at an aged care facility.

"Never mind him." She refocused on Warren, leaning in. "Tell me about you."

Warren went on to explain about his life. She held a polite smile and nodded at his stories about his family and a long career in metal welding, which had eased off into a newfound passion for small-scale wire sculpturing, all the while dispersing her own input into the conversation.

Just as her pulse finally came down from her earlier excitement, her two-hour window with Warren ended, and in an instant, her pulse picked up again.

Mr. Dark and Mysterious would be waiting for her. She had a date with someone supposedly experienced in *trouble*. Someone who might be able to show her the way...

She stood and patted Warren's shoulder, promising to return with the other volunteers in two days' time.

It's only a drink. I can do this. Or bail if I really can't.

A care worker wheeled in a cart with blue lunch trays, while Sophie waited at the common room's exit, one of the last volunteers to leave. Only, her handsome stranger still sat amongst the tables and the other residents, while his elderly partner brushed past in a hurry to get out.

For a brief moment, a beautiful smile tugged at his soft-looking lips, but then he dipped his chin and those same lips curled into a wicked grin. She waited another few beats, expecting he'd stand and follow her out the door.

But he didn't.

Her body stiffened. She spun around to peer outside through the glass sliding doors, where the lady he'd sat next to ambled through the parking lot, then ducked into a white hatchback. The taillights flared red, and the car pulled away.

Sophie whipped back to her sexy stranger. Her stomach flipped. A care worker slid a lunch tray in front of him, his new flinty glower saying there'd be no drink.

She'd heard of young people taking up residence in nursing homes, but never before had she actually encountered one. It often took some injury, disability, or condition—something that required twenty-four-hour assistance—to land someone non-geriatric in a place like this. Often because there weren't enough places in more appropriate facilities, especially if someone lived rural. Rural, as in, Roseford.

Pain radiated through her chest, and her heartbeat throbbed loud in her ears; even worse was the burning in her cheeks and the sickening cramp in her tummy. She forced herself to turn and place one foot in front of another. To get the hell out of there.

The man she'd hoped would kick-start her sexy, new life wouldn't be "catching her later". *He wouldn't be going anywhere.* He wasn't even a volunteer. *He was a resident.*

Two

THAT AFTERNOON, Sophie sat alone at The Keeper's Arms, Roseford's only pub. The lighting was subdued and a subtle, but not completely unpleasant, smell of stale beer punctuated the air. Judging by the empty seats, the large venue was at half capacity.

She nursed a white wine on the table before her, and her bruised ego brought strain to her heart. At the very least, she deserved a break from making her own lunch and scrimping over every dollar she spent to be at this pub now.

Her embarrassing encounter at the home left her unfocused and regretful, with little idea of what had truly happened, or why that guy had picked her to torment. Her heart pounded at how much she'd failed at her first attempt at breaking from her boring existence in the hopes of finding a man.

She twisted the wine glass in front of her, the thin stem not quite as cold as the lump that nestled in her chest. A dazzling stranger had jumped at the chance to toy with her. To humiliate her. To chip away at her unstable confidence. Why? Why her? Did she look like a woman easily fooled? Clearly, she did.

The way his all-seeing stare had cooled to flat malice...

She swished the citrine liquid in her glass and then knocked back a big mouthful. Even the biting taste played on her dread. He'd banked on her naïvety. That she'd never pick him for a resident. A man in his thirties, much less mobile, much less seemingly mentally aware. *Jerk.*

She didn't know his name. Didn't know his story or his motivation. But sure enough, she wanted to hate him.

And yet… Something held her back from that very thing. Something about him plucked at her intrigue.

He didn't appear to have anything wrong with him… Well… Except for his not-so-charming personality.

She scoffed under her breath and shook her head at her stupidity. Maybe she hadn't moved quite as far from that innocent girl she'd once been, but she could start by letting the whole ordeal go. She'd come to this country for experience, and the dazzling jerk had given her just that—though not the positive encounter she'd hoped for.

Her lunch arrived, and she pushed a fry into her mouth, savoring the comfort of carbs whilst using her spare hand to reach for her phone. She needed to hear a friendly voice and had promised to call her best friend and housemate in London.

"Sophie!" Hannah Taylor's voice chimed in clear as a bell. "How are you doing? Meet anyone cute yet? Oh God, the house just isn't the same without you. Talk, girl. Tell me what's happening."

Tension slid from Sophie's body. Hannah was the least difficult person she knew—well, except for the whole being messy thing, and Sophie always having to clean up after her housemate, which did complicate her life more than needed. And then there was Hannah's strange passion for collecting charity shop handbags and leaving them all over their tiny apartment… "I'm fine, just settling in. Tell me how everything on your side of the pond is doing."

"Hmm. Well, not much going on, really. You've only been away a week. Oooo, but I'm sure you'll be devastated to hear that I saw Randal Berry leave his apartment with a new, leggy bimbo on his arm." Hannah giggled.

Randal Berry was their downstairs neighbor, a guy Sophie had a not-so-secret crush on. A crush spanning the entire six years she'd lived in the two-story building.

"Don't say that." She reached for her wine glass again, gulping down another sip of reality-obscuring liquid.

"What? The bit about Randal having a new girlfriend, or the part where she's a bimbo?"

"Both. But the bimbo part especially. It's beneath you. And she could be a nuclear physicist for all you know."

"Yeah, but she's totally not. Come on, Soph, you know Randal doesn't date anyone with an I.Q. higher than a potato."

Sophie pulled her wine from her lips and tried not to choke. Hannah did have a point. And Randal did have a type. Tall, athletic, blonde... not very bright... All the clichés and all the things Sophie wasn't, not with her medium brown waves and shorter than average build. He'd never go out with a visually standard nerd such as herself. Which was probably why she liked him. The man was unattainable. A relationship was never going to happen. Though really, she had no desire to change for a man, so she'd painted herself into a corner with that particular infatuation.

She cringed, and her earlier tension returned. Just today she'd tried to "aspire" again and here she sat, drowning her sorrow and using her best friend for distraction. A small wave of guilt took over, because there was one man that she'd forgotten in all her musing. *Hector*.

She'd dated Hector for far too long, in part because he seemed a safe bet. But she'd learned that a safe bet wasn't all that safe when life ticked over and mutual misery provided their only connection. They'd used each other as a crutch to shy away from taking any real risks. Not that her recent attempt at risk-taking had paid off, but at least she could say that for the first time in years she was trying.

"How's Hector?" She dipped another fry in sauce, pretending her friend could see the casual gesture as the intended diversion from a completely un-casual question.

"He dropped off a box of your things yesterday." Hannah's voice lowered, quieter than before. "To be honest, he seemed a little sad. He said he might shoot a message your way to see how you're doing."

A heaviness settled in her chest. Truth be told, she'd kind of blindsided Hector with the whole break up, then jumped on a plane for a four-month rest from her years of study and long clinical hours.

But even her exit, and his general immaturity when maturity mattered most, didn't stop her from wanting to see his life improve. Especially since he'd graduated with his computer science degree a full year ago and still hadn't landed a full-time job. "If you hear from Hector before I do, tell him I hope he's well."

Hannah released a heavy sigh. "Oh Soph, it's not your job to fix everyone's problems."

"I'm not *fixing*. I'm being polite."

Though she had to admit, guilt did have a lot to do with her politeness. She'd escaped London at the first viable chance; she'd used the double-whammy of Luke's engagement and the fact that his fiancée, Agathe, was pregnant, as an excuse.

"Fine, next time I see him, I *might* say something, but... Just so you know, I think you're giving him false hope, and this is totally going to bite you in the ass one day."

Sophie speared a chicken tender on her plate but waited before eating it. Hannah had already given her many huge lectures on no longer putting others' needs ahead of her own aspirations, and she wanted to avoid yet another one. "Maybe you have a point."

"Damn right, I do. There are boundaries to every relationship, Soph. Let Hector sort himself out." Hannah paused but released another sigh when Sophie didn't offer a rebuttal. "Anyway, tell me more about how Australia's treating you? Something other than 'I'm fine'."

"It's too early to say for sure." Sophie pressed the cold bulb of her wine glass to her forehead—a refreshing breather from the weight of this conversation, much less her earlier loss of pride with the guy from the care home. "I've moved into the cabin and started my first day volunteering at the local aged care." She made a point of omitting anything regarding The Jerk. "I'm working with a lovely man named Warren, who I'll visit every Wednesday and Friday."

"And aside from that, you'll be taking time to yourself, right?" Hannah had opposed Sophie's volunteer gig from the very beginning; said it would be mixing work with what should be a holiday. Of course, Sophie didn't see it that way. "I've only ever known a Sophie who works herself to the bone. I can't wait to see my friend get a good rest and a decent shag for a change."

Sophie startled, pulling the glass away from her forehead and a small amount of wine sloshed to the table. "I... Ahh... I'll try?"

Hannah let out a raucous laugh—one so robust it reminded Sophie why she called Hannah a friend in the first place. The woman had a way of keeping her on her toes, and pointing out when she'd sold herself short.

"You're blushing right now, aren't you? Oh, shit"—a car horn blared through the phone, half drowning Hannah out—"gotta go. Running late. I love you. And honey, work on not working, all right?"

The call ended before Sophie could reply, but Hannah's sentiments lingered. No amount of oddball shenanigans from an attractive aged care resident would keep her from what she wanted—the chance to restart her life. Nor would those shenanigans stop her from returning in two days and upholding her promise to see Warren again.

Three

"You've got to be fucking kidding me."

Sophie blinked as The Jerk's words struck her harder than a sledge hammer to the face. Her mouth hung open, her worst nightmare unfolding before her very eyes.

Minutes prior, she'd entered Roseford Aged Care to a caregiver rushing toward her—the caregiver's blue eyes flared, her wide shoulders heaving as she relayed a rushed story of how Warren had passed away from an unexpected heart attack two nights ago. Sophie's own heart sank in the few seconds it took to absorb the shock of how a guy who echoed her father had also died in a similar fashion.

This detail brought back the day she'd received the call to return to Scarborough because "time was running out", only she'd arrived to her father's side an hour too late. His body was still warm. His spirit long departed.

So, she'd stood mere meters from the home's exit, reeling, her palm pressed to her aching chest, when the same caregiver ushered her deeper into the center. *"Not a problem, dear. We have a suitable replacement resident waiting for you."*

A lie!

There was nothing *suitable* about her new resident.

Now, she sat blinking, a hot sliver of anger blooming beneath her ribcage. This man was no resident. He was a sore thorn in her side–a burned piece of toast in a hurried attempt at breakfast. Except the toast had slipped from her fingers on her way out the door and landed butter-side-down on her doorstep, too germ-ridden to attempt eating… Or something like that.

Either way, she did *not* want to be partnered with this man and his perpetual deep brown stare.

Her attention slid to his lips; her politer nature made her question if he'd really just dropped the f-bomb upon seeing her. Definitely not because those lips still sat undeniably full and enticing. Surely lips that looked like that didn't swear?

She drew a slow breath and grappled with the shock of her predicament, then took a second to glare at the caregiver who'd delivered her to this menace of a man. Hopefully, the glare mirrored The Jerk's sentiments of, "You've got to be fucking kidding me", but the caregiver only grimaced and disappeared out the common room door.

Sophie turned back to her tormentor; the small scar at the top of his forehead adding to his diabolical bully act.

I should get up. I should just go.

But her fingers dug into her chair's textured armrests, and a deeper voice whispered that any self-respecting psychiatrist would at least try to figure this guy out.

If anything, a unique learning opportunity sat right in front of her.

Most patients in aged care were just that. *Aged.* People who'd lived long, full lives. Everyone, especially staff, knew to expect death. When someone like Warren died, as sad as his parting was, there was also the knowledge that he'd had a lengthy chance to achieve his dreams. But that wasn't the case with the guy seated before her. He was young with a temper. That temper alone offered clues that maybe he wasn't done with life.

And even if he wouldn't make being around him easy, maybe Sophie could still help. No one got into medicine for *easy*. And she knew a thing or two about vulnerability and skepticism, so maybe she could try to learn what The Jerk's deal was. Though she'd probably need to start with not referring to him in her thoughts as "The Jerk".

Besides, she'd made a vow to be braver in life, and now that chance presented itself, she couldn't let this smart mouth break her down. His past toying might be on the vanilla side of what she'd encounter one day, anyway.

She tilted her head back and glared down her nose at him, making it clear she'd sized him up and wouldn't be intimidated. "Yeah, well… I'm not so eager to see you either, but here we are."

The muscles in Orlando's face tightened, and a wayward glare slipped through his attempt at an unruffled smirk. *Who knew Miss Neat and Nerdy had an attitude?*

He'd long regretted the home's director, Candice Olsen, badgering him into participating in this half-baked volunteer program. But then, he still held a deep need to get out of the center occasionally—to escape the sight of wrinkled skin and urinary drainage bags—to engage with the outside world.

And in order to do that, he needed more funding. He needed a dedicated carer. Which according to Candice, increasing his chances of that meant pretending he gave a shit about fitting in. Even though one look at him made it blindingly fucking obvious he didn't fit in.

He pushed past his usual fatigue and brain fog and refined his smirk on Miss Neat and Nerdy, then dropped his voice to a low rumble. "You were eager enough to see me last week. Very eager, as I recall."

Nerdy's face went rigid, and her ivory-eggshell skin turned paler still.

He'd seen that look a million times over. She wanted to tell him to fuck off. Well, good. He'd honed a knack for convincing people to leave him the hell alone. Or to at least give him a bit of space. And any minute now, Miss Nerdy would play right into his hand.

She cocked her head to one side, her pretty lips forming a soft smile. "You want me to get angry at you. You want me to leave."

Her steady tone embodied sweet control; and the ever-present tension in his jaw relaxed for a brief second. This wasn't how his attempts at prodding anger usually went.

Miss Nerdy's light green eyes glittered. She thought herself clever. Like she'd conjured the weakest piece of advice from some book titled *Psychology 101*—some shit about mirroring his emotions—and figured she'd be special enough to get through to him.

He brought tension back to his jaw. Just because this woman deluded herself into believing the world less of a shitty place for having her in it, didn't mean he owed her any kind of proof of that belief.

"Congratulations. I hope you didn't need a degree to help you figure out the bleeding fucking obvious, but just to aid you with the next step, maybe you could make good on your observation and leave."

Miss Nerdy's face didn't shift an inch, the soft-looking skin over her freckle-dusted cheekbones remained perfectly still. "No. I think I'll stay just to tick you off."

She, and her small frame, all five-foot nothing of her, sat defiant and firm.

He frowned deeper for noticing.

Granted, this woman showed more pluck than he'd credited her for, but funding be damned, he didn't need another do-gooder digging into his life.

He'd had and missed his chance at being known. His last chance had disappeared the day his ass landed back in Roseford. In this care facility. He didn't want one more person asking him to do things he didn't care to do. To talk about things he didn't want to remember. As if his life wasn't already its own special variety of fucked up.

His chest muscles bunched, and his stomach churned, just enough to remind him not to show Miss Nerdy how much she'd already ticked him off.

"Fine." He crossed his arms and sat back, making it clear he wouldn't make this pleasant. "You must be one of those women who enjoys a little punishment."

He made a show of looking her up and down, keeping his gaze

extra slow and creepy. The corners of her eyes creased with another self-satisfied smile, and her expression only brightened—like the intended creepiness in his gesture went right over her head.

Not the reaction he'd hoped for.

She looked the picture of innocence, the floaty, pale yellow tunic she wore atop black jeans and brown knee-boots adding to that effect, as if she belonged on the cover of *Earthy Provincial Magazine*. If such a magazine existed.

She settled in her seat, mirroring his posture—yet another thing she must have picked up from *Psychology 101*—though Miss Nerdy's oblivious nature meant maybe she wasn't that clued in after all.

Her green eyes fused with his, more serious now. "Why'd your last volunteer quit? Did your charming personality scare her away?"

He gave a little shrug and buried a need to chuckle at her dig. He'd never been one to intentionally hurt or embarrass others, except to maintain what little personal space still remained to him, which Miss Nerdy wanted to infringe on. So, he wouldn't mislead Miss Nerdy into thinking he'd co-operate. Better to crush her dreams now and send her on her way. Just like the last lady.

"Not exactly."

"What then?"

He shrugged again. "She was a sore loser."

"Oh?"

He put on his best smirk, leaning over the pale gray table between them, reeling her in, setting Miss Nerdy up for a mighty fall. "She didn't think I could get you to agree to a date."

Miss Nerdy's cheeks sank before defensiveness kicked in, and she narrowed her eyes. "I know that's not what happened, but good attempt at covering up just how repellent other people find you." Her gaze dropped to her hands, betraying a smidgeon of shame over her lashing out. "Why did you ask me out on a date, anyway?"

His stomach clenched at her whispered tone. He'd noticed her pain last week too, the second his lunch tray landed on the table in front of him, and she'd realized he wouldn't be leaving with her as promised. Right then, she'd witnessed everything she needed to know about him. About the ridiculous shit-show called his life.

He gave a loud sigh and waited for her attention to return to him. No point apologizing. He didn't want her to like him. Any *like* she might have would only be an offer of charity.

"Just wanted to see if I still had it in me." He gave her a wink, though his jest held more truth than he admitted. "Thanks for the confidence boost."

A small muscle over her jaw ticked. Perfect. The last thing he needed was another person convinced they could affect anything akin to positive change in him. There was nothing positive about where he was headed.

"That was a cruel trick." She maintained a death stare, despite her choked voice.

"Life is cruel. Get used to it."

Her face held momentary tension, before she looked back down at her hands and shook her head. "I don't know why you're here, but I know they wouldn't put a person like you in a place like this unless living in the outside world was impossible." She lifted her gaze, expression softening with something resembling sincere compassion. "Your life can't be easy. I can see why you view the world as cruel. You're right, it can be."

A ball of angry heat ignited in his chest; his breath surged, harsh and hot. People rarely voiced their observations. They sure as shit never presented those observations with any sort of kindness—usually only as a rage-filled explanation of why he'd turned into one giant pain in the ass.

But then, he didn't want kindness. Didn't want compassion. He sure as heck didn't want Miss Nerdy's wrath-inducing empathy.

He knew how to deal with opposition at every turn. What to do with people's anger when he didn't fall on his knees in gratitude for help that he had zero option but to accept. Yet...

He jutted out his chin. His abrasiveness counted for nothing with this woman, and his head hurt more than usual—probably her fault too. Well, maybe a blunt order would work. "What's your name?"

Miss Nerdy maintained her peaceful smile. "My name's Sophie. And what about y—"

"Right, Sophie. I want you to leave."

Her expression fell, and bonafide hurt turned her pupils into wide pools. He'd seen that look on her before. *The moment she'd learned the home was his home.*

She glanced about the room, as if she cared what the others thought of her and this scene. Her stare landed on him again, her mouth agape and ready to question, but he refused to let her question anything. Just because she could come and go as she pleased didn't mean he had no power. "Leave. Now."

"Orlando."

He jolted.

Shelley, the soft-headed staff member who'd delivered this insufferable woman to him, broke his stare-off. She stood over his left shoulder and let out an exasperated sigh. "I hope he's not giving you trouble, Miss Tindall."

He trained his attention back on Miss Nerdy, refusing to reward Shelley's interruption.

Sophie blinked, though to her credit, her stare did not part from his either.

"Orlando?" A small, sarcastic smile crept across her face—as if she took great joy in learning his name. "He's no trouble at all." Her attention stayed eerily glued on him, though she spoke to Shelley. "In fact, he's all charm. Really. However, it might have been helpful to know you'd be partnering me with such a *remarkable* resident."

"I. Ah…" Shelley released a nervous chuckle. "Candice told me you're on track to be a psychiatrist one day. I thought you'd… appreciate the challenge?"

Orlando's muscles pulled taut.

A psychiatrist? Hell no!

That was the absolute last thing he needed.

No wonder this woman had latched onto him and refused to let go. *Fuck.* She probably saw him as the ultimate "fixer upper". Not old and decrepit. Not like the other losers in this home. Though unbeknown to her, just as bloody doomed.

Her gaze bore into him, her chin raised as if his dissatisfaction pleased her to no end. He mouthed the word, *leave.*

She gave a smirk, followed by a nod as if to say, *fine.*

The air shifted as she stood, and brought the scent of daisies and spring flowers because, of course, Miss Nerdy would smell sweet like a meadow full of delightful spring blooms.

She turned to Shelley. "It was nice to meet you." Then looked down at him—both literally and figuratively, her eyes glinting once more. "Orlando, I'll see you next week."

Four

Sophie stalked toward the Aged Care center's exit, only for her feet to spin her in a hard right turn down the corridor, toward an office she'd visited back when she'd first signed up to be a volunteer.

She stopped and stared at a closed door, her mind racing with the wild hope that Orlando hadn't noticed her detour. The name "Candice Olsen" hung on a sign before her, the job description "Center Director" underneath. Her hand worked of its own accord, and her knuckles connected with the door's glossy white wood.

Despite the volunteer gathering's chatter farther up the hall, her loud knock reverberated around the fluorescent-lit corridor—or maybe her nerves simply heightened her senses to every sound around her.

"Come in." The muffled female voice called from the other side.

She looked about, checking to see if anyone witnessed her out of character master stroke of daring, then seized a last second of calm before pushing the door open.

A woman in her early forties peered up from her desk; a woman Sophie had met briefly weeks ago. She had medium-length hair in the most stunning shade of bright copper.

"Hi." Sophie paused for a mere second, doubting her action. "I'm sorry to bother you, Ms. Olsen, I'm Sophie Tindall. We met—"

"Yes. Yes. Come in." Candice beckoned with her hand, her bright blue stare serious but not unwelcoming. She was likely busy and in a rush to know what Sophie wanted. "I remember you."

She pointed at a chair across from her. Sophie did as directed and took a seat. "I've just been placed with Orlando, and I was hoping you could spare a few minutes to talk."

Candice sank back in her seat and let out a heavy sigh, hands coming away from the laptop in front of her. "And let me guess, you want to be placed with someone else?"

"I'm not sure if you're aware, but he's not exactly the most welcoming resident."

Candice spluttered a small laugh void of any real joy. "Oh, I'm aware, but if it makes you feel any better, he misbehaves the same for everyone."

Sophie gave a slow nod, still pondering how best to serve her thoughts out loud. "Orlando needs help." And though some of his words hurt, she knew enough to understand the people most likely to strike out were also often the ones concealing the most damage. "I have no desire to be partnered with anyone else just yet, but thank you for offering."

Candice's chin jerked back.

Sophie, on the other hand, noticed that she hadn't taken a healthy breath since the moment she'd first sat in front of Orlando. She took that big breath now and exhaled on her explanation. "I understand there are limits to what you can tell me, but if there's anything you can share about him, anything that might make my job as his volunteer easier... I'm in Australia for four months, and I don't want to waste time muddling my way with him. So, I'd appreciate any and all of your help."

Candice broke with a genuine smile—one that brought a sparkle to her eyes and hinted at cunning—as if she knew Sophie's reluctance to leave would be exactly what Orlando didn't want but perhaps desperately needed.

"You mean you're not running for the hills? His last three volunteers gave up after barely one session, two at best."

Sophie shook her head. "He's not exactly my ideal candidate, but running away won't be helpful to his wellbeing or my reasons for taking this placement."

Candice extended a long, contemplative look, her wheelie chair creaking as she leaned even farther back. "Then I guess I better make good with compelling you to stick around." Her face eased. "I can't get into too much detail, especially since so much of Orlando Piras's condition remains a mystery. In my layman's understanding, he's somewhere on the neuromuscular impairment spectrum, with behavioral and cognitive issues limited to his episodes. No memory loss, no impaired judgment, no lowered attention span, or delusions outside of his episodes.

"He has some general fatigue and brain fog most days. Mobility-wise, he can manage well enough most days, prefers to stay active in the center gym. We've added a few extra pieces of equipment to encourage this, as lack of movement after an episode might mean losing his ability to move in totality. Our grounds are extensive enough for simple exercise and fresh air, but his episodes are when he really needs us. That's when he forgets who he is and fails to function as any normal thirty-six-year-old man would. There are particular times during his episodes when he's a danger to himself and others."

Sophie thought back to Orlando, to the harshness in his eyes, the sheer size of him...

"So, he's violent?"

Candice shook her head. "No. Not at all. Not intentionally, anyway. We wouldn't have him here among our residents if that were the case. Let's just say you wouldn't want him driving a car or at home alone when one of his episodes hits. He can't fend for himself in any way. And I'll be honest with you, Miss Tindall, Orlando's family is well known and loved in this town. I know Orlando sticks out at this center, but Roseford is one of those towns that looks after their own, and he wouldn't be here if he didn't have to be. And trust me, everyone has pulled a lot of strings to afford him a place at our community-owned center and around people who know him. His attitude might wear on us from time to time, but our residents and staff still want him around."

Sophie frowned. She couldn't imagine what made Orlando likable enough that so many people would shift and bend to accommodate him, but perhaps, as Candice had said, the blind acceptance was a symptom of a tight township.

Sophie's mind already went to piecing together this man and his condition—though the details remained vague enough to make it hard to draw any clear conclusions. Her volunteer status meant she had no real right to pry into what tests he'd undergone, specialists he might have seen, or even the duration or course of his illness, much less his prognosis.

She had no other option but to turn to what she *could* do—what her current role entailed—enriching Orlando's life. Maybe if she got him to ease up on the *sealed-fortress-of-doom* persona, he'd offer the information she needed to *truly* help him.

"Is there any way you see me breaking through to him?" She refocused on the woman ahead, her mind already forming a rough game plan. "Anything he needs that the center can't provide?"

Candice nodded, as though she admired Sophie's train of thought. "Yes, actually. Orlando's government funding was cut drastically months ago, and because of this, his dedicated carer is only funded for a couple of visits a week and only for a couple of hours. That's not enough to take him out for much more than a walk around the block or a coffee down the road if they're really quick." Ms. Olsen shrugged. "Our staff is pressed enough for time and can't dedicate too much attention on any one resident. He used to get full days out, and his overall mood has taken a huge hit since those stopped."

Sophie's tummy did a small flip, the impossibility of Candice's suggestion already sinking in. "You want me to take him out? I'm allowed to do that?"

Her and Orlando on an outing together? She just couldn't see that happening.

Candice nodded. "Granted, if you can get him to agree first."

Sophie gave a shaky laugh. "I'm almost certain he'd rather see me jump in the nearest lake and never return."

Candice leaned forward, elbows rested on her desk, gaze set in a pointed stare. "Sophie, Orlando will never admit it, but he needs help. He needs purpose and things to be passionate about—despite the degenerative nature of his condition. You might not be in Australia for long, but you're the first volunteer who hasn't spoken one word to him and run in the opposite direction. The fact you cared enough to knock on my door..." She paused, allowing the silence to speak for itself. "You sure can't make him feel much worse than he currently does. Orlando isn't our easiest resident, but he's not irrational, either. If you keep showing up, he'll notice. And what he does with your continued presence is anyone's guess, but it's up to you to stick it out to see what happens."

Five

"You didn't tell me you're a psychiatrist."

The muscles along Sophie's spine squeezed in response to Orlando's narrowed stare and the way he'd practically spat the word *psychiatrist*, as though she might as well have been a *parking inspector* or *evil overlord*.

"That's because I'm not a psychiatrist." She fought back a need to return his scowl, doubt scrubbing at her decision to visit him again.

Befriending this man was about as easy as befriending a death adder. Scrap "befriending", she'd settle for him simply not scowling. Clearly, his low opinion of her hadn't softened since their last meeting.

"I have a medical degree, but I'm yet to specialize in psychiatry, which is what I intend to do next. Besides, we never got to the point of swapping pleasant small talk. Remember? Nor were you welcoming enough to ask what I do. How was I supposed to tell you anything about myself?"

He unleashed a harsh squint, scowl shifting from mean to mocking. "So that's your schtick? Find a pet project here until you can unleash yourself on some real patients."

"Not exactly. The medical degree means I can already be 'trusted' with 'real patients' if that's what I choose to do." She leaned one elbow on the table between them, a casual gesture to weaken his attempt to diminish her qualifications. "But what I really want is to specialize in old-age psychiatry. This volunteer position is about getting to know the demographic I plan to work with."

His voice cracked under a burst of laughter. A few residents in near proximity turned and glared at him. "And then you got lumped with the dumpster-fire young guy. How's that for meeting your 'demographic'?"

"Well. Yes." She sunk back, a pit of shame opening up in her belly.

Despite being the person in the power position here, this man made her feel smaller than a gnat. And still, she was the one with the ability to get up and leave if she wanted to. Orlando couldn't. He had little control and possibly resorted to grasping at hers.

"Warren would have been perfect, but it seems he had other plans. I should make it clear though, my volunteer work isn't about me fixing anyone. I'm here to understand the issues and lives of whoever I'm partnered with." She looked him up and down. Maintaining her composure. With his good looks and the cocky attitude, appealing to his vanity might work. "And I wouldn't exactly call you a 'dumpster-fire.'"

She offered a soft smile.

He returned a flat stare. "What about a walking disaster? Or a clusterfuck?"

Okay. So, her niceties didn't move him. "Is that how you see yourself?"

"Is that you psychoanalyzing me?"

"No." She mirrored his blank stare. "This is me attempting to have a normal, human conversation."

An uncomfortable silence drew out, and his emotionless stare lingered. "And how's that going?"

"I think we both know, not very well." She focused on the large windows to her right—taking a momentary break from the standoff. An extensive garden waited outside, edged in rose bushes and fruiting trees. The tranquil image offered a reminder that few discomforts—including this encounter—lasted forever.

She willed her attention back to him, vowing to tough out his resistance. To test her grit. She'd dealt with worse than this man.

A satisfied smirk broke the hard line of his lips. "So, ask to be reassigned."

She leaned in, matching his innate intensity with a glare of her own. "One thing you should know about me, I don't give up."

And every desire to surrender stoked a decades-old fire within her, a fire built on mistakes she still needed to make up for. Mistakes when it came to herself. Mistakes when it came to others. Mistakes she couldn't let define her forever. Even if that meant not letting a small volunteer role such as this get the best of her. She'd help this man, even if helping meant sticking around just so he could mouth off at her.

She could take a bit of attitude.

She'd worked too damn hard to give up so early.

Orlando shrugged. Maybe he didn't care, but the mild dart of his gaze said her presence did rattle him.

"Orlando." His attention snapped back to her. "Rather than resist this, wouldn't it benefit you to just go with the exchange? Perhaps we could help each other—"

"Sophie, honey." He slanted forward, gaze smoldering and dark. She saw through his wolfish act—but the heat in that stare, the heat focused solely on her—sent butterflies through her middle either way. "There's nothing in this world I want from you."

The spell in his eyes burst quicker than a balloon held to a flame. She sucked in a breath. Still... She could fix this. "I know about your funding cut. I have a hire car while I'm living in Roseford. If you'd prefer, I could take you out for—"

Laughter broke from him again, and he slumped back into his chair. "Wow, you really are keen to go on that date with me, aren't you?"

Arrogant prick. She glared at him. Was she even allowed to think of him as an *arrogant prick*? Hadn't she just vowed to stop calling him The Jerk, even if only in her own head?

Sure, she'd heard worse about patients from more senior doctors, but that didn't make their negative approach right, nor did it give her license to stoop to judging a patient weathering a hard time. That said, Orlando's ribbing definitely upstaged anything her brothers ever dished out—and that was saying something. And sure, he had a right to feel sore about his life, but that didn't mean she had to let him treat her badly.

Sophie gave a slow shake of her head and fell just short of *tutting* at him. "One minute you're beating yourself up, next you're back to being God's gift to women." She took a drawn-out pause for no other reason than to make him wait. "Orlando, honey, I wish you'd make up your mind."

The smile on his face froze, but even that didn't slow him down much. "Since you seem to know all about my funding, I'm going to take a punt and guess you went straight to the top and spoke to Candice?"

"Yeah, I did. I take this role seriously."

"Right. Well. You're acting like a horny-as-fuck stalker. So, lay off the seriousness." His gaze bore into her. "I'm not interested in your help."

Shock waves ran through her body at the "horny-as-fuck" line. She might have traveled across the world to live a little, but that was more about gaining experience than being *horny*. Not that any of that was this guy's business... "Even if my help means more freedom than you've had in months?"

"The answer's still no."

"Explain to me why."

His crinkled scowl did a swift scan over her. "I don't have to explain shit to you, Miss Neat and Nerdy. Or are you confused because your text books never gave you a game plan on how to deal with a person like me?"

Neat and Nerdy. Though she'd always figured she gave off a "clean cut" impression, her heart still squeezed at the mockery in his tone. He knew less of her than she knew of him. He couldn't understand the origins of where "neat and nerdy" came from.

She waited for her composure to return. For her heart rate to settle and the hollow in her middle to fill back up again. Hoping to force something from him other than defiance. Hoping to hit a nerve as he'd done to her so many times already. "So, you figure you're a losing hand, and you might as well give up altogether?"

He scoffed out a hard laugh. His elongated stare made it so she could almost hear the wheels of thought turn over in his head, as he calculated the severity of his next blow. "Losing hand? More like losing my mind. You know, I'll be long dead before you nab your first boyfriend. What are you, twelve? But you can call the death sentence I'm living a 'losing hand' if that makes you feel better about nosing around in my business."

"I'm twenty-eight." The words fell limp out of her mouth, while the other words *death sentence* pinged around in her skull with no exit point for release. "I'm just small." There she went again, spewing useless phrases. Meanwhile, she struggled to wrap her thoughts around how a man so commanding could also be supposedly dying. "You don't have to carry the burden of what you're dealing with on your own."

Pathetic reply but better than her last two attempts.

He let out another tight laugh. "Nice try, but no."

She squeezed her eyes shut. Vexed. Down. Out of her depth. "Why even participate in the volunteer program if you won't let me help?"

She reopened her eyes; he merely held her stare, though a small muscle ticked in his jaw. The creases on his forehead and cheekbones seemed to soften for a second there. Maybe he did care about his impact on her.

He turned his head and broke eye contact. "Drop it, Nerdy."

The hanging silence revealed little more than the ironic, cheerful mumble of other volunteers and their partners around her. Orlando's pointed stare returned to her face—not so cheerful—and her heartbeat thudded loud in her ears.

His silence spoke louder than words. His harsh approach indicated there was more to discover. Like he had a story. A mountain of hidden pain. And no miracle placation could win him over. So maybe she'd have to come to terms with being no different from every other volunteer who'd left.

She wanted to leave this surly man too. Leave him right here where he sat. But she couldn't. Not just yet. What if Candice was right? What if he needed a friend more than he let on?

"I…" Though she spoke mostly to herself, her voice rasped on a brittle sound. "I want to help."

What more could she do? He gave her nothing.

His hard glare softened once more. Maybe, for the briefest second, he doubted his approach. "I know. But you can't."

She opened her mouth, ready to ask for a proper chance. To plead with him to ease up on her just a little. But all her possible words died on her tongue.

Orlando's posture snapped into a poker-straight position. His eyes flashed wide, panic-filled, and so dissimilar to the stoic man she'd encountered twice already—like he'd lost control of all movement—like confusion swallowed all his confidence.

Every muscle on his face pinched. Split-second desperation filled his gaze. And his deep-chocolate stare lost all depth. His eyes glazed over. His warm, olive skin paled.

The common room's thick, eucalyptus-scented air clogged her throat. She lunged for him—shook his arm—but hard layers of muscle and bone failed to respond. She turned. Searched for help. A large, male nurse bolted toward her in wide, loping strides.

"It's happening again."

Sophie's jaw loosened. She spun back to Orlando. A goofy grin pulled his mouth wide like a clown tripping on acid.

He was gone, missing in a place inside his own mind, a place no one else could follow.

Six

Electricity coursed through Sophie's legs. *Run.* Not the instinct of a would-be psychiatrist. But logic had fled.

Beads of sweat formed over Orlando's forehead, while her skin prickled with panic. This man was having an episode, and in his moment of need, her mind drew a blank.

His fingers trembled; the slow but constant tremor spread to his arms with increasing violence. Within seconds, his entire torso shook, and a childish laugh broke from him. Then he shrieked.

Volunteers and residents turned. A security guard she'd noticed on a couple of occasions joined the nurse, and both men hooked their fingers under Orlando's armpits.

"Come on, Buddy. Let's get you to your room while you can still walk." The nurse lifted him to his feet. Untrue to character, Orlando followed without protest. The nurse leaned forward and peered around Orlando's broad chest to address the security guard. "We'll sedate him there."

Sedate? Why? Did this man pose a risk? Sophie jumped to her feet. Overcome with an unexplainable drive to protect.

"Kayla." Orlando's high-pitched cry tore across the room. He sounded like a lost child. His frightened stare pointed at her. "Kayla. Come with me. Please."

She glanced around, and the entire room stared at her, their collective gaze asking, *What will you do next*?

A sick sensation rushed her body. Orlando thought *she* was Kayla. *But who was Kayla?*

She clenched her eyes shut. The urge to run resurfaced. Her chest constricted under the mounting stress. Maybe she'd made another mistake. Maybe she didn't belong here after all. Maybe his problems were more than she could handle…

And I call myself a doctor?

She shuddered against the question.

Where was her fight?

She had to find her professional grit and help this man. For herself. For *him*.

"Kayla." Orlando's face disappeared around a corner, twisted and pained. "Please. I'm scared."

Her left foot moved of its own accord, propelling her forward and across the room, making the decision for her. "Hang in there. I'm right behind you."

By the time she caught up, he already lay sprawled across a single bed in a sparsely furnished room, a moss-green wool blanket beneath him.

"Kayla." He panted in heavy breaths and reached out a shaking hand, the rest of his body convulsing. The security guard kept one hand pressed to Orlando's chest, the other held to his now bare upper thigh, pinning him while the nearby nurse readied a syringe.

Despite the poison Orlando had served her earlier, she stood at his shoulder and took the hand he held out to her. "I'm here."

He needed her. Now. And she had a moral duty to be there for him.

The strength of his fingers wrapped her palm, and he tugged her in. She stumbled and almost collided with the security guard.

"Stay." Orlando's wild eyes darted around her face. "Please stay."

She swallowed on a ball of emotion and nodded.

The nurse administered the sedative via intramuscular injection straight into his thick thigh. Orlando's eyes squeezed shut, and he shuddered, resisting what was happening to him in this small way.

She rubbed her thumb over the back of his hand. "I'm not going anywhere."

She kept a soft whisper, and her cheeks burned at her overwrought reaction. As if she'd never seen a man sedated before, much less performed a few sedations herself. As if she'd never seen someone with a neurological disorder. She had. Many times over. She'd done placements at several major hospitals... *So why was this man different?*

His hold on her eased. She refocused on the details of his face—his eyes still closed but lacking strain, his cheeks slack and void of expression. The drugs had worked, more effectively and quicker than she'd expected. *He slept.*

She jerked her head up and sought out the nurse, who was busy covering Orlando's lower half with the green blanket. "What did you use on him?"

The security guard stepped back and gave her a direct line of sight with the male nurse. "Ketamine, ma'am."

"Ketamine?" She frowned. "Isn't that a bit much? He wasn't violent. He didn't resist you. Wouldn't Midazolam have been better?"

The nurse's soft smile returned, the security guard already on his way out the door. "I know, ma'am, but we have orders. Orlando doesn't get violent, but he gets distraught. He, himself, prefers the Ketamine over Midazolam as it means less prolonged drowsiness, and he doesn't have to wait out the episode. What you just witnessed was mild. His bigger reactions in the past have been frantic to say the least. The potential for accidental harm to himself or staff increases if we let an episode continue."

"I don't mean to criticize, but it sounds as though his episodes aren't all that managed."

"Yes, ma'am." The nurse's gaze shifted to a nearby wall, as though he weighed up how much to tell her. "If we played by the rules, Orlando would be on constant behavior-modifying drugs, but when we did that, he was pretty zoned out and even more miserable than he is these days. You might not agree, but the staff here decided we were happy to manage him as is. It's a big facility, we make room for him, and as you saw, he's mostly compliant. Even though he's a cranky type, we consider him family here, and he does stuff for us by way of the occasional maintenance job or whatever else he keeps himself busy with. He's a team player in his better moments."

Sophie turned back to Orlando with his deceptively calm face. So much about what she'd heard about him through others didn't connect with the moody man she'd met—including what Candice had said about the other residents wanting to accommodate him—even though Warren had also warned her about him being "trouble".

And since she was thinking about things Candice had said... "Candice mentioned Orlando's condition is degenerative."

The nurse nodded, proceeding to snap off his blue plastic gloves. "That's the assumption. Young people in his position don't tend to have long life expectancies. If not due to their condition, then from the medication, or just the day-to-day emotional wear of being in a home."

Sophie took a moment to consider what life would be like for someone in Orlando's position. Candice had said he needed to get out more. That the lack of outings affected his mood, much less the physical ramifications of being cooped up inside day in, day out, away from anyone his own age.

She turned to the nurse again, thankful to have yet another person to grill about Orlando, since the man himself wasn't all that forthcoming. "Is he always scared during an episode?"

The nurse gave a soft chuckle. "No, ma'am. Sometimes he passes out cold. Sometimes he acts like a happy-go-lucky kid. It seems he's reverting back to something, you know? But with episodes like today's, he starts off afraid and spirals into pure terror. Once that happens, he's near unstoppable. We have to control the episodes early. He was lucky you were here, miss. I don't know who Kayla is, but he seemed to look to you and settle some. I think you took the edge off."

She buried the name Kayla in her memory—both the desperation with which Orlando called it and the fact he'd used that name on her. *Why? And why her?* Somehow, she'd have to find a way to weasel that bit of information out of him.

The nurse made soft rustling sounds behind her. "If you need any help, press the buzzer on the side table there, and someone will arrive soon. Otherwise, I'll be back later to check on him."

She nodded her thanks and kept her attention on Orlando, fingers returning to the back of his brawny hand. The warmth of his skin slowed her galloping heart and stilled her enough to take in more details in his near-empty room.

Most long-term patients tended to personalize their rooms in some way, either with photographs or knick-knacks from their former lives. But Orlando's room had none of that—just a bigger-than-standard TV on a chest of drawers in the left corner, a small stereo on a table to the right. No photos. No knick-knacks. Not even a left-out item of clothing to show he even lived here.

The lack of stuff seemed important. Like he denied his existence at the center or perhaps refused any memory of his former life.

And what sort of life had he had, anyway?

She studied his face, those stormy eyes closed to reveal little more than a row of thick, black lashes—those eyes for once at ease. His dark olive skin still sported a sheen of sweat, but his breathing had at least settled.

And despite his peaceful exterior, she doubted this man ever found peace. Not under the weight of what she assumed was forced bravery. Not with all that buried emotion. His stony act signaled he didn't care, though from how others spoke of him, a different Orlando existed altogether.

He cared a lot and about a lot of things. But he'd had years to practice apathy.

His wide-eyed fear during his episode, the raw pain as he'd called her Kayla... all told a story.

Kayla. He cared about her, too.

Sophie could only imagine what it took to be him. Almost ten years older than her, but if not for his condition, with decades of life ahead of him. So then, a life deteriorating in a nursing home, and a man with little to no hope of ever returning to who he'd once been.

He was right about his younger age putting him outside of her target demographic, but her help didn't come with an age limit. She'd signed up for a career in care, and sometimes that care entailed dealing with an impending end. And whether Orlando expressed it or not, he needed her. Needed someone to not give up on him.

Seven

"KAYLA." Orlando's voice crackled on the name, his throat dry and brittle like fallen leaves. "Kayla, you still there?"

His head throbbed. He wanted to see, but his heavy eyelids kept fluttering closed. He groaned, turning his head to his left. Honey-sable hair and eggshell, pale skin flashed before his eyes. His eyelids snapped closed again.

Not Kayla. She had auburn hair and a deep tan.

A cold chill ran through his body. He forced his eyelids open again. Ivory skin. Sea-green eyes? *Shit!* Definitely not Kayla. The cold chill morphed into a burning ache—one that coursed through his veins, poisoning his daydream.

Idiot, Kayla's dead. I live in the old folks home now.

Shit. Shit. Shit. Shit. The burning in his veins intensified. He hadn't heard or uttered the name Kayla in decades. Why now?

A groan rumbled deep in his chest, the sedatives always too slow to wear off. The reality of who sat beside him sank in. *Sophie.*

"What are you doing here?" Gravel wore at his throat, though the pain at least distracted from the knowledge this woman had watched him lose all sense of himself.

"You were in a bad way." Her hand brushed his arm, and an

enlivened shiver ran through his entire body—her soft tone sounded measured and intolerably comforting. "I didn't want you to wake alone."

He let out a rough laugh, then coughed when that didn't feel so good.

As if he didn't wake up alone every other day—episode or not.

She pressed a cool glass to his lower lip, ignoring his attempt to laugh off her presence. "Here, drink."

Chilled water coursed over his tongue, trickling down his raw throat like a blissful balm. He drank, slowly, fighting the urge to chug the whole damn glass. Experience had taught him not to over indulge, that would bring nothing but nausea and vomiting, and this poor woman had seen enough.

He scowled at her, still sipping, questioning his need to spare her, much less categorizing her as poor when he normally considered her just a plain old pain-in-the-ass.

She kept the glass to his lips a little longer as if she understood his need for caution. A memory of smoke-filled air circled his thoughts. *His former life.*

The sting of sun beat down on him. The protection and torture of his heavy coat. His hands stained black. Tall gum trees impersonating ghosts, hundreds of years of growth gone up in literal flames. Before him stood a graveyard of burned-out giants, stretched as far as the eye could see. But then came the pure relief of throwing off his helmet. Of removing his mask. The choking smell of scorched earth, dry air, and timber. Followed by that first sip of water…

He pulled away from Sophie and the glass, and then sank back into his pillow, eyes shut to block out the haunting memory. "Thank you."

But even his small show of gratitude hurt.

He couldn't go back—the past as much a scar on his soul as his illness. Though a knotted sensation worked through his core now, and a far more recent realization rose to the surface.

What exactly did I do during this latest episode?

His eyes flung open, and he stared at Sophie. Kayla's name still singed his lips, and her presence filled the room like yet another ghost. "You can go now."

He couldn't be certain if he'd meant the words for Kayla or Sophie, but he didn't need to turn to the woman beside him and see pity on her face.

"I will. Soon." Her even tone matched her neutral expression, and she showed no judgment. "I just want to know you're okay first."

The knotting in his belly unfurled, releasing his sense of shame, only to make room for hot anger. Her willingness to stick around annoyed him more than the idea she might flee in disgust. "I'm fine. You can go."

"Who's Kayla?"

The direct question hit him swift as a slap. He squeezed his eyes shut and whispered an obscenity. "None of your business."

Her chair scraped against the carpet. He opened his eyes to her standing over him. "Fair enough. I just hope you know I mean well. I'll be back in two days as per the volunteer schedule. If you're feeling up to it, we can talk then."

The fire within him roared, and he scowled his contempt. Even her white cotton tunic taunted him like some kind of flag of innocence, the kind of untouchable goodness he couldn't measure up to, even on his best day.

He shifted against the wool blanket on top of him, the one scratching and irritating the skin of his belly through his thin t-shirt. The light from the open window shone too bright.

He hated having his window open. Who'd opened his bloody window?

Even the rose bushes outside, with their pink and yellow blooms, seemed too cheery, too pink–their overly sweet aroma in the air a sharp invasion of an outside world he couldn't access. A world he no longer belonged to.

And the woman before him was much, much worse.

That pleading gaze... The one she'd used just moments before he'd blacked out. A look that had brought him idiotically close to accepting her help... Everything about *her* was just too suffocating to his already limited sense of personal space.

"As I recall..." He caught the flinty edge to his voice and went with it. "You were ready to slap me minutes before I spazzed out. Now what? You saw a hint of how fucked up my life is and you feel sorry for me?" Miss Nerdy's pupils dilated, black pools surrounded by crystal green waters. As if recovering from an episode didn't pain him enough, now he had to add the guilt of hurting her to his current misery. "If it weren't for Candice's nagging about my need for more funding, I wouldn't be putting myself through this volunteer program, do you understand? Heck, the funding isn't much motivation anymore, so cut it out with your puppy dog eyes and wrangling me into talking to you. Nothing you have to offer will make my life any less aimless than it already is."

Her jaw hung open for a moment, before she clenched it shut again. "I'm not here to cure your condition. I don't even know all that much about it. All I want is to improve your quality of life in any way you'll let me."

He snapped his gaze away from her and stared up at the ceiling. "Well, you can't, and I don't want you to. So go."

"You want to get out more." Her voice held a stern edge now as she regained her defenses and rose to the argument. "I can help you with that."

"After what you just witnessed?" He huffed out a short laugh, refusing to look at her. "You still want to take me out? Are you insane?"

"I'm a doctor, remember?" She paused, as if she figured he needed a moment for that information to sink in. As if he could forget. As if he hadn't encountered enough well-meaning doctors. "I'll get the home to give me the run down on the best course of action should you have an episode. Ms. Olsen seems to think it's doable. All I need is your consent."

"Well, you don't have it." He glared at the ceiling and tried not to growl.

She'd clearly taken time to think this through. And even though he should have jumped at the chance to get out, a deeper part of him still resisted. "In fact, given what you've seen and that you're a psychiatrist, I'd say you're taking this role way too seriously."

She crossed her arms in his peripheral vision, her white tunic shifting—calling for his attention, though he tried not to conjure up the mental image of how the fabric might bunch and dip between her small and perky breasts.

He squeezed his eyes shut again, making it appear as though he wanted to block her out—not a total lie—though, really, he'd just annoyed himself. How had he already noted she had small, perky breasts?

Because I can't help myself. She's young, and beautiful, and smart, and puts up with my bullshit. I'm one low-life, dirty bastard. That's for sure!

Well, clearly two years surrounded by oldies hadn't killed off his last shred of virility. Though, damn Sophie even more for jolting that particular aspect of his past back to life.

He turned to her, her arms still folded in seductive confirmation of how he'd figured she'd appear—her pinched stare, along with her petite but solid build, reminiscent of a feisty, little dancer.

My tiny dancer.

He shuddered, recoiling at the desire to stake any kind of claim over this woman. To call her *his*. She wasn't his. Not by any stretch of any mile. And the challenge in her stare made him want to prove her wrong for ever trying to help him. The very sight of her compact figure looming over him in his bed made him want to pick her up and have his way with her. To prove he wasn't the helpless soul that life seemed set on making him.

Fuck.

She tilted her head to one side. "What about me makes you uncomfortable?"

Fuck again. Wrong question, lady. Wrong timing too. Not with where his thoughts wandered…

He turned his attention back to the ceiling, even more disgusted with himself, even more confused. Why now? Why did his libido surge back to life now? And why with this damn woman?

He frowned ahead. "Everything about you makes me uncomfortable."

"Okay. Fine. I'll be back in a couple of days. Until then, you can either think of somewhere you'd like to go, or I'll come up with something myself. And…" She huffed out something similar to a sigh, mixed with a groan, as if reluctant to offer her next words. "And if I truly do make you uncomfortable, then I promise to keep my mouth shut the entire time we're out. At least that way, we'll both get to enjoy some freedom without the bickering."

His stomach hollowed at one particular word. *Freedom.* That word embodied everything he'd wanted in recent years, doled out so casually from this woman's lips. She clearly took her freedom for granted. Though he couldn't blame her. So had he.

And yet. She offered freedom, at the expense of her ability to scour for more information, a compulsion probably near impossible for this well-meaning do-gooder.

"I know doctors are said to have a God complex." He kept his attention away from her. "But you take your deity status to a whole other level."

She released a soft laugh, one that skated over his skin in light tingles. "You're welcome to think what you want. In fact, I'd say your skepticism is a natural response."

"Thanks for the validation." And simply because she'd made his skin tingle... "But you should know I plan to have you removed as my volunteer."

"Sure. I mean, you doing the ditching would be a nice departure from volunteers walking out on you, right?" The door knob creaked, alerting him to her impending exit. "So, you make that request, and I'll await the call telling me not to come. Otherwise, I'll swing by in two days to pick you up."

Eight

"IS THIS A BIKER BAR?" Sophie perched on the edge of a bar stool at Hell Cat Tavern and cringed at all the leather-clad, bearded dudes dispersed in small groups around the dingy space. The sour stench of stale beer and sweat surrounded her, probably permeating the cotton of her favorite beige tunic.

It was just before noon on a Friday, and some of the guys appeared more bedraggled than others, as if they'd continued their drinking session from the night before. Orlando sat beside her, his large palms cupping a giant mug of beer, while he gave her an exaggerated shrug in reply. "Could be a biker bar. I've never really noticed." He turned his attention to the room and released an audible sigh. "Ahhh. I've missed this place. You were right about getting out more. I feel better already." He spun his darkened gaze back to her, eyes narrowed, as though he knew just how out of place she felt. "And wait till we check out Teasers later on. You'll love it there."

Teasers was a strip club, and his stare dared her to backtrack out of her promise to take him wherever he wished.

In her two days spent fretting over this man's power to fire her as his volunteer, she hadn't once considered he'd try to use her offer of help as a form of torture. Maybe she'd just been so glad to simply not get fired that she'd blanked out on his true nature. *Silly woman.* Then again, maybe he really was into biker bars and strip clubs, and this was what he simply wanted to do. Though an unexplainably optimistic part of her brain still refused to accept that notion as fact.

She took a deep breath, meaning to release a sigh, but instantly regretted her decision. The stink of sweat and beer assaulted her nostrils again, and her stomach twisted in revolt. Either way, biker bars or sweat stench aside, she wouldn't break. She'd stick out her promise to Orlando. After all, she'd wanted more life experience, and here she was getting some.

"I'm sure Teasers will be lovely." She tilted her chin and sipped at her orange juice—orange juice she'd needed to convince the barman three times not to add hard liquor to. "And you're right. You do look happier, and I'm glad our arrangement works for you."

She offered Orlando an easy smile, withholding her judgment in exchange for embracing his venue of choice. He ticked an eyebrow. As if her optimism annoyed him. "Watching you try to fit in here brings me happiness. You're not exactly a 'Hell Cat' kind of girl."

She gave a strained laugh, sweeping her gaze over the room until her focus landed on a biker seated with his back to her. Bum crack and hair spilled from the space between his tight leather vest and his even tighter leather pants. She cringed, half expecting his pants to explode and someone in his near vicinity to lose an eye from a wayward metal button or something. Though she hoped not. That would mean she'd have to roll up her sleeves and administer first aid, which meant even more bad things for her favorite beige tunic.

"You're right." She flicked her gaze back to Orlando, eager to forget the impending leather pants disaster. "I'm not a 'Hell Cat' kind of girl, but I'm willing to make sacrifices. I understand how being stuck in the care facility day in, day out might turn you into a grouch."

"Or maybe I'm just an asshole." He gave her a deadpan stare. "Did you ever think of that? Maybe I'm an asshole who really loves checking out strip clubs and women with big boobs?"

He gave the room a casual glance as if he hadn't just said the word boobs. But then her face heated, his unnerving attention stopping at her not-so-big chest.

"Sure." She shrugged, convinced he was messing with her. "But I figured taking you out couldn't make you more of an asshole."

His expression turned flat again, and he drew out a silence.

Her stomach churned, so she spoke once more. "Can I ask you something?"

He turned back to his beer, giving the impression he'd finished messing with her for the time being. "I can't promise I'll answer."

When he wasn't busy scowling, his side profile revealed lips that curved so beautifully upward and a well defined jaw beneath a thick, dark layer of stubble. If she didn't know him, she'd describe him as *masculine perfection*, but she did know him, so the best she could conjure was *attractive trouble maker*.

She sighed, getting on with the task of trying to help him. "Why are you in an aged care facility? Surely some better suited housing situation could be arranged for someone your age?"

He remained silent, this time tilting his beer in the palm of his hand, inspecting its foamy surface. "I lost my job some years ago due to my condition and had no more money left after my last hospital internment. I needed immediate care, and Roseford Aged Care is close to where my next of kin lives." He shrugged. "The center was willing to take me."

"Oh?" She settled back a little, the lack of snark in his reply an encouraging sign. "So, you have family here? Have you always lived in Roseford?"

His gaze darted over in a sidelong glare. He said nothing.

"Okay." She bit her lower lip, unable to keep from pushing her luck. "But if you *do* have family in the area, could they also assist in taking you places?"

He pulled his attention from her. Quiet. Focused down on his beer again.

"I get visits. That's enough." His voice was a mix of gruff, soft control. "I don't expect anyone to burden themselves with whether I might spaz out while I'm away from the center. I still don't know why you bothered."

She cringed at his harsh use of the words "spaz out", but at least she'd gotten him to divulge something about himself. How long till she could get him to discuss his condition? His current treatments, tests, and prognosis? She'd encountered so many cases during her placements where patients languished simply because they didn't have the right specialists or care. Maybe Orlando was one of these people. Maybe at the very least, she could act as a temporary medical advocate.

His glare eased, and his deep chocolate gaze lingered on her face in an unreadable expression. "My turn."

She jolted out of her train of thought. "Sorry? What?"

His sly grin returned. "My turn to ask a question."

Her shoulders drew tight. She wanted to say no, but...

He gave a small chuckle as if her discomfort amused him. "Let me guess, being a psychiatrist and all, you figured you'd ask all the questions and I'd just sit here like a good little boy and tell you all my sad stories."

"I'm not a psychiatrist. And that's not what I thought."

That last part wasn't one-hundred-percent true. He was right. She'd never really considered sharing anything personal about herself.

He tilted his beer at her. "Not a psychiatrist, *yet*. And you forgot about the part where I'm not your patient. This is supposed to be a two-way exchange, remember?"

She gnawed her lower lip once more, gaze accidentally sliding back to the biker's butt-crack again. A sudden shudder ran up her spine, and she turned to Orlando. "Okay, fine. Ask."

His eyelids narrowed, as if readying himself to analyze every detail of how she responded to whatever he said next. "Why would a woman like you choose to live out her life in a safe little bubble?"

The muscles on her face turned involuntarily lax, and her heart sunk in her chest. "What are you talking about? A 'woman like me'? What bubble?"

Am I really so obvious?

And what other things had he learned about her from their limited exchanges? Hadn't he been too busy with his own distant brooding? Gosh, why was she so rattled? Why wouldn't her mind quit firing one question after another? Which, ironically enough, was yet another question.

He turned away from her, attention fixed forward, as though he could hear the confusion pinging around in her head. "I mean, you'd be a smokin' hot woman if not for the potato sack clothing and uptight personality."

She tipped her chin down, mouth agape at her loose-fitting tunic over steel gray leggings and knee-length boots. Okay, maybe she could see how her beige top resembled a potato sack, but had he really just insulted her favorite tunic?

"I'm not uptight, you're just too much of a prickly bastard to let me relax long enough for you to get to know me." He whipped his gaze back to her, but her mouth had run away from her and wasn't ready to stop. "And let me get this straight. You've decided from my choice in clothing, I must be a closeted nun?"

"Am I wrong?"

This time her mouth didn't gape so much as waver. She snapped her jaw shut, refusing to succumb to his attempt to shame her. "No, you're not, but I'm working on it. And you know, maybe sometimes looks aren't what they seem." She flicked a loose strand of hair from her face. "Happy now?"

"No. You haven't answered my question." He placed his beer on the counter and leaned back. "If I'm not wrong, then what's with the sheltered act?"

"It's not an act. Some people are introverts."

"Yeah, some people." His all-knowing smile sent a shudder of doubt through her belly. "But that's not the whole story with you, is it?"

"I don't know what you're talking about."

He didn't respond right away, which in and of itself added discomfort. His deep gaze seemed to search for some kind of confirmation before he nodded, as if he'd found his answer despite her avoidance. "I've seen fear and confusion on enough faces to see it in yours too."

The weight in her tummy turned into a mammoth boulder nestled low in her gut. He spoke of fear, something she had in spades. Fear of failing. Fear of falling short. Like she was doomed either way, whether she made a go of her life or not. Maybe that's where the confusion part of his remark kicked in. Because most days, she doubted the decisions she made. And she might be one to linger back, but no fear or confusion had ever stopped her. At least, not forever. The fact she'd come on this holiday proved she could take risks. Which reminded her, she really did need to ease up on Orlando's problems and return to her mission of finding a man. Maybe then she'd stay occupied long enough to worry less about her not-so-elderly resident.

Still, there was one positive to his shocking insight—his statement offered a clue to the life he'd once had. The one where he'd "seen fear and confusion on enough faces". What did he mean by that? Though something about his confession made her feel more settled in his presence. She doubted much could ever surprise him.

She blinked, using the cold glass in her hand as a distraction. She did owe him some sort of clarity. "I've watched others mess up their lives simply because they didn't tread carefully enough. I don't want to make those same mistakes."

Orlando didn't need to know that *their lives* was actually *her life*. She'd never come close to talking about this. Not with her ex, Hector. Not with her best friend, Hannah. What would they think if they knew the truth? One thing was for sure, they'd never see her the same again.

So perhaps the transient nature of her relationship with Orlando offered a pleasant kind of false courage. Even if she did find herself mostly responding to him in indirect riddles.

"And an entire life can pass while you're busy treading carefully." He offered a wry smile. "I've seen plenty of that too."

"Are you speaking from personal experience?"

"Just the opposite. Though personal experience might mean messing around too much led me to the same result. So maybe you're right about not treading carefully." He paused to release a heavy sigh. "Anyway, we were talking about you. Who are these 'others' you mention, the ones who apparently messed up their lives?"

She broke eye contact and feigned interest in the various colorful bottles of liquor behind the bar. If this man had taught her one thing, it was that answering undesirable questions with silence constituted acceptable currency within the parameters of this relationship.

"Right." He spoke with a grumble, before casually slapping a hand to the counter. "I've had enough of this charade." He shot to standing. "Let's go."

"What? Already?" She frowned, her thoughts snapping to her cringe-worthy next task of going to Teasers. "You're not going to finish your beer?"

He laughed, eyes glittering a little too much for her comfort. "If you haven't noticed, I haven't taken a single sip of my beer. I'm not dumb enough to add alcohol to all the meds I'm on."

She peered down at his full glass sitting on the counter. "Why did you ask to come to this bar then? Didn't you want to relive 'the good old days'?"

The scar at the top of his forehead crinkled as he smiled. "I've never been to this bar in my entire life. And as far as I know, Teasers doesn't exist." He pulled a navy-blue jacket over his shoulders. "But as I said, watching you try to fit in here sure did bring me a great deal of happiness."

Nine

HILLTOP ON HIGH was Roseford's most popular cafe, famous for its rustic look and cozy high tea service. Three-tier cake stands with floral country-kitsch patterns stood on most tables, while their occupants sipped from matching kitsch teacups. Sophie sat at a table on the back patio; the wide, wrap-around area unsurprisingly reflecting the cafe's name in that it perched atop a big hill overlooking a picturesque scene of Roseford's rolling hills.

Her laptop sat propped open before her, while the summer sun heated her skin. She dragged her gaze away from the view of gum trees waving in the breeze and a glass-like lake winking from the valley's base. Back to her latest research. Or anti-research, since she used the cafe's complimentary WIFI to browse a local dating site that Luke's fiancée Agathe had urged her to try.

"You know they have phone apps for that now?"

Cold shock zipped up her spine, and she squeezed her eyes shut—needing a moment for shame to subside before she could face the voice's owner. Though she maintained a tight cringe, she opened one eye and peered up at Candice Olsen. "Thanks, I tried, but the cheapo phone I took with me traveling doesn't support any kind of newfangled software."

Candice gave a warm smile. "Don't look so pained, it must be difficult being young and single in a far-flung town like Roseford." She pointed to the seat across from Sophie. "Mind if I sit?"

"Make yourself comfortable." Sophie snapped shut her laptop and welcomed the opportunity to wrangle more information out of someone about Orlando.

"This place is always a little crazy in the warmer months. Thanks for sharing your table." Candice lowered herself into the chair and placed a little sign with her order number down beside her. She leaned forward, fingers interlaced. "I heard you witnessed one of Orlando's episodes."

Sophie paused; her mild progress with him at Hell Cat had somehow faded his episode to the background of her mind a little. That small experience gave her more to associate with him than his condition had. Or maybe he'd spoken to her for a few minutes without any disdain and blindsided her with the things he'd noticed about her that most people didn't.

"Yes." Her mouth remembered Candice sat watching her, even if her brain hadn't. "Though I can't claim to know much more about his condition than I did before."

"Well…" Candice flopped back in her seat and dropped a sigh. "All I can say is what you saw was minor."

Sophie focused on her closed laptop and disappeared into her thoughts for a moment. "I did ask him why he wasn't in a different facility, given his age and care requirements. All I got was that he needed ongoing help, and he didn't want his family taking on his burdens."

"Often there aren't the right resources when a young person experiences a life-changing injury similar to Orlando's. A lack of options may mean they can't stay in their own home and aged care is the only solution." Candice gave a tiny shrug; the structured seams of her moss-green blazer gave her shoulders a square shape. "Orlando wasn't lying about not wanting to be a burden on his family. He has a younger brother who has a successful career interstate, and though his elderly mother lives in Roseford, she's in no condition to handle a guy as big as him when he's in the throes of a bad episode. I can understand why he doesn't want her looking after him."

Sophie maintained her silence, unsure whether to ask for more information or shut up and count herself lucky. She now knew Orlando had a brother interstate and his mother lived in the area... and one other potential detail...

She leaned forward, daring to plow for more evidence. "Orlando is in care because of an injury?"

"That's the assumption, yes. Though a few other factors cloud any real certainty."

Candice's order arrived at the table—a chicken sandwich and espresso—and Sophie waited so the woman could enjoy a first sip of coffee. Her attention wandered in the silence, to Orlando and his little stunt at the biker bar. The way he'd toyed with her, gotten her to take him to a place he had no interest in visiting beyond watching her twist in discomfort. Yes, he'd been a little more open to confiding in her, but he'd toyed with her all the same.

"I want to help him." Her cheeks burned with what might have been a blush, as if she'd offered up some deep, dark desire rather than a concerned volunteer's basic impulse to look after her resident. "But he doesn't want my help. He wants to make my life hell."

Candice let out a short laugh and lowered her coffee, as if she feared her laughter might make her spill her hot beverage. "I wouldn't go that far. He seems to actually like you."

"No, no, that can't be right." The heat in her cheeks released, only to give way to a series of quivers in her belly—a visceral protest against the notion Orlando might *actually like her*. "He threatened to fire me the other day. And yesterday, he made me take him to a dingy biker bar, where he proceeded to laugh at my discomfort. I'm pretty sure he finds great joy in making me want to quit."

"Hmmm... Yes." Candice skimmed a forefinger over her coffee cup handle and nodded to herself. "Actually, he did tell me the other day that he wanted you gone, but I guilted him into reconsidering."

Sophie released a shaky chuckle, thinking back to his non-guilt-ridden shenanigans at the bar—his fake beer drinking and the fake desire to visit a strip club afterward. "Guilt? Is Orlando even capable of that emotion?"

"Sure is. I told him how much the volunteer program meant to you—that getting booted would reflect badly on your study and future work placements." Candice took a big bite of her sandwich and chewed, as if convincing Orlando of anything was a non-event to her.

"B...But that's not entirely true. I already have my degree. Volunteer work is completely irrelevant in relation to my career. As far as anyone would be concerned, this is purely a recreational pursuit."

"Yeah, he said something similar, but I fudged the details a little, you know. I said that having international experience on your resumé will look better than none at all, and that's why you signed up to volunteer in the first place. That you're hugely over-qualified, and you could be enjoying your holiday, so given how far you've traveled to work with someone, he better not disappoint you."

Sophie's jaw hung loose and her face felt bloodless. Not only had Candice twisted the truth to a painful degree, but Orlando had been close to dismissing her after all. *Then*, by some crazy miracle, he'd taken pity on her. Not that she needed his pity. But the fact someone as guarded as him even *felt* pity, much less toward her...

Her nerves were a live wire sparking and flailing, and she reached for her cup of tea in the hopes she might find some kind of calm.

Candice's stare bore ahead. "You're judging me right now, aren't you?"

"A little, yeah. I'm not sure I want to work with a resident who's been manipulated into working with me."

"My little white lie benefited everyone, didn't it? Orlando now has someone to take him out—I don't think you understand how huge that is. You got to keep your volunteer placement. And I got my most unwilling resident out of the center for a couple of hours. Even my staff were happy, since he was decidedly less difficult for the remainder of the day. So, I'm calling this a win."

Sophie peered around the large cafe with its packed tables and cacophony of chatter and clinking cutlery. The smell of sugary cakes from the kitchen mingled with the hill's fresh grassy scent. Her gaze skimmed nearby faces, only to land on Candice's again, just as a new realization struck.

Yes, the cafe was busy, but it wasn't *that* busy. There were more than a few empty tables left.

"There's more to you being here than needing a table, isn't there?" She waited as Candice's complexion dropped to an ashen shade. "You care about Orlando, and there's something more specific than his outings that you're worried about."

Candice broke eye contact, shoulders suddenly rigid as her earlier nonplussed attitude evaporated. "Young people in care require so much more community access. In particular, they need people close to their own age. People like you. All I want is for Orlando to receive help while he still can."

"Because his condition is degenerative?"

"That's the assumption." She returned her gaze to Sophie. "But no, it's because he requires so much more than someone to simply walk him to his room and sedate him when his episodes are at their worst. It's the aftercare that's a literal soul-crusher—when he needs physical rehabilitation and a heck of a lot of intervention." Candice's fingers tightened around her blue floral coffee cup, as though she held back a tide of frustration. "Speaking as one professional to another, in the last year alone, he's had two major episodes. Both left him immobile for months on end. His body simply forgets how to walk, how to move; though he recovers oddly quicker than most accident victims, so I guess that's where the belief comes from that this is more neurological than physical. Either way, each time he has to relearn how to do so many things all over again."

Sophie's lungs compressed, her next breath hard to take. No wonder she struggled to get him to engage with the outside world. "He essentially has to start from scratch with every major episode?"

"Yes. And no one knows quite why his brain reacts the way it does, just that he's in the strange position where his condition isn't bad enough to have him take up a hospital bed, but it's prohibitive enough that he needs constant help."

Sophie let her gaze wander toward the hills, with their sunlit pastures intersected by low wire fences. A few of her prior thoughts on

Orlando clicked into place. Why he was always so grumpy. Why he always seemed ready to check out of life.

Imagine having to start over and over and over again...

Candice rested a flat palm to the table, beckoning for Sophie's attention. "I know he's not easy, but I choose to focus on his ability to get back up after each and every set back. I don't know how he does it, but I do wonder how much longer we can keep convincing him to try. There's so much more going on in that man. So much more than the bad temper he puts on show.

"Something's changed in him lately, and I'm worried. More worried about him than any other resident in my care. And trust me, I'm doing all I can to make the place livable for him—bending so many rules—making so many allowances. And everyone else in this town feels for Orlando too. Do you think anyone here would put up with his stuff if there wasn't a sense of looking out for our own?" She peered down at her hand on the table and winced. "He's losing his spark, Sophie, and I'm getting really worried we might lose him completely. Not to his illness, but to himself."

Sophie's mind ground to an immediate halt, and the clash of cafe sounds seemed to stop around her. Nothing but the beat of her own rushing heart filled her ears. Coldness filled her veins as if her blood itself lost all heat. Soon, a great shiver ran up the sides of her ribcage, and her entire body shuddered in response. She knew exactly what Candice meant about losing Orlando to himself. And the gravity of that meaning cut bone-deep.

She didn't want to believe it. She didn't want to imagine someone as stubborn and unassailable as him taking his own life. But she'd tended to enough suicide attempts during her hospital residencies to know these things could be unpredictable.

She fought to locate her words—but words didn't come. Men were statistically more effective when it came to suicide attempts. They had a knack for finding permanent, and often more gruesome, results. But the one thing she'd heard time and time again—families and friends often had no idea the patient had lost their will to live.

Anyone in her field understood that even the most resilient people could falter under life's curveballs. And just like illness, depression didn't discriminate.

She caught Candice's eye, her pulse still fast. "Orlando needs a psych assessment."

"It's been done. Whatever he said to the psychs, they decided he was of sound enough mind and didn't present anything inconsistent with someone in his position. He's never made an actual attempt at ending his life, and he refused any offer of further help." Candice sent forth a tight glare. Maybe she figured Sophie hadn't been listening, or that her statement hung doubt over Candice's ability to provide care. "There was only so much pushing I could do. Why do you think he was pissed about your dreams of becoming a psychiatrist? He thought I'd planted you to spy on him."

Candice leaned back in her chair as she awaited Sophie's reply. New ease slid across her face, hinting that she'd finally released a great weight off her shoulders, only for that weight to shift right onto Sophie.

A dull pain radiated down her back, the force and magnitude of Orlando's situation, and now her own, settling in. Heck, she couldn't even be sure Candice's assumption on his mental state was all that correct. He'd passed his psych assessment after all. Either way, she couldn't tell him what she knew. Not yet, anyway. Any progress she'd made with him was too fresh with too little trust established. He'd only push her away. For good this time.

And suddenly this unplanned meeting felt too complicated and too much to bear.

This tranquil Australian holiday didn't seem quite so calm after all.

She stood and lifted her laptop along with her, her appetite for tea and dating websites gone. She couldn't even decide whether to thank Candice for the forewarning—or berate her for not leaving the information about Orlando's mental state trapped firmly in its box.

"I'm sorry." Candice's brows pushed together in seeming remorse as if she saw that this conversation wasn't wholly appropriate or appreciated. "I only told you because I need you to stick it out with Orlando until I can at least sort more funding for him—or until I can think of something else to keep him distracted. I know it's a lot to lump on a volunteer. I'm only asking you to do what you can, within the limited months you have, because of your academic background, because Orlando seems receptive to you, and because I believe you can open some windows of possibility for him. Please. Just be the friend he needs right now. Okay?"

Ten

ORLANDO DRUMMED his fingertips over the gray Formica table, as the care workers wheeled in the last few residents. The drumming reverberated in his ear. *Thrum. Thrum. Thrum.* Until abrupt recognition made him stop.

I'm nervous? What the fuck is that about?

He took a deep breath and forced the tension from his shoulders. What was there to be nervous about? Nothing except the daunting truth that talking to Sophie Tindall somehow injected new interest and cheer into his day. Interest and cheer. Two sentiments long absent in his world. As if her visits kept him going.

Well, what a scary thought. Fuck, I'm pathetic.

A burst of laughter erupted out of him, and an elderly woman nearby shot forth a judgmental glare.

Maybe he *was* pathetic. *Stupid too.*

Any enthusiasm he had for Sophie wouldn't hold back his miserable fate.

She's a distraction. Nothing more. Got it?

Yes, his decline would arrive soon enough. He had to remember that. No point getting too invested in this woman.

He gazed around the room, at all the frail bodies with trembling fingers and papery skin. His peers. Though some days, he had even less control over his body than most of this poor lot. Chances were, maybe a few would outlive him.

"Eager to see Sophie today?" Shelley stepped into his view with her smug grin, no doubt pleased her harebrained attempt to match him with Sophie had lasted this long.

He jutted his chin toward the giant brown cardboard box in her hands, ignoring her invasive question. "What's that?"

Her grin widened, and she reached into the box. A smaller, glossier carton landed on the table in front of him.

"Puzzles. For today's session. I'm sure you'll love it." Her overly bright tone denoted sarcasm. She'd been around long enough to know he never showed enthusiasm for anything, much less puzzles.

He scowled, his muscles heavy under the usual effort of working past his lethargy.

"Oh, I love puzzles!" A genuinely happier, distinctly British voice cut in. Sophie appeared from behind Shelley.

Orlando's cheeks lost all rigidity, his scowl hiding at the sight of Sophie's beaming smile.

"At least one of us does." He'd meant to grumble the words, but only managed muffled dissatisfaction. Some unexplainable corner of his conscience didn't want to dull her joy.

Shelley winked at him, she'd noticed his muted response, then turned away to distribute more puzzles. Sophie plonked into the seat opposite him and her large, brown handbag hit the ground beside her.

"Nawww, two kittens. I love kittens." She leaned over the table, gawking at the puzzle box, a little too close for his comfort. The fresh scent of spring flowers jumbled his senses.

She lifted her gaze, bringing the most stunning view of sparkling hazel eyes—green pools streaked in umber and gold—too close to his face. "It's only one-hundred pieces, but both kittens are gray, so that might add some fun complexity."

Her innocent passion kicked his heart against his ribcage and lightened his lethargy. He wanted to laugh but didn't. "I know I've called you Miss Nerdy before, but could you at least try not to prove me right?"

She rolled her eyes, darting her hands out and prying the box open. "I forgot who I was talking to, Mr. Sour Lemons."

He opened his mouth, ready to insult her back, but nothing happened. Again came that rising need to laugh, almost as if just having her near was enough to momentarily melt away years of anger and bitterness. He lost all desire to fight her at the sight of those spindly fingers making fast work of flipping the upside-down puzzle pieces.

So, he joined in, keeping quiet as he turned any piece so the cardboard backs stayed down, and the mottled colors peeked up. Occasionally, he dared to lift his gaze and her eyes rewarded him with a glint. As if simple things like cat puzzles really did bring her joy.

His heart stumbled again.

Damn. Damn her.

He'd done enough damage to everyone who came into contact with him already; he couldn't bring this woman down too. Besides, what the hell was he thinking? Sophie hadn't shown any romantic interest in him whatsoever. Not since that first meeting, where she'd accepted his offer of a date. Not since finding out he was a resident. Not since he'd continually proved to her what a grade-A asshole he was.

And why *would* she be interested? Hell, why would he? No good would come from letting his emotions run wild here.

He shifted pieces around, avoiding any eye contact. "You're looking extra chipper today. Did some cute boy ask you to the social?"

Fuck.

Even when he tried, he couldn't help but give her shit, much less attempt to gather something of her personal life. He'd grown used to rubbing people the wrong way. The mere fact he wanted to rub this woman in any way, much less *every* way—right and wrong—meant he didn't know how to stop tormenting her.

She separated an edge piece from the others and put it aside. Her gaze rose to him, and the corners of her eyes creased with a cheeky grin. "No. You might refer to me as being twelve, but I'm a bit too old for socials. These days my excitement levels require a little more action than a slow dance and an awkward kiss."

His cheek muscles slackened, and his brain shorted for a reply. She paused and then laughed. "I didn't think it'd be so easy to put a look of shock on your face."

He gave a slow shake of his head and returned his attention to the puzzle. "I didn't expect you'd open our conversation with a commentary on your sex life."

He forced his thoughts from what sort of *action* might actually arouse her excitement, just as his hand brushed hers over a puzzle piece.

Her skin was about a million times softer than his and a few shades paler too, while her small stature and Britishness nudged his mind to all things soft, feminine, and classic. The smell of freshly brewed black tea. New cut flowers on a bedside table. Crisp morning light over pristine white bedsheets. A naked Sophie laid out on those bedsheets…

Instant heat spread through his chest and electricity coursed through his extremities. His heart didn't just kick, it seesawed on the edge of exploding.

He snatched his hand back but too late.

Her stare slammed into his, pupils wide and mouth agape. Maybe she'd felt the same surge of electricity. The same shock of need. And if she didn't, then why did she blink at him? So silent. So still.

Her eyelids fluttered some more, and her attention slid down to the table. Neither one spoke. Neither one of them acknowledged the awkward gravity. Which was fine by him.

"So, in light of our biker bar adventure last week…" She kept her head down, gaze firmly averted. "Maybe you could suggest somewhere you'd actually want to visit next time?"

"A lake." He cleared his throat and made himself form a more substantial sentence, though his hands ached to reach out and swipe the light tendrils of sable hair fallen from her ponytail and framing her face. "On the outskirts of town. I haven't been there for a while. Years even. I want to go there."

The lake bordered the back paddock of his childhood home, a deeply personal place where he and his now-dead father had once upon a time spent hours fishing and talking shit together. Those long-lost hours meant even more to him now—now that only one of them still survived. At least, for the moment …

To Sophie's credit, she'd witnessed one of his episodes and not run screaming into the night. She'd even endured his farce adventure to that dive biker bar. So, maybe he could trust her with the lake too.

"Sounds like an adventure." Her bright tone brought him back to the moment. "How about next week?"

He nodded, not intending much of a reply given where his thoughts went now. But then memories of the lake and his dad were always hard to escape once he got thinking on them, and he couldn't handle that pain, so he made a joke instead. "Just be sure to wear sunscreen. Next week will be a hot one, and you Brits are like vampires."

She gave him a crinkled scowl, as if she didn't quite understand, so he offered up his punchline. "Can't handle direct sunlight."

A loud crack of laughter erupted from her—one the circled around the room. He peered around to find residents and volunteers alike wide-eyed and slack-jawed, as though he and Sophie had suddenly become the nuisance kids in class, and no one believed he'd made the woman beside him laugh rather than cry.

He turned back to her and nearly startled at the genuine chuckle rumbling through his chest. He picked up a puzzle piece, vowing not to overthink his reaction, joining the piece to the few she'd already assembled.

Just as that piece fell into place, his stomach churned, and a strong burning smell entered his nostrils. A smell of charred food. Headache-inducing. Eggy. Like stove gas...

And something else... Something... Something similar to singed cloth.

A fire alarm shrieked. Loud. Painful. His chest constricted. Skin prickled.

That smell. So overwhelming. Like a tidal wave arching over him, seconds from crashing down.

The sound. Familiar. Terrifying. The wail frayed his nerves. His control stripped. It told him to go. So his body worked of its own volition, using what little energy he had to launch him into survival mode. He scrambled to the floor, panic and memory converging as one. The reaction mimicked one of his episodes. *But different.* At least he didn't disappear into his mind.

No. His mind sparked and fired under a barrage of commands. Instinct and action took him over. He grabbed Sophie and dragged her down with him, then barked out an order. "Get down. Stay down."

Eleven

"W...W...WHAT'S HAPPENING?" Sophie's knees collided with the hard linoleum floor, instant pain radiating up her legs. She wanted to cry out but didn't have the time. Orlando's hand hooked under her armpit, and he dragged her along on all fours toward the doorway.

"Smell that?" He gave a half-yell, gaze wide and hyper-alert.

She turned her head to her right, then upward—where residents, volunteers, and staff shuffled out the door in calm compliance with the fire alarm. Her wrists already hurt from crawling, something no one else did. "You mean like someone burnt lunch?"

Everyone peered down at her. Many snickered as they left.

Orlando's attention darted around the room.

"And hear the alarm? This is serious." He huddled, head ducked at the common room's archway, hand held up for her to stop behind him. "Listen. Stay low. Okay? The air's cleaner down here. The gas won't get us so much as the lack of oxygen from the smoke, so you need to stay low. Do you understand?"

He peered around, as if blind to all the people scraping past. She sniffed at the air. No gas smell, no visible smoke, but the open fear in his eyes forced her to nod and play along.

An announcement mumbled over the home's speaker, something

about a small fire in the kitchen. Already extinguished. No huge deal. But residents might prefer to go outside for fresh air while staff worked on clearing the smoke smell and switching off the wailing fire alarm.

"The men. Where are they?" Orlando knelt back and looked about him, as if he hadn't heard the announcement. "They should be here."

"What men? Orlando, what men?" She reached out and put a hand on his shoulder. Maybe if he felt her, he'd return from whatever world he'd lost himself in.

"The fire crew. Don't worry, we'll be okay. I'm sure they'll be here any minute." He put his hand over the one she held to his shoulder and patted. Her heart twisted from his show of concern amidst his panic. He seemed to be having some kind of flashback, perhaps a post-traumatic-stress reaction. Something with more physical and mental control than what she'd witnessed with his episode. "In the meantime, I'll get you out safe, and then I'll run back in for the others."

He used his spare hand to swipe at the sweat beading on his forehead, and it was then she decided to let him have this moment, to not embarrass him with the reality of what was really happening.

The alarm went silent. But still, Orlando didn't seem to notice. His breaths panted hard and fast, and he pushed beyond the common room door, around the corner, and motioned for her to follow.

As people filed back in, she and Orlando crawled out, and she yielded to his world. He crawled along, looking back every so often as if to check that she was okay. Even in distress. Even in this moment where he believed his life in danger. He worked to protect her.

A pair of white nurse's shoes stopped inches from Sophie's fingers on the floor. She tipped her head back and craned her neck. Shelley stood over her, head slowly shaking as if to ask, "What the hell are you two doing?" But Sophie held a hand up, signaling for Shelley to stay quiet, to let Sophie handle this.

Shelley frowned but nodded anyway, then retreated.

Orlando's alert control seemed telling in itself. His considered movements hinted at experience. Like he knew his way around an emergency. Like he'd done this before and relived some kind of ingrained trauma where survival trumped flipping out.

He pointed a strained smile her way, an offer of reassurance. "We're almost there. Can you make it a little farther?"

She nodded. Quiet. Overwhelmed at this glimpse at who he might have been outside the home's protective walls and the ones he'd built around himself. A tight lump swelled in her throat. *Poor Orlando.*

Even as he struggled now, she felt completely safe. If this situation were real, he'd still be looking out for her. That first unnerving time they'd met, she'd recognized something in him. His intense stare. His overpowering masculinity. His stillness. For all his problems, this man still held a moral code and maintained a sense of honor.

They reached the sliding doors, and only then did he stand, offering a hand to help her up too. Her knees stung in painful protest, and she peered down at her red palms, cringing at all the germs she'd just encountered on the center's floor. Not that she had much time to cringe, because he grabbed her wrist and hurried her into the parking lot.

Wind whipped her hair about her face, and the lot was full of volunteer's cars. He looked about again before pinning her with a soft stare, where dark circles shadowed his eyes. He appeared truly strung out, even more than normal. "They're not here yet. I hope you don't mind. I have to go back inside. I have to help the others. Dammit. I thought these days were behind me."

He let go of her and turned, but she launched forward and recaptured his hand. "Stop. You don't have to go."

He peered at the home's doors. Uncertain. A man fighting a battle within. *Stay here in safety with her, or risk his life going back in.* His gaze latched onto hers. "They're in there. I don't have any other choice. I have to go back."

Still, everything about his rounded shoulders and hollow tone said, *"But I really don't want to."*

In his mind, he'd just saved her. Maybe it was time she ended his torture. Maybe it was time she repaid this perceived rescue.

She pulled him closer and cupped both her hands over his clenched fingers, encasing his hand.

"It's over. Everyone is safe." She held his gaze, keeping her tone and touch soft.

Sweat drenched the front of his navy-blue shirt, but she reached out and pressed her palm to his chest, repeating the words. Her hands offered sensory distraction—her words pleaded for him to believe her. She wanted to offer escape from the demons in his head and strength where his currently faltered. "It's over. Everyone is safe. Including you."

His brow creased with deep lines, a sign he concentrated hard on what she'd said. The firm set of his jaw released, he broke eye contact, and his gaze shifted to the center's open doors, cheeks relaxing as if he finally saw what she did. No fire. No smoke.

"It's over?"

She held his hand tighter and offered what she thought he might need to hear. "Yeah, you're okay. You're safe."

His stare snapped back, eyelids widened, while his black pupils grew large. Two jerky breaths lifted and fell beneath his ribcage, like a shattered man jolted from a dream, working double time to dam his emotions.

His reaction prompted her to take a risk, to wrap her arms around him in yet another offer of comfort. She expected him to fling her away. To call her irrational. But she also expected he'd had more than his fair share of abandonment. So maybe she needed to be brave. And maybe he needed something different.

Moments passed, and he didn't fling her away. He didn't call her irrational.

He merely paused slightly before his body sunk against hers, and his arms engulfed her in a reciprocated embrace.

Her heart swelled and strained, as he shook in her hold, heavy breaths brushing the small hairs along the nape of her neck. And she clung to him, absorbing this vastly different Orlando—someone she hadn't encountered up until now–someone he probably didn't let *anyone* encounter.

Don't get too used to this. This moment will end. He'll go back to being the hardheaded man I'm used to.

She took a long breath and shelved the reminder, savoring his solid warmth and uncharacteristic openness. She could appreciate the hardheaded man. The hardheaded man had a good reason for being.

That hardheadedness protected him. The hardheadedness likely kept him alive.

"It's okay. It's okay," she whispered and patted his back. For all he'd been through. For this glimpse at his former life—a life no doubt worlds away from the one he lived now.

She repeated the words until she'd convinced herself he might believe them, even though he offered no confirmation of his own. This man, strong and vital, shaking in her arms—the result of constant physical setbacks and psychological scars.

What it must take to be him, to wake every day. A young man trapped in an old man's life.

To miss out on so much stuff that most people took for granted, with no remedy in sight.

For a brief moment, earlier today, she'd rejoiced at seeing him in a cheerier mood; like maybe Candice's suspicions—which had already been assessed and dismissed—really didn't hold much truth. Though Sophie had planned on asking him some subtle questions, that plan had been shot to pieces and replaced with a starker reality.

No wonder Candice feared for his mental state.

But now Candice wouldn't be the only one looking out for him. And even through Sophie's bewilderment, what she really felt was awe that he'd survived this far. That a different man existed when Orlando's defenses were down.

His shaking stopped, and he pulled back, but not enough to let her go. "Sorry about that."

She shook her head, unable to meet his gaze, her attention pinned to the dip at his throat. "What sort of a wanna-be psychiatrist would I be if I couldn't handle a little emotion?"

She tried for a reassuring smile, but her lip trembled, refusing to cooperate. Her reference to her work offered cheap deflection in exchange for his display of raw vulnerability—though she did need space and time to unpack what she'd seen.

She forced her gaze to meet with his. The color in his face hadn't returned, and he looked spent.

"Come on." She stepped out of his hold, a part of her wishing she didn't have to. "We'll start the slow walk back inside."

Twelve

SOPHIE RACED her fingertips over the keys of her laptop, her elbows digging into the glossy red timber of what she'd just been informed was a native Australian Jarrah wood dining table. She shelved any enthusiasm for the expensive slab of timber, and her brother's bragging, and focused on entering Orlando's full name into her web browser.

Agathe took a seat beside her. "I propose Sophie and I do a bit of shopping and sightseeing tomorrow. Let's say, from eleven onward? That will give her time to sleep in after bar-hopping with Max tonight."

Sophie tilted her screen down, trying not to draw attention to her search results and why she'd asked to access Luke's WIFI.

Max sauntered past, beer in hand, mischievous grin in place. "I hope you mean because we'll be getting in late rather than Sophie getting drunk. Otherwise, you clearly don't know this woman. You'd have to pin her down and hold her mouth open to get her to drink anything more than a couple of white wines."

Moments away from clicking a link that seemed to offer a lead, Sophie glared at her brother. "Hey, just because you're all for wild nights and puking into gutters, doesn't mean I have to be. I hate being drunk."

The constant whoosh of cars and city lights infiltrated from outside the double-story brick house in South Melbourne, a strong reminder she wasn't in Roseford anymore. And speaking of reminders, Max's words jogged her memory on why she didn't drink much, the true reason far more painful than the one she'd given. A reason her brother had probably long forgotten, though she never would.

He leaned his hips into the back of a chair across from her, smile still strong. "Yeah, cos you're a control freak, and you struggle to let go, my dear sister. But I'm going to try my damnedest to change that tonight."

"You don't have to try anything. I'll play along, I promise." She clicked the link and continued her farce of being only half invested in the screen before her.

Max meant well, but he'd accomplished world fame for partying and having no clue. About anything. Ever. And he clearly didn't have a clue about her. Though he was right about one thing. She did struggle to let go. And *letting go* had been one of her reasons for traveling abroad. Except, she'd abandoned that goal since meeting Orlando, so she'd do her best to let loose tonight. "As long as you promise not to —" Her gaze reconnected with her screen and a short gasp fell from her. "Oh…"

Agathe leaned over, her shoulder pressing into Sophie's. "Well, hello. Who's that? Is he someone you're talking to on that dating site I suggested? He's gorgeous."

Luke charged into the room, the bottle of wine he'd gone looking for in hand. He crowded in behind Sophie, yet another uninvited person staring at her laptop. "Hey, why are you using my precious WIFI to look up photos of "gorgeous" firemen?"

An icy chill washed over Sophie's skin. *Gorgeous* didn't sum up the man on her screen.

Magnificent, maybe.

Every woman's wildest dream, for sure.

But more heart stopping than any of that, the man staring back at her was Orlando. Yes, eyes twinkling and smile beaming, with zero cares in the world. *Orlando.*

He was an immaculate cliché of masculine beauty with his chiseled jaw, glossy black waves, his golden olive skin... Even the scar atop his forehead somehow added a human edge to his perfection... Though what held her frozen most was the attention-grabbing fireman's uniform. Not just because a set of perfectly sculpted, six-pack abs peeked out from his open jacket—though that didn't help her frozen state—but because the uniform confirmed a massive detail about his former life.

"He..." She swallowed, needing more time, unable to connect this man with the one who pretty much cussed her out at every meeting. But it was him. It was most definitely him. The shadows of this dream man still lingered in the Orlando she knew now. "He's my resident at the nursing home."

"No way." Max crowded in, too. "That's no geriatric geezer. That's, that's..."

She stared blankly ahead. "Orlando."

No. Not a geriatric at all.

She scrolled down the page to a photo of him posed beside a child at a community event. Rainbow balloons hovered on strings behind him, and he wore a wholesome smile. The article said something about him taking part in a "sexy" fundraising calendar for the local fire service.

She scrolled farther again. To another photo. *Holy hell.*

This time the heavy jacket was gone. Broad pectoral muscles accompanied his rippling abs. Smears of strategically placed black ash lay painted over his torso and thick biceps—a homage to someone vividly young and vital. A hero. *A firefighter.*

No wonder he'd freaked out at the alarm the other day.

She saw past the provocative photo long enough to make sense of their last encounter, of all the things he'd left behind, his past resurfacing at the first sign of smoke and fire alarms. The trauma he must have endured to react that way. The emotional scars he carried beneath the ones his condition already caused. He was a man who paid for the privilege of just staying alive.

And even as her brain absorbed the implications of the images before her, her body reacted. Skin warming. Heat pooling between her thighs. While a deep gnawing guilt grew in her gut.

Any attraction to this man wouldn't be right. There was nothing official about her role, but she'd made a promise as his volunteer. To help. Not ogle. And even as that promise crossed her mind, so did the visceral memory of his arms around her.

The man on her screen looked like a god, or maybe just an airbrushed version of what his job entailed. Someone beyond reach of anything or anyone. When the man she'd met was very much human.

"No wonder you've barely left Roseford." Max elbowed her in the shoulder.

"It's not as if he struts around the home looking like that." She gave him a playful shove back, a deceptive move in light of the roiling sickness within her. She stared at her screen, at eyes full of gleaming welcome. "In fact, I'd say there's next to nothing of this man left."

Except, of course, for that hint of *something*. The something as he'd near collapsed in her arms. A hint of inherent good. A man who'd tried to save her, to save others, at risk to himself. And maybe this hint formed another layer to his rage. Orlando was lightning trapped in a bottle. A force of nature bursting to fulfill a purpose. His once beautiful and strong body now a cage.

She closed the laptop, face hot, shame burning a hole in her chest. Another thought entered her mind. Researching his past had been a bad idea. She'd crossed a line. Orlando wouldn't be happy if he knew.

Max's devilish grin pulled her attention. She didn't want to know what he thought, so she peered up to Luke, who leaned over from behind her chair, face almost above hers. "I've seen that look on her face before. She's adopted another stray bird."

"Except this time, it's not a bird." Max wiggled his brows. "It's a sexy fireman with abs of steel."

"Stop it." She slapped Max's arm, hard enough to assert her seriousness, gentle enough not to hurt. "He doesn't flash his abs during my visits. And as far as I know, the six pack is another thing of the past."

Why on earth am I even discussing Orlando's potential abs?

And even in her protest, her treacherous mind pulled up the memory of his firm body pressed to hers—how Candice had said he exercised to keep himself sane—the intimate knowledge that at least something of those abs had survived...

Damn. Damn. Damn. Why couldn't she get her thoughts to behave?

Agathe waved her hands out in front of her, beckoning for attention. "Hang on a minute. Stray birds? What are you guys talking about?"

Luke gave his fiancée a light peck on the cheek and took a seat beside her. "We all grew up near a forest back in York. Occasionally, a local cat would bungle a kill, and Sophie would swoop in to save any injured animals. At least, she'd try. She'd drive everyone crazy with her latest find, get so invested, when ninety-nine percent of the time the poor little critters never made it."

She scowled at her brother. "Yeah, but occasionally one would. And it paved the way for my medical degree, didn't it? So, my 'investment' wasn't all for nothing."

"Yeah, and one-hundred percent of her finds would tweet or squeak up a storm all night, every night." Max pressed the heel of his hand to his forehead. "Man, I can't even count how much sleep I lost each time she brought home an injured stray."

A small chuckle escaped Luke's lips. "If it'd been up to Sophie, she would have skipped school and collected stray creatures every day."

Sophie slumped back in her chair. "Well, I didn't. And despite what you say, my education didn't suffer one little bit."

Luke peered around Agathe. "Soph, you know what we're getting at here. Do the best you can with this guy, but don't get too caught up."

"Who says I'm getting 'caught up'?"

Max crossed his arms, making it clear he didn't believe her attempt at indifference. "The fact that we haven't seen you nearly enough this trip. Or maybe the fact it's a Saturday night, and you're spending your time researching this guy rather than hitting the town with me already."

She pushed her laptop away and held both hands up in surrender. "Okay, fine. I get it. Let's go."

"Yes!" Max gave an excited hiss and turned to the kitchen counter, where he collected his dark gray sports coat from one of the bar stools. "I'll race you to the front door."

———

But later that night, against all warnings, Sophie didn't keep her thoughts off Orlando. The Ruby Room's loud dance music sent vibrations through her body, while the bar's swinging strobe lights flashed blue, yellow and red across the walls and roof. Max had disappeared to the men's room, so she rummaged through her purse which sat on the bar top.

The photo of Orlando actually smiling clung to her memory. She had a hunch, one she wanted to confirm. Her limited and expensive phone data allowed her to perform yet another internet search, while she ignored the fact she'd already spent two hours of her night *not* meeting people.

Her gaze darted about her phone screen, where one particular headline stood out amongst the blurs of blue and black text on a white background. Some article about a chemical fire.

Bingo.

She clicked on the link.

Orlando's name came up in the first paragraph.

"Hey there, beautiful." A bass-heavy voice interrupted her reading.

She focused on her phone for a split second longer, gathered some mention of Orlando hailed as a hero, something about being taken to hospital with minor smoke inhalation, before ripping her attention away and onto a cute guy standing before her, one hand rested on the bar, an amused smile on his face.

She gave him a quick half-smile back, before holding up a forefinger. "So sorry, just one moment."

She returned to her phone, aware that Max would never let her live down the uncharacteristic rudeness. Hopefully he wouldn't spot her trawling the internet over talking to the actual live human standing beside her.

"So, so sorry." She skimmed another article, not experiencing quite as much guilt as she should have.

This article was about the same fire, which had occurred three years prior. She got to the part where there'd been a lawsuit. Her eyelids flared.

Orlando had wanted compensation for his treatments, better care, and a deeper investigation into his condition… but then he'd dropped the lawsuit.

"Riveting reading, I assume?"

She peered up. Mr. Clean-cut-and-cute beamed another, wider, perfectly straight-toothed, blindingly white grin.

"Absolutely." She jammed her phone into her pocket and extended a hand to him. "Thanks for waiting. It's nice to meet you."

Clear blue eyes twinkled, and he took her hand. Her enthusiastic offer to shake seemed novel to him. To her defense, she wasn't up with the latest dating rules and sucked at playing cool. So maybe a handshake wasn't the done thing? She didn't know.

"Nice to meet you too." He turned her palm over and kissed the back of her hand. "Can I buy you a drink?"

Mr. Clean-cut-and-cute dripped charm by the bucketload; his pristine looks and unfettered smile gave the impression he'd never experienced a single dark moment in his life. She gave a quick nod. His light appeal was a welcome change from all things serious. All things Orlando.

She gave the handsome stranger her drink order and spent the next two hours talking to him, glad for the distraction. Glad she'd somehow attracted a man's attention, much less someone so well-put-together. All the while, she withheld her focus from Max, who hid in a far-off corner with a group of people he seemed to know, throwing her an occasional, encouraging thumbs-up.

By the end of the night, Mr. Clean-cut-and-cute gave her a peck on the cheek and his phone number. His name was Branden. An executive in some giant city-based company. A banker? Accountant? Lawyer… *Something…*

Honestly, she hadn't committed much of what he'd said to memory. Just as her brothers had warned, her one-track-mind struggled to focus on the charming guy or his pleasant retelling of his perfect life, even though she should have. Even though she had nothing against "perfect" or Branden.

Only, a different kind of perfection had her captured. The broken kind. Or as her brothers had put it, her "injured bird".

Thirteen

SOPHIE KILLED the engine to her red hatchback, then leaned forward to peer through the rain at the warehouse and the giant, blue sign on the warehouse's side, the words "Aero Syntech" confirmed she'd stopped at the right place.

Her attention dropped to the passenger seat and a glossy pink cardboard bag containing the spoils of yesterday's shopping trip with Agathe. A few new clothes, but mostly lingerie—something other than beige or high-waisted—both of which she'd promised Agathe she'd ditch just in case she met and decided to go home with another charming Branden type.

Her cheeks heated every time she looked at that bag. She couldn't see herself having enough courage to wrangle an encounter with any man, much less wear the racy garments in front of anyone.

But, oh, how I want to.

She sank back in her seat and took a steadying breath, running over her questions thanks to a phone call she'd made that morning. A phone call that led to this one stop before heading back to Roseford.

Aero Syntech had been the chemical warehouse mentioned in the articles about Orlando's injury. She'd managed to arrange a private meeting with a guy named Sam. Though his role and what he knew about Orlando's case remained a mystery.

A loud knock boomed against her window. She jolted and turned to find a man in a heavy white lab coat and a clear rain poncho standing outside. Fat droplets of water streaked her window, adding to the nerve-wrenching, ominous vibe of this encounter.

"Sophie?" The man's steady question came with a short burst of foggy breath against her window's cold glass.

He was a good twenty years her senior, his glasses speckled with rain, and strands of sandy brown hair sticking out from his plastic hood, but plastered to his forehead.

She gave a hasty nod.

He stepped back, allowing space for her to open her door. "It's me, Sam. We haven't got long before my lunch hour is up. We should hurry."

She scrambled with her door, failing to pry the handle open on the first attempt.

Once again, she had poked around in Orlando's life, and who knew what this Sam guy had to say or whether this risk would pay off. She stepped out and shut the car door behind her. "Thank you for meeting me."

"I feel bad about what happened to your friend." Sam spoke against the loud rain, and he tipped his head to one side, indicating she should follow. He hurried through a gate in the long chain-link fence, toward the factory.

Meanwhile, gray-white clouds hovered far above, hitting her with a stinging, white glare, and she had to crane her neck just to compete with his tall, lanky build and make eye contact with the back of his head.

"You're not supposed to be here, understand? So, if anyone asks, you're an old friend of mine who's thinking about studying chemical engineering."

She clambered to keep up, a whipping wind adding to her bumpy sound as she spoke. "I can do that. Can you tell me what happened the day of the fire?"

"Sure. We had a couple of tradesmen repairing the building's exterior. Some of the inventory had been shifted around, when some numb-nuts stationed a pallet of experimental chemicals outside." Sam pointed to an area to the building's left, as if signaling where the incident had occurred. "A perfect concoction of high winds, high summer temperatures, nearby work setting off sparks, and drums and drums of highly flammable chems. You know what happened next."

Yeah, she knew what happened next, though it remained to be seen whether what he described had anything to do with Orlando's life-changing condition.

She sped up a little and got in stride with Sam. "But it was a relatively benign fire, right? Big blaze, but no casualties. Orlando was the only victim, and even he was out of hospital after a basic overnight stay."

"That's correct, and the warehouse admitted to holding more fuel load than it probably should have. I saw the huge plumes of chemical smoke and changing winds that day. Your friend worked one of the farther trucks minus a breathing apparatus, which I later learned is normal if not working too close up. But then the wind shifted and smacked him and a few others head-on with smoke."

"And that's where his injuries occurred?"

Sam gave a short laugh. "If you mean the smoke inhalation that landed him in hospital that night, sure. But the other stuff, the stuff he sued for? No. I can tell you now, he didn't get those here."

She glanced about, uncertain why this guy would agree to meet with her, only to reveal she'd hit a dead-end.

"And you'd know that, how?" She positioned herself next to a door and stopped walking. Maybe if Sam thought someone might catch them talking, he'd make quick with the details. Especially now that she realized she'd never clarified who Sam was exactly. "I'm sorry, what is your role at Aero Syntech, anyway?"

"Let's just call me a run-of-the-mill engineer. If you have access to Mr. Piras's court documents, then you'll figure out who I am soon enough. I testified at one of his hearings."

She crossed her arms and buried a growl; his vague reply made her think he was holding back. "About the court case, any idea why it got dismissed?"

"You don't know?" He jolted a fraction. "Insufficient evidence."

And just like that, the tables of suspicion turned. The vertical creases in the center of his forehead, along with his narrowed stare, implied he knew her presence here wasn't all above board.

She peered to her right, to a window on the door, wanting a chance to look inside without showing obvious signs of snooping. "I gathered that much, but the very fact you're standing here makes me wonder whether you agree with that judgment?"

Her shoulders sank as she leaned back and found the window was actually frosted over.

Sam gave a shrug. "It's the opposite, actually. Your friend sued the fire association for exposing him to toxic chemicals and Aero Syntech for having those chemicals improperly stored. And as I said, Mr. Piras was completely obscured in smoke with no breathing apparatus on. And because other unprotected firefighters caught the same cross winds and are doing just fine, the company had strong grounds to claim they weren't totally in the wrong. So again, insufficient evidence."

That sounded like bullshit reasoning to Sophie, and she wanted to say as much.

In her experience, each person's body was unique. Multiple people could be exposed to the same contaminant and react in vastly different ways. But then, antagonizing Sam would get her nowhere. He wasn't a judge. And no doubt Orlando's lawyer had sought medical counsel in deciding how far to push his case.

So far, Sam here was turning out to be a wasted trip.

"I'm going to need more details." She softened her tone, scrubbing any hint of rising frustration. "Why the secrecy over this meeting? Why are you meeting with me if you believe Aero Syntech is innocent?"

"Look, Ms. Tindall. I'm not just any engineer, I'm a chemical engineer." He pointed a thumb at the building beside him. "The suits in there would have a stroke if they knew I was talking about Mr. Piras without the presence of their high-priced lawyers. Not that they'd ever allow me to talk to some random off the street. I'm meeting you in good faith." He stuffed his hands into his white pockets, the tension across his forehead easing on a look of open concern. "Beyond what I saw that day, the other reason Aero Syntech called on me to testify was that I'm a key developer of the chem that burned in that fire."

"In other words, you're confident that whatever Orlando inhaled couldn't have caused his issues?"

Sam gave a lopsided smile, leaning in a little. "The chemical that burned that day is called TL-20. It's an experimental fuel that releases lower emissions when used in large commercial aircraft. Don't get me wrong, I don't recommend inhaling any kind of chemical smoke, but TL-20's fumes simply wouldn't cause the specific reactions Mr. Piras suffers from now. Lung damage. Sure. Cancer? Maybe after long periods of exposure. But not psycho-centric episodes. Not what I saw in the videos Mr. Piras's legal defense made me watch."

A frown dragged at his lips, and Sam turned unnaturally quiet. Perhaps whatever Orlando's lawyers had shown him still weighed heavy on his conscience. Maybe he wasn't just covering up for his employer after all. Maybe Sam's presence had more to do with sympathy than guilt.

He relaxed his shoulders and continued to yell over the rain. "I'm meeting you because I feel for Mr. Piras. He and his team stopped a fire that could have had a much worse outcome. They ran in when everyone else ran out. And if you're here to get help for him, then you're standing in the wrong place, and that means potentially everyone else around him is looking in the wrong places too. Which means you all need to regroup and start looking elsewhere."

She stifled an urge to share the news that it appeared no one looked in the wrong places because everyone had stopped looking altogether. Especially Orlando.

Still, she'd come here to help him. If she wanted to regain her holiday, much less her life, she needed to settle on a resolution. So far, that resolution involved doing as much as she could to get Orlando the right treatment. That way her overbearing investment in his life could end.

"How do I know this isn't an attempt to send me looking in the wrong direction?"

"Here." Sam dug around in his coat pocket, movements jerky. She'd crossed a line and really teed him off this time. He thrust a small notepad and pencil into her hand. "Give me your email address, I'll send you a list of TL-20's ingredients. If that's not putting my job on the line, I don't know what is. Find someone in the know, and they'll tell you that nothing in TL-20 would cause Mr. Piras's condition. Especially not from one exposure."

She peered down at the notepad jammed into her hand, her heart pounding at how much she'd overstepped her place in being here to begin with.

Max and Luke were right; she'd made this whole Orlando thing way bigger than intended and way too personal. Now poor Sam wanted to throw his career away to appease her curiosity. Yet, she'd come too far and knew too much to turn a blind eye. And if nothing else, she'd at least well and truly taken the plunge into her new world of being brave.

She scribbled her email address on the tiny page, face hot, shoulders drawing upward. "I'd appreciate it if you didn't tell anyone I met with you today. I really am trying to do the best by Orlando."

Sam outstretched a hand and retrieved the notepad. "Likewise. And good luck, Ms. Tindall." He wrenched the door handle down, and the industrial sounds of forklifts and various other machinery broke through. "I hope you find what you're looking for."

Fourteen

"YOU LOOK DIFFERENT."

Sophie whipped her attention over to Orlando seated beside her on the ground at the lake's edge, her skin tingling under the strong afternoon sun and that he'd noticed her floral sundress with the mustard-yellow background. "Yes. The dress is new."

She tucked her knees in and folded her arms over the top, her chest straining that she might have opened herself up to another one of his barbs. Still, even if one did come, she needed him in a good mood in order to learn more about his condition.

"You don't usually do color." His low and easy rumble somehow ensured that him noticing a change in her appearance didn't diminish his cool act one little bit. "I thought black, white, and beige were your thing."

She smiled over at him, squinting against the glare from the lake. "I wanted a change."

A small, gray stone sat nestled between his large fingers, and tiny flecks of dirt stuck to his skin. She could have sworn he mumbled something along the lines of, "You don't need to change," but she couldn't be sure.

She sharpened her attention on him. "Sorry, what was that?"

Maybe the jovial Orlando she'd witnessed in her internet searches would come out to meet her.

With one careless flick of his wrist, he tossed the stone into the lake and turned back to her. "I said, 'Good to see a change from the usual headmistress look.'"

Just like the stone he'd pitched into the water, her stomach sank, and she scowled for half a second. An awkward silence dragged, but she didn't even care. Orlando deserved more time to stew in the juices of his backhanded compliment.

The soft lapping water at her feet should have soothed, but each minuscule wave against her toes only advanced her anger. She had a mind to ask why he was so sour. Why he had to take his moods out on her—someone only seeking to help—and the one person willing to talk to him for any extended period of time. The one person who took him places. Who endured his bitterness. And, unlike the center staff, she wasn't even being paid for the *privilege* of minding him.

"I. Ah." His lowered voice snapped her thoughts back to him. "I should thank you for your help the other day."

His forehead creased with what she could only describe as a confused glower. Her mental tirade halted. His gratitude was the last thing she expected. Then again, he had a way of leading her into traps, so maybe she needed some caution.

"You *should* thank me, or you *want* to thank me?" She narrowed her eyes, still peeved at his earlier negative feedback. "There's a big difference, you know."

The muscles on his face released, and his haunted stare took on extra shadows, as if saying thank you wasn't second nature to him, but he'd push himself to say it, anyway.

"I want to thank you. You put up with a lot from me, I get it. And you handle stuff I figure most normal people have already run away scared from. Thank you."

A burst of heat exploded in her chest, and something unfurled from deep within her—something akin to an icy pond melting under extreme conditions, leaving only warm and welcoming waters.

"Nothing about you scares me." She cleared her throat, but she couldn't take back the husky whisper. "Does that make me abnormal?"

Nothing about his temperament or his condition *did* scare her, but there were other things about Orlando that shook her to her very foundation—the myriad of ways he could hurt her if she made the mistake of getting too close—the ways she could likewise hurt him.

His analytical stare held for a long and heart-stopping moment, until he eventually turned away. "That or you're foolishly brave."

"I think I'm none of that, but your gratitude is appreciated either way."

His gaze narrowed on the lake, giving the impression he didn't quite know what to reply or what to make of her. Though frankly, the confusion was mutual.

She took a deep breath, set on changing the subject. "Tell me about this place." She nodded out to the tall gum trees lining the water's edge and a well-worn jetty with a single tethered rowboat to her left. "Why did you want me to bring you here?"

He shrugged. "I came here a lot as a boy. Just wanted to pay the old place a visit."

A small bird perched on the edge of the rowboat, tiny gray tail swinging in a joyful side-to-side motion. Maybe if she got him to talk about the easier details of his past, there'd be room to broach the subject of her research and her plans to help him. "Roseford would be a nice place to grow up."

"In some ways it was, though I'd kinda always banked on a life away from here."

His shoulders drew a little in a begrudging sign that he expected her to ask for more detail, which was a good sign she should probably ask nothing. Besides, she already knew what his dreams had entailed. Where those dreams had led. Though Orlando had no idea she'd dug into his past. Or that she'd met with Sam at Aero Syntech.

She was yet to abandon her suspicion over the claim TL-20 had nothing to do with Orlando's condition. Sam was a chemical engineer, likely a damn good one too—but he wasn't a doctor. Heck, even if he had been. Even if Orlando's own lawyer had received advice from a doctor who agreed with Sam's ideas about TL-20—advice that had maybe pushed Orlando to drop his case—she'd seen firsthand that there were doctors, and then there were *doctors*. Each one had their own strengths and skill sets. And finding the right specialist care could make all the difference to Orlando's life.

"What about you?"

She startled at Orlando's question but stared ahead, the cool wind off the lake brushing her face and bringing with it the water's earthy-sweet scent. "You want me to tell you where I grew up?"

He scraped a patch of dirt with the heel of his brown leather boot. Maybe he too didn't expect the sudden interest in her life. "Yeah. What's with the accent?"

"York." She offered a gentle smile. "I grew up in York."

He faced her, wrists curving over his bent knees, long fingers pointed toward the ground. "And what does a childhood in York entail?"

"I guess it would be similar to life in Roseford. I grew up in a small town, only with a different landscape. I had the ocean and cliffs nearby, and the forest closer still. My younger years were magical, really."

He frowned, suggesting he'd grasped her positive assessment and still heard the somber notes underneath. "And you still left."

"I wanted to experience life away from my small town." Actually, she'd practically run from her small town, but she couldn't say that. It would be selfish to bog him down with her own sad tales. "I also wanted to study."

And she'd been great at study—making the most of city life, not so much.

"Right. So, you stepped out in search of excitement and"—Orlando let out a short chuckle—"decided to specialize in geriatric psychiatry?"

She shook her head at the irony. Geriatric psychiatry didn't seem all that glamorous or exciting to most, but there was a certain beauty in working with the elderly.

"My high school used to do this whole community linkage thing." She paused, making sure he'd understand she really did care about her job. For his sake, more than hers. That everything she did was because she wanted to see the people in her care do well. "Students would partner up with a resident at the local nursing home, not too dissimilar to the volunteer program here in Roseford. The lady I was paired up with was named May. The sweetest woman I'd ever met, with some of the saddest stories. The thing that really struck a chord with me most was how she'd lost her younger brother in a downed military ship during WWII. How half a century had passed, and her eyes still misted when she spoke of him, and how that very story would soon disappear with her own passing.

"Every week I had a meeting with living history, and it was an honor to bear witness to what she had to say. I'd never had much contact with elderly people before that point, but May changed my life. She made me want to do my bit to help make these people more comfortable, more heard in a world often in too much of a hurry to listen. Our society shifts in ways that repeat old mistakes over and over again, and I don't know—" She toyed with the hem of her dress, a lump forming in her throat. Would Orlando understand, or would he simply mock her as usual? Though to his credit, today his bitter appraisals were mostly absent. "I guess I figure if we all cared about our elders a bit more, maybe we wouldn't feel so isolated or aimless ourselves."

His focus honed in on her, and she wondered if maybe he knew she spoke partly about herself. The drawn-out silence put new strain in her muscles, and she refused to look at him in case anything she did tipped him off further.

"You make them sound like saints."

The tension in her body eased. If he noticed anything, he thankfully didn't let on. "I guess living in care, maybe you have a different opinion?"

He shook his head at the lake. "I try not to mingle with the locals."

"Why not?"

"The oldies don't tend to stick around long, if you know what I mean. My situation is depressing enough."

His subdued tone formed an uncomfortable ache around her heart, and she dropped her attention to her sandaled feet. "Right. Sorry."

She'd been stupid to overlook that detail. A detail no doubt more painful given he'd grown up around many of those residents, only to get a front row view to their decline. And of course, according to Candice, there was the added weight of how those same residents made allowances to ensure he received care at the center.

She rose to her feet, wanting to shake away the disquiet weighing heavy on her shoulders. "Is this fresh water?"

"Not sure I'd drink it." His voice settled behind her, but the shame of her blunder kept her from facing him. "Safe enough to swim in, though."

She closed her eyes to the soft breeze on her face and took a slow breath, the air sweet and smelling of sunshine and muddy earth. "I can't remember the last time my feet touched water, outside of a shower, of course."

Nowhere in the world could she see clear lakes surrounded by gum trees. No amount of time in this country would ever be enough to uncover the mysteries of its overwhelming, natural beauty. Just the other morning, a mob of gray kangaroos had decorated the wild grassland outside her cabin. They'd grazed in a heavy mist over the valley, and she'd awoken to peaceful magic all around—a secret dance of nature unfolding for her eyes only.

She kicked off her shoes and went about gathering the hem of her long dress, ready to test the water.

A shuffling sound from behind her pulled her attention to Orlando jumping to his feet.

"What are you doing?" His eyelids flared.

"I thought it might be nice to wade in a little. Why?"

He didn't answer, just sent her a flinty glare, that glare dropping to her exposed knees.

A quick laugh broke from her. "My shoes are the only thing coming off, trust me."

His gaze met hers again, brows bowing at the center. "This partnership is awkward enough without having to see your skinny ass."

Laughter tore through her again, but she turned away to sink her ankles into the water. "Nice to know you still noticed my ass despite my 'headmistress' clothing."

She chuckled to herself, imagining Orlando rolling his eyes behind her.

He didn't respond, so she left him to his silence, wading deeper now. The sensitive skin behind her knees tingled at the water's cool touch, sending a thrilling shiver through her body. "You know, you don't have to sit there scowling at me. You could always join me."

"I'm not sitting, and I'm not scowling."

She whipped around, heart thudding to see him standing in the water about three meters away. His heavy boots lay abandoned on the shore, and she opened her mouth to voice surprise. But his hands swept out in front of him, collecting the lake's surface until a light shower of water hit the front of her dress.

The cold impact sucked air from her lungs, and she gaped at her water-speckled dress.

A wave of instinctual laughter clashed with another instinctual drive to seek revenge. She swung her foot out and kicked water back at him, instant regret holding her in place as the giant spray slammed into his stone-blue, cotton shirt.

She expected a growl, for him to swear and retaliate and give her a serve of his usual stick-in-the-mud attitude. What she didn't expect was for him to laugh.

The joyful sound alone kept her off guard, and one huge, man-sized kick of lake water hit her square in the face. She let out a shriek and spluttered to expel water from her mouth.

Her hair hung in thick, soggy tendrils, plastered to her face and shoulders. Her dress clung to her body. But the afternoon air was warm, and Orlando's laugh kept her warmer still. The low rumble of it... The way his eyes lit with his wide smile. His jeans were wet from mid-thigh down, his fault from his backfired revenge. But that smile...

He held the same smile from his photos. The one from his past. A grin that beamed and brought light to his face. Genuine. Unfettered. Real. Energetic and amused. And not on a computer screen, but just meters away.

He smiled for *her*.

She had so many questions, starting with, when had that smile last made an appearance? But she refused to ruin the moment.

He spun away. Another laugh rose from his wide chest, and that laugh cracked the air, unabashed and spontaneous, as if he couldn't stop even if he wanted to. He was like a child playing in the rain, the lake one giant puddle to frolic in. The gleam in his eye lifted her, and before she knew it, her inner child soared too.

He doubled back toward her—as though he figured she'd wasted enough time. She squealed and ran in the opposite direction, but she wasn't fast enough.

Somewhere in the pandemonium, she dropped her hem in the water. Her legs tangled in the material. So much for trying to look stylish.

She tripped, her face inches from the water, only for a strong hand to grasp her elbow and pull her up.

Orlando drew her to him so swiftly, her forehead almost collided with his.

She puffed against more laughter. "I didn't know you had that in you."

"Neither did I." He paused, his gaze darting over her face.

A clump of hair clung to her forehead, obscuring her vision on one side. She moved to clear her eyes, trying hard not to focus on his tight grasp on her elbow or the blossoming heat filling the space between their bodies.

"I would have brought towels if I'd—" She lifted her attention to him staring at his hand at her elbow. One sharp lift of his chin, and his attention met hers.

"If I were any other man." The air between them prickled. "If I had any kind of future, I'd—" He clamped his jaw, not finishing that sentence.

"I…ummm…" Her heart thundered, and she had no idea what to say or do next, but when his gaze dropped to her lips, her senses locked further.

Did she want Orlando—with his haunted stare and undoubtable beauty—to kiss her? *Oh, yes.* Should she let him? *Hell, no.*

A kiss would mess up their professional partnership.

Sure, there were no strict rules about volunteers getting involved with residents. She'd even heard a story or two of senior marriages stemming from such introductions. For those in care, when it came to intimate relationships, it was vital to maintain as much privacy and autonomy as possible.

But more lay within her doubts than the way they'd met. She already struggled to distance herself from this man—her internet searches a case in point. She'd get attached.

She hadn't come to Australia to fall in love. Far from it. But she was the type to fall easily and fall hard—and that was without considering just how complex falling in love with someone in Orlando's position would be. So, maintaining her space would be for her benefit as much as his.

She'd be leaving in mere months. And his life remained complicated enough. As much as she wanted it, a kiss would be unfair.

And still...

Oh goodness.

Her tummy flipped.

She'd just weighed up the probability she'd fall in *love* with Orlando. She really needed to regain her grip.

"I researched you." The words shot from her mouth, her need to avoid any intimacy with this man landing her in a different kind of trouble.

He reeled back and let go of her arm. "You, what?"

"After your flashback the other day, I researched you. I know you were a firefighter. I know about your accident. I know about the lawsuit. I even visited Aero Syntech and spoke to an engineer there." Her body tensed.

What am I even saying? Why am I saying it?

Her stomach flipped again, for an entirely different reason than to run from her earlier attraction.

Dark anger burst in his eyes, his deep brown pupils seeming to turn black. But in her usual fashion, she couldn't stop rambling. Also in her usual fashion, she would not stop rambling until she'd obliterated every last chance he'd want to kiss her... Even though she still so desperately wanted him to. "I've made some phone calls. Depending on the replies, there's a small chance I can get you some help."

There. She sounded like a right clueless idiot. Even to herself. *Bravo, Sophie.*

Orlando blinked, and his teeth ground together, a ripple of muscle flexed and released over his jaw. Perhaps he sifted through all she'd said and couldn't make sense of any of it. "You dug up information on me?"

"Nothing that isn't already publicly available." She cringed. She really was a level ten clueless idiot. "You know what I do. Give me a chance to alleviate your situation."

"You dug up information on me, then turned up at Aero Syntech, and then made phone calls like a bonafide creeper?" He shook his head, stepping farther away; face contorting a little, as though the woman he'd potentially wanted to kiss had vaporized and turned into a toad. "I've had all the offers of help I can deal with. Nothing's worked. I don't need you doubling down on me too. That's not what this relationship is about."

A sick sensation spread through her gut, while his displeasure cast a heavy net around her shoulders, dragging her beneath the lake's surface.

"I'm not 'doubling down'. I'm not even asking you to do anything." She'd meant well. Really, she had. Even if his hardened features made it clear he didn't see her efforts quite so positively. "I've seen a number of cases turn around with the discovery of something that was previously missed. I want to make sure that's not you. If you'll just humor me, I'll—"

"You'll, what?" His features hardened. "You'll imply I haven't already thought about every possible scenario? As if my lawsuit tanking and being told I was clutching at straws wasn't humiliating enough? Do you even hear how condescending you sound right now?"

"I just thought—"

"Let me guess." His words cut forth, as if he couldn't hold back even if he tried. "You thought maybe your 'almost' psychiatry qualifications could be enough to fix me? Is that it?"

The weight of his accusation held her in place. Or maybe it was the kernel of truth that bothered her so.

She'd been arrogant to think she knew better than anyone else involved in his care. Or maybe some corner of her heart didn't believe that life could really be over for a man so otherwise strong.

His expression eased and a slight softness entered his glare. Maybe he too heard the harshness still reverberating around his words. "Sophie, I don't need another doctor. I need you to—"

He pressed the heel of his hand to his forehead and spun away, as if he second guessed whatever he'd meant to say.

"Tell me." She stepped forward but fell short of offering her touch.

"This is way more honesty than I've had in years." He kept his back to her, but his tone dragged husky. "For a second there, playing in the water, I felt like a man again. A man without a death sentence looming over his head. A whole man." His broad shoulders rounded, the rough-spin of his cotton shirt stretching over his back. He turned to her, dark clouds gathering in his eyes, despite the perfectly clear sky around him. "For one brief moment my problems disappeared, and then you jumped in with your own special brand of verbal castration. I don't need another doctor, Sophie. Do you hear me? I'm not some charity case who can't take care of his own shit. What I needed from you was an equal. At the very least, I needed a friend."

The word *friend* echoed in her skull, and the hollow in her stomach collapsed into a bottomless sinkhole. She'd failed him, indeed, overstepped her mark; completely missed the simpler elements of what she should have provided from the very beginning—a meaningful connection with the outside world—a life for him beyond Roseford Aged Care's walls.

Everything I'd started to give him already.

But *enough* was rarely enough for her, and she'd underestimated the value of all the gradual softening she'd already drawn from him. She'd all but ignored his achievements thus far.

And she'd hurt him in the process.

She lowered her attention to the easy waves pushing at her sundress. "I'm sorry. I—"

She lifted her chin, owing him some direct eye contact and a decent look at her guilt as she apologized. He inched forward, like he planned to speak.

"Orlando?" A different voice called out from afar.

Sophie spun around to an older woman, perhaps in her mid-seventies, power-walking across the sandy bank. A path of golden yellow dust rose behind her, and she held a hand high in a quick and excited wave, a black Staffordshire terrier trotting along beside her.

Orlando frowned, rapt attention no longer on Sophie.

"Mum?"

Fifteen

"WHY YOU HERE?" Orlando's mother spoke to him in a strong Italian accent, and Sophie sank back, a set of magnificent blue-green eyes glittering her way. "And who this?"

Orlando cleared his throat, cheeks relaxing though his brow was still tight, failing to completely obscure all signs of his earlier anger. "This is Sophie." He nodded toward her minus any eye contact, then made his way out of the water. She followed his exit, feeling less than worthy of his mother's attention. "She's my volunteer from the home. She's been deemed competent enough to take me out."

A slow grin widened on his mother's mouth, and she threw herself toward Sophie in an enthusiastic embrace. "Thank you for helping my boy. I so happy Orlando has a new friend his age." She backed away, her knobbly, bent fingers brushing wisps of hair from Sophie's face with a sense of motherly affection. Her care and warmth exuded from the quick glance she threw Orlando. "She's pretty, no?"

Orlando clenched his jaw, appearing to hold on to a need to remain polite. His mother didn't seem to notice the tension passing between her son and his "new friend". She peered back at Sophie. "You both come to my house. I live near. I feed you."

Sophie's muscles locked in protest. "Oh. No. I can't."

The staccato words were less gracious than she would have liked, but she really couldn't impose on Orlando's mother after having just disappointed him. And especially not in light of how deeply she'd already allowed herself to get pulled into his life.

"You take care of my boy, I take care of you." Orlando's mother grabbed Sophie's hands and drew her closer. "Please. I will also give you towels."

"Mum." Orlando spoke on a low growl. "She said, no."

His mother waved a hand in a dismissive gesture. "Where your manners, Orlando?" She hooked her arm around Sophie's and gave a sharp tug. "Sophie comes and so do you. It's Italian hospitality."

Sophie stumbled along, scooping up her sandals, her sincere moment of joy with Orlando long gone. She couldn't look back at him. Not to plead for help. She didn't deserve help. Nor could she put her foot down and hurt his mother by refusing to eat at her table.

Orlando trudged a few paces behind, the black Staffordshire terrier trailing farther still, as they crossed through a thick line of gum trees.

"My name is Marcella." His mother spoke in a bright whisper, though the scores of wrinkles on her forehead signaled a woman well versed in worry. "Orlando is in a temper, yes?"

Sickness turned within Sophie's tummy, her dress dripping water down her legs, adding discomfort as she walked along. Still she gave a shaky nod. "It's my fault."

Marcella held a momentary silence, as if assessing what exactly Sophie might have done to upset her boy.

"It will be okay." Marcella's decisive voice cut through, and she patted Sophie's hand. "Everything be better with food. Orlando's father take him to the lake for important talks as a boy." She lifted her posture along with her voice, including Orlando in the conversation. "It's nice he think to take you here too."

Sophie's skin prickled as Marcella insinuated she knew all too well that Sophie and Orlando had been embroiled in their own *important talk*—one they hadn't quite finished before Marcella showed up.

"Sophie's a grown woman." Orlando's grumble sliced through the hanging quiet. "You don't need to hold her hand."

Marcella peered over her shoulder. "With you in your temper, I do. You scare your friend. You make her upset already."

Cold guilt ran through Sophie's veins. She turned back to him, not exactly sure what she hoped to achieve, except perhaps a silent offer of apology. His tight stare spoke of anger, but his rolling silence said he would not rat her out to his mother about looking into his past.

His attention switched back to his mother. "Let her go. We're joining you. Isn't that what you wanted?"

"*Si, tesoro mio.*" Marcella let out a heavy sigh and released Sophie's hand.

A red brick house sat atop a small hill up ahead. The sky behind its corrugated-iron roof had already faded to a vibrant pink-orange with evening rolling in fast.

Marcella's dog brushed against Sophie's left leg, tongue lolling to one side as it peered up. She leaned down and scratched the dog's head. An ambush of licks drenched her palm in doggy slobber. She laughed. "Aren't you a beautiful one? What's your name?"

"Nero." Orlando's clipped tone sent her back to standing. The dog didn't seem to care. The sound of his name sent him darting toward Orlando, and in a well-synced series of steps, Nero leaped into his arms.

Marcella shrugged. "Nero was Orlando's. The dog live with me now."

Trust Orlando to name his dog after a fiendish Roman emperor.

A long hush took over, and they made it to Marcella's door. Marcella went inside and pointed Sophie toward the bathroom to wash the remnants of dog slobber off her hands and find a towel; meanwhile, Marcella went to the kitchen to call Roseford Aged Care and alert them that Orlando would be returning late.

Once back in the living room, Sophie overheard Orlando tell his mother he needed a rest. She rounded the corner to find the shadows beneath his eyes supported his claim, while Marcella wandered over to her son and touched his face with slow tenderness. "Go, rest. I will talk to Sophie."

Orlando opened his mouth, like he second-guessed leaving his mother alone with Sophie, but then he walked toward the door anyway.

He slowed beside her, voice a hushed whisper, eyes narrowed. "Don't use this as an opportunity to dig up more information about me." He sauntered out the door and called behind him, "I'll be back out in half an hour."

Marcella's blue-green eyes lit up, and she motioned for Sophie. "Come. Come. I'm excited to meet one of Orlando's friends."

"I'm not sure he'd count me as a friend right now." Sophie followed into the adjacent kitchen, heart heavy, overcome with a need not to allow her role in Orlando's life to bring Marcella too much hope.

"He likes you." Marcella opened a retro-looking, lipstick-red fridge —a fridge that matched an equally red oven set into blond, woodgrain cabinetry. "He's angry at you. But he likes you."

The sun disappeared behind a far line of trees through the kitchen window, turning the world outside a deep indigo hue. Meanwhile, Sophie sought conversation away from whatever Orlando may or may not feel for her. "Who's Kayla?"

Though Orlando had warned her not to ask questions about him, this one fell from her mouth before she could stop herself.

Marcella straightened, fridge door still gaping open. "Orlando told you about Kayla?"

Sophie shrugged a shoulder, chest constricting. "Not exactly. I was there when he had an episode, and he called me that name."

"He thought you were Kayla?"

She nodded, unnerved with the clear interest. "Who is she?"

"Kayla is Orlando's friend from when he was little." Marcella peered down, and for the first time, her face lost all excitement. She refocused on the open fridge door, silent, as though deliberating over what to say.

She eventually collected a bowl of salad greens and placed it in the center of the small dining table.

"Orlando, he care for Kayla a lot, you know? Many people not happy that our family come from a different country. We look different. Speak different. Orlando not fit in. But Kayla never worry about what others think. She was his only friend for a very long time, and because of her, other children begin to like him. They give him a chance. And because of that, then some parents accept our family too. And even though Orlando and Kayla know each other forever, when they are in high school, he had… What do you say… strong feelings for her."

For some inexplicable reason, Sophie felt her organs sag within her body, and the unease of that sensation took her to the dining table for a seat. Somehow though, she stayed fully invested in learning more about Orlando's past. About a little boy isolated for no other reason than he had olive skin and was born to a migrant family. And a solitary girl who came along with her brave brand of friendship.

And even though Sophie didn't know what it was to be excluded over race, she knew such experiences left marks on a child. Marks that often altered self-belief all the way through adulthood. Orlando undoubtedly hadn't forgotten his ill treatment. Chances were, his condition made up just part of why he acted like an outsider. Why he'd wanted a life away from Roseford.

She peered back at Marcella, wanting to know more. "And what happened when they were in high school?"

Marcella pressed a switch on her red kettle. Clearly, she had a love for all things scarlet.

"Eventually, they do start to date. Kayla loves Orlando, Orlando loves Kayla…" She paused, gaze glued to the tile floor. "They skip school one day and go to the beach. Kayla get stuck in the tide, but there's no one else but Orlando to help. But he can't save her. He didn't know how. They call it a rip tide. He didn't know you swim along the shore, not toward it. He too nearly died." She closed her eyes and sucked in a slow breath. "I think this is why he maybe want to be a fireman. Save people, you know? Why maybe he never want a serious relationship after that." Marcella snapped her eyes open and swatted a hand as if to shrug off the topic.

"Survivor guilt."

"Sorry?"

"Your description indicates he tried to make up for Kayla's death with his subsequent life choices." Sophie let out a sigh, while Marcella poured water from the boiled kettle into a large pot on the stove. "Though, it's hard not to wonder how different his life would be if

Kayla hadn't died. No firefighter. No accident. Maybe no neurological condition."

Marcella added a small palmful of salt to her boiling pot, though she managed to peer over at Sophie as she did it. "Orlando told you about the accident?"

Sophie shook her head. "I figured it out."

"I bet that make him happy." Marcelle laughed. Pasta went into her pot now. She shot Sophie a sudden sideways glance. "Oh. That is why he is mad with you. Yes?"

Sophie gave a sheepish smile. "I'm trying to help. He's not onboard with that idea."

Marcella dropped the empty pasta packet into a bin under the sink, renewed lightness crinkling the skin over her cheekbones. "You think you can help?"

"I don't know. I have a medical degree, but I'm as green as a doctor can get, though I have witnessed a few cases where further investigation helped." She lifted herself out of her seat and padded over to the counter for the bag of green beans Marcella had left out. "It's a long shot, but I doubt looking deeper into his treatments over the years will make Orlando's situation any worse."

Marcella stared in silence for a moment, her hand coming to rest over Sophie's. "Thank you. Orlando won't say it but I will." Her fingers curled around the back of Sophie's hand—fingers boney but her touch tender. "Someone else is trying to help my boy, this is very special to me. But if you don't mind, please don't talk to him about Kayla. It makes him sad." Her gaze stayed locked on Sophie's, sandy-brown brows releasing their tension. "You care for him. No?"

Heat washed over Sophie's torso, and she dropped her attention to the counter where Marcella's hand covered hers. Orlando would be royally pissed if he walked in right now.

She slipped her hand away and reached for a small knife on a nearby chopping block, deciding she would help top and tail the beans.

"Not like that. No." The breathlessness with which she spoke made it hard to believe her own lie.

She didn't know what she felt for him exactly. The more she learned about him, the more she wanted to know; the more her heart ached for him to let her in, the more she needed to distance herself.

And still, she'd been the one to shrink away when he'd eyed her lips less than an hour ago. He'd wanted to close the distance between them. She hadn't. But here she was again, asking questions. Getting too close. Her head ached from the merry-go-round of clashing thoughts.

Marcella set a red bowl beside Sophie for the beans in, though the woman's gaze stayed on her until she caved and offered returned eye-contact.

"Before his accident, Orlando had a lot of women. After his accident, I'm the only woman he sees." Marcella's continued flat expression resembled someone going through the motions of a story that hurt to retell. "For all the 'I love you', not one woman stayed. I don't blame them. My son ran out of money in the city and had to come back to Roseford. None of us knew what was wrong with him. We still don't. Only that it will maybe get worse. Maybe kill him." Her voice cracked on the last line, a woman doing her best to hold herself together. She gave a hard swallow, working at control, eyes red-rimmed, but dry of tears. "I'm his mother. It's no other woman's job to look after him. I stay. I want to stay. Mothers stay, you know?" Her thin fingers curled into the countertop, trembling. Her voice wobbled, too, and a tear finally trickled down her cheek. "If he could let me, I would go with him."

Sophie lowered the knife, her forearms limp under the weight of Marcella's words. *Go? Go where?* She frowned at Marcella's tear-streaked face, so happy minutes earlier.

Did she sense the same things Candice did? That Orlando might not want to live for much longer? Or was Marcella speaking more broadly about the possible degenerative nature of his condition?

Bile rose up Sophie's throat, but she swallowed it down, her own wave of emotion threatening to spill over. In another life, she'd come close to knowing just what Marcella did, but as fate would have it, she couldn't claim any personal experience of motherly love. Not like Marcella described. Not the sheer desire to follow a child to the grave if that were the only place that child could go.

Her shoulders sagged, and she gave a surrendering sigh before turning to Marcella and pulling the woman into her arms. Muffled sobs broke against Sophie's neck, but she held still, allowing the woman a moment to grieve.

Minutes passed before Marcella pulled back, gaze suddenly brightened. Maybe a good cry had been all she needed. "If Orlando were okay, you would be with him. No?"

Sophie shook her head with taut vigor. "I can't. I—"

"Orlando was always popular with women." An exuberant smile tugged at Marcella's cheeks, as if she wasn't all that interested in Sophie's explanation. She sniffed, using the back of her hand to swipe at another tear, before giving a soft chuckle. "He was always restless. A curse. I used to worry he would never settle down and give me grandchildren, but now I know there are bigger things to worry about than no grandchildren... Anyway, he never let any woman be a friend. Not after Kayla. You are special. I know this."

Sophie snorted out a laugh, then pressed a hand over her mouth to stop herself. "I'm sorry." A few seconds passed, and she mumbled through her palm. "I'm almost certain that right now he'd rather see me disappear under a moving bus than call me a friend."

If he'd been angry about her researching his past, heaven help her if he knew about this chat with his mother.

"I know my boy. And I like you too." Marcella took the idle knife off the counter and started on the beans Sophie had failed to complete. "If things were different, meeting you would bring me hope—"

"But there's nothing—"

"Let me finish." Marcella held up a hand, sending forth an insistent stare. "I know you say he not like you—maybe you believe that—but if I say nothing now, I will forever have regrets." Her pale cheeks showed the full weight of her wariness, and she returned to cutting beans as if she couldn't look at Sophie as she spoke. "Please don't break my boy's heart."

Sophie's jaw slid open, and for a few seconds, words refused to form in her brain. "I have no intention of getting involved with Orlando."

Marcella continued to hurriedly trim beans. "It's my job to love him, no matter what. Enjoy your time in this country. Find out what you can for Orlando's illness. But if you feel for him, let him go. Save yourself. Don't let my boy love you, only to watch you leave." Her words were rapid fire, and she shook her head as she spoke. She cut, strain and speed culminating in jerky, fevered movements. "You know about his condition. He cannot follow you. Get on with your life like any young woman should. His life is hard enough without watching more people leave. You will break him. You understand? Just like Kayla did. Maybe worse. Leave loving him to me." Her chin jerked up, her gaze latching onto Sophie's. "Please."

Sophie's blood coursed through her body at a wild and straining pace. Every muscle felt weak, and she wanted to fall into a pile on the floor—or maybe she wanted just to fall *through* the floor and disappear. Her mere presence had obviously made this woman's life worse than it had already been.

For the longest time, her mind blanked. Sure, she found Orlando attractive, but she'd never once entertained the idea of a relationship beyond her being his volunteer. Marcella's warnings and gray-tinged face spelled out why.

"I understand." Her mouth wobbled into a reassuring smile, while she vowed not to argue or offer excuses, even if Marcella's assumptions were way off. "Thank you."

"Thank you for what?"

Sophie swung around to find Orlando standing in the doorway, his attention switching between her and his mother.

"Your mum was giving me some advice about the locals." Sophie smiled at her cleverness, her claim not a complete lie since Orlando *was* a local. "How was your rest?"

He stared at her, the skin over his cheek bones taut, like he recognized her deflection but hadn't heard enough to press her on what had passed.

Marcella walked over to him and placed both hands either side of his face, forcing him to break his stare-off with Sophie. Her fingertips skimmed his cheeks, like a mother soothing a small child. Her son. Her son who required all the gentleness she could muster.

"Sit." She stroked his cheek with the pad of one thumb. "Food will be ready soon."

Orlando held his mother's gaze, expression unreadable. His tight jaw said he didn't appreciate the unmissable sorrow on her face, but the softened edges around his eyes betrayed his usual pretense that nothing got to him. That he never worried.

Orlando worried about Marcella.

Sixteen

"My mother warned you to stay away from me, didn't she?"

Sophie maintained a hurried stride on her way back to the car, annoyed at Orlando's question and that he, with his longer legs, managed to trudge even farther ahead of her. If anyone was going to be pissed, it should have been her.

She hugged herself, the gesture not enough to fend off the cold night or the icy strong winds skimming off the lake. "What makes you think your mother warned me away?"

"I know my mother." His hands hung in curled fists at his sides.

"It's dark. I can barely see where I'm going." She frowned at his hulking physique and those long legs stalking farther and farther away. "Will you slow down already?"

He didn't slow down. He stopped completely. Then whipped around to give her the full intensity of his devilish, dusky glare. "Happy now?"

She drifted past, at least glad not to have to look at him. "I will be when we get to my car."

In truth, she couldn't blame his snappish mood, much less her own. Marcella's parting stare had held a vivid *remember what I told you* vibe and hadn't been at all subtle. Any chance of a pleasant goodbye had been shot to pieces. Orlando took one look at his mother, then at Sophie, and marched instantly off into the gloomy night.

The memory made her cringe, and she figured, despite the fact she'd gotten ahead of him, Orlando probably needed a break from people making decisions behind his back. So, she breathed in the lake's damp and muddy scent and dispensed the truth. "Fine. Yes, she did warn me. But I like your mother, and I understand why she did it."

No. Actually. The warning stung. And she'd felt no better than a child being slapped on the wrist for something she hadn't yet done. She understood, sure, but understanding and appreciating were two different things.

The thud of his feet grew louder, and he soon sidled up to her, though she tried to ignore him. "And what do you plan to do about her warning?"

She focused on the glittering water ahead—black, though speckled in moonlight—her tiny car a shadowy blob to the right. "Nothing. The warning was baseless."

A second of silence, save for their panting breaths, passed long enough for her to wonder if he'd speak again. "Why? Because Saint Sophie could never have feelings for Screwball Orlando?"

Her belly churned, and unease sent her state of mind further off-kilter. His blunt words failed to hide the low huskiness in his tone, a huskiness that suggested her reply might hold more importance than he let on. And maybe her tummy churned because she did have the feelings he spoke of, and his mere question hinted his awareness of that fact.

"Both your mother's warning and your question just now are redundant." She swallowed hard, hoping with all hope he wouldn't drill down on her need for denial. "I would never cross that line with you. Never."

He barked out a laugh. "Never is a strong word, one I'm not sure you'll be able to keep. And which line would you never cross exactly? The non-existent one between volunteers and patients?" He walked in stride with her now, close enough that his body heat caressed her left arm, the lightness in his tone in itself unnerving her. "You're the only one drawing lines, Saint Sophie."

She shot him a glare, only to witness the maddening view of his mischievous grin. Why did her need for caution always seem amusing to him?

"My work means something to me." She picked up her pace, her car not far now, though her feet sank into the long grass with its swishing, dense brush. "You're not serious about wanting to cross any lines with me. And don't call me 'Saint Sophie'. You don't know the first thing about me."

A growing rasp of grass behind her announced his fast approach. He soon positioned himself ahead, forcing her to a standstill. "But you know everything about me, given your research into my life and all. And that's fair?"

"You know why I did that."

She glared, shifting to get away from him. He sidestepped, stopping her, making it clear he wanted this conversation. Even if she didn't.

"What I find interesting, is how your professional integrity flies out the window when it comes to digging up my past, but despite whatever *you* think you know about me—" The devilish grin returned, eyes glinting against the moon. "Let's just say I don't need the internet to figure you out."

She rolled her eyes. Maybe if she let him talk, he'd let her and this conversation go.

"Fine." She huffed out a breath, theatrically bored. "Tell me what you know. It's cold, and I've more than earned the cup of Earl Grey tea waiting for me at home."

He scowled, clearly disapproving of her glib approach. "You're passive and indecisive. For the most part, you struggle to stand up for yourself. Worst of all, you look after other's needs without factoring in your own."

As much as she disliked what he had to say, his confident appraisal held a dangerous edge of truth.

"You think I'm naïve, don't you?" Tension bunched the muscles at her chest, making it harder for her to breathe against all his quips about her being a "nerd" and a "saint". How dare he fling her attempts to care for him in her face and use it to make her sound stupid and weak? "And let me guess, you think these attributes are also my fault?"

He lifted a palm to the sky, only confirming the statement, and stoking a need to find out about his other perceptions. "I'm sure you think your heart is in the right place."

She pressed her jaw tighter and held back on defending herself, if only for the moment. "Tell me what *you* think."

"I didn't ask you to look into my life. You either did it under the naïve impression you could help, or to satisfy your curiosity because you had more malicious reasons." He trained his heavy gaze on her, as if he saw every thought running through her head, analyzed it, then hung those thoughts out for all to see. He inched a little closer. That mere inch was enough to churn her guts anew. "I know which version I'd rather believe. In which case, you'd do better to protect your heart and not get so invested in things that will hurt you."

"Things that will hurt me? As in you?"

His smile crept up on one side, the rest of his expression flat. "I'm a losing bet, remember?"

She barked out a laugh, jabbing at his pumped-up certainty that she would ever get so invested in him. "I'm not looking to get involved with you, Orlando. Though I am glad you've noticed my commitment to your care. It's my job not to give up on people. And since my intention is to work with the elderly, pretty much every case I take on will end sooner rather than later. *Losing bet* or not, you don't need to worry about me getting hurt."

His eyes narrowed, but he remained silent, suggesting he didn't believe her future career would be her sole reason for meddling.

Perhaps he genuinely disliked being nothing more to her than a case. *Well, tough.*

She lifted her chin, ready to set him straight on the limits of this relationship. "It takes more strength to let others in than it does to keep your guard up. I acknowledge that must be exhausting for you, but all the flaws you point out in me lack perspective. Where you say I look after others at the expense of myself, another might say I'm hardworking and I enjoy a challenge."

He stared at her, unblinking. "Whoever said that is an idiot."

She locked her muscles in place. "Do you always have to be so rude?"

"On the subject of you and me? It seems so, yes."

"There is no 'you and me'."

A tiny smirk cracked his stony glower and he made a *tsk* sound. "Naïve. Or maybe it's denial?"

"You're being ridiculous."

She took a step forward, moving to leave.

He took a wide sidestep, halting her exit yet again.

His glower returned harder than ever, jaw set, like he'd had enough. "You really think my observations here are wrong? That I lack perspective? Well, I have a little perspective for you..." He drew nearer, the direct hold of his deep, dark pupils seeming to bore into her soul. Her heart thundered. The close proximity took up all her air and fanned whatever growing attraction she might have had, yet stifled, toward this man. "Where you demand gratitude for your help, I hate being treated like a spectacle. I'm not a puzzle for you to solve, Sophie. I'm not an experiment. I'm sure as heck not some animal in an exhibit for you to observe. Passive might be your 'thing', but it's never been mine."

Her heart squeezed. She let out an awkward crackle, before finding her voice. "That's not what I intended."

"Nevertheless, that's how you made me feel."

A gust of wind *whooshed* over the long grass. She peered down at her feet. The mere fact he talked about his feelings should have been a good sign, but those feelings entailed pain, and she'd been the cause.

"Not that long ago, I was an independent man with decades of life ahead of me." He paused, attention veering toward the lake, which seemed to stretch out forever into the night. "I have nothing now. Nothing except the same conversations with the same dying people at the home. The monotonous routine of every meal served at the same time every day, every day playing out almost the exact same way. Except for when I've had a bad episode.

"And then it's the need to have someone I barely know wipe me, bathe me, turn me over so I don't get bed sores. I can't even rely on the comfort of my own mind functioning as it should." He reached out and tipped her chin up, forcing her to see him. To see the reasons why he was rude and often grotesquely direct. "You want to know what makes me tick, Sophie? The answer is nothing. A person in my predicament doesn't waste their energy on dreams and desires. And you, in all your academic brilliance, should already know that. There was no point to your digging, and that's what makes you naïve."

He gave his head a slow and steady shake, not much different from a stern teacher scolding a child, though a muscle twitched in his cheek, belying his defenses weren't quite as impenetrable as she'd figured. "And no matter how much you might think I fail as a man, I deserved to know what you were up to. I have nothing, but I never once gave up my right to tell you to shove your job and your research."

His last words hit her like a hard slap to the face, so much so her skin burned of its own accord. He was right. She didn't deserve to be in the same space as him.

He'd deserved to know. And she deserved his take down now. She'd known that truth the second she'd carried out that internet search on him. She'd not only been naïve, but she'd been downright condescending in confessing her failure too.

She bit her inner cheeks, shame snaking its way through her insides and adding to her sense of unease. But even then, she still fought to be right, and she fought an urge to point out he would never have agreed to her help.

She'd come to Australia to rough her life up a little. To learn about herself... But now as she got her wish, she skulked away at the image reflected back.

"For what it's worth—" She forced herself to maintain eye contact, to offer a win in light of her mistakes. "I don't see you as a losing bet or an incomplete man. You were dealt an impossible hand, and I'm in awe you've held together as well as you have." She paused, hoping he'd take heart of what she had to say next, minus discovering another detail she had on him—Candice's hunch. "I hope you continue to do so for a very long time."

He gave a little flinch, his head tilting to one side, as if her words affected him, or maybe he'd gleaned her knowledge of his potential wish to end his life. Her heart squeezed. Her skin prickled. But ever so slowly, one corner of his lip curled up.

"So Mother was right." A light burst to life in his eyes. "You would if you could."

"I—" Her mouth wavered open and closed for a few seconds, delaying her ability to respond. "I didn't say that."

"See what I mean?" He turned on his heel, this time the first to head for the car. "Indecisive."

She stood stunned in his wake, attention glued to his back as she tried, but failed, to chase after him. She couldn't believe he'd turned the conversation on its head, but then again, this was Orlando. He took *heartfelt* and made it into a joke.

She growled under her breath, spell broken, and trudged after him.

She eventually reached the car, where she got in and started the engine.

The drive back to Roseford Aged Care consisted of her staring ahead and refusing to look at Orlando. Not that he seemed to mind. He spent his time gazing out his window, flashing an occasional dumb grin from the corner of her eye.

When she did pull up to the home, she counted the seconds until the infuriating man would open his car door and leave.

But he didn't leave.

"Sophie." His voice held a gentle quality, the low rumble adding intimacy within the tight confines of her car. "Look at me."

She blinked ahead, fingers tightening around her steering wheel. "No. We've done more talking today than in our entire time knowing each other. Let's call it a night."

A heavy silence drew out. Perhaps he waited for her to change her mind. But he'd already referred to her as indecisive and passive and naïve, and she'd prove him right in falling for yet another of his attempts to embarrass her. She wouldn't give him that chance.

He blew out a loud breath, and his seatbelt clinked as he released the buckle.

"Fine." His door popped open, but he still failed to leave, the bite of cold air hitting her side. "The thing is, I know I don't have what it takes to be what you need." Next came the rustle of movement, and in her peripheral vision, he stepped out—only to lean in and poke his head through his open door. "But I would if I could, too."

Seventeen

SOPHIE DIPPED her brush into the orange watercolor paint, her movements scaled down to avoid any accidental clashes with Orlando. They sat side by side in the home's common room, a photo of a farmhouse backed by sunset clipped to the easel, a photo she and Orlando were tasked to reproduce on canvas together.

"So how is it that your mum lives in town, but she never takes you out anywhere?" She focused on the painting—on the pink and orange hues—anything to avoid looking directly at *him*.

"Trust me, she's tried." He dabbed green paint at the farthest edge of the canvas, seeming equally invested in maintaining his space. "I told her not to. Everyone in town already knows I'm an invalid. I don't need to parade myself through the streets with my mother clutching my hand and crying at the sight of me."

Sophie's heart squeezed, and she looked about to see if any of the many fellow residents or volunteers overheard Orlando's cruel description of himself. *An invalid.* A deeply derogatory term meaning literally *not valid.* Which Orlando was anything but, especially to her.

She frowned, lowering her brush half an inch. She understood why he wanted to shield his pride in public, but Marcella loved her son, and raw emotion had flowed in thick waves off the woman whenever she discussed him. And then there was his clear protectiveness over his mother, so maybe he cared as much about safeguarding her pride as he did his own.

"Your mum loves you." She collected more orange from the pallet, while considering how Orlando might benefit from redefining his relationship with his mother. "And why do you care what anyone in town thinks?"

"Sophie, my mum is in her mid-seventies. She should be looking out for herself. Besides, she's not all that good in an emergency." He let out an exasperated sigh. "One time she thought someone was breaking into her house, and she called me, who lived hours away in the city, to ask what to do."

"I mean, that's not completely unreasonable. Many people call those close to them in an emergency. Not the best course of action, but understandable."

"The point is, she should have called the police first, and she wasted precious minutes panicking on the phone with me. I don't want to put her in a position of having to manage me in an emergency."

She shifted her hand to the canvas, just as he moved his to paint a patch of sky beside her sun. Their knuckles nearly touched, but he redirected his movements, guiding his brush back to the pallet between them. For a man who'd boldly declared *he would if he could*, he sure was being skittish today.

Sophie glowered at her portion of the painting, unsure what to make of his current evasiveness, while also miffed he'd limited his mother's involvement in his life over one mistake.

He cleared his throat, perhaps a distraction from the literal near brush of his hands. "The point is, she worries enough. If something went wrong, she'd spend her remaining years blaming herself."

Sophie gave a gentle nod, and a steady silence drew out, her heart plodding under a slew of conflicting thought.

Maybe she should come right out and discuss what he'd said the other day. Wasn't it best to deal with issues of impossible attraction in a direct manner? Maybe in a clinical sense. But the human side of her, the side that maybe did feel something for Orlando—as a man, not as a *project*—couldn't find the courage to broach the subject.

She glanced sideways, to his occasional downward gaze at the paint palette, that gaze giving him an air of sadness. Her energy dipped in response. She recalled his heavy tone as he'd told her he didn't "have what it took to be what she needed". The way his eyes had grown darker, as if the brutal honesty pained him as much as it had her.

"You never talk about your parents." He spoke low and warm, but the abrupt sound of his voice jolted her focus back to the canvas.

"There's not much to tell." The cold creeping through her body begged to differ. "My mother lives in York, has done all her life. Now all her kids are grown, she spends most days in her garden or socializing with her lifelong gal-pals. And Dad... He..." Her words snared on a sudden lump in her throat. She took a long breath, allowing her emotions to settle. "He died a few years ago. A bad heart. You know. Kind of sudden."

Orlando paused and turned to her, her gaze momentarily fusing with his, before she got too overwhelmed and peered back at the emerging artwork.

"It still hurts even when you know it's coming."

She gave a quick nod. "You speak from experience?"

"My dad died seven years ago. If you ask Mum, he worked himself to an early grave."

He began painting again, and she joined him, the light from the wide window behind her reflecting off the wet canvas. "Why does she believe that?"

Orlando let out a rough laugh. "He did everything he could to keep the farm running, but a few bad years and a shaky economy overshadowed his efforts. The house and the lake you saw the other day are just a small portion of the original land belonging to our family. My parents were forced to sell off two-thirds a couple of years before Dad died. And Mom's right. The stress and disappointment did kill him."

She willed her eyes to stay pointed forward but failed, her wobbly tone also taking on a life of its own. "I'm sorry."

Her focus trekked down to the dark, thick stubble over his strong jawline, his full lips commanding her attention.

A shock wave of need quaked heat through her body, and she yearned for the days where she saw only hard scorn and denial in his eyes. This new, softened look, along with his sudden ability for candid conversations, felt impossible to ignore. He should have shut her out after he'd learned of her digging; instead, he opened to her even more.

I would if I could, too.

Arggh. Her heart fluttered, nerves unsettled. Would she? If she could...

She turned away from him. From answering that question. The pressure of his stare too much.

Even if she could... Orlando's defensiveness served a purpose. At the least, it helped him survive. And then there was Candice's warning...

Strain constricted the muscles in her throat, but even then, speaking in that moment sure beat thinking. "It must be hard on your mother. You know, living alone."

From the corner of her eye, Orlando dipped his chin, as if taking a moment to consider his words. "A lot of Southern Europeans of her era weren't overly welcomed in Australia. My parents had a hard enough time relocating from post-war Europe, without the decades of blatant racism and being shunned by some folk here. I guess times changed, and most people in these parts got to accepting us eventually, or maybe they look out for us now out of guilt for how they treated us back then. Who knows? Either way, my parents had each other through it all, and they had a bond only death could break. Which it did."

He dropped his brush into the cup of water designated for cleaning off paint, and slumped back in his seat. "The ending was bad. So yeah, Mum pulled the short straw, but she got more love from my dad than a lot of people can ever hope for. I doubt she'd take a refund on their time together just to spare her the grief of that ending."

Sophie sank deeper into her seat, too, twisting the end of the brush between her fingers. Orlando's resignation from their task zapped her own desire to paint, much less that the deep tragedy in his words hinted he would be one of those people who'd never have the chance or the decades to experience the relationship his parents had shared.

That sentiment alone made it hard to forget the phone call she'd received that morning—an answer to a few enquiries she'd made before spilling the truth to Orlando about looking into his past.

He wouldn't be happy if she told him about the call, he'd accuse her of more meddling. But to look at him and do nothing? To know that one way or another, his days might be numbered, or at the very least, he'd likely never regain all he'd lost. Maybe she had a duty to tell him either way.

Her attention shifted to the rustle of other volunteers standing and packing up. A wall clock to her right signaled an ended to their time together for that day. She needed to decide whether she should tell him. In order to do that, she needed distance from this man. So, she stood, her purse strap already halfway up her arm.

"Don't leave yet."

She startled at the gentle command, her gaze catching his. The depths of his eyes were endless, and they swallowed her whole, keeping her in place.

He grinned and sudden lightness ruptured whatever tension lingered between them. "I like having more than octogenarians for company. Stay, please. Or if you have plans, take me with you. Just don't leave yet."

She flicked her attention to the tiny stampede of volunteers filing out into the parking lot. Her brain yelled to turn him down flat, but where he'd once forced her out the doors, now he finally invited her to stay. She couldn't find it in her to reward this hard-won acceptance with rejection.

"It's nice out, and I'd planned on enjoying the good weather." She refocused on him, her heart in an inexplicable flitter. "I've been meaning to visit the beach along Manna Gum Grove. I wouldn't have to go alone if you joined me."

Orlando's smile stilled, and his gaze drifted over her face, like he saw her fraying nerves and her heavy doubt. Like he too understood the risk in prolonging this visit.

"I know Manna Gum Grove well." Stern tension marked his

features, as if avoiding any sudden move that might awaken her ability to say no. "I can show you the nicer sightseeing spots."

She gave a tight nod and turned on her heel, drowning her misgivings with a rapid-fire response. "Grab whatever you need to take with you, and I'll meet you by the doors. It's almost lunchtime, so we'll swing by my place and fix something quick to take with us."

Her cheeks burned; thank goodness she had her back to him. Not only had she signed up for an impromptu beach adventure, but she'd just invited Orlando to her cabin.

Sophie leaned into the open door of her fridge and searched for what was left of the lunch meat she'd bought yesterday. The muscles between her shoulders burned under the stare she envisioned Orlando pinned her way. *Envisioned* because she'd struggled to look at him from the moment she invited him to the cabin.

The lunch meat lay wrapped in thin, white deli paper at the back of the top shelf; she pulled it out and ferried it to the kitchen island.

"I hope you don't mind sandwiches." She spoke down to her hands, unable to get her mind around the rough-edged man propped against the far wall in her kitchen, or to come to terms with her stupid plan to feed him.

He didn't respond, which only added to the twitchy sensation in her gut. This was ridiculous. This was her place—at least for the time being. He didn't get to make her feel uncomfortable in her home.

She reached into a drawer and peered up at him as he gave her a slow head shake. His lack of words and full attention caused her fingers to fumble, and she dropped three teaspoons whilst searching for a butter knife. The high-pitched, metallic ting shattered the painful quiet.

She huffed out a groan. Annoyed at him. Annoyed at herself. "Will you please say something? You're creeping me out."

She had two brothers. Had just come out of a long-term relationship. She'd been around plenty of men and performed a great many medical assessments on them. Why did this particular one bother her so much?

A smile broke across his face, as though he'd been only half-aware of his leering, and her admission cracked some unspoken barrier.

"Sorry." His focus switched to the wood-paneled walls around him. "Quaint little cottage." He refocused on her and shrugged, as though the simple observation was the best he could offer.

She paused her bread buttering and glared at him, before gazing around the small, but light-filled kitchen—black stone bench tops to her left, cutesy paneled windows above the sink behind her. "This is my brother's cabin. Luke runs a successful tech business. He's somewhat of a star." She returned to the sandwiches. "So go-figure, he has a spare house or two. Me, on the other hand…"

"Let me guess." Orlando's rich voice came as a warning for her not to peer up, in case the look in his eyes matched his tone. "You've racked up years of student debt so you can learn important skills to help others. There's nothing wrong with your career choice, Sophie. The world would not function if we were all businessmen."

She warmed at his genuine defense of her career. A job he'd given her hell for earlier. A job where she witnessed the best and worst of people, and often had to deny her humanity in order to work fast and avoid becoming overwhelmed.

She dared to look up, to his softened smile. If he truly did hold respect for her job, perhaps now was the time to tell him about her earlier call. That she'd nabbed the assistance of a specialist willing to look into his case…

She opened her mouth, ready to blurt out what he'd see as her latest misdeed, but he pushed himself away from the wall and sauntered toward her, drying her ability to speak.

"Let me help you." He picked up a tomato from the bench. "It's only fair."

She snapped her jaw shut and handed him a serrated knife. His powerful hands enveloped the slim handle, and he went to work slicing the tomato—drawing her focus to the ripple of muscle in his thick forearms.

For a brief moment, she had a sense of standing outside of her body. Like none of this was really happening. Orlando was making sandwiches in her kitchen, and somehow, they managed to hold off on the fighting long enough to have a normal conversation. *Much less* his presence felt easy and pleasant—even though her nerves remained set to fluster.

She buried her confession about the specialist. *Perhaps another day.*

For now, she'd settle with maintaining the *nice*.

"I don't know how you do it." Her heart sank the second the words fell from her lips.

So much for maintaining the nice.

He peered up at her, and his direct stare signaled he understood her reference.

"Neither do I." His jaw muscles strained a moment, before finding release. "Most days I don't want to."

She nodded, heartsick at the toll of his daily battle with his condition. "I kind of figured that much."

He drew in a loud breath and put his knife down, before he curled his fingers into tight fists and pressed his knuckles into the kitchen island's rustic wood top. "I feel bitter most days. I can't go back to what I had before the episodes started. I can't find hope in any kind of future because I simply don't see one ahead of me. The last three years have been me trapped in the middle of a raging storm with no escape. Every day is incrementally worse. Every day takes me further away from what I used to have. But something's changed."

His chin tilted down, but he lifted his grave focus onto her. "Lately, I get glimpses of calm within that storm. I'm trapped, but sometimes there's this new kind of stillness. Moments to breathe within the panic. Does that make sense?"

Her eyes prickled, but she gave a weak nod. She'd weathered storms too. Personal ones. Ones that engulfed her whole and spat her out, aimless and afraid. And even though his admission unlocked her own painful memories, she held her emotions together. For his sake. For his willingness to include her.

"You're accepting your circumstances." She offered a soft smile designed to reassure. "The limitations. The inevitabilities."

"And I've found someone that makes my days a little more bearable."

He held her stare. Immovable.

His open vulnerability came with a purpose. Or more precisely, a challenge.

Clear thought ran from her mind, leaving her deficient in words, though his resolute gaze demanded an answer.

She'd come to admit an interest in him, at least to herself, but she'd never once considered marring this semi-professional relationship with something more personal. She'd also never imagined he'd be the one doing the marring.

Her ability to speak wore down to a rough rasp. "You're supposed to hate me."

He straightened and loomed over her from across the island. Elbows locking. Brow flexed and stern.

"I never hated you. I recognized your ability to ruin the neat solitude I'd built for myself." Hard tension pulled his shoulders wide, making him appear broader than ever. Finally, she could see the man his mother had described, the one quick to run into burning buildings, the one confident with women. And that same confidence took him around the kitchen island. He drew near, and his close proximity coupled with his swarthy features made her pulse race and breaths short. "You don't give up, and for all your prodding, I've learned one truth. The only thing I hate about you, is the hope you bring, when hope for me is dangerous. But hope doesn't keep me going, Sophie. Your visits do. Each day you're not at the home is just time between when I get to see you next."

She needed space to breathe, space from him, and took a step back. "That kind of dependency isn't fair to you."

"Incorrect." The word shot from his mouth, fierce and certain. "I'm not in control of where my condition takes me, but don't let that confuse you into thinking I'm not in control of my mind. Not once has my competency come into question. You can ask Candice about that one. I know what I want. The question is, do you?"

She dug her fingers into the rough counter, his iron resolve rendering her momentarily speechless. "What I want is irrelevant."

He stepped forward, disallowing the space she'd claimed. "Maybe to you, but not to me. And what you want is written all over your face. Every time I look at you, I see your mind ticking away. I bet you wish you could make that ticking stop, huh? Maybe break free of yourself just long enough to live a little. Isn't that why you left London?"

Her muscles locked. He seemed to know at least some of her reason for being in Australia. But she needed to save herself now. Needed to redirect him. Anything to keep Orlando from digging out more truths or setting any more challenges. God help her if he articulated her desire for a short-term lover.

She eased her shoulders down, attempting to conjure a sense of calm. "My precise job as your volunteer is to help make your life more bearable. It's understandable you'd look to me for an escape."

His gaze darkened. "That's one piss-poor attempt at deflection. If you truly want what's happening here to be fair, then I sure as hell wouldn't mind shaking up your world the way you've shaken up mine. And I dare you to tell me that *your job* is the only reason for all this energy pinging between us."

Her mouth fell open, ready to throw forth a quick rebuttal. But nothing came. All she could do was stare. She couldn't lie. She also couldn't admit to her feelings—no matter how much his all-encompassing presence made her want to. And even then, her lack of confession wasn't just about her job, so much as a literal inability to speak her mind when it came to anything that mattered. When it came to *him*.

From the moment she'd met Orlando, she recognized his capability to shake up her world. And part of her deep-seated concern had always been about whether she could withstand anything he had to offer. Maybe he was right. Maybe her status as a volunteer did present a poor reason for deflection. And maybe, in many ways, her state of mind was just as fragile as she'd assumed his to be.

Her focus shifted to the low-scale commotion of a gusty wind outside, and the creak of windows.

He drew near, as though she'd run out of time to fight the tug-of-war he'd extended, her heart clenching in response.

"I see."

What exactly did he see? And why did she feel like some newfangled discovery under a microscope?

He stood close enough that his heat touched her, the front of her body enlivened, caressed with warmth. His palm engulfed her left cheek, and the challenge faded from his eyes, replaced with a new kind of tenderness. Somehow, her heartbeat settled.

In all her confusion, two things remained indisputable. This man had innate power over her, and for all his brooding, she trusted him. She felt safe.

"If you don't want this." His arm locked around her waist, and he tugged her against him. "Just say so." His voice dropped to a whisper, as though for once he wanted to be the one to comfort her. "I never sought you out to help me, Sophie. I'm not your patient. I'm a man in my own right, and I want you. Do you understand?"

Her mind struggled with the reality he unfurled around her, and she produced just about the only action she could manage—a slow, dumbfounded nod.

He drew his face closer still, and a small smile tugged at his lips. "Then I'd like it if you didn't try to distract me this time."

Blood rushed her veins. Her skin prickled under an attack of nerves. He'd seen through her blurted confession at the lake when he tried to kiss her. And still, her every muscle burned with sparks of desire. The touch of his hand to her cheek and his spoken certainty settled her into following his lead.

His lips closed the space between them, and before long, his full-bodied kiss commanded hers, overriding and inescapable—as if he'd decided her chance to protest had passed. His movements mirrored the man himself. Dark. Hot. Powerful. Somehow robust and gentle all at once.

She should have said no, should have pushed him away, but already, he'd taken her too far. His tongue swept her mouth, claiming her. His strong hands held her pressed to his large frame.

And even as he kissed her, she wanted more. His touch intoxicated and left her no choice but to melt against him, to relish all he gave, and for once surrender to losing control.

Seconds passed, and she unearthed the courage to kiss him back.

He rewarded her with a growl. His hands swept down her body, wild energy coursing from his fingers as they curled around the backs of her thighs, and he hoisted her off the ground.

She cupped his face and pulled him in for a deeper kiss. He carried her across the room, then pushed her hard against the wall. An exhilarating burst of air escaped her lungs. Her body responded with a burning sense of recognition. She ground against him, hoping to sooth the needy ache tearing through her body.

As much as she wanted to blame herself—to call this moment a lapse in judgment—Orlando was right. He *was* a man in control of his mind, and he proved it every time he set her in her place. She'd never once questioned his self-awareness, never once doubted his ability to know what he wanted.

She clung to him, her fingers raking through his thick wavy hair, whilst vividly aware he was right about something else. She had used her position as a volunteer to run from him. To run from herself. But now, for once in her overly-controlled life, if just for one fleeting moment, she wouldn't shrink away from what she desired most.

Eighteen

ORLANDO HAD LEARNED that anyone in his predicament could not waste time. And after weeks of watching Sophie blush and stumble through every exchange, he wasn't about to lose this chance.

He'd also once read that what people missed most after a big loss was the mundane. Things like: a favorite meal, a parent's hug, a much-loved book lost through the years. What he missed most was the assumption he had any kind of future. He missed fitting in. Stability and direction. But Sophie in her kitchen, carrying out the mundane tasks of making sandwiches and dispensing with easy talk, had brought another thing simmering to the surface. Something he thought he'd never have again. *Connection.*

The scorch of her lips now tore open a space in his heart, a pain he chased, despite settling for less than what he truly wanted with her. That ever-elusive future. He couldn't imagine her desire for him running as deep as what he held for her, but at least for this moment, she was his.

A dull ache bore into him from her fingers clinging hard to his shoulders. He relished that pain too. A reminder of her need, as he held her lifted and pinned to the wall. For once, someone *needed* him. He was more than a compliant patient doing what he was told.

She pulled her lips away, panting. "This is the most absurd thing I've ever done."

"It's not my brightest move either, but making good decisions hasn't gotten me all that far, so..." He slid his hands over her thighs, pushing her loose red sundress until it bunched around her waist, his touch an incentive for her to stick with him. He'd be damned if he let her overthink this. "Let's forget about using our brains for a while and focus on our bodies."

She shuddered, sucking in a sharp breath. His blood surged at her uncontrolled reaction, but seconds later, her hazel eyes clouded in seriousness. "I'll regret this."

"No." He held her gaze, dismantling her stern approach. "No. You won't."

"You'll regret it too."

The pain in his heart vibrated through his body, another hint he couldn't let her back out. "I can't think of anything I want more."

The throb in his chest deepened into a sharp needling, the truth in his confession a surprise even to him. A part of him prepared for yet another of life's rejections.

"You're okay, aren't you?" Her gaze searched his, the darting movements betraying more misgivings. "You'll be okay?"

Her question left him momentarily speechless. Never had a woman he planned to sleep with asked if he'd be okay. He couldn't imagine why it was so important to her, but he nodded. "You?"

She nodded, too, hand rising until her knuckles skimmed his jawline.

"I'm scared, but I still want you." She let out a staggered laugh. "Or maybe I'm scared *because* I want you. Or maybe it's how much I want you that's the frightening part."

Her touch and words ignited a flame. Based on what he'd witnessed of her personality, she'd probably never done anything quite this spontaneous before. Compared to him, she was sweetness personified. But then there was her courage, compassion, and quick intellect. And the gleaming truth that she was too good for the likes of him.

But still, she wanted *him*.

And yes, he saw her wide-eyed fear. This situation had her lost, but for a change, they shared equal standing. Or maybe he had the ability to help her here and, therefore, had the upper hand...

Little Miss Neat and Nerdy was about to get a lot less "Neat and Nerdy", and as for him, he hadn't been with a woman in years. Yet, the constant panging in his chest told him this one time with Sophie wouldn't be enough. If there were more time, he'd do so much more. Take things slow. Lay her down. Explore every inch of her. He'd taste her. Repay her for all the ways she got to him.

But there wasn't enough time. Not for her. Certainly not for him. And he needed to get Sophie Tindall out of his system.

Her fingers shifted to the nape of his neck, and she pulled him closer, initiating the next kiss. Hunger and passion mixed with force, and her lips unleashed an untamed desire. A wild fire allowed to run free, or a woman held back for far too long.

He pressed his body to her, allowing her to feel him—all of him. Matching her intensity. Encouraging her bravery. He wanted to strip her naked right there and then, but as ready as he was, she needed a moment to warm up.

He pushed his tongue into her mouth, his lashes slow at first, then more commanding, mimicking what he wanted to do to her at the lower point where their bodies pressed. Her gentle whimper prompted his hands up her ribcage, and she ground against him, escalating his need.

His palms found her breasts—rewarding her courage, rewarding himself—kneading her small, firm, perfection through her dress.

She ripped her mouth away, her gaze failing to meet his. "I know you prefer a woman with bigger breasts."

Her pupils were wide and truly apologetic, the comment a reference to his ribbing weeks ago at the biker bar, back when he'd teased her with a potential trip to a non-existent strip club. Of course, his assholery would come back to bite him now.

He touched his forehead to hers until her gaze met his again. How could he have done anything to make this woman doubt herself?

"The only breasts I can think about are yours." He brushed his thumbs over her dress's thin fabric, the hard pebble of her nipples prodding through whatever equally thin bra she wore underneath. "They're flawless, and so are you."

Her eyelids fluttered closed, her body sinking against the wall, though her cheeks lifted with a small smile. "What about my potato sack clothing and uptight personality?"

A low chuckle broke free of him. "Potato sack or not, I'd prefer you with no clothes on. So if you'll let me get back to it, I was about to help you with the uptight thing."

She gave a soft laugh, but he nipped at her neck, where the scent of spring daisies floated off her smooth skin, and the laughter she held turned into a needy gasp. He wanted to devour her, to purge himself of his intense need for this woman. At the same time, he'd only just started and didn't want to let her go.

His mouth found hers, and he slid his hands under her dress until he felt the rasp of her lace underwear. Tongues meshed. Breaths drew heavy. One need rose and then another. He needed to be inside her. Needed to feel her gliding over him, and watch her come undone at his touch... But not just yet.

First, he shifted her underwear until his thumb met with her slick center. She gasped again, inching higher and away from him, like even that amount of stimulation was too much.

He drew light circles over her flesh and soon she relaxed, her keening cry calling for more.

The brush of her breath to his neck brought on his own excited shiver. He claimed her mouth, swallowing her moans. She bucked against him, gathering speed, until he buried his fingers within her, and her climax exploded.

Not waiting for her to finish, he freed himself; before he slid his length into her, having to stop halfway. She clenched around him. Resistant. Seconds passed as he gave her time to soften and relax. When she did, he entered her fully.

Her eyes closed. She called his name. And he nipped her plump lower lip, losing himself in a kiss, before he moved within her.

Her head tilted forward, and he buried his face among a cascade of exquisitely soft, sable hair. She gave another moan and tightened. His heart soared, and he plunged harder, deeper, faster, putting himself to work until he found a solid rhythm. She wanted this. Wanted *him*. Never before had he felt so needed. She was perfection—too perfect for him—but he'd take her. All of her.

He increased speed, and with each of his thrusts, small puffs of air escaped her lips; her body trembling beneath his until she gave out a long, great cry. Every corner of the tiny kitchen reverberated with her beautiful sound—the call of her unrestrained pleasure—of his victory and pride. Neither of which he'd had in years.

He picked up speed, made way for his impending release, only for a heaviness to settle in his heart.

No. Not heaviness. *Fear.*

He teetered on the edge of losing control—so similar to what occurred during his episodes—the dizzying sense already building. Would he be okay? Would letting go with Sophie induce an episode? Would this be yet another moment stolen from him?

Her eyes flung wide open, and she gasped with continued need. She wanted him to join her, to see him tumble too. But uncertainty battled lust as he threw himself at the mercy of whatever happened next.

He buried his face into her free-flowing hair again, his orgasm building with more intensity than he'd ever experienced and way too fast to stop now. He'd have to trust her. He didn't trust himself. But she'd seen him crumble before. *Sophie. Perfect Sophie.* She'd forgive him. Surely, she'd forgive him.

Pleasure struck—a million shooting stars racing past him faster than a freight train. He dug his fingers into her hips. Trying but failing to maintain control.

I can't control this. Trust her. Just trust her.

And, oh, how he trusted her. Maybe a little too much. But he trusted her all the same.

This was about more than mere sex or finding validation as a man. *This* was something he thought he'd never have again. *This* was something other than his usual daily grind of life within the same walls. Something beyond the same battle between soul-crushing routine and the agonizing uncertainty of what his condition would do next.

A guttural groan tore from deep within him, the sound disappeared into her hair and the wall behind. He poured himself inside her. Literally. Figuratively.

Long minutes passed before he found direction again. He'd lost himself, yes, but not as much as he could have. Fear had held him back. He'd trusted her, when maybe he shouldn't have. She'd looked into his past after all. Though even in her more dubious decisions, she always meant well, and what he trusted in most was her goodness.

His racing mind settled, as did his body. He leaned back to search her gaze. Her focus held his, pupils wide and directionless. *At least he wasn't the only one.*

She stroked the scar along his hairline, as though even now she embraced his imperfections. He blinked down to his own fingers tracing the edge of her chin, the room so impossibly quiet, save for the sounds of ragged breaths and his blood pumping loud in his ears.

And with that silence, clear thought descended like slow settling snow. He pulled his face farther from hers, a shock of realization flooding in.

Yes, he'd taken an unwise emotional leap, but then there was something else he'd just done. Something far more reckless.

Nineteen

SOPHIE GRABBED HIS COLLAR, halting his escape. "No. Don't."

Her attention skittered over his ashen complexion, and his gaze settled down at where their bodies met. The moment she'd felt the heat of him spill within her, she'd known what seemed to only dawn on him now.

They hadn't used protection.

"I'm so sorry." Even as the words fell from her mouth, she couldn't say what she apologized for, just that her thoughts raced in an attempt to make sense of all that had just occurred.

He withdrew and lowered her to the ground, hot wetness clinging to her thighs. She focused on his sunken cheeks, confirming his shared alarm.

Her chin wobbled, and she let go of his collar, grappling to control her emotions. Orlando shook his head, expression firm as if his usual defenses had kicked in. "This is my mistake. I'm the one who messed this up, you got it?"

She gave a small nod, lips parted, though no words escaped. She'd loved every second of being with him, had traveled halfway around the globe seeking this very encounter. Well, maybe not this *exact* encounter…

Tears stung her eyes. Her heart drummed now for a very different reason. How could she have gotten so carried away?

Because *Orlando*. Of course.

The man stole all logic and turned it into pure and unavoidable impulse. Not that she really believed this was all his mistake. There'd been his ability to short her logic, sure, but her inability to control herself when it came to him was also to blame.

She turned toward her kitchen and paced in small circles, patting her open palm to her forehead over and over again. *Stupid. Stupid woman. The same mistake again?*

And even in her panic, she knew better than to fall apart. He didn't know her story. Nor did he need to know. Moreover, she refused to give him another reason to feel worse about his life.

"No. I'll handle this." The platitude broke from her, weak and reedy. "It's okay."

"To hell it is." His harsh tone cut across the room. "It won't be *okay* if we've just produced another freak like me."

Her hand slipped down to her chest, and she rubbed the heel of her palm over her boney sternum, choking back a sob, thankful that at least she made no sound. As much as she wanted his support, she knew better than to expect any.

"I'm just as responsible. I wanted this. The heat of the moment got to me, that's all." She kept her back to him, cheeks so hot she needed to obscure her face in an attempt to buy time until she could escape. "And we don't know for sure there's any genetic factor to your condition."

Even though her body still pulsed and hummed from the most arousing sex of her life, her thoughts jumbled and flew at her fast. She had no space to worry beyond just how stupidly carried away she'd gotten.

His hand landed on her shoulder. "Look at me."

She jolted at his touch. "No. I need to go."

She shrugged him off before he saw whatever pathetic expression marked her face and stormed toward the bathroom. He stayed silent in her wake, though in all truth, she was thankful she couldn't hear much beyond the pounding of her feet on the wooden boards, minus the sounds of him following.

She got to the bathroom and plonked down onto the closed toilet seat, where a heavy sob tore through her chest and echoed within the small enclosed room. She wriggled free of her underwear and wiped away all evidence of sex. She must have made one pitiful sight.

Her muscles vibrated, weak from adrenaline, but she forced herself up to the mirror, where splotchy marks covered her face. Her eyes were puffy, and her cheeks were red. She'd achieved her goal. Gotten laid. But the spontaneity and frosty outcome proved far more than she'd ever planned on.

She should have been happy—and in all truth, for a brief moment, she had been. He'd made her feel so utterly alive. Given her a profound experience she'd likely never match. But all that was before she realized their grim mistake.

She peered down at her hands, uncertain what to do about the shaking, much less her splotchy face. She'd have to deal with him. He'd take one look at her and know she wasn't handling this "slip up" as well as she pretended.

Would it kill him to see I'm human?

Maybe it literally would. And any resulting hurt would be her fault.

Stupid. Stupid woman.

She turned on the tap and cupped her hands under the running water, attempting to hold back a great need to vomit the lunch she hadn't even had the chance to make, much less eat.

Even as she washed, new tears sprung free.

Wait. I'll cry all I want once he's out of this house.

So, she pulled in a slow breath and tried to forget that she'd jumped in without thinking—made herself vulnerable—jeopardized her fledgling life improvements and sold herself short professionally.

Even though what they'd done wasn't off limits. Even though he said he didn't see anything wrong in their attraction. She had her own limits, and she'd broken them with this exchange.

What a terrible fall.

She splashed her face one last time and did a simple calculation.

She was midway through her monthly cycle. The timing was right. Or more precisely, wrong. Either way, she could very well be pregnant. The morning-after pill might have been an option—if she could find a local drug store. But given her past, she just couldn't go down that path. How would she explain an unplanned pregnancy to her mother? Much less her brothers who'd warned her of exactly this? And how would she finish her studies as a single parent, or practice in her chosen field?

Goodbye holiday.

Goodbye clear and easy life plan.

Goodbye to her last throes of youthful spontaneity or freedom.

God, she couldn't think. Had to get out of this room. Get some air. She'd sure as hell made a mess of *spontaneity and freedom*. Maybe she should just fly back to the UK and cancel any final *adventures* in this country.

A light knock sounded at the door. She paused, still not ready to face Orlando.

"Are you okay?"

She squeezed her eyes shut and shook her head. No. No, she really wasn't. And even his question got in the way of her need to hate him right now. He had his hang-ups too. And rightfully so. He deserved a moment to blunder his reaction, his comment about creating "a freak" case in point, but she didn't have the ability to handle him and whatever fevered thoughts entered her head.

She snapped the faucet closed and took one last steadying breath, then opened the door to him standing before her, his espresso-dark eyes dulled slightly. "I've called a taxi. I'll get myself back to the home."

"I can't let you do that." *Though she wanted to*. Not because she thought less of him, but because she simply wanted to hide. To have many, many hours to get her head around what was the second most confusing moment of her life. Her fingers curled tight around the door handle, her tone about as flat and hollow as her heartbeat. "What if something happens to you?"

His attention danced around her face, assessing her, no doubt filtering in the signs of her devastation. His mouth wavered, as though he wanted to say something, but seconds passed, and eventually he frowned. "I'm not totally useless. The center is ten minutes up the road. You have the look of a woman whose life has just ended, and it's my fault. So, I sure as shit don't expect you to drop me off at that pathetic place I call a home."

He turned, and she failed to find it in her to insist on the lift. At the very least, she'd call the home in twenty minutes to ensure he got back safe.

He took only a few paces from her before he spun back around. The tiny muscles in his cheeks softened. "I'm sorry, again. We both need time to think things through." She glanced down at his hands curled into fists at his side. Maybe he too held something back. "The only upside to this whole disaster is I've had every test under the sun. Aside from the potential 'freak factor', you can at least rest easy you haven't caught anything from me today."

She winced at his second reference to his contribution to a child as the freak factor, but she gave a shaky nod, still unable to speak.

He gave her one last long look, and then walked away.

Twenty

ORLANDO PINNED his focus on his hands clasped together on the table in the common room. Fifteen minutes had elapsed since the beginning of the volunteer gathering, all while his fellow residents and their volunteers surrounded him, and Sophie was nowhere to be seen.

Idiot. Isn't this what I wanted?

And if that wasn't the case, then Sophie leaving to get on with her life sure as shit should have been. He'd made the biggest mistake, and of course she wouldn't want his baby. Then again, maybe everything would be fine. Maybe he hadn't burdened her. Maybe she'd decided to do the smart thing and stay away.

He lifted his gaze, to the room's entrance, where Candice Olsen powered through, pulling a tear-stained Sophie by the crook of an arm.

Candice stopped before his table and nudged Sophie gently forward.

He zeroed a glare at the director, but her expression pinched in equal warning—an uncharacteristic gesture for a woman dedicated to all things compassion and healing.

"Watch your step, Orlando." She turned away, then shot him one more scowl from over her shoulder, leaving Sophie seated across from him.

His heart strained at the red around Sophie's eyes, her face unusually pale, even for her. "What is this? What's happened?"

She pulled her body into a poker-straight stance, shoulders raised and hands squeezed between her tight, blue-denim-covered knees. "I told Ms. Olsen everything. I quit the volunteer program."

His gut churned. His breath momentarily stalled. She really was leaving him. And then, his old friend anger struck like a lightning bolt. "Why the fuck does Candice need to know anything?"

Sophie startled, only for an eerie calm to wash over her. "I'm worried about how what happened between us might affect you. Believe it or not, Candice is on your side."

He glared at her, wanting to get to the real issue here. They had a lot to sort through. Or maybe they didn't. Maybe that's just what he wanted to believe in order to delay letting her go, even though letting her go was the inevitable thing. The best thing.

"I pay Candice to be on my side."

"I feel that in light of what's passed, and this being our last meeting, I should explain myself." She took a shaky breath, as though she held back more tears. "I'm sorry. I just can't escape the feeling that I've used you in some way. I came to Australia with a goal of getting some life experience. For myself, for my work. And one of my goals included meeting men, for…"

She held a hollow look and stared out the window to her right, face crumpled, clearly unable to finish that sentence.

"Well, if it weren't for the disastrous ending to our last encounter…" He gestured down at his body, meaning to lighten the mood, though probably doing the opposite while looking ridiculous. "I'd say, 'use away'."

He narrowed a glare to the wide-eyed gape she lobbed back. He didn't feel used, but his blood near boiled at the mention of other men. That he'd been wrong in his assessment of Miss Neat and Nerdy being somewhat rusty.

Maybe there'd been others directly before him. Maybe she'd leave this room and move on to someone else in her quest for "experience". What she did with her body shouldn't have bothered him. But it did.

His hands clenched, and he struggled to accept the forlorn

expression on her face as being anything real. Once again, life and another person were leaving him behind.

He damn well wanted to punch a hole in the nearest wall.

She cleared her throat, as if resetting her composure. "I know why I found myself attracted to you, and I was wrong. As to why you were attracted to me, there's a good chance my therapeutic role has caused something called erotic transference, and—"

"I know what transference is." His voice snapped out, and the sick sensation in his gut turned into a rolling ball of white-hot anger. "I was a fireman, remember? I have a basic understanding of psychology. I know about hero worship. How people get romantic delusions and attachments to those administering assistance. And for the record, that's not me."

She blinked at him, either to gain a moment to regroup, or to provide him time to calm down. Which wasn't about to happen. "Yes, but—"

"I resent you implying that I lack the self-awareness to know whether I have feelings for an idolized version of you or not." The raspy strain in his voice rose. "That I'm a passive victim who can't see who you are beyond how you meet my needs. I know you. I know exactly why I did what I did. We talked about consent and how cognizant I was, remember? You're taking the coward's way out. You're leaving now because whatever passed between us has you scared."

Her mouth fell open, but no words came. His cheeks burned, and he had a sudden sense that everyone was listening. Well, if they did, he didn't care. He'd alluded to having feelings for her, when in reality, he was falling in love. What a shit of a moment to realize *that*.

For the first time in a long time, shame sent tingles down the back of his neck. Shame. An emotion afforded to those with something to lose in the first place.

But I do have something to lose now. Don't I?

Heavy silence settled between them. Her mouth wavered, while his heart seemed to stop altogether. If she asked him to elaborate on his feelings, he'd deny everything and claim a slip of the tongue.

Did he really love Sophie Tindall?

She took a sharp breath, as though her senses returned. "I just want to know you'll be okay."

The way her gaze flittered around his face, brows pressed together, complexion pale. She knew something.

Maybe she sensed just how dark his thoughts got at times. He'd been stupid enough to admit to her that her regular visits gave him something to look forward to. Clearly, the unintended shift in responsibility weighed heavy now she planned to leave.

Then again, anger wouldn't help here. It never had where she was concerned, and he didn't want anger to be his parting gift.

"You know my story doesn't end well." He softened his tone, willing his taut muscles to release. "Given your career choice, you should get used to bad endings."

He'd seen enough death and tragedy to know. Poor Sophie had little idea just how much her career would change her. How others' pain could seep into her bones, and she'd wear that pain wherever she went. One day, much of the hope and innocence he adored about her would be replaced with cold reality, like a bitter poison winding through her system. And one day, she'd wake to a sense of merely passing through, a sense those outside of her job wouldn't understand. They'd call her pessimistic. Tell her to lighten up. But then she'd learn to build her own defenses against it all. Just as he had.

And everyone would always assume she was okay, when maybe she wasn't.

She gave a shaky nod, and a tear spilled down her cheek. The first actual tear she'd allowed him to witness. "This is for the best, isn't it?"

"Yeah." He gave a weak smile, though the lump in his throat made speaking hard.

He drank in every last detail of her face. The ill-deserved concern dilating those mottled brown, gold, and green eyes. The downturn of her peach-pink lips. The wisps of hair kissing her cheekbones. It hurt to look at her too long, to know she'd soon turn and leave.

She bit her lower lip and nodded again, her hands unfolding to reveal a piece of paper tucked within her palm. "I have something for you."

She slid the paper over the table toward him, the table itself an unnecessary barrier between them. A barrier he wanted to push aside so he could take her in his arms one last time. But even that would send them backwards, when he really just needed to be thankful for the physical distance and let her go.

He scowled down at the folded page, unwilling to touch it lest it be another thing to draw him to her. "What is it?"

"I figured since this is goodbye, it wouldn't make much difference to reveal the extent of my meddling." She jutted her chin out toward the page. "These are the contact details for Professor Faith Bandara, a neuropsychopharmacologist. I pulled some strings with my professors back home, and they recommended her above anyone else. She specializes in the effects of drugs and various chemicals and compounds on cells. She's brilliant and practices in Melbourne, and she's willing to dig deeper into your case."

His shoulders drew together, and he pushed the paper back toward her. "You're right, this is meddling. It's also patronizing. I don't want your professor."

She frowned and pushed the paper back. "Keep it anyway. She's only willing to look into your case with your consent. If you change your mind, she'll start out with an assessment and some initial pathology, but it's really up to you to get the ball rolling. I can't do anything more."

"I never asked you to do a damn thing for me in the first place." Though he did want things from her now, things that were more important than chasing down another dead-end doctor. "In fact, I expressly told you I've been through all of this with a million other doctors."

Her new frown dragged deeper than the last. "I might be leaving your life, but there's no reason you can't still get help. Please don't make this an ugly ending."

He reached out his hand and slapped it over the piece of paper on the table, then dragged the page back toward him, closing his grasp to scrunch the page. An immature, childish, and dismissive gesture, sure, but she'd been right about him not appreciating her meddling, much less that this ruined what could have been a heartfelt goodbye. "Happy now?"

Another flash of pale displeasure streaked across her face. "Since you're set on ending things this way, maybe you can answer me one last question?"

He released a grumble, suddenly wanting her to put him out of his pain and just leave already. "What?"

"If getting better were an option… If tomorrow you woke up with a different future ahead of you… What dreams would you have for yourself?"

He reeled back. "What sort of a fucked-up question is that?"

"You had dreams once, yes?" She merely returned his glare with a weak smile. "They were enough to make you strike out of this town and embark on a life of your own making. What were they?"

He raised both hands and pointed out the room. "Look around you, Sophie. Look at how I live. Look at *where* I live. The only dream anyone in this place has is that the end comes soon, and it isn't too painful. Whatever dreams I had are moot, now."

He leaned in and summoned all the ice he could into his stare, raising his hand with the paper still crumpled in it. "And if your conversation on dreams is a lead-in to tell me that this scrap of paper here is the answer to all my prayers…" He shook his head slowly. If he was going to let her go, then he'd make damn sure she had every reason to leave and zero reason to come back. He owed her that. He owed it to himself too. "Then save the bullshit and do as I ask. Just go."

A few seconds passed before his abrasiveness hit its target. She gave a single, solid nod and launched to her feet. "You're a hypocrite. You accuse me of being condescending, Orlando Piras, but you're the king-of-all-things condescension. And I'm almost certain that was the case before you ended up here. I've only ever tried to help you—to do exactly what I promised the day I walked through those doors and got lumped with your sorry ass."

She pointed to the main doors, doors she'd any minute now walk through, never to return. Her hands curled at her sides, and her cheeks glowed a furious red.

"And you, I might be carrying your child, and all you can do is grumble and sulk and attack. You want to fool everyone here into thinking you're some unshakeable tough guy, but I've seen you ruffled.

As much as you think you know me, I know you too. You're really just chicken-shit scared, so much so, you can't make one easy phone call in a final effort to save your own life." Angry tears streamed down her cheeks. "I might not be the worldliest person ever, but unlike you, I try. And I don't give up on people. I tried here. I really did try. Your mum was right. At some point long before your condition, you decided you weren't going to let anyone in. So, bravo, Orlando. You've made a fool of us both."

Her voice ricocheted off the walls, and the common room lay inordinately silent. All eyes had turned to her. She swiped at her tears with the heel of her hand. Only then did her glare break from him long enough to take in the room.

But her watery expression didn't waver, and for the first time ever, she seemed unaffected by what others thought. She gave him one last crumpled glance and turned in a marching gait for the exit.

The sight of her back made her leaving more real. Instinct took control, and he launched to his feet. "Sophie."

She swung around. Eyes wild and demanding he not stop her. "I'll be in touch if there's any news about our slip-up the other day, but you're right, we're better off not knowing each other." Her face scrunched, indicating another wave of hurt took over. "I was an idiot to believe I could make a difference here."

She clapped her hand over her mouth, and her shoulders shuddered. And just like that, she turned and raced out the door—a woman holding back her cry long enough to leave him.

Twenty-One

"PUT THE PHONE AWAY."

Sophie followed Agathe's order and pressed the hang-up button on her phone. "I was just about to—"

"Nope. It's not enough." Agathe sat across the table at the harbor-side bar, chin dipped low, the reflective light from the water behind her illuminating her brown skin a lustrous gold. She outstretched a hand. "I need you to hand the whole phone over. Now. Otherwise, we have no chance of enjoying this weekend."

Sophie groaned. "Fine. But I want it noted that Hannah called me, and your phone hasn't stopped dinging since we left Melbourne."

She slapped the phone into Agathe's hand. Impromptu weekend in Sydney or not, nothing could distract from all things Orlando.

Agathe held her giant, multi-colored purse agape and dropped the phone inside with extra ceremony. "What can I say? Luke's a stress-head, and he wants to know every detail about how me and this baby are doing. Besides, Hannah's call was merely my tipping point. Whatever redemption you're looking for is not gonna happen on that little device. He's gone, Sophie. In fact, you're the one who did the leaving. Remember?"

"I know." Sophie peered down at the bright yellow mocktail—a fancy word for fruit juice and soda water—the one she'd ordered under the pretense of supporting Agathe on her alcohol-free weekend. She hadn't found the strength to break it to her new friend that she might not be the only pregnant woman at the table.

"Anyway, since I've had to marvel at the harbor view alone while you wrapped up that long-winded conversation, maybe you can tell me who Hannah is." Agathe's deep-brown eyes sparkled against the midday sun. "Oh, and Randal, and Hector. I had no idea Miss Sophie Tindall came with a past."

A past? Sophie's breaths tightened. She didn't just have a past. For a time there, she'd had a whole other existence few knew about. Not even Hannah. And history seemed set on repeating. She swatted a hand in dismissal. Yet another thing she couldn't get into with Agathe.

"It's not as exciting as you think. Hannah is my best friend and housemate. Hector is my ex-boyfriend. He's a nice guy, but our relationship fizzled. And Randal Berry—" She let loose with a strained laugh. How could she have ever been so silly? "Randal lives in my building. I had a mini crush on him, and Hannah likes to give me updates on his love life, but…"

Sophie pressed her lips together, not quite sure how to finish that sentence.

Agathe stabbed a straw at her drink, ice cubes clinking. "But let me guess, you forgot he existed the second you met Orlando?"

Sophie's heart slowed to a heavy, plodding beat. She frowned at the severe accuracy in Agathe's guess, thinking deeper on her time in Australia thus far. How she'd assumed Orlando's lure had crept up on her, but a closer look revealed an attraction had existed from day one.

"And Hector too. I forgot about him, too, despite how long we were together and how much I sympathized over the way that relationship ended. It's as if I met Orlando, and everything else faded." She buried her face in her hands. "Urghhh… I'm such a wooly-brained idiot."

She lifted her gaze to Agathe's reassuring smile. "It happens to the best of us."

"No, this stuff never happens to me. The vast majority of my adult life has been dedicated to study. To making one well-thought-out decision after another." She lifted her hand to her face again. Her cheeks burned, the pleasant, midday sun suddenly too hot and muggy on her skin. "The more I think about what I did, the more I uncover just how much damage I've inflicted on our lives."

Agathe shook her head through an uncomfortably long silence.

"What?" Sophie frowned. "What is it?"

Agathe shrugged and picked up her glass again. "This is going to be one long and dull weekend if you don't loosen up quick-smart, especially since there's not a drop of alcohol between us." She held her glass higher, inspecting the near glowing contents. "And since I'm the one who's engaged, I'll need you to carry the baton for us both. So, I have just one question for you…" She lowered her glass to the table and shot Sophie a sly grin. "Which one do you prefer, Blondie or Mr. Tall, Dark, and probably Loaded?"

Agathe gave a small nod toward a blond, surfer-looking waiter and then an immaculate-looking businessman, with deeply tanned skin and a navy-blue suit.

Sophie felt her eyes pull wide, and she hunched over the table to whisper, "You don't seriously expect me to hook up with some stranger while wallowing over Orlando?" She peered over at the men, her stomach flipping at the mere thought of approaching either one of them. "Besides, you make it sound like they don't even get a choice."

"Nooooo." Agathe's smile broadened, eyes sparkling anew. "I said nothing about hooking up, though I won't tell anyone back home if that's what you do." She wiggled back in her seat. Too cool. Too confident… Or at least for Sophie's liking. "Just give one of them your number. The sole benefit of me having to endure your long chat with Hannah was that I got to watch both dudes checking you out. So, don't you worry about their choices. Hell, give both of them your number, if that's what'll pull you out of this slump."

Sophie crossed her arms and leaned back in her chair. "You can't be serious."

"Serious about us having fun this weekend? Hells yes." Agathe patted her tiny baby bump. "I'm on borrowed time here. So as much as I want to support you, you better believe I intend to enjoy my last shreds of freedom before this little one arrives. And I'm certainly not going to let you kill the vibe with your broken-hearted act. You need this just as much as I do. Maybe more."

Sophie stared down at her abandoned drink, and mumbled, "It's not an act."

"Whatever." Agathe swatted a hand. "So, here's step one of my plan. You go over to one of those gorgeous men and slip them your number. You know, just to prove your heartsick little self can do it and that a world of men still exists beyond Orlando, Hector, and Robert—"

"Randal."

"Whatever. I'm pregnant, and my brain can't keep up with you." Agathe swatted her hand again. "Anyway, you can slip those two hotties your number, *or* you can spill the beans to me about your Orlando drama. I know you've been holding out on the details. I figure if you release some of those icky sads holding you back, you'll start enjoying yourself again."

Sophie tucked her chin in and scowled at Agathe through her lashes. "Everything I know about mental health tells me your ultimatum is a really bad idea."

Agathe pointed a finger, smile still firmly in place. "Yes, but it's better than whatever you're doing now, right? And judging by the color in your cheeks, I'd say you're already feeling a tad better. So, what's your choice?"

Sophie huffed out a weak laugh, her focus falling to Blondie and then Mr. Tall, Dark, and Probably Loaded. For a long moment, she contemplated saying nothing—that perhaps the simplest course of action would be to hand out her number and deal with the potential calls later. But a new sense of guilt flared, green-lighting the probability she'd be surrendering to easy escape; in other words, keeping quiet to avoid speaking on what bothered her most about all that had passed between her and Orlando.

A tight band squeezed around her chest, good old guilt rearing again. Afternoon sunlight passed through the glass before her, reflecting rainbow fractals across the table. The vibrant colors helped to distract, ever so slightly, from the tension in her body. Would Agathe judge her if she knew everything? Maybe. But there was at least one thing she could say for herself.

"While I sit here with you in a different city, lapping up a beautiful day on the harbor, with plans for a civilized night at the ballet, Orlando sits within the same stale walls he's been in for the last two years. The same walls I left him in. The walls he now can't escape because I'm not there to help." A lump formed at the base of her throat, the surrounding muscles seeming to swell further, while no amount of swallowing erased her discomfort. "There are so many unfair things about his world, and for a brief moment, it was my job to bring some kind of happiness to his life. I failed him. Not only did I fail him, I was the one who always had the privilege to walk away. And I did. I walked. I practically ran. I added to his burdens, and then I ran."

Her chin trembled, but she clenched her jaw long enough to regain composure.

Agathe reached out a hand and placed it over Sophie's. "But it sounds as though you did improve his life. He accepted your help when at first he wouldn't. It seems he changed a little for the better. And then you found that professor willing to help him, right?" She gave a half smile as if to offer reassurance. "He made progress, and that's easier said than done. I put up one heck of a fight when Luke urged me to get help. Hell, we busted up over it too. You have no idea where your influence will lead Orlando. Maybe his life will continue to improve from having known you."

Sophie shook her head. "I don't think so. Orlando was right when he said the referral to the professor is a long shot. And if that's the only thing I helped him with, it's not much. I expended so much energy defending my interferences when he really just needed support."

"Okay, sure. Let's say you screwed up, which I don't entirely think you did." Agathe shrugged. "But what more can you do now? You offered him the professor, and he threw that idea in your face. Meanwhile, you're twisting yourself in knots over a bust up with no remedy, which by the way, I'm still unclear why exactly you two are fighting to begin with."

Sophie felt her hairline prickle with sweat. Though Agathe knew she and Orlando had had an encounter, Sophie still couldn't bring herself to share the whole story about her potential pregnancy. "I know. I know. And the silliest thing is, I'll have to deal with combative patients like him in the future. So, the fact I'm struggling so much to let this one go—the fact I couldn't even carry out a volunteer position without getting things so incredibly wrong, only makes me think I've wasted all my years of study on an ill-suited career."

Agathe scooped up her drink and toyed with it. "Yeah well, I mean, I'm sure the whole getting it on with a patient is a huge no-no if you're their actual psychiatrist, but that wasn't the case here, right? There was always a personal element to your work with Orlando, though maybe neither of you banked on just how personal things would get." She paused to sip on her drink. "You're not the type to make rash decisions, Sophie. And almost no one is immune to being swept away, not when there's someone they truly connect with. I was so angry and forcibly alone for years before I met Luke, and as much as I fought to stay away from him..." She smiled, sudden light entering her expression. "We ended up together, anyway."

Sophie's mind filled with the sounds of people talking and the rumbling of a passenger ferry on the harbor. She wanted to give in to Agathe optimism, but just couldn't. "That's not going to happen with Orlando and I, even without factoring in his condition. I love living in London. I want to finish my studies. Either way, I'm returning home when this holiday ends."

Agathe scooted closer, brows pulling down in clear sympathy. "Sure, but my point is, Orlando is a bloody gorgeous man, close to your age, with an incredibly sad story. You'd be a lacking human being if something about the people you encountered didn't affect you from time to time. And"—she pointed a finger as if to demand more attention—"he voiced a clear attraction to you from the very beginning, before you ever knew his deal or became his volunteer. You know, when he tried to set up on that bogus date. Don't forget that. And you felt the same attraction for him, otherwise you wouldn't have said yes to that same bogus date." She dropped back into her chair, point made. "Accept this experience for what it is and find a way to forgive yourself. Take it from someone who knows, second-guessing your past will only swallow your future."

Sophie drew small circles with her fingertip on the white-linen tablecloth, as an even sadder realization settled in.

When it came to Orlando, she simply wouldn't get the closure she desired. No ballet or fancy bar would save her from knowing Orlando was right. His life would have no happy ending. With or without her in it.

And maybe he'd been right about another thing. Maybe her meddling did come with an ulterior motive—her wanting to avoid the cold, hard truth that someone as vivid and vital as him could still meet a cruel and early end.

There'd be no silver lining. No absolution for what he'd endured.

Certainly nothing for them as a couple.

Now, all she had left was uncertainty over her immediate circumstances, and a sickening sense this whole holiday had turned out to be far from the fun "shake up" she'd wished for.

"There's that sullen look again." Agathe huffed out a sigh, "Clearly, this talk has done nothing to improve your merry-making abilities."

Agathe dug around in her bag, the coin fringe tinkling, her phone in her hand within seconds.

Sophie frowned, her heart entrapped. "What have I done now? What are you doing?"

"First, I'm putting out a social media post asking if any of my Sydney-sider friends want free tickets to the ballet tonight." She tapped away at the screen, a bright and mischievous smile pulling at her cheeks. "And then I'm going to find out what's shaking over on Oxford Street."

The heat returned to bother Sophie's cheeks, and her stomach roiled in protest. Despite her mood, she'd been looking forward to the ballet. "Oxford Street? What's on Oxford Street?"

Agathe's dark eyes glittered as if she'd morphed into some kind of evil genius. "Drag queens. Male strip shows. And since I can't drink, and you won't, watching other people get absolutely obliterated." She returned to her phone, shimmying her shoulders in a little dance to go with her monologue about drag queens and male strippers. "You'll love it."

Orlando lay in bed while the not-so-muffled murmurs of a volunteer meeting traveled down the hallway. He let out a heavy sigh and rolled his eyes, fixing his stare to the beige ceiling.

He'd missed two volunteer meetings so far, with zero interest in joining another, not since he'd finally succeeded in driving Sophie away. He didn't want a new volunteer. He'd learned his lesson. Never again.

And even if his budding psychiatrist did return, his condition and inability to offer more than a few good times and a bucket load of regret meant he couldn't speak to her again. He'd done enough damage. He needed to let her move on.

A hard knock came at his door, but he made no effort to respond.

The door handle squeaked, and soon the whole thing swung open. Candice Olsen stood over him, hands fisted on her hips. "Ignoring me won't make me go away."

"What if I outright *told* you to go away? Would that work?" He turned his attention from her searing judgment and back to his neutral ceiling.

"Oh, hahaha, Romeo." Her dull and stagnated tone held no real humor. "It's been more than a week since you and Juliet put on your woeful, *star-crossed-lovers* act. Are you going to hide in this room forever?"

"I'm not hiding." He ignored her dig at his last-ever encounter with Sophie—an encounter that had indeed been woeful and way too public for his liking.

"Really?" Candice leaned over and stuck her face in his line of sight. "Then what are you doing? Meditating?"

He let out a sarcastic laugh, eyeballing her back. "No. I'm giving up."

A long pause filled the room. Sure, his words were dramatic, but they'd sure as fuck mess with Candice.

Her small flinch indicated he'd achieved his goal, but judging by the twisting pain in his chest, maybe his lie about giving up did hold some morsel of truth. That he'd given Sophie a piece of his heart without even knowing.

He raised a brow, a gesture designed to throw Candice off the topic of his wellbeing. "Sophie told me you know everything about our time together. Don't tell me you want a recap of the gory details?"

Candice leaned back, expression flat. "Funny. I can't say I'm happy about the extra drama your showdown brought around here, but you're a grown man, and not the first resident we've had pair off with a volunteer. Though the last couple to do that got married rather than fall just short of clawing each other's eyes out. Despite your condition, Orlando, you're hardheaded enough to leave no doubt you were a willing participant in whatever relationship developed between you and Sophie."

He kept his flat stare trained on her, pretending her less-than-professional description of his personality didn't bother him. "It wasn't a relationship, Candice. It was fucking."

She grimaced, before settling on a pinched glare. "Yeah, sure. I saw the look in your eyes when she asked what your dreams were. The woman got to you. Even blind Mr. Larson up the hall could see that. And now, I'm left with the sole job of diverting your crusade to spend the last years of your life moping over her."

"Is that why you've come to bother me today?"

She lowered her chin, as if to say, *What do you think, dipshit?*

"Right." He returned his focus to the ceiling, ignoring the fact Candice was right and so was Sophie. That his injury was not the sole cause of his isolation. That he didn't want anyone getting too close to him. And he truly hadn't. Not until her. "What I do with my 'last years' is none of your business."

"Wrong." Candice pointed a finger and leaned forward enough to loom over him. "What you do is precisely my business: mine, my staff, and every poor sod who has to deal with you. And we're all worried about you. We've been worried for a long time, way before Sophie happened. We've all jumped hurdles to keep you here and help your family, you're just too knuckleheaded to see it. We thought you were making great strides with Sophie in your life. She was the best volunteer we've had for a long time. But of course, just like all the others, you had to push her out the door. So, call my presence right now whatever you want. Me, I'm calling this an intervention before we all do truly give up on your sorry ass."

Intervention? A cold sensation ran down his body, but he refused to let her see how much her intervention bothered him. As if losing Sophie didn't hurt enough. He'd let her leave, believing she'd made no difference to his life.

The biggest kicker? Sophie Tindall *was* the difference. Even just the fact he'd allowed her enough access to his world to *make* that difference…

Now he just wanted to be alone. To wallow in his loneliness. Striking up more concern would not help his goal.

"Aren't you supposed to be on my side here? You know, offering me warm milk and cookies in light of me getting dumped and all?" He gave Candice a hard glare, the untruthful kind that mirrored everyone's impression of him being *knuckleheaded*, pretending he'd be just fine.

She let out a sigh, like she saw through his act. "I would if you made an attempt to show you cared. We've tried being on your side and look at you." She held a hand out, gesturing at his supine position on the bed. "So, have it your way, Orlando. I'm cutting you loose from the volunteer program. I'll stop trying to convince you to interact with the outside world. If you want to stay in your room and brood until your last dying day, who am I to stop you? But if you really did ever give two hoots about that poor woman, then the least you can do is call the number on the paper she left for you." She pointed to the torn page still sitting on his bedside table. "Call the last professional willing to put themselves out there to help you."

"And why would I do that?"

"Because you love Sophie."

"I told you." He put on a snarky grin. "It was just fucking."

Candice merely blinked at him and held a short silence. "You think a few swear words will throw me? I hear worse from Mrs. Boyle when I demand she take a shower, and that's on one of her more pleasant days. Save your energy and stop wasting everyone's time."

She gave him one final death stare and shook her head as if to say, *I can't believe what an asshole you're being.* "If you really didn't care, then you wouldn't still be holding onto that piece of paper. And now that you've had a chance to mope over the loss of your girlfriend, maybe you could help us all by trying to get better for a change."

Candice turned and left, falling just short of slamming the door behind her. He stifled the urge to yell out. To make some joke about how the paper only remained at his side because of the center's shitty housekeeping.

But genuine pain swelled deep beneath his ribcage and pulled him up short.

He looked about him. At the empty room. Symbolic of everything missing in his life. For weeks, Sophie's unrelenting presence had urged him on. But now, he had Candice and her all-too-clear message. He'd disappointed everyone. He was a man-sized vacuum sucking up all the air wherever he went.

And somehow, he now had even less than before.

Sophie had offered change. She'd offered hope. That day in her kitchen, she'd given him back a piece of himself. Not just because of the sex, but from the way she'd looked at him. Her unwavering stare. Her open vulnerability. Her trust. Like she saw him as a man, not a problem.

And then there'd been something more, a kind of acceptance, as though she didn't just see him as a man, but she saw *him*.

He turned his head toward the torn page and pushed down a desire to skim his finger over her handwriting for the millionth time.

A rip ran along the page's edge. A rip he'd caused while losing his temper, as well as the unmistakable anguish that had filled her eyes as she'd run from him.

But despite what anyone insisted, he had no business in messing with change or hope. And because he had none of either, he'd dashed her hopes, too.

He dragged at his next breath, and sadness burrowed ever deeper. Maybe he couldn't have her, but he did still owe her for the differences she had made. And maybe, just maybe, he owed himself.

He'd spent decades denying it, but he did have a dream. A dream of finding someone like Sophie.

And now that he'd found her, maybe it was time he imposed on her life the way she'd imposed on his.

Twenty-Two

"YOUR VOLUNTEER GIG went bust two weeks ago. Why are you still living Roseford? Come back to Melbourne with me."

"You're right." Sophie peered over at Luke in her kitchen, one hip leaned against the counter, a beer in his hand, while she constructed a salad for their lunch. "I have no reason to stay in Roseford, it's just—"

"Let me guess." The silver kettle dinged behind her, and he disappeared for a moment to pour hot water into a waiting tea cup. "You're hoping things will turn around with that Orlando guy?"

She frowned and pointed at her brother. "That was *not* what I was going to say."

He gave her a silent look, one that hinted at disbelief.

"I enjoy having my own space." She focused on seasoning the salad, careful to use chili instead of pepper like Luke preferred. "What with two rowdy brothers growing up, and then nosy Hannah as a housemate, this is the first time in my life I've had an entire house to myself."

"Hey." Luke stabbed a teaspoon in her direction. "I wasn't 'rowdy' and as I recall, I was off on active duty those last few years you were at home. You should have had heaps of peace there. And I thought you liked Hannah, so what makes her so nosy?"

"Sorry, you're right. I do like Hannah." A slow grin pushed at her cheeks, and she shook her head at the emerging salad, as if it might somehow understand what she'd meant. "But I enjoy having a crack at a life where I have to navigate all challenges for myself. You know what I mean?"

He offered a gentle smile, one that showed just how much her older brother had changed in the years since he'd left the British military. He'd checked out a hardened and confused man, only to start a successful tech company and find love in Australia. "Yeah, I do. And if you really want to continue the self-discovery thing, I'm happy to set you up with a place of your own in the city too. You're not limited to Roseford."

Now that things had ended with Orlando, and they'd had zero contact in two weeks, perhaps the time had come to spend her remaining weeks in Australia closer to the action in Melbourne.

She washed her hands in the sink and returned Luke's smile, truly grateful to have someone to count on. "Thank you, I'll think about it."

"Listen, Soph. I didn't drive here just to nag you into coming back to Melbourne." He added some milk to the teacup and placed it beside her, then stepped back, a slight rosiness spreading across his cheek. "Agathe told me about how broken up you are over Orlando. I wanted to check you're okay."

She held back a chuckle at her brother and his clear discomfort in addressing his little sister's love life.

"I knew that free trip to Sydney would come with a catch." Despite the subject matter, she couldn't resist the chance to have fun at his expense. "Did Agathe also tell you about our exploits at that club on Oxford Street? The drag queen show, the male striptease act, our invitation to hang out with the guys backstage afterward..."

Luke's expression sagged, his brilliant green eyes turning dark. "No, she didn't tell me any of that. She's smart enough to understand there are limits to how much I want to know."

She laughed, impressed with her brother's ability to ignore the wilder details of his wife and sister's interstate adventure. Her time in Sydney helped with her goal of learning to loosen up, whilst gaining a break from all the Orlando drama. And she wanted a break now more than ever.

She'd was due to take a pregnancy test in the next few days, though she tried not to overthink that detail or what she'd do if she turned in a positive result.

Every small churn in her belly, every instance of exhaustion, played on her mind as a possible sign of early pregnancy.

Luke took a sip of his beer, his gaze not once leaving her. "But let's make one thing clear. I don't like Orlando." She flinched at the bold statement—exactly the words she didn't need to hear in light of her predicament. "He's damaged, and worse, from what I hear, he's been cold toward you. I don't see any future in whatever you two shared."

Her body felt hot and her mouth dry. Luke meant well, but he overstepped with his criticism of Orlando, a man he'd never even met. "That's a patronizing statement if ever I heard one. And who decided I was looking for a future?"

He paused his beer bottle at his lips, half-choking in a loud spluttering cough. He placed the bottle on the counter, whilst pressing his rolled-up sleeve over his mouth.

"If your defense is that you were just looking for a good time, you could have had that with anyone other than your volunteering resident." He cleared his throat, still struggling with the aftermath of his wayward mouthful of beer. "And despite your shock tactics, you don't fool me. You're much too cut up about this whole thing ending."

She shrugged a shoulder and went about prodding at the salad with a pair of metal tongs. "Fine. Maybe Orlando was a little more than a 'good time', but who are you to talk about damaged? Weren't you the one who went off the wall after your military service? And then there's Agathe. You said yourself she had a lot to work through when you two first met."

"Off the wall?" Luke let out a derisive laugh. "As a would-be psychiatrist, I think your terminology needs improvement. And as for Agathe, I'll be the first to admit working through her stuff nearly ended us." His voice tapered off, gaze slipping from her and over to a vase of plastic sunflowers on the counter. "It wasn't an easy time. I don't want the same for you."

She dipped her chin and inspected the ground between them. "I know. But despite all of that, Orlando's still a good guy dropped into a terrible situation. Before things turned sour between us, he'd displayed genuine change and lost that coldness you mentioned. He was funny and playful and would have had far more in common with you than you think. He's the type of person to throw himself on the line if called to do so. I'd appreciate it if everyone just took a step back and cut him some slack."

She lifted her gaze to her brother, his bottle-green stare searching hers. "Sure, I get it, but by the time I met Agathe, the worst of her damage had already occurred. Your guy is still drowning in the thick of it." Luke towered over her, so tall despite her being related to him and a total short stack. He sidled up to her, his hand patting her upper back in a seeming attempt to soothe. "Just tell me you'll be careful."

She gave her brother a quick nod, her throat contracting over her ability to form words. No matter his blunt approach, he only looked out for her.

"Neither of us have anything to worry about, okay? I haven't spoken to Orlando in two weeks, and I don't plan on changing that. And I have every intention of returning to the UK. I'm not giving up on my studies for anyone, 'damaged' or not. I've worked too hard and for too long."

She took the salad to her kitchen table and sat. Luke must have been satisfied with her assertion, because he said nothing else and followed to take a seat across from her.

They ate in comfortable silence, while she contemplated that perhaps his instincts to protect her were right, even if he hadn't been there to witness the full impact of her past. His work overseas had left him unable to save her from her bad choices back then, both when she'd been younger and in more recent years with Hector. Not that it had been his job to save her. But his concern now felt like a loving hug softening the crush of all things hurtful.

If only there'd been less of an age gap. If only she'd had him around all those other times she needed help.

Her phone rang, and she pulled it from her jeans pocket, still chewing as she answered. "Hello?"

"I got a call from Professor Bandara."

Adrenaline rushed her body. Her heart swelled within her chest—medically impossible given the circumstances—but something felt awry in there all the same. She regretted having been too lost in her thoughts to check her caller I.D.

"I need to show for an emergency appointment this afternoon." Orlando's unmistakable gravel pulled her from further analyzing the strange workings of her heart. "I'm not going alone. You're coming with me."

Her chin wavered, and involuntary tingles washed over her skin.

Eventually, she managed a breathy, "What?"

"Your professor had me do some blood tests. She wants to see me about the results." The matter-of-fact tone. The one with the slightly annoyed edge. *So, Orlando.* She wanted to dance. She wanted to cry. "You got me into this. I'm sure as heck not going alone."

Sophie squeezed her eyes shut and shook her head, the shock refusing to recede. "I can't go with you."

The desire was there. But she just couldn't.

"Why not?" His voice rose. Hard. Angry. Abrupt.

Luke tilted his head and mouthed, "You okay?"

She waved a hand—a sign for him to not worry.

"You know why not." And with that first bit of reasoning, her rational thought flowed smoother. "We can't see each other. Why don't you get your mother to go along?"

Luke lowered his cutlery to the table, denoting he'd figured out who she spoke to.

A terse laugh cracked into her ear. "Because your professor has either good news or bad news, and Roseford Aged Care doesn't keep hard alcohol on hand to help me deal with whichever type of news this is. Plus, someone in my position can't be expected to also deal with whatever my mum's reaction might be either way. It has to be you."

"Well... what about one of the nurses?" A small tremor worked its way into her fingers holding the phone, though she couldn't pinpoint if from Orlando's insistence or Luke's now-seething scowl. "Surely, they'll have to organize a car to drive you to your appointment in the city, anyway?"

He released a heavy sigh. "Look, I'm not getting any staff to take me. You're the one who pushed for this, Sophie. The one who found Professor Bandara. I would have thought you'd want to see this through. Call it part of your research. Aren't you interested to know how this all ends?"

She bit the inside of her cheek, holding back from pointing out she'd already *seen things through* two weeks ago by ending whatever volatile relationship they'd shared. Hadn't passing on the professor's details been her parting gift?

But then again...

She'd also done a lot of legwork researching Orlando's past, visiting Aero Syntech, finding the professor, and then getting her onboard. And Orlando was right. She *was* interested in how this would all play out... In her role as a medical student, of course... Not as someone in any way still attracted to Orlando Piras.

What if she encountered another patient like him one day?

Plus, she'd never met a neuropsychopharmacologist before. Especially not one as esteemed as Professor Bandara. She'd be giving up a hugely unique chance at gaining more knowledge.

And despite the strained relationship, whatever news the professor had to share might have big implications. She couldn't leave Orlando to deal with this alone.

"Okay, fine." She ground the words out, already certain she'd made the wrong choice. "I'll go with you."

"Great." A loud knock sounded at the front of her house. "Let's go."

She startled, her attention shooting to her front door. "You're not outside already, are you?"

"Yep. Like I said, let's go." His voice projected in stereo, his warm timbre rumbling through her phone and again from outside.

"What? Right now?"

"Right now. Open the door."

She shot to standing, and her focus hit Luke. He gave her a sidelong glare.

She turned and marched across the room to the front door, her brother's thudding footsteps close behind.

By the time she opened the door, Orlando had his back to her and his arm raised, waving off a taxi. He spun around, and her heart gave a painful palpitation against the ache of seeing him again—of knowing in that moment just how much she'd missed him. Even though she most definitely shouldn't have.

"I'll wait here if you need a few minutes." His tone softened along with his gaze.

Rigidity ran across his shoulders and along the strained and ropey muscles at the front of his neck—like he hadn't forgotten what had transpired the last time he'd entered her house. Like he wanted to avoid making that mistake again.

His impossibly dark gaze flicked to a point behind her. She turned to Luke standing over her shoulder, glaring at Orlando, jaw muscle ticking and cheeks taut, and a burning glare that said, *You broke my sister's heart. I want to break your face.*

But she'd been just as much to blame. Probably more. And Orlando didn't deserve any retribution. Only Luke, in all his loyalty, didn't seem to care. She couldn't leave these two men alone. So, she presented her brother with a beseeching look and gave up on the idea of finishing her lunch or taking a moment to change her worn jeans and faded black t-shirt.

She offered Luke a weak smile. "You'll be okay to lock up, won't you?"

Twenty~Three

"I'VE BEEN THINKING about the end." Orlando eyed Sophie, her fingers white-knuckled around the steering wheel. They'd been driving for twenty minutes, and still neither had said anything. "This isn't how I want to go."

His throat constricted even as he admitted that, but he needed to show her he was trying.

She glanced his way before refocusing on the road. "I need you to define what exactly 'this' is?"

He looked ahead, ignoring the pit opening up in his stomach. From experience, specialists only ever took emergency bookings when they had news—good or bad—not to share they'd merely found nothing. The importance of his fast-approaching meeting with Professor Bandara weighted heavy on every breath he drew.

"I mean freezing people out, giving up, making rash decisions. I want to stop doing all of that." He swallowed at the knot in his throat, voice thick and syrupy as he tried his damnedest to hold on to his thoughts; all while he searched for the words to explain himself to this woman he'd tried so hard to shut out. "And you. More than anything I regret how I've treated you."

A short laugh shot from her mouth. "And forcing me to drive you to the city after I ended things doesn't count as a rash decision?"

"No." He thought of all the things that had brought him to this moment. Candice dressing him down. His subsequent call to Professor Bandara. The phone assessments, blood tests, and then the call this morning. And of course, now, him taking this chance to rope Sophie in on a city-bound road trip. "Me calling you wasn't rash, it was a tactical decision. Walking out on you after we'd made love, losing my cool when you decided to ditch me, now *that* was rash. Trying to make things right, isn't."

Her attention stayed on the road ahead. Nothing about her still demeanor revealed much of her thoughts. "I'm not sure I'd call what we did *making love*. And you walking away that day didn't hurt me so much as my own lapse in judgment. And I'm not totally sure I regret ditching you."

Strain compressed around his ribcage, and he pulled at the car's seatbelt that suddenly sat too tight, or maybe it was his shirt. But he didn't wear tight shirts, so it must have been just him. He didn't want to believe she had no regrets. Because he sure as hell did. And he missed her. Not just the physical attraction, or even the outings, but *her*.

Then again, maybe he'd moved this conversation along a little too fast. Perhaps he needed to lighten up.

Isn't that what he did best? Lighten up or take the mickey out of someone or something until they either laughed or left him alone. But he definitely didn't want Sophie to leave. He'd tried that and hadn't liked it. Now he wanted to learn to live with what little he had, but in a new way. And having Sophie at his side would, if even for a short while, make that transition into a new way of living a heck of a lot easier.

"If what we did wasn't making love..." He smiled, while the light floral scent of her skin drifted over him and tugged at his memory. "What would you call it?"

A deep blush rose up her neck and blossomed over her cheeks.

He chuckled to himself.

She turned to him with a startled gaze.

"What?" She switched her attention back to the empty country road with golden grass plains on either side. A reluctant smile wobbled and then broke fully across her previously hard-set lips. "Some of us aren't as free with the colorful language as you. That wasn't a fair question."

He turned to his window. Whatever she called it, she'd loved what he'd done to her. He could still recall the heavy sigh of her body as he'd had her against that kitchen wall. And he'd loved having her too. More than loved it. At least for one heavenly moment, before all hell had broken loose.

She cleared her throat, drawing his focus back to her. "If I had to call what we did anything…" She held a tiny whisper, as if speaking to herself, yet that whisper cut loud enough to overcome the rev of the car's engine and the road's rushing winds. "It was the most thrilling moment of my life."

He stared at her, silent, her honesty slapping the smile right off his face. She stared ahead. Silent too. Not acknowledging what she'd just said.

Meanwhile, sparks of joy danced through his body, and goose bumps prickled his skin. Even though the lack of protection had marred what they'd done, maybe she didn't hold all that much guilt after all.

A smirk pushed at his cheeks. "You might be able to trade in the whole sweet and prudish act now."

He meant it as a joke, but she returned his smile with a sadder one of her own, then shifted her gaze back to the road. "I never was a prude, Orlando." She wrung her hands over the steering wheel, knuckles pointed as a result of her tight grip. "I keep telling you. You don't really know me."

The downward tilt to her voice, along with everything else about this whole encounter, was a precious stolen moment. It begged him to absorb every last detail of her. Because no matter how hard he worked to find a way to get her to see him, no amount of time together would be long enough.

"I know. I'm sorry."

She gave a small nod to his husky whisper, and another unreadable expression washed over her face. "Since we're being honest, I don't think I can take any more of your belittling. You really hurt me when you scrunched up the paper with details I'd worked so hard to get, and the way you barked barked at me to go... I get why you did it and that I was wrong too, but I didn't come to you that day aiming for an altercation. If you insist there's nothing professional between us, then I can't say I'd endure any friend or lover lashing out at me like that."

The slight waver in her voice suggested her stoic energy had more to do with protecting herself than shutting him out. His mind spun from what she'd said. In one breath, she admonished him for hurting her; in the next, she referred to him as a lover.

She glanced his way, and her lower lip momentarily tucked between her teeth. "In other words, it was one painful encounter too many. So, if one of your goals today is to instigate a reconciliation, I'm not sure I'm ready to forgive you."

It was his turn to look away. Witnessing what he'd done to her, that he'd given her multiple reasons not to trust him, raked nails over his heart. He'd inflicted one cruelty after another, yet only now did he compute the magnitude of his constant moods. Heck, and not just on her. Everyone.

He'd taken all the toxic energy whirling around in his heart and passed it on to anyone who dared cross his path. According to Candice, even the staff and residents at Roseford were on the verge of being done with him. These same people who endured thankless tasks day in, day out; and he, the antithesis of brilliance, had driven each and every one of them away.

He needed to deal with his mess. *But how?*

Maybe he didn't deserve Sophie's forgiveness. But he wanted it. More than he wanted anything. Despite the complete irrationality in that desire.

He was a man condemned, and she was everything he couldn't have. What he'd failed to achieve in his former life.

She was bright and beautiful. A gentle soul with an iron edge. A woman with a whole life ahead of her. A woman who dredged up every hope he'd packed away. And every wonderful thing about her delivered a messed-up reminder he had nothing to offer in return.

Nothing except maybe love. And maybe even that would be gone soon, too.

Who could say how long his malfunctioning mind and body would hold out? After all, the appointment they barreled toward now would either solidify or refute his death sentence.

But he needed to know this woman still thought him capable of redemption, because if someone as pure-hearted as Sophie couldn't see it, then maybe his life really had been worth nothing.

He blinked at the road, feeling hollower with her beside him than in all their weeks apart. As always, more his fault than hers.

"I'm sorry." He stared off into the distance, and the sound of his voice seemed to come from way down deep in his belly. "I've been a real asshole."

But she gave no reply, so he looked at her with her attention still pinned ahead.

Slow and silent minutes passed where she merely clenched her jaw, and visible tension dug shallow ridges along her forearms. "What you don't seem to factor in when you're being an asshole, is that everyone has their own hang-ups and pressure points." A tear rolled down her cheek, and she swiped it with the heel of her hand. She whipped her attention at him in one quick, hot, and angry stare. "You've all but admitted in the past that you know what pressure points are, but you press and press until those around you buckle and break. I know you just want everyone to leave you alone, but we're trying to help you. Have you ever considered the toll administering that help takes on the people in your life?"

The air chilled his skin, and he found himself speechless. He did often think about the constant effect he had on others. The price of his illness. How achingly dependent he was on others. How his bad attitude wore everyone down, including himself. But then, honest anger took less energy than faked happiness or groveling gratitude.

His heart hurt as the toll of knowing him played across Sophie's taut face, with its streaming tears, and the dent under her cheekbone from her gnawing on her inner cheek. The sight of her twisted a knife in places he'd assumed long numbed.

"Thanks to Candice, I'm starting to," he whispered. His learned hostility had become rooted in his very being. He could try. He would have to show her. And though words and promises were as helpful as using a sieve to catch water, he offered more words. "I wasn't always like this."

His inclination to bargain now made him wonder if he'd been mistaken in roping her into this road trip. Maybe his continued presence would only damage her further.

She drew out a long silence, followed by a sigh. "I'm sure you weren't. Time and circumstance changes everyone, Orlando. I've seen pictures of you from back in the day. You used to smile on occasion." The jest didn't lighten her voice. "You say there's nothing impulsive about pulling me back into your orbit, but you can't know that. Not without really knowing me. And you don't know me, Orlando. You don't know the first thing about me. You certainly don't know why I'm 'prudish' or have a deep need to avoid risk. You seem to assume that's just how I'm made. But you have no idea how much that day together cost me. All you have are a bunch of assumptions, when I'd bet my life every one of them would be wrong. You're so wrapped up in bitterness, you don't know how wrong you are."

He stared at her. "I want to know you."

A dull, soulless laughter broke from her. "Why? So you can use the truth against me? You've done just that with every other sore point, observation, or insecurity up until now. I return to the UK in mere weeks, and according to you, you're a 'lost cause'. So, why would I ever trust you? Why would I put myself through the wringer of recounting anything that might hurt me?"

He frowned, again drawing a blank. "I don't know. You're right. I haven't earned anything from you."

The hollow laughter returned, like her anger kicked up another notch. "You know, I hoped you'd return to my life, but now that you're here, I'm only just realizing how mad I am. The fact that you've already given up on getting me back only adds to my mistrust."

Her raised voice and palpable fury spoke volumes. He'd done enough. She was right. He didn't deserve her. What on earth had he been thinking?

"You should stop the car. I have my wallet. I can get myself to

Melbourne." The countryside flicked by, and he tried to gauge where exactly outside of Roseford they were. "Go home, Sophie. I've only made things worse."

"Oh, for fuck's sake." The enormity of her swear ricocheted around the car's tiny cabin, and she lashed a hand out and grabbed his wrist, as if she figured he'd throw himself out of the moving vehicle just to get away from her. "You're the one who reopened the wound here. You don't get to wriggle away so easily."

This scene, with her yelling and latching onto him, losing all control, while insisting he not wriggle away, held a comical edge. His earlier words about not ending his days as someone who gave up returned to haunt him.

The need not to give up tethered him to this car. He didn't just owe trying to *her*. He owed it to himself.

So, he tried.

He turned to her, pushing his usual resistance down, and attempting a different approach. An approach that required something other than defiance. An emotion he hadn't touched in years.

Empathy.

"Sophie." He eased his tone and allowed his own vulnerability to shine through. He needed this possibly more than she did. "Let me help. Tell me what I need to know."

Each of his days in more recent years had been about survival. His own survival. And everyone else's needs had ceased to exist. When for a large part of his life, being of service to others had been his entire world.

She peered over, eyes glistening and cheeks sunken, as if she didn't know how to respond. "You won't see me the same way." Her voice was small, reedy, her shoulders rounded. "I can't."

"You've supported me through an episode and a flashback, and neither one sent you screaming away into the night. Give me a chance to repay the favor. Besides, maybe me not seeing you the same isn't such a bad thing. As you said, you're going back to the UK, and I'm a lost cause, so what have you got to lose?" He offered a strained smile, his head aching from all the extra energy this sincerity drew from him.

She blinked ahead, posture slumping another degree. "More than you know."

He reached out and touched his fingers to her upper arm, where her muscles bunched beneath his touch. "Try me. Please."

She lashed her gaze his way before her focus returned to the road, and she blew out a heavy breath, as if needing time to weigh up whatever she had to say next. "I'm not 'Neat and Nerdy' by choice. It's a learned behavior. A survival technique. I haven't always been a 'prude', and the one time I did step out in the name of adventure, I learned a painful lesson."

She grimaced ahead, as though she'd already said too much, when in reality, she'd revealed very little at all.

He kept his attention on her, not wanting to miss a single detail, despite her not looking his way. "What lesson was that?"

"That every decision has a price. And that price can impact everyone around you."

Twenty-Four

SOPHIE STOPPED the car at an empty intersection and waited for a lone light to change. The ensuing quiet between her and Orlando made the tick of the indicator seem inordinately loud. She took a long and shaky breath, using the silence to build her courage. *Oh God, am I really about to admit this to him?*

"I had my first boyfriend when I was sixteen. He was eighteen. I was always a model student with top grades, but I wanted out of that stereotype. Having a boyfriend, along with the things we got up to, made me seem so wild to all my friends. I could sense the amazed jealousy every time we talked. It was more admiration than I'd ever experienced, as if acting out justified greater rewards than being well-behaved ever had."

She turned to Orlando, a concerned frown gracing his face, as though he already didn't like where this story was going. Why? Why was she telling him this?

Calm down. Maybe he's right. What do I have to lose?

She'd carried this secret for so long. Even those who knew the truth did their utmost not to speak about it. But she needed Orlando to understand. So, she pushed on.

"Of course, my parents didn't know. I feel like such an idiot admitting this now, but he lured me in with his ability to sneak me into clubs, buy me alcohol. He had a car when all my peers were walking. Stepping away from the 'wholesome' role, regaling my friends with things none of them were doing, it was one big rush. Besides, Luke was off on active duty, Max was busy training for his swimming comps, and I was the reliable quiet one in the family. So, my parents didn't think twice about me coming home late. They assumed I was studying at a friend's house. I didn't even have to lie, beyond omitting the truth and letting them fill in the missing details."

Her stomach churned, a hot sensation burned her from the inside out.

She'd thought herself clever, lying, spending time with people who were older but not all that invested in her wellbeing. "I knew that boy was using me. He didn't really love me. But then, I was using him too."

"Sophie…" Orlando's voice dipped, pleading in a way that said he knew where this story went, but hoped for a different outcome.

She gave a weak smile, one that would only confirm his misgivings. "You already see me differently now, don't you?"

The muscles over his face hardened. Maybe he disapproved of her ability to read him. Maybe he already thought less of her. Maybe he regretted chasing her out of her house and into this car. But all he gave her was his continued stare and a simple demand. "Tell me what you're getting at here."

She let out a sigh and sunk back against her headrest. *Here goes…* If he wanted to reject her over this, so be it. She'd condemned herself to losing him two weeks ago, anyway.

"One particular weekend got way out of hand. I can barely recall what happened beyond us taking the train from Scarborough to London and crashing on the floor of my boyfriend's friend's flat. Well, that's where we left our stuff, anyway. We didn't spend much time there since it was an all-weekend clubbing event, and we proceeded to get completely wasted. The only other thing I remember is having one drink after another and spending the next two days paying for it with the headache from hell." Her chin trembled. The headache and fatigue had been minor consequences. The worse stuff came not much later. "I treated my body like a dumping ground. Except, what I didn't know was... It wasn't just me I was hurting that weekend."

Orlando's clothes rustled against the car's leather seats, and he shifted his torso toward her. "What do you mean exactly? Tell me what happened."

She couldn't bring herself to return his stare, so she blinked at the road—her head shaking a silent and numb denial of his request—though she knew she had to finish this story.

"Two days later, I was at school and I started getting these cramps. My lower abdomen and back hurt more than anything I'd ever experienced, and I was doubled over in pain during math class. It was completely surreal. My best friend kept rubbing my back and asking if I was okay. And I kept saying, 'Yes, yes, I'm fine', and bargaining that it was just unusually strong period pain. Maybe just a result of dehydration from my big weekend. But the minutes kept ticking by, and in my heart of hearts, I knew something was really wrong." Her lips took on a life of their own, forming the words to a tale that sounded strange and unfamiliar out loud, even though it was her story.

She turned to him for a second, her eyes stinging, cheeks cold as though her circulation had lost the will to flow that high up her body. "The teacher eventually sent me out of the room, and I was about an hour into lying in the nurse's office when the worst of the bleeding started. About an hour after that, my mum sat beside my bed at the nearest hospital and a doctor stood before us informing me I was experiencing a miscarriage. My heart shrunk. I wanted to curl up and stop existing. I hadn't even known I was pregnant and I'd drunk myself to oblivion just days prior, I'd done this to myself. I'd been so foolish."

Her throat felt drier than a scorched field, but despite the pain of delivering her words, she focused ahead and rasped out her final sentiments on the matter. "I'd done this to myself, but I'd also ripped a potential new life out of this world, too. It was all my fault. For being so blasé. So naïve. I can't ever for a second forgive myself for that mistake."

A heavy hand landed above hers on the steering and wrenched the car into a sharp swerving motion off the road. She screamed, instinctively slamming her foot on the brakes and working to pull the wheel in the opposite direction.

"Let go. Pull over." Orlando's hand fought hers again, and she did as he asked since fighting him held the strong possibility of directing the car into a tree.

The car swung into a dip at the roadside; she planted her foot on the brake again, and the tires crunched the vehicle to a stop.

Her body flung forward, inertia running its course until her shoulders flopped back into her seat.

"What about your appointment?"

Her question sounded ridiculous against the panic of swerving all over the road.

"Kill the engine. We can spare ten minutes."

She killed the engine, and the churning in her gut gave way to a hollow sensation.

What now? Had she waited all these years to talk about her past, only to find she'd picked the wrong person? As much as she wanted to deny it, Orlando's opinion mattered. His harsh tone still rung in her ears, along with the engine's soft tick, tick, ticking, as though it too needed a moment to recover.

"Jesus." He pressed the heels of his hands over his eyes. "Sophie." Her name came out on a low growl, and he dropped his hands to his lap and pinned her with that dark, inescapable glare. A glare that always saw too much. "Please don't tell me you've been beating yourself up over that for all of twelve years. What happened was a tragedy, but how many other sixteen-year-olds lie about their age so they can hit the clubs and get wasted? Too many to count. Hell, even I was into the same shit at that age. You made a mistake. An inexperienced, never-been-out-in-the-world, sixteen-year-old mistake. And there were two of you involved. So, as much as I understand your guilt, you can't claim full ownership of what happened."

His words hung in the air, slow to filter through. She peered down at the steering wheel while her shoulders rounded. She felt small. Exposed. Completely vulnerable in the worst kind of way.

Forgiving the past wasn't as simple as admitting to a mistake.

"Logically, I know that. But people beat themselves up for less."

How could anyone love her knowing what she'd done? Who she'd been? If even for the briefest time. Perfect Sophie Tindall didn't exist. In fact, she was so fatally flawed, her actions had quite literally cost the life of an unborn child. "Over the years, I've had so many reminders of just how wrong I got it. Of just how much I need to make sure I never make those same impulsive decisions again. Except—"

"Except you made almost that same exact mistake with me." He frowned, eyes darkening as he made the connection to that afternoon in her kitchen, where they'd had sex but hadn't been careful, and her frantic escape from him minutes later.

"I had no idea." His tone softened, but his eye contact remained. "I'm sorry."

"Please don't apologize, I don't deserve it. And like you said, you didn't know."

"Not knowing isn't an excuse. I was selfish and so wrapped up in my own dilemma after we..." He reached out a hand and placed it over hers. "I own every bit of my part in all of this. Including the part where this has reopened a wound for you."

She squeezed her eyes shut and drew in a breath. Somehow his compassion hurt more than the disgust she'd expected. "There are people like Agathe, people who have lost a child, or people who have tried over and over and over again, only to never get the baby they so desperately want. Then there are monsters like me. I could have had a child, and I not only ruined it, but I also felt a sense of relief that one never eventuated. Whenever I think about that day, every thought is worse than the one before it."

She leaned her head to the steering wheel, spare hand pressed to her middle. Even though Orlando sat less than a meter away, she felt so alone. He might have shared responsibility, but no one could wear her pain for her, and she deserved every last bit of it. For being so cold. For spending all these years running from something she'd so recently and carelessly repeated again.

His hand squeezed hers. "That first time, you were a kid playing at being an adult. You weren't ready, and you have no idea how you would have adjusted had things turned out differently. And you can't compare yourself to Agathe. I doubt she'd want you owning hers or any other person's hardship." He kept his tone low, as though coaxing her away from a proverbial ledge. "I don't know much about her story, but I'm guessing you were in very different stages in your lives when you both fell pregnant. What's right for one person isn't right for the next. You had things to sort through and a heck of a lot of growing up to do back then."

She turned to him, a rise of panic sweeping through her body. "But if I'd only stayed home that weekend. What was I thinking? I was only sixteen."

"Sophie." His insistent tone, along with his exasperated sigh, commanded she listen. "You're the one with the medical degree. You know more than I that some pregnancies survive much worse than what you did, and some don't. You also know that the human brain isn't fully developed until the mid-twenties. Teens are hardwired to make idiotic decisions, to rebel sometimes. I should know, I've pried far too many young bodies out of smashed-up cars as a result of drunken joyrides gone wrong. And just like pretty much every other teen, you thought you were invincible and older and had more control than you really did. Some people just get through those years more unscathed than others."

She opened her mouth, ready to argue, only to snap it shut again, her mind racing. "You're taking this way better than I thought."

He huffed out a laugh. "Yeah, well. Let's just say I also have first-hand experience talking people off ledges, and I've heard some pretty crazy-ass stories. Though yours does still surprise me."

She gave him a lopsided smile, her level of brokenness still high but not as stratospheric as before. "Well then, there you are, I'm not as innocent as you thought."

"No." He reached out and touched her cheek. "You're even more so."

"You can't believe that. I've repeated the same mistake, and I'm older now. I didn't enter your life as a lover. I was supposed to help you. I should have known better."

"And you're also human." His frown returned, more severe this time. "Listen to me, I'll never consider what we did a true mistake.

And I understand why you're cautious. Why you were keen to break away and that what we did brought you close to that confused sixteen-year-old you once were. I'll always regret getting so lost in my own shock. No wonder you didn't want to see me again."

"I understood you were fighting your own demons."

"That's not an excuse."

"It kind of is."

They watched each other in silence, and sense of mutual understanding passed between them, offering the one positive out to this whole ordeal—they at least knew each other a little better.

Orlando broke the silence first. "I'm just starting to realize that both you and I have complementing needs. We've been so caught up in trying to protect each other that we kept missing the mark. I didn't give you enough credit to manage your life. I assumed you wouldn't be able to handle disappointment or my condition, much less my general shitty attitude. And you"—his hand squeezed gently around hers—"you decided I'm too psychologically fragile to handle anything beyond a volunteer-resident relationship. And that's not fair, either."

She kept her mouth closed, knowing she should reply; for the most part, agreeing with him but unable to commit to where she stood when it came to this relationship.

He offered a soft smile, perhaps his recognition of her struggle. "Regardless of what the doctor has to say today, I want to continue knowing you. On one condition."

She quirked an eyebrow, falling just short of a genuine laugh. "You're the one trying to convince *me* right now, remember?"

His eyes took on a joyful gleam, his gaze flitting over her face with a new kind of lightness. "I remember. But you're going to forgive me, anyway, I know you will. You're just as intrigued about where this will all go as I am."

She gave him a sideways glance, reminding him she thought he was full of himself. But he was kind of right, and she wanted to hear what he had to say all the same.

"Whatever happens, I promise to do my best to shut down my cagey-bastard act, but you have to promise not to mess up your life for me."

She gave a nervous laugh. "Don't worry, I never had a plan to mess up my life for you."

He rolled his eyes, the *cagey-bastard* making a minor appearance. "Whatever. Just promise not to get swept up and forget why you came here to begin with. Got it?"

"Sure. Whatever you command."

Somehow, she'd missed this man's cockiness.

A distinct shadow clouding his eyes indicated he wasn't impressed with her snarky answer. "Promise me you'll return home and continue your life as planned. You'll keep studying. You'll keep living. No matter what. Whether I live or die, Sophie. Promise me you won't stop being you, and you won't break with your goals."

His hold on her hand tightened again, and his strong tone sent cold fear rushing through her body. All his talk about dying, she didn't want to think about that. Whether he spoke of dying naturally or taking matters into his own hands, she wanted him to share in her denial. Or better yet, share her hope. To reassure her everything would be okay.

"Orlando…"

But his dark gaze held firm. "Promise me."

"Fine." She gave him what he wanted, surrendered to the knowledge he would never offer her the benefit of sugar-coating his future. "But I'm still not convinced us knowing each other is a good idea."

He shrugged and let go of her hand, as if pleased to have her agreement either way. His suddenly relaxed demeanor seemed contrary to what she expected of a man about to learn his fate.

"We'll iron out the details later. For now—" He jutted his chin toward the empty road ahead. "We have an appointment to get to."

Orlando sat on one of the five maroon fabric chairs within Professor Bandara's waiting room. Sophie sat to his left, her fingers interlaced with his. A middle-aged, female receptionist sat behind a high counter, tapping away at her computer, the *clack-clack-woo* of her printer breaking whatever small calm existed within the room.

He counted all the purple shapes on the massive abstract painting on the right-hand wall. Twenty-five. When that was done, he moved onto the green. Seventeen. His palms grew sweaty, and his grip around Sophie's hand tightened. She wriggled her fingers, like maybe he'd cut off her circulation.

"Sorry." He loosened his grip.

She shifted sideways to face him. "Are you okay?"

He opened his mouth to admit that maybe he wasn't, but the door at the room's farthest corner opened and a woman with South Asian brown skin and chin-length black curls stepped out. She held a small smile and looked to him with eyes as dark as his own. "Mr. Piras?"

He nodded and stood a little too fast, his heart already racing from the wait.

He took the longest walk of his life into the professor's office, all the while refusing to let go of Sophie's hand. And while he walked, he made a promise to himself and the universe at large. That regardless of what the professor said, he'd spend whatever limited days he might have supporting Sophie and adding value to her life, rather than thinking about himself and his bitter existence for a change.

Professor Bandara lowered herself into her black leather chair and dispensed with quick pleasantries. "I'll get right to the point and spare you the technical jargon." Her eyes glittered and the corners of her crimson-covered lips crept higher. "You are the proud owner of an enzyme I'll affectionately call ACRUNase. It was an ordeal for myself and my team to find, hence why we required so many blood samples from you, along with your past MRIs. Sorry about that."

He blinked at the professor's sympathetic cringe, his mind spinning out of control, while completely blank at the same time. He wouldn't have cared if she'd asked for half the blood in his body and access to his dwindling bank account, as long as he got some answers.

When he failed to offer any reply, the professor gave a tight smile, and continued with what she'd been saying. "So, the thing about ACRUNase, it's incredibly rare. For certain people, it has the potential to alter nerve, muscle, and general brain function when exposed to particular influences. Do you understand what I mean, Orlando?"

Her chin dipped, and she stared up at him, as if she considered he might be a bit slow. To her credit, they'd only ever spoken on the phone, and he'd so far only managed a tight, "Hi," on his way through the door.

But her words did filter through, and his muscles and thoughts froze in place, his cheeks cold and sagging as though all the blood had drained from his head.

What the professor had just described sounded like the answer he'd always searched for—and nothing—all in one.

"Influences?" His throat prickled and lumbered as he forced the question out. "You mean, the TL-20 at the Aero Syntech fire site?"

"Yes, exactly." She nodded. "I tested your blood samples against separate compounds from the TL-20 ingredient list Sophie supplied and got a definite reaction out of one set. Though I suspect the accumulation of some third element, maybe something such as stress or viral exposure or anything really, might explain why your episodes are intermittent and differ in duration."

He turned to Sophie, the only other person in the room with a medical degree, hoping to decide how excited he should be. She held a gleaming grin, cheeks lifted and eyes aglow, signaling perhaps he could afford to lighten up too.

He refocused on the professor, not yet ready to cash in years of crushed hopes on a premature chance to celebrate. "What does this all mean for me?"

"It means what wouldn't affect most normal people, messed with your brain like an over ripe banana in a blender. The day you put out that fire, you walked into a perfect storm, and all hell was unleashed on your body and your brain. Our job now is to try to find a way to switch off the hyperreaction your body has been stuck on since that day—which is what your episodes essentially are, a hyperreaction."

He frowned at the word "hell". Hell was what he already lived in. What he needed most, was for the professor to confirm he'd finally earned his way out of hell and had something a little more like earth to look forward to. "Can you fix me?"

The professor shrugged. "Maybe."

"Just maybe?"

He got a sly smile back from the professor and turned to Sophie. "As Ms. Tindall can confirm, we doctors don't like to give guarantees." She gazed back at him, the smile hardening, and a sterner look taking over. "I'm confident I might be able to customize the right combination of drugs to block the ACRUNase production in your body. If I can pull it off. If my theory is correct. Then you'll be okay."

He held onto his frown, his long-time safety blanket, unable to find it in him to believe her. "You mean there'll be no more episodes and this nightmare will be over?"

She gave a silent, but steady nod.

He slumped back in his chair, the air knocked from his lungs.

His attention fell to the ground and the swirling, teal patterned carpet below. Years of pent-up hopelessness slipped from his body. He shook his head, face hot, eyes stinging, unable to form proper words.

I might be healed one day. I might return to my former life. I might actually have a future.

But it couldn't be true.

Good things like that didn't happen to less-than-worthy people like him.

"But Mr. Piras," Professor Bandara called for his full attention, and he whipped his focus back to her. "I need to be very clear. This will be a process. A potentially very long process. Next to nothing is known about your condition, so you'll be a guinea pig of sorts on this, do you understand? I'll need time to adjust dosage, medication, and my approach, depending on how you respond."

He heard her words. Nodded to say he understood. Yet no warning would put him off trying to get what had eluded him for years. And there wasn't much this doctor could do to him that others hadn't done already.

"Whatever you need." His voice came out a rough croak.

"I have another warning." Her jovial smile from earlier seemed long gone, but he cared little for her gloominess. She held the keys to his cage. Nothing else mattered. "Even if I do cure you, there's no promise this won't happen again. That means you need to steer clear of as much chemical exposure as possible. That means you won't ever return to your former job as a firefighter."

His ribcage compressed, and his body felt suddenly heavy, but he nodded all the same. He'd never expected to live beyond the next few years. Any dreams of returning to his old job had been long packed away.

The professor's eyes sparkled anew, and she grinned, a woman whose natural default expression might be a permanent smile. "I have a good idea of where to start with your treatment." She spun her office chair to a set of cupboards behind her, and very soon a white plastic pill bottle rattled within her palm. She slid the bottle across her desk and waited for him to grab it. "You won't get this stuff from your run-of-the-mill pharmacist. I had two of my best underlings compound these for you. We'll adjust dosage and mix based on your feedback and reactions."

He examined the pill bottle and expected it to glow, like some kind of beacon or the holy grail. But no, it was just a little white bottle with his details printed in black across the label.

Still, he turned to Sophie, the sudden lightness in her eyes prompting him, for the first time in years, to envision a whole new world ahead of him.

"This must be a lot to process." Professor Bandara's voice turned his head toward her again. "You can, of course, contact me with any concerns or reactions you might have to your new medication. Just know, this whole left-of-field discovery is very exciting for me and my team. We're not going to let your case slide by without giving it our full effort. But before I let you go, do you have any final questions?"

He flicked his gaze back to Sophie and nodded. "This enzyme, is it genetic? Will it affect any future children of mine?"

A heavy weight seemed to bear down on his chest as he awaited the professor's reply.

"Yes." The professor held a strong tone, one that didn't hide from the truth. "But here's the good news. Like anything of this nature, now we know you have it, we can help any affected future offspring. Again, whatever switches this enzyme on, appears to be very specific. Quite often with these types of disorders, one can be a carrier and live their entire life without any reaction. That would be true for any children you have." Professor Bandara sank back in her chair. "Your earlier assessment questions stated that no one else in your family has presented with this issue. So, I'd say that, up until now, you've just been one really unlucky guy."

———

Orlando stood beside Sophie in the elevator on the way down to the hospital lobby. A dumbstruck silence stretched between them, though they'd shared a few skittish glances before continuing the status quo of watching the shiny metallic double doors ahead.

"I'm not going to say I told you so, but..." Her low, yet sing-song whisper echoed around the tiny space.

"Really?" A small laugh bounced from his chest. "And I guess you're also still not convinced us knowing each other is a good idea?"

She released a stifled chuckle. "Shut up."

He gave her hand a gentle squeeze, and said nothing, glad that for once worry didn't underscore either of their moods.

She turned to him, so he returned the gesture, only to find her smiling up at him. "Just don't you forget, I said yes even before the professor offered her glimmer of hope."

Twenty-Five

"YOUR BROTHER, Luke. He wants to kick my ass, doesn't he?"

Sophie stood outside her open car door and smiled at the unique sound of Orlando initiating the conversation for a change. "Probably Max too." She swung the door shut and laughed, fawn sandals crunching over the sandy gravel in the parking lot at Lacey River—a stretch of thick bushland half an hour from Roseford. "But Luke has had his fair brush with complicated relationships, and as intimidating as he seems, I think he'd be willing to give us the benefit of the doubt."

Orlando slung her black backpack, containing their lunch, over his shoulder. "So that means we're an 'us', now, huh?" He grinned back, the expression uncharacteristically light. "I don't blame your brothers, really. I'd want to kick my ass too. Then again, I have zero regrets over storming the cabin."

She made a show of raising a brow, a folded picnic rug clasped in her right hand. Orlando led her down a track; his palm on her lower back sending a soft wave of heat throughout her body. "I missed your friendship, Sophie."

She leaned into him, despite the churning in her tummy, as if the roles had reversed, and she'd become the skeptical one.

Professor Bandara had unleashed her surprisingly positive

diagnosis just days ago, and already Orlando exuded an air of bright new hope. Candice reported a marked ease in his attitude, though that change had started days before Professor Bandara's appointment, as if he'd made a sudden decision to invest in himself.

This shouldn't have been a bad thing, but Sophie needed to know he'd be okay. That he'd genuinely improve, both physically and mentally. But she couldn't pinpoint what would cause him to reawaken from the slump he'd been in.

His quick change scared her. Like his enthusiasm might burn out, and his sudden rise would lead to an equally sudden fall.

What would happen should the professor's treatment fail? Should Sophie's *own* relationship with him fail? Or he not be as accepting of her return to the UK as he'd claimed?

"Have you noticed any improvement yet?" She spoke with the echoes of Candice's warning in her ears. "I mean, with the medication."

She held her breath, not easy given the quick pace he kept down the gnarled bush track. All the while, she awaited his reply, afraid of yet another regret to haunt her through the decades.

"Not really." His broad shoulders took up the limited space on the path, his torso far taller than hers. He turned to her, lines scoring his cheekbones. "I can't imagine a day where I'll feel totally out of the woods. I'm not buying into hope just yet. I've been down this road too many times."

On a surface level, she wanted to believe him, to ease her guilt about just how deep she'd pulled him into trusting her, but his change alone signaled he wasn't quite as disengaged with hope as he claimed. "What hope exactly aren't you buying into?"

He twirled a thin gum leaf from a nearby tree through his fingers, then tossed it back to the ground as he walked on. "That a man who's lost everything can still have a future." He gave a tight laugh, as if the gesture alone could erase the heavy expectations pressing down on both their shoulders. "That he could have..."

His husky tone tapered, as though he fell short of uttering his dreams out loud, or at least lacked the heart to finish the thought.

Her own heart beat faster, cresting on a sharp ache. She wished to know what a man like Orlando wanted, and yet, given how temporary her presence would be, maybe she had no right to pry. He'd said as much the day she left him at the care facility.

The rushing of water pulled her attention, and the track thinned until a wider clearing opened up, one that revealed a great, brown river with white caps smashing over protruding rocks along the banks. She paused a moment to watch, to catch her breath.

Everything about this place invited contemplation. From the glaring midday sun, to the joyful kookaburras and white cockatoos in the nearby gums. Cheery wattle trees dotted the landscape with bright patches of yellow. Across the river, a gigantic sheet of flat, gray rock made up the steep mountainside, and a mass of tall trees battled to grow from between the cracks.

She'd taken time to learn a little about the Australian bushland as part of her travel experience, but she wasn't all that confident in her powers of identification. She pointed to a small, dark bird, darting and circling the water's swollen surface. "Is that a willie wagtail?"

The same bird swooped closer, and Orlando's gaze followed its path. "No. That's a welcome swallow. Notice the red chest? The local indigenous people watch for its appearance as a sign of the start of a new season." He turned to her, squinting against the sun. "I guess we'd call it spring, but they have about seven seasons and their own way of tracking things. Their weather calendar is more accurate to the area than the four European seasons we all follow."

She couldn't help it; she let out a small laugh. "I'm beginning to think you calling me 'nerdy' was more a case of self-recognition."

He smiled and turned back to the water. "A lot of firefighters in these parts have a basic understanding of indigenous seasonal change. Plus, I grew up running wild around places like this. The first people have been here for over sixty thousand years, and they know the land better than anyone. So, when those same people forecast a season high in heat and wind, and you're the one slated to fend off any resulting fires, you'll take any bit of help you can get."

She watched the bird a while longer, the scent of the damp ozone rising from the river's edge. The alien landscape differed so greatly from dreary London or the oak-and-birch-dappled forests around her hometown of Scarborough. She could never dream of asking Orlando to leave this place. To uproot himself from everything he knew. *Again.* And for her this time. Even if the professor's plan miraculously worked...

She sucked in a breath at her runaway thoughts, far too dangerous considering the limits on this relationship.

"I don't want to be your friend." The words slipped from her mouth, and she regretted them instantly. Her statement could be easily misinterpreted as her not wanting to know him at all.

"I don't want to be your friend either, Sophie." He reached a hand out and stroked his thumb over her chin. "You and I could never be just friends. We're all or nothing. When I said I missed your friendship, I only meant it as an entry into picking up where we left off."

His hand slid down her arm, and he interlaced his fingers with hers. His dramatic statement was more truth than she could deny. They'd tried to maintain distance, in a number of ways, but failed every time. Still, she needed to be clear.

"You know I can't stay. We have no choice but to accept less than *all.*"

"I know."

"Then what *are* we? Not friends. Not lovers. What?"

"Are you looking to name this?" His attention dipped from her eyes to her lips. "I have every plan to have you again, multiple times if you'll let me, but—" He captured her gaze, deep-brown eyes drawing her in. "I'm never going to call you a fuck buddy, Sophie. You're more than that. You're... You're my spark." He frowned, before an easy smile lifted his cheeks. "We burn bright and hot, but not forever."

She laughed, nudging at him, skin tingling at the hard and heated feel of his ribcage. "Nice firefighter analogy." But then her laughter wobbled under a swell of broken emotion. "And you're okay with that? Not forever? Because no matter what happens, there'll come a day when we won't know each other."

The swell grew, overwhelming and taking up an inordinate amount of space within her chest. If she didn't get hold of herself, she'd turn into a blubbering mess. She couldn't do that. Not in front of Orlando. He'd contended with so much misery already.

His hand tightened around hers, as though he saw her struggle. "Want to know how I get through one day after another? How I survive the knowledge that things will probably only get worse?"

She gave a shaky nod, peering down at their joined fingers because she'd lost the strength to look at him.

"My survival depends on not thinking about the future. Any chance of me enjoying anything depends on not thinking about what's coming next. So..." He lifted her hand and brushed his lips over her knuckles. "Stop thinking about the day we won't know each other. Think about now. Think about how *this* feels." He pressed a drawn-out kiss to the back of her hand, and her skin responded with instant heat.

Her eyes closed to the skim of his breath, his words already sinking in. The hurried *whoosh* of wind through the trees added to her drunken feeling. "You make escaping reality sound simple."

"For now, it is." He pulled her hand away from his lips and cradled it in his palm. "It won't be for much longer. I know that."

She peered back up at him, an empty feeling opening inside her, a hollow she instantly recognized only he could fill. That knowledge alone meant she would collide with disaster if she didn't get some other details straight.

She'd always been one to have her life planned out; as long as she played things safe, things tended to work. But this situation was far less than perfect. The only thing that did work was how well they got along, which seemed enough for her.

When he looked at her, her former obsession with leading an ideal life evaporated. So maybe she could be okay with the limits and just enjoy what they had, but first...

"I plan to stick to our agreement. I plan to return home. Just as I promised." She turned her hand so their palms pressed together. "But I worry about you."

"You shouldn't."

The importance of what she had to say formed a hard ball in her throat. This relationship's trajectory hung on whatever happened next. She couldn't go further with him unless she spoke now.

"I have to worry. I absolutely have to. And you have to understand my obligations both as a woman and as a doctor, just as you had obligations as a firefighter back when you were one. There's a duty of care here I can't ignore any longer. Even if our relationship has never been anything formal."

She lifted her gaze to his frown, perhaps he suspected he wouldn't like what she had to say, though right now he remained silent.

"I need you to let Candice line up ongoing psychological care for you."

He jolted, mouth open as if ready to protest, but she held up a hand and cut him off. "If you're allowed to stipulate conditions, then so can I. And this is my one condition. I can't shoulder the pressure of your wellbeing alone, especially knowing I'll be leaving."

"But I don't need a psychologist."

"Oh, come on, Orlando." Her voice rose, and she inched back, ready for a fight. "You're having flashbacks. If not for your condition and circumstance at the home, then get help with how to handle those. And if not for the flashbacks, then to help me feel confident I'm not crossing any line here as your sole place of support."

His gaze shifted away from her. On the surface it appeared he distanced himself, but the lax skin over his cheekbones suggested deep thought rather than rejection.

A fluttery feeling spread through her stomach. She needed an answer and that answer had to be yes.

He turned back to her, frown still set, forehead pulling at the middle. "Okay."

Her shoulders dropped as his gravelly agreement seeped through to her brain. She'd envisioned an argument—her storming off to the car, him storming after her, and a frosty ride back to Roseford Aged Care Center together.

"Really?"

He gave a short nod. "I won't add more doubt to your life. And… maybe you're right about the other stuff, too."

She held back a laugh. Partly because of his reluctant acknowledgement, but also out of relief. He'd gone a long way to elevating the huge burden she'd carried in the weeks since her talk with Candice. More than that, he'd be getting extra help.

She reached out and cupped his face in her hands, then landed a hard kiss to his right cheek. He reeled back a little, like her excitement surprised him.

Still, she had more to say, perhaps something closer to what he'd want to hear. "The one perfect thing about our situation is that maybe we can both get what we want here."

He tilted his head in questioning.

"I mean, you're worried I'll sacrifice everything I want in order to be with you. And I get it, I tend to help others, while failing to grasp at what I want. But you've forgotten something else." She gave a sharp smile, taking joy in the confused crinkling of his face. "This *is* me grasping for what I want. I want what you've already proven very capable of giving me." His scowl gradually lightened, a sign he'd read the subtext of what she got at. "Up until now, you've wanted to live, but couldn't. I want to live, too, but I don't know how. And I'm asking for your help. I don't do spontaneous, Orlando, but you've given me glimpses of just that. For once, fear didn't stop me. And as much as we fumbled that day in my kitchen, this is still something you could help me with. Because... because I trust you."

Her heart stammered at that last confession.

His eyes pulled wide; maybe she'd caught him off guard. Then his posture lifted, indicating he liked what he'd heard, that she'd handed him a ticket to something he hadn't had in years.

For a short time, he'd be needed. He'd have a relationship where he wasn't the only one requiring help.

His eyes glinted like polished onyx, if polished onyx could hide a brewing plan. "I'm sure I can arrange that, and with surprising frequency. But since you're after spontaneity, maybe you could be the one to show me what you want?"

Her jaw slipped loose. She peered around her, to the river with its forceful current. "What? Right now? Right *here*?" Granted, no one had walked past in the entire time they'd been talking, but still... "I think you're throwing me in a little too deep."

He let out an easy laugh before a devilish grin took over his features. The same grin he'd given her that first day he'd offered her a fake date. Though *this* devilish grin didn't mock so much as play.

"I'll help you." He drew nearer, voice low and rough. "Spontaneity starts with a kiss."

Those simple words shifted a space in her heart. A space that allowed room for the trust she'd mentioned. And she did trust Orlando. She couldn't quite define why, but she did. Completely.

Her heart pounded; her senses heightened, even the brush of a cool breeze on her sun-warmed skin grew her aching need for him. But he held still, just watching her, and it was then she twigged that he wanted her to initiate his mentioned kiss.

He leaned in, larger-than-life, as though he saw her grapple with the situation.

"You can do this."

His coaxing whisper suggested she could back out if she wanted to. She was safe if she changed her mind. But she *did* want this. She wanted him. She'd wanted him since that first meeting, even as he messed with her and left her running in anger.

And now here he was, wanting her too.

She stood on her toes and reached for him. And in an instant, their lips met.

He remained still, allowing her to find her way. To explore. She lifted her hands and stroked his neck, marveling at his play of muscles dancing beneath her fingertips. Her nostrils filled with the scent of clean skin and soap, of manly musk, all of which melted her further. His chest rose and fell, his body taut, the strain of a man holding it together for her.

She paused. Overwhelmed. Then pulled away, resting her forehead to his as she waited for her bearings to return.

Since when did any man make room for her?

Since never.

Not with Hector. His passionless love-making had been sparse but efficient. Not with the boy from her teen years. His hurried and selfish attempts couldn't even be called anything close to *love-making*. But both men had praised themselves as heroes. Heroes she'd been supposedly lucky to date.

And then there was Orlando.

He never praised himself. Not without a heavy dose of sarcasm.

He'd been the antithesis of a hero. Her villain. Someone who'd set out to block her dream of doing good things, even though in some ways he'd succeeded.

She opened her eyes, drunk on wonder and a man of total contradiction. A man fast becoming her undoing.

His eyes held humor, but his brow twisted in mild worry. "Don't give me that look."

She smiled, choosing to focus on the lighter side of his expression. "What look?"

The twist in his brow untangled, and his smile mirrored hers. "Like you're about to adopt me or something."

A quick laugh had her head swinging back. "Haven't you noticed? I've already adopted you."

"I know." He stroked her jaw with the pad of his thumb. "Come with me."

He took her hand and led her farther up the creek, over a small, stony cliff most people wouldn't bother climbing. They descended to where a large rock face and the cliff's base met with a thick line of weeping willows. From the smoky scent, she figured these willows were native. Long, leafy tendrils spilled over and brushed against the straw-colored tall grass.

He pulled her farther through the line of trees until he had her pressed against the cliff behind. "No one will see us here." He gave a curled grin. "But we'll need to be quiet."

She giggled, genuine joy mixed with nerves, as his hands traveled up her arms.

Warmth flowed from the rock behind her and into her back, turning her body languid in his hold. He tilted her chin up, kissing her again, his large body engulfing her in this intimate space where the trees served as a tent, the interior thick with river sounds and the *chirrup* of insects.

But his lips blocked everything, and suddenly all she sensed was *him*. Her hunger for him grew as they fought to explore each other, his hard length pressing to her belly and lighting a fire within her.

His hurried fingers bunched the hem of her dress, and she responded by fumbling at his pants until she freed him. Their breaths were rushed, ragged and raw, as though they couldn't get to each other quick enough. His hands moved to her shoulder straps, and he tugged them past her arms. She wore no bra and stood exposed all the way to her waist.

He leaned back, assessing her. A second of self-consciousness roiled through her. As much as she loved the open look of awe, he'd called this her show, and she meant to take control.

She gripped his shirt in her hand and pulled him closer. He smirked, rewarding her bravo. She ground her hips against him, her voice a tight whisper. "It has to be now."

He pressed his nose to hers, his fingers curled to the rock beside her head, the other hand curved around her bare waist, strumming her skin and sending electric shivers through her body.

Next, he crushed his mouth down on her until his tongue plunged deep, his long fingers traversing lower until they met with her hot, wet core. She let out a whimper, but he swallowed the sound, as if possessing her so completely spurred him on.

Her excitement had blossomed in the delicate moment he'd told her to kiss him, but things weren't so delicate now. Heck, she didn't want delicate. Not gentle. Or sweet. She wanted Orlando. Resilient and rugged. Simple and sometimes crude.

She found her voice, demanding once more, "Turn me around."

He pushed back and out of her hold. His lust-filled glare paused before he released a low growl and reached out.

He spun her as asked, and her face brushed warm rock, his breaths heavy, in sharp bursts against her ear. Next came the crinkle of a condom wrapper. And then the harsh relief of him entering her in one hard thrust.

She tipped her head back, reveling in the moment, hips tilting out of an instinctual need to deepen the connection.

His lips nipped and sucked at her shoulder, and he moved within her, low and indulgent glides, until her moan broke free, and she begged for more.

Sophie Tindall never begged.

She waited. Patiently. Without a word. And as a result, she *never* got.

His large hand snaked down her back, over her ass, and lower to her thigh. She clenched beneath him, anticipating his next move, only for his hand to reverse trajectory. This time over her waist and up between her breasts, his fingers stopping at the base of her throat. He moved within her and held her there, suspended in his tight embrace. Erotically trapped. She dug her fingers into the rock, her other hand joining Orlando's on her hip.

He pounded into her, rough but deliciously controlled. Her excitement grew, and each thrust sent new shock waves through her body. Her heart rate lifting. Blood heating. Her every cell and nerve alive and elated.

And just as her peak rose, his fingers entangled with hers, moving her hand to the front of her hips and between her thighs.

She sucked in a breath, flutters twirling through her body. His fingers met the electric juncture of her excitement, and his hold on her hand meant she joined him in touching her. Slow and strong, circling caresses kept her captive. The soft pressure of his hand at her throat and his rhythmic thrusts overwhelmed her body. She couldn't keep up, and her ability to hold together imploded.

His movements turned harder and faster all at once again, until her voice ground on a strained moan, one that morphed into a needy cry. She lost control and sagged in his arms—a state of total and inescapable surrender. He plunged deeper still and released his own groaning pleasure.

Minutes passed while the clouds of desire cleared. He spun her around, unleashing a torrent of desperate kisses on her lips.

Like he couldn't believe what they'd just shared.

Like he needed to make sure she was real. That this moment was real.

Her laugh broke through the anguished tension, and he gentled his hold, pulling back as they watched each other.

A lot went unsaid, and a new truth settled in. One that burrowed down to the depth of her bones.

She didn't need words. She didn't even need the mind-blowing sex. The one thing she did need would never be hers.

She closed her eyes and buried her head against his shoulder. Breathing in his musky scent.

She couldn't have him. Not forever. But she'd try to be thankful, just as he'd told her. Thankful for what they had. Thankful for the air in her lungs. Thankful for the sun through the trees. And for the beautiful man in her arms.

The man who—with touch alone—set her free.

ORLANDO

In the spirit of doing things we never do, I have one thing to say before you close your eyes tonight...

Sophie stood in her bathroom with its giant wicker baskets filled with lush towels under the wood vanity. She pulled the ivory towel already wrapped around her wet hair, her phone in her spare hand as she replied to Orlando's text message.

And what is that?

Her phone pinged.

I wish you were here now.

She smiled, instant warmth spreading through her chest.

That's sweet. I miss you too.

Wait. I wasn't finished.

She brushed her tangled locks cascading over her fluffy white bathrobe and waited for him to complete his reply.

> ...So I can get you naked and scare the
> bejeezus out of Mrs. Davy next door with the
> sounds of us boning.

Instant laughter echoed within the tiny, steam-filled room, and she scrambled to keep from almost dropping her phone.

> There's NO way I'm agreeing to that!

She could imagine Orlando's smug smirk now, proud of his cleverness in setting her up for a dose of his smutty humor.

> Sorry. Too much? Don't worry. The old folk's
> home is off limits anyway. Too depressing.

> Too depressing, huh? Well, since we're being
> brave, and in the spirit of 'doing things we
> never do'...

She sent the message, leaving him to stew for a few minutes. Meanwhile, she leaned against the vanity, second-guessing her idea before forcing herself to stick to her vow of bravery.

Her black satin and lace slip, one of the pieces of underwear bought during her shopping trip with Agathe weeks ago, hid beneath her bathrobe. She stepped into the bedroom with its full-length mirror outside the wardrobe door and shrugged off her outerwear, letting the slightly cool air hit her skin.

She tilted forward, striking a pose with one hip popped to the side, lips pouted, and her hand in front as if blowing a kiss. The other held her phone, camera ready. And then she took a photo.

And then she hit send.

She tried her best not to hyperventilate in the seconds it took for him to reply.

> HOLY SHIT!

She clapped a hand over her mouth, her heart racing. Maybe the hyperventilating would start after all. She needed more to go by than, *Holy shit!*

As if the man read her thoughts, her phone pinged again.

> Jeez, woman! Damn Mrs. Davy, get yourself down here now. Or scratch that, I'll be right over.

A hysterical laugh tore from her, and the panic truly set in. The last thing she needed was for Orlando to go missing from the home and a midnight search party to turn up at her door.

Her fingers trembled as she typed out a hurried reply.

> No. No. No! Don't you dare leave the home. I'll see you tomorrow, okay?

A few moments passed, and a message arrived.

> Okay. But please wear the black lace under your clothes when you visit. ;)

She laughed, heart beat settling. Still not quite used to Orlando's brand of excitement. Still not sure she'd ever get used to it, only that she savored every little encounter they had. For once in her life, she felt sexy, powerful, adventurous. She had a man who rewarded her small moments of courage. Someone who truly saw her.

Maybe, even if this did have to end one day, it wouldn't be all bad. She'd come out a stronger, more rounded person for having known him.

She typed one more message.

> Dream on, Lover Boy. xox

And got a final reply for that night.

> Thanks for giving me something to dream about. I'm not just talking about the black lace.

Twenty-Six

TWO WEEKS HAD PASSED since Professor Bandara's diagnosis, and now, Sophie stood with Orlando in Luke's spacious dining room, a sense of mild optimism bouncing between them. So far, Orlando had suffered no episodes. He'd also completed some sessions with a psychologist Candice had visiting the home, and even those progressed well.

Sophie had come to the city with him today for an appointment with Professor Bandara to assess how his new medication was taking. Luke had extended an offer for them to stay at his place before braving the long drive back to Roseford in the morning.

Now, Luke rushed past with a stack of white plates in his hand, his footsteps heavy on the high-polished floor. "So, how'd the appointment go?"

When Orlando didn't answer, she turned to find his gaze paused at Luke's impressive Jarrah dining table, a burgundy runner and crystal candelabras intersecting the middle. His attention moved across the room to the casual-but-still-expensive custom, designer, silk curtains.

She shrugged, deciding he needed a minute to settle in, so answered for him. "Right now, it's a case of *no news is good news.*"

"And what do you think"—Luke stopped setting plates and focused on the man standing next to her—"Orlando?"

Orlando dropped his gaze from the equally custom, equally designer, and very arty light fixtures. "I don't like to get ahead of myself."

His short reply plunged the room into a lead-filled silence. The two men stared at each other before Luke shook his head and gave her a *what the hell?* side glare.

Orlando caught the glare, and his jaw set firm, leveling his own scowl of mutual loathing.

Her shoulders sagged, and she dipped her chin so she wouldn't have to look at either man. She'd wanted to show her brother that even if she could only have Orlando for a short time, he wasn't a bad bet and deserved acceptance. And she'd wanted to show Orlando a normal night out with her family—something he hadn't had in so long.

She'd thought she knew both men well enough to guess they'd get along. But neither was having it.

Luke, a man who was usually nothing but kind and welcoming, returned to placing the last dish, the dismissive gesture shutting everyone out.

"So." Agathe bustled in, smile in place. Max followed close behind. "Buy anything interesting while you were on Collins Street today?"

Sophie laughed, though the sound seemed to get stuck partway in her throat. "Does window shopping count? Most shops were closed by the time our appointment was done, and the theater crowd was already rolling in. We ran out of time."

"Oh, well." Agathe held a light smile and lowered some wine glasses to the table. "Hopefully you'll get other chances to collect more souvenirs. You know, beyond the ones we've already purchased." She gave Sophie a not-so-subtle wink.

Orlando cleared his throat, the following mild splutter concealing a poorly hidden laugh. He'd figured out what *purchases* and *souvenirs* Agathe referred to.

Luke's attention passed between his wife and Sophie. "What souvenirs?"

Sophie sent Agathe a wide-eyed glance, pleading with her not to mention the lingerie they'd bought together weeks ago. Her cheeks burned, but she infused an edge of low warning in her voice, "Agathe..."

Orlando's eyes gave a wicked glint. "Agathe's right. Sophie, you really should do more shopping before you head back. In fact, we should go first thing tomorrow morning. Examining your new purchases brings genuine enrichment to my otherwise empty life."

Agathe's mouth dropped open; she seemed to have deduced he'd already reaped the rewards of Sophie's lingerie shopping. Seconds later, Agathe slapped a hand over her mouth and a giggle shattered any notion she shared the same doubts as her husband about Orlando's ability to socialize.

"If that's the case, maybe *you* should be the one to buy her something tomorrow." Luke frowned. His rigid voice indicated he at least understood the conversation's sexual undertones, even if he'd been excluded. "Though Collins Street might be out of your price range, buddy."

The room fell silent. Luke and Orlando commenced another stare-off, while Sophie, Agathe, and Max peered between each other, uncertain at what might unfold next.

Luke understood full well neither she nor Orlando could afford much of anything—especially not anything from one of the designer stores on Collins Street. Not that either one of them cared. The dinging trams and the lively street buskers had been enough enjoyment for their evening, both of which had been free—and most importantly—something they'd experienced together. And then there'd been the clash of old-world buildings against modern skyscrapers and geometric art houses. Her days with Orlando were numbered, and time, more than stuff, was what she grasped for most.

But then, Luke's rude statement had nothing to do with his attitude toward money, much less those that didn't have it. Luke himself hadn't come from privilege. He was the last guy to care what any person had in their bank account, and far from a snob, despite current impressions.

That being said, her brother did seem trapped in some moronic protective-older-sibling act, enough to make it clear he didn't think Orlando was good enough for her. Not because of money. But perhaps because he'd hurt her before. Still, Luke's attempt to protect her was turning him into a grade-A jerk, and she wanted him to stop.

She took a small step, about to unleash on her brother, but Orlando's hand shot out and stopped her.

"Thank you for welcoming me into your home." He turned to Agathe, omitting Luke from his gratitude.

The subtle slap down was far more elegant than what she'd had in mind.

Agathe offered a gentle smile, her gaze narrowing at Luke. His jab about money was below him, and everyone knew it.

"Well." Max plonked himself down at the table and held up his knife and fork. "Looks to me like there's too much talking and not enough eating. I made the ribs, so I get dibs."

His lips split into a wide toothy grin, indicating pride over his rhyme.

Sophie led Orlando to the table, and whispered, "You'll like Max. He's the family clown, but there's more going on in his head than he lets on."

Orlando took a seat beside her and looked down at her from his extra height, his dark gaze dancing around her face. "You're worried Luke will make me feel bad. Don't."

She turned back to Luke, who chatted to Agathe. From the strain across her cheeks, Agathe wasn't ready to forgive him yet, and he wasn't ready to apologize. "He's not usually this obnoxious."

"I know."

She jolted back. "You do?"

He lifted his hand to grasp hers, all the while his smoothed-out features emitted a calm so different to the prickly man she'd first met. She'd only just begun to get used to this new and unperturbed version of him, occasionally wondering if his stillness had been a feature long before his health deteriorated, destabilizing his world.

Maybe he'd bought into the hope Professor Bandara offered.

Or maybe their blossoming relationship made all the difference. Not just to him, but to her too. And not simply because of the life-altering sex. He challenged her. Forced her to be okay with impermanence.

Because of Orlando, she'd be forever changed.

Because of him, her world opened to new possibilities beyond a life of meticulous control.

"Sophie." His softened voice returned her to the conversation. "I can handle your brother."

She offered a weary smile, his reassurance not enough to abate her concern.

He turned back to the table, his grip tightening around her hand, a signal for her to bear with him.

"Luke." The strident boom of his voice killed any and all chatter, and with that boom, a cold wave of reality washed over her.

When he'd said he could handle her brother, he hadn't meant to reassure her of his lack of offense, he'd stated an intent to literally *handle* her brother. As in, right now. In front of everyone.

Her skin turned instantly hot, and her insides quivered. Luke glared at Orlando, silent, expression rigid, as if anticipating what would happen next.

"I know you don't like me." Orlando's battle mask reappeared in the form of a lifted chin. "And I understand why."

Luke eased back in his chair, a seeming challenge to Orlando's direct approach. As a prominent CEO and former army man, Luke wasn't all that used to people being bold enough to confront him.

"You do, do you?" He kept a measured voice and his gaze steadfast. Her brother was a bright man, one who knew when to tread carefully. He'd recognize someone as well-lived as Orlando likely possessed the ability to hang him with his own words. "You're right, I don't like you. But more than that, I don't trust you."

Orlando said nothing.

"Luke." Agathe's voice broke past the silence, her gaze darting between the two men. "Maybe you could give Orlando a—"

"No." Sophie reached out a hand, though the hard demand surprised even her. "Let them talk. Luke doesn't owe Orlando any fake sympathy. And if I've learned anything first hand, it's that Orlando can stand his own ground."

Agathe threw a split-second, wide-eyed glare, as if to say, *Are you crazy? These two will kill each other.* Then she grumbled something under her breath and settled back in her chair.

"It's because I've hurt her before. And maybe because you think this—" Orlando gestured between him and Sophie "—isn't built to last?"

Luke scoffed. "I thought the whole premise of your relationship is that it's a temporary arrangement?"

Orlando paused, and the momentary silence squeezed a portion of life from her heart. She hated reminders of her inevitable return home. Her eventual life without Orlando.

"Sophie has much brighter days ahead of her without me, I know that. We both know that. And so do you." Orlando nodded toward Luke. "But our inability to be together long term doesn't cancel out what we have now. Sometimes, a few shared moments is the lasting thing you take with you, even if the relationship doesn't survive. Sometimes, there's no other choice but to accept the limits of what you have. And sometimes, those small moments are more than what many get in an entire lifetime."

For a moment there, Luke held an unnatural stillness, before his posture collapsed ever so slightly. "I appreciate that. But your sentimental motives aren't enough to make me trust you."

"But you trust Sophie, don't you?"

"Sure." Luke shrugged. "As much as anyone else close to me. She's family."

"Then your mistrust toward me is irrelevant. She's capable of making her own choices and living with the consequences."

Luke's gaze flicked over to her. The soft focus in his bottle-green eyes gave the impression his mind harked back to sixteen-year-old her and her subsequent decade of *living with* one particular consequence. Or more precisely, beating herself up over it.

But even Luke couldn't deny that she'd knuckled down and turned her life around, albeit by checking out of life and locking up her heart. But she *had* done her fair bit of living and *did* deserve his respect.

She sat a little taller. A dare to her brother. *Defy me and you'll pay.*

Luke turned back to Orlando and gave the smallest of nods. He understood. He agreed.

And in an instant, the room's energy changed—less prickly, with space for easy banter.

Eventually, Luke regaled Orlando with the tale of how Max, a co-founder of his successful tech company, Tiluma, had quit when it became clear he wasn't at all suited to working in an office.

"The breaking point came when he got the entire building shut down by fumigators on the same day we had a major investor visiting."

Agathe laughed and shook her head. "He not only almost ended Tiluma, but damn near ended Luke and me."

Orlando chuckled around a quick sip of his water, then set his focus on Max. "How did you manage that?"

Max gave a sheepish shrug beside her. He, Luke, and Agathe all replied in unison, "Bring your dog to work day."

Sophie seized the opportunity to draw out the crosstalk and chimed in. "Or more exactly, some flea-infested stray that Max invited into the office."

Orlando pressed his knuckles to his mouth and restrained another laugh. The extreme lightness in his mood made her heart dance.

This was the most laid-back she'd ever seen him. He and Luke got along just fine now. The tension from earlier long forgotten.

Orlando fit in. There were no episodes. No flash backs. She'd succeeded in providing him with a normal night.

"Yeah, well." Luke grumbled and he gave his brother a playful side glare. "That stray almost ruined the entire company."

Max pointed his beer bottle at his brother, eyelids flared in opposition. "Hey, I also managed to save the company, don't forget that. You have to admit, Brett turned out to be a much better fit as an investor than Ernest Schneider would have been."

Luke rolled his eyes and busied himself with a sip of his beer, rarely one to admit he was wrong.

Orlando jutted his chin to Max. "So, what do you do with yourself these days?"

A rosy hue spread across Max's pale cheeks, and he shook the shaggy blond surfer waves from his eyes. "Not much, to be honest."

She laughed and leaned into Max with her shoulder. "He enjoys the yearly profit share he receives from the company, while trying to 'find himself'. Isn't that right?"

A grin pulled at her cheeks, and she turned to gauge Orlando's response, but something about his sudden frozen stare made the smile fall from her face.

He lowered his gaze down to his hand on the table, the careful gesture imploring her to look. There, his little finger on his left hand trembled. A small movement. Barely noticeable. But uncontrolled. And a very, very bad sign.

She met his gaze. An ashen tone stole brilliance from his golden olive skin. He peered down once more. She followed his line of sight. And the tremor claimed his next finger.

A sense of alarm shot through her body, her own hands shaking, but for a whole other reason. She needed to take quick action and help him.

She glanced at the others. The conversation had already moved on, while she and Orlando had been left behind. His eyes now pulled wide in a silent plea. He needed help. He needed her to get him out in a way that didn't alert everyone to his problem. He'd made a point of notifying only her, sign enough he didn't want the others involved.

She had little time. Her one idea was a long-shot. It would have to do.

She dropped a forkful of pasta from the side of her plate, into the lap of her teal dress. A large portion of white-sauce clung to the fabric.

"Oh, hell!" She leapt from her chair, the pasta landing with an awkward splat between her feet. She kept her voice loud, dragging attention away from Orlando. "Oh, I've made a mess. I'm so sorry."

"Don't worry about it." Agathe stood, hand outstretched, waving her forgiveness. "You go get yourself cleaned up, and we'll take care of everything here."

Sophie turned to Orlando, twisting her voice to play up her panic. "Would you help me?"

He rose in haste, his chair scraping against the floor. "Get to the bathroom. I'll find you a change of clothes."

She sent him a pinched smile, one that hopefully portrayed

gratitude and not alarm. He jammed his still-trembling hand into the pocket of his black pants and followed her out of the room.

Twenty-Seven

"IS IT ANOTHER EPISODE?" Sophie slammed the bedroom door closed and turned to Orlando. She pressed her hands to his cheeks, taking stock of two positives—he was warm and his pupils were even in size. At least his circulation and brain function weren't altogether shot.

"I don't know what's happening to me." He doubled past her and slumped back against the closed door, breaths loud, but shallow. "I don't know…" He shook his head, shoulders now trembling too. "No. This. This is different."

His words rushed out, and sweat trickled down his temples. Her own muscles turned weak at the signs of his alarm.

Any moment now she might lose him to that childish voice again, the one reserved for his episodes. Or maybe something else entirely would happen. If she couldn't get him to slow down, then she'd have no choice but to call an ambulance. Then her entire family would know everything, and goodbye to his wish to save face.

He peered down at his right hand, the shakes having spread wider, producing a staggered tremor to his voice. "I…I don't. I don't…" He glanced up, pupils blackened and lost. "Help me. I can't stop it."

She wrapped his hand in hers, offering the warmth of her enclosed palms, trying to distract him. Her insides set heavy like concrete. Her hope sank with every passing second. What if everything she did wasn't enough?

Think. Don't give up yet.

What do I do if someone is having a panic attack?

Okay. Good. If she proceeded under the assumption that his trembling might be psychosomatic, then maybe she could stop this thing in its tracks.

"Orlando, look at me." He continued shaking but did as asked. She kept her voice gentle, steady, predictable. Attempted to play the role of a buoy amidst his mind's raging tempest. "Tell me what you need."

His gaze skittered around her face. "I..." A frown weighed his twisted expression as he struggled to control his words, much less his face. "Breathe. Help me breathe."

She peered at his chest. His sternum was heaving up and down, so, actually, he could breathe, but perhaps not enough as a result of whatever he experienced.

She rose a hand and pressed it to his cheek. Another sensory distraction. Another point of contact to help center him.

"Okay. Let's slow down. I'm going to count to ten, I'll go slow and you just try to slow right down with me. One... Two..." She counted, while a play-by-play of all they'd achieved in the last couple of weeks ran through her head. Everything hung in the balance. Especially the ramifications of Professor Bandara's treatments perhaps not working. That maybe Orlando's death sentence would be back on the table. Perhaps all the lightness and laughter he'd recently regained would go...

She couldn't stand for any of that. Though the dart of his gaze down at their joined hands seemed to convey similar thoughts crossed his mind. "You're doing great. Five... Six. Let go of your muscles."

She shifted a hand lower and rubbed her thumb over the thick tendon at the side of his neck. His gaze jolted back to hers, as if searching for a lifeline. As much as she'd needed him, he needed her more.

"The damage is done, Soph." His voice wobbled, similar to a man neck deep in a semi-frozen lake. "I'm falling apart, and your family thinks I'm crazy."

"You'll be okay, and they haven't noticed a thing." She brought her body closer to his, hoping to keep his thoughts on her. "Now focus for me, please. Seven… Eight."

His muscles spasmed. "They know we've disappeared together. They're not stupid. They'll figure we're either getting it on, or I'm having a spaz attack."

She locked her arms around him, losing sight over which of them needed the other most. The room's soft light and warm plum and burgundy tones did nothing to heat the chill working through her body. "I'm having a problem with my dress and you're helping me, remember? Besides, it doesn't matter what they think. Orlando, please, I need you to focus on slowing down."

"No. It does. It matters." He rushed his words, overly loud and uncontrolled, hitching between phrases. He pushed back, his stare landing on her, a man grappling for what precious seconds his mind afforded. "As much as I didn't want to, I found a new home with you. I care what you think." An uncontrolled shudder worked through his body. He clenched his eyes shut and stopped, as if pausing to fight off his trembles. "I care about the people you care about—the same people who care about you. What they think matters. My being here will affect how they see you when I'm gone. I don't want to embarrass either of us in front of them."

Her chest caved at the mention of him being gone, and she worked fast to suppress a surge of tears burning the backs of her eyes. Again, Candice's warning played on her mind. Where before he would have lashed out in anger, now fear reverberated through those pleading dark eyes. *Fear and vulnerability.* Where was her brash firefighter? The man who unleashed more passion in one minute than most summoned in their entire lives?

His broken honesty broke her, too. She wasn't a miracle worker. She was at best a newly minted doctor. And whatever had a hold of him lay always one step ahead. Just out of sight. Just out of reach. A mystery taunting her from afar.

And this man had endured years stripped of dignity, years of choices pried from his hands. Just when he thought he might get his old life back, this new incident set him adrift again. That he might have to face her family in his rattled state, with broken edges exposed. Perhaps her family's potential judgment would be his limit, amongst so many already shattered limits.

Pure instinct prompted her to throw herself toward him. She had to turn this around. Had to give him some small win. "Hold me. And don't let go this time."

Where he once would have scoffed, he merely did as she asked. His arms enfolded around her, and he shook. The tremors passed right through him and into her. She could feel his need and his pain. Like one of her injured birds.

His violent storm picked her up. Transported her back to her childhood. Back to her mother's arms, where all things bad could be made good again.

And that's when, for some inexplicable reason, she began to sing.

A lullaby her mother had gifted her.

She sang and she swayed.

A song for a child afraid of the dark. A child afraid of the blind unknown. When darkness held all that might hurt, much like the uncertainty Orlando experienced in each episode.

She would not let him go. Not until the fear subsided. Not until he found his calm, just as her mother had done for her as a child, and again that night when a scared sixteen-year-old Sophie sat on the edge of her white hospital bed crying. When she'd willed herself to get up and continue on with life, while everything within her refused to move.

Her mother had held her. Allowed her to cry. Until fat tears darkened the shoulder of her mother's emerald green sweater.

That same lullaby guided her now.

A song about Scarborough. Her home. *Parsley, sage, rosemary, and thyme...* A playful song, with a haunting melody. A song that offered relief. Protection. A reminder of times gone by and how small she was against the scheme of all history. That maybe, because of that, everything would be okay.

If only she could erase Orlando's pain, and just like the song did for her, offer him a comfort.

She opened her eyes, her voice still carrying the sweet, ancient melody. Orlando's purposeful breaths now skimmed her neck.

His shaking had stopped.

He squeezed her tighter, then stepped back and let go completely.

Though his gaze met hers, it lacked its usual fire. His attention shifted sideways. Shutting her out. As if reality stepped in to keep him from her reach.

She offered a smile in the hopes he might need a minute to regroup. "You're okay? This one wasn't so bad, right? Maybe the fact I was able to bring you back is a good sign? Maybe the meds are still doing their job?"

His attention snapped back to her, though his face still gave nothing away.

"Yeah. Maybe... Thanks." He turned for the door, his fingers already wrapping around the handle.

She'd helped him, yet his shuttered demeanor now made her heart drop to a sluggish beat.

"Let's get back to your family."

Orlando found his place at Luke's table, the scuff of Sophie's movements trailing somewhere behind him. He knew he shouldn't have walked from her, not after she'd just pulled him back from the brink of whatever the hell had just happened. But tonight was a reality check. A *much needed* reality check. A reality check on just how much he didn't belong. Not with these people who were too undamaged, with too much to look forward to.

She took a seat beside him and from his peripheral vision, her stare burned into him. Understanding. Compassionate.

But a mess like him could offer no more than a tangle of humiliating outbursts on top of non-existent prospects. He needed to release her. Sooner rather than later.

"Seems Sophie didn't bring a change of dress after all?" Luke stared at him with a quizzical look.

"Oh, that." Sophie gave a tight laugh. "Everyone here knows me well enough, and I'll probably head up to bed soon, anyway. I figured I didn't need to do the whole outfit change thing."

She gave a playful shrug. A very fake, somewhat strained, playful shrug.

The muscles in Orlando's jaw bunched. She didn't need to cover for him. He wasn't a cyclone and she his clean-up crew. If anything, he'd come to Luke's house to support her.

He gritted his teeth, tempted to admit they'd left the table because of him. Him and his stupid condition. Him and the fucked-up dream that brought him to this home with her family to begin with. That maybe he could be normal. That maybe he could have a relationship with Sophie beyond their secretive outings alone together. That he could learn how to live again, if only for a short while. Well, clearly fucking not.

And all that, for what? He wasn't getting better. His attack just proved Professor Bandara and her magic meds didn't work.

He recalled the bargaining scrunch of Sophie's face, her unwavering stare, and the way she'd pleaded with him to breathe with her. And then how she'd sung him a song, trying to get him to stop shaking...

Christ. Watching her joy give way to panic had brought him as close to torture as the attack itself.

And something as close to a lullaby as anyone could get, of all things, had stopped his episode. No experimental science. No highly esteemed professor... No. *A song. A bloody song.* And one that might as well have been for a child.

In the early days of his episodes, he'd read all he could about neurological disorders—including how music could sometimes soothe patients with dementia. Music was apparently intrinsic to every human culture. Its effects were imprinted on even the most inaccessible parts of most people's brains. And Sophie, with her song, had played him like a fine-tuned fiddle. It seemed that, in the heat of an encroaching episode, his mind had been reduced to the base level of a baby.

How fucking pathetic.

He sucked in a quiet breath, allowing an inevitable truth to sink in;

one that acknowledged what he needed to do next. He couldn't keep bringing her down.

I don't deserve her. Why can't I get that to sink into my thick skull?

As hopeful as she'd been, he didn't share her hope. Sparing her from impending heartbreak would be his best parting gift. She was too good for him in so many ways. Her future too bright. And even in the best-case scenario, even if he got his life back, he'd be starting out all over again with nothing to his name.

She deserved better. She deserved more.

Agathe turned to Luke with a joyful spark in her eyes—a spark Orlando hadn't ever witnessed in Sophie—perhaps because, unlike Sophie, Agathe had more than just hard work and a bitter ending to look forward to.

Agathe turned to him next, beaming grin still in place. "Well, if Sophie's set on wrapping things up, before you both go, Luke and I have a question to ask you, Orlando. Would you like to come to our wedding next week? You know, as Sophie's plus one?"

Sophie twisted in her seat, her body angled toward him. Her hazel focus locked to his. Once again, no joy lit her eyes. Certainly nothing resembling the joy Agathe displayed. Only wide hopefulness. Wide hopefulness with a heavy edge of doubt. The same sad look she gave him every time she expected he'd say no. The look of a woman used to disappointment.

Or more precisely… disappointment *from him.*

A hard lump knotted within his chest, twisting and writhing, burrowing deep. He wanted to say no. *Of course, he did.* Tonight's near episode meant he couldn't predict what would happen at the wedding. But he owed Sophie. He owed her so much. More than he could ever repay. She held impossibly still, her face holding an optimistic glow…

His presence at the wedding meant the world to her, and without him, she'd almost definitely go alone.

So, he nodded.

A held breath hissed out of her. A hiss of relief.

And there it was, the glitter of joy now lighting her eyes, her sad smile momentarily gone. For that alone, he'd endure another night out. Or more precisely, one *final* night out.

He reached for his glass of water and downed a large gulp. Somehow, he'd have to keep his battered mind together and get through another evening without letting her down. Without turning himself into another burden. An evening a thousand times more important than this one.

Soon, dinner wrapped up and everyone said goodnight. He walked back upstairs with Sophie. The moment the bedroom door closed, she rounded on him, face pinched in concern. Or hurt. Or maybe anger. He couldn't quite tell.

"What happened after your episode tonight? You closed up on me. You shut me out."

He tugged his collar open, his neck itchy and all too hot. His gaze dipped to the white smudge of pasta sauce still marking her dress. A mess she'd orchestrated to bail him out of trouble.

"It's nothing." He turned away. *Turned from her. From his own lie.* Then distracted himself with ripping open buttons on his shirt and then pitching the light fabric onto the bed. "Whatever happened rattled me, okay? I'm fine now."

He couldn't tell her the truth. That he saw everything with her and his medical issues spiraling down and out of his control. The more he confided in her, the more she dug her heels in. She'd never leave him. Not willingly. Perhaps not even to fulfill the promise she'd already made. She'd sacrifice herself to the end. And the mere knowledge of her sticking around and ruining her future brought vicious pain to his heart.

She couldn't save him. *Shouldn't* save him. Saving him had never been her job. A job he'd specifically asked her *not* to take on. But she'd taken it on anyway.

And tonight's near miss only proved how much that misstep would cost her. She'd sacrificed enough. He couldn't let this continue much longer.

The soft padding of her feet neared behind him. He stifled a jolt, his darker emotions imploding, as her hands slipped around his waist. "Are you sure you're okay? Tonight worried me. I can't imagine how it felt for you."

His muscles tensed at the press of her warm cheek between his shoulder blades.

Why did she have to be so damn compassionate all the time?

He turned and gripped her wrists to his chest, exchanging his need to shield her for the open conversation she deserved. "Tonight was a warning, Sophie. Don't get ahead of yourself. Okay?"

She offered a gentle, knowing smile, and flattened her palms to his chest. Just as always, her touch seared into his skin, sparking an unavoidable need. "It'll be okay. You'll see."

"Sophie, you can't say—"

She stood on her tippy toes and pressed her soft lips to his. "I can. See..." She kissed him again, her sweeter, more playful way of silencing his doubts. "It'll be okay."

The scent of spring flowers and something uniquely her teased his senses. He groaned against another of her feather light kisses, clinging to an urge to warn and protect. "Sophie."

"Orlando." She lowered her heels, and her head leveled with his chest, her attention lifted. "It'll be okay."

She raised a brow. Challenging him.

Somehow, she'd found it in her to unearth a good mood—making him one heck of a giant asshole if he spoiled her optimism with his need for bleak predictions and caution. Besides, at least until after the wedding, they had more time. And she had the ability to turn his caginess into contentment. Doom and gloom could wait while love and affection shone a little longer.

Only she could deliver him from the shrieking pit of nothingness he lived in most days. He would have to end this soon. But not tonight.

Tonight, she was still his.

Twenty-Eight

SOPHIE TUCKED her hand into Orlando's, her muscles relaxing at the live harp music drifting through the small, ornamental garden. A gathering of about sixty friends and family settled in collective silence, while Luke stood mere meters away from her out front, face pale and gaze glassy at the top of the aisle. The last bridesmaid swanned her way down, and the final murmurs died. Agathe appeared from behind the russet vine arch at the back of the crowd—her dress a gorgeous fairy tale puff, billowing ice-white lace and satin into the aisles. Her bouquet was a giant ball of burgundy roses, and a single large rose sat perched behind her ear.

The white dress glowed against her nutmeg skin, the bursts of red added extra drama and warmth. A charged quiet hinted at the gravity of what was about to take place—a ceremony of promises and forever, hopes and fears. A day to bind two lives together for eternity.

Agathe stopped beside Luke beneath the circular arch, another thick forest of burgundy roses framing her and her future husband.

The celebrant neared, and Max shifted into position just behind his brother.

Luke. *Oh Luke.* Gone was the pale skin and glassy gazing, his features lifted and eyes sparkling for the woman beside him.

Sophie's heart squeezed, and Orlando's grip tightened in sync around her hand. Did he feel it too? The sense of rightness in the world. A dreaminess. That maybe, just maybe, *they* might have this one day, too.

Tears prickled the corners of her eyes, and the muscles in her throat strained. She was being foolish and certainly getting way ahead of herself. All she really wanted was for him to enjoy this day. To forget the darkness of his near-episode last week. To adopt the professor's nonplussed attitude and focus on the positive. He hadn't escalated to a full-blown episode, and with his meds now tweaked, maybe a similar happy future awaited him as well.

Though maybe not with her.

She drew a strained breath and focused on the scent of red roses and how Agathe's deep crimson lips spread into a wide smile. Because of love. Because love had cured all. Or at least, that had been true for Agathe. Her life before Luke was far from any fairy tale.

She'd endured the senseless death of her child. The end of a marriage. And years and years of destructive behavior and isolation. And though her first days with Luke had been tumultuous, love *had* won in the end.

Sophie shuddered, an involuntary reaction against the subtle changes that had occurred between her and Orlando in the last week. More a change in mood and energy than anything she could put her finger on. He peered down, as if her shuddering caught his attention, but she shook her head, letting him know she'd be okay.

Not the best. Not what she wanted. But *okay*.

Just okay.

She pressed her hand to her lower abdomen, around about where her uterus would be, heart sinking further. Yet another portion of hope had slipped away. A last portion of hope she still struggled to share with Orlando, but a lost hope she'd have to tell him about either way. But how could she have held onto this particular hope without ever even knowing she'd cared?

She squeezed her eyes shut and crammed her rising guilt.

How would Orlando react?

Hush. Everything will be fine. Orlando's problems will improve. He'll go on without me. And he'll never, ever again think about hurting himself.

She opened her eyes to Luke sliding a plain gold band onto Agathe's trembling finger.

Damn it. She needed to focus, or she'd miss the whole wedding.

The celebrant rang off more sentiments, and then the happy couple shared a passionate kiss. Guests whooped and cheered, while tears rained down her cheeks.

She was happy for her brother, heartbroken for herself.

I'm a losing bet, remember?

Orlando's words echoed in her head, as if the man standing next to her remained that same, angry resident she'd met months ago. But he wasn't that man anymore. And he wasn't to blame for her heartache now.

She'd been the one with choices. The one who could always cut and run.

But she hadn't. And her pain now was all her fault.

Every day took her closer to leaving him. And something worse. To learning he might never recover. If that happened—if he hurt himself—a piece of her would stay forever broken too.

Orlando locked an arm around her waist, heat engulfing her hip where his hand lay. His smile beamed down at her in a look of happy sympathy. "Sucker for weddings, huh?"

She laughed and gave a quick nod, wiping away her tears with an open palm. "For some reason, watching my smelly older brother get married makes for a cathartic experience."

His smile grew, his glinting, brown eyes setting her heart to flutter before he pulled her into a tight embrace, her head tucked under his chin, her face buried against his navy-blue suit jacket.

The scent of freshly laundered fabric and woodsy-sage warmed her senses. He usually just smelled of soap and man, but this new fragrance turned her stomach hollow—simply because he never had reasons to dress up, much less wear suits and cologne. For better or worse, she'd changed his world. And he'd changed hers.

"Come on." He planted a kiss on her cheek and pulled back, her heart stumbling as his thumbs wiped away her last remnants of tears.

"As the groom's sister, you'll have to pose for photos, but after that, we're free to escape to the reception together."

From rag-tag country boy, to stupidly confident fireman. To now. The guy with nothing going for him except a limited life within the walls of an aged care facility... Luke and Agathe's wedding reception brought Orlando worlds away from anything he knew.

No expense had been spared, and everything about this place, from the orange light spilling from the chandeliers, to the scent of cinnamon and clove hanging in the air, screamed, *You don't belong here.*

But then, Sophie. Sophie was here. And therefore, so was he.

He couldn't have made her come alone. Not when she'd asked. Not when presented with the one thing he *could* do for her. The one thing guaranteed to make her happy, when so much about their union was constructed on the graveness of a ticking clock. And also because... well, frankly... he loved her.

He loved her.

He tugged at his collar, his shirt a discomfort after years of growing accustomed to wearing t-shirts and sweat pants. At one point in his life, a dressy shirt and tailored trousers had been his second uniform. He'd lived to go out. To put on a show. To pull in a new woman. The mere act of wearing a suit now made him feel like a fraud. Which only made him wonder how many people at this event knew his story and thought the same.

Did anyone here look at him and see a freak on display? Maybe. Or maybe no one did. Still, the whole suit charade, coupled with this reception and all its extravagance, only rubbed in just how much he could never compete with Luke or Max's financial wealth.

Even if his condition disappeared tomorrow, he had no money. No security. No means of providing for Sophie in the ways he wanted to.

And even with all the impossibilities and differences, he still managed to damn-well love her.

"Will you dance with me?" Her sweet voice pried him from his doubts, and he took in the details of her floor-length peach dress. The fitted cut matched her slender build and innate grace. A row of delicate glass beads circled the high collar, lighting her already glinting hazel eyes. How on earth would he let her go?

The woman belonged here. In a place as lavish as this. He didn't.

But then, she held out a hand to him, and he had no other answer. "How can I say no?"

She laughed, nudging him with an elbow as he took her hand. "You never had a problem saying no before."

"We wouldn't be together now if I'd made it easy for you." He led her toward the sparse dance floor. "We both know you prefer men who play hard to get."

He tugged her into him, and she laughed again. He relished the trilling sound and her soft warmth. He would have to say no to her *soon*. Would have to break it to her that their relationship needed to end. Though the precise word would be more like *goodbye* rather than *no*.

Her head came to rest on his chest, blessing him with her light scent of daisies, but then she pulled back enough to look at him, eyes glittering. "So that was your plan all along? Reel me in with angry glares and fake trips to biker bars?"

An ache unfurled in his chest, but he offered a lopsided smile, wanting to enjoy this exchange while he could still be the one to hold her in his arms. "What can I say, my sick idea of charm?"

She threw back her head and laughed once more, offering the concession that he'd made her happy. At least for tonight. "You definitely picked a riskier form of flirting."

God. That effortless laugh. Those flecked, hazel eyes. Her ability to make him dance with her in a crowded room when months ago he would have flatly refused.

She'd broken so many of his barriers, given him a last chance at being a man. He'd be forever grateful. But a woman like her belonged with someone else. With someone who had more to offer. And keeping her would be cruel, if not impossible.

She stared at him, her attention darting about his face as though she read his thoughts. "Orlando?" Her hand rose to cup his cheek. "I have news. I don't know whether to call it good or bad, or how you're going to feel, but..."

His heartbeat plodded, as if conserving energy for the shock of whatever she had to say. "Share it anyway. Let me decide."

"I...ummm..." Her gaze dropped to his chin; it seemed she struggled to hold a direct stare. "I thought maybe the outcome would be different. I mean, I was almost three weeks late, and I guess I was too scared to take a test, but I figured sometimes I'm irregular any—"

"Sophie." He frowned, wanting her to stop rambling and get on with the plain truth of whatever news she had to share. "What are you trying to say?"

Her gaze shot up to his, and she held quiet for a second.

"I'm not pregnant." She bit into her lower lip, like she hadn't meant to blurt the harsh truth. Her focus left his face and slipped down to his chest. "I got my period a few days ago. I'm not pregnant. And I thought you should know."

His shoulders sagged, and his hands ached with an urge to let her go—not out of rejection or judgment—but because of one biological truth. His last fleeting chance to father a child had just passed him by.

He pressed his jaw shut, unsure what to say. Unsure of Sophie's feelings, especially in light of her past. His potential for keeping this woman had just diminished even further. Or maybe, he'd been handed a small gift. Another opening to set her free.

What poor child would deserve me as their dad?

"Orlando?"

She frowned up at him. He shook away the thought. Somehow, he felt numb and on fire all at once. The news was sobering, painful, somehow predictable, yet too much to process.

He gave her hand a gentle squeeze, then pulled her close to land a kiss on the top of her head.

"I can't call this good or bad news. It's..." He swallowed back a need to say much more. "It's sad."

A couple just a few meters away gave a soft laugh, the clinking of champagne glasses complemented the mellow jazz quartet playing on the stage. The subdued light illuminated a defused halo of red around

Sophie's sable hair. Despite the heavy topic, a sense of intimacy danced around her.

"You probably don't want to hear this"—she looked down again, chin wobbling—"but I'm calling this bad news." She peered back up at him, eyes glistening as though she clung to a wall of emotion. "You know my past. And these last months with you, I didn't expect to feel this way." She gave a shaky laugh, trying, but failing to recover composure. "Getting knocked up right now would have been terrible timing. I'm still not ready to have a kid. Neither are you. God, I don't even know what to call this thing between us, but..." She squeezed her eyes shut and took a long breath. "But I'm still disappointed. And I can't help thinking, if things had been different, if I was pregnant, then I would have... I would have... I would have found a way to make it all work."

Her body shook along with her words, and he pulled her into him, tucking her head beneath his chin and offering a soothing, *shhhh*. She didn't need to explain. He understood. Though he couldn't say if he had the right to wish for a different result.

The sad sheen in her eyes. Her words of regret. So much about this woman dug an agonizing pit in his stomach. And with every encounter, she dug deeper into places and desires he'd had no idea existed within him. And then *this*. Holy hell, this moment did things to him. To hear she'd wanted *his* child all along. To know that if circumstances were different, he'd want the same. That he'd bundle her up and kiss away the pain and promise they'd try again someday soon.

But circumstances weren't different, and it wasn't safe to get any more attached.

His life was a twisted joke.

To find her.

To love her.

And after tonight, to do the humane thing and let her go.

She turned her head against his chest and obscured his view of her face. "Urghh. I'm sorry. I sound irrational."

He lifted her chin and cupped her face, forcing her to look at him, and then he pressed his forehead to hers. A million volts of electricity surged through his body, prickling his back and lifting the hairs along his arms. She was right. Her wanting his child was irrational, but then...

"Sophie, the only irrational thing about all of this is that I'm at a wedding with you tonight instead of at the home staring at my ceiling, alone, as I have been every day for years before you barged into my life. And of all the impossible things, that I get to hold you in my arms, and that you feel anything for me. At least for now..." He stopped to watch the concerned wrinkles on her forehead smooth and a slow smile grow over her cheeks.

The mere sight made his throat clog and his voice drop to a hoarse whisper. "You're beautiful. Unselfishly kind. You're more than I could have ever wanted or imagined. The only irrational thing about you is that you're with me. Do you understand? And for that reason, it's a damn good thing you're not having my child."

She moved to talk, but he shook his head, demanding she listen and stay crystal clear on just how much they couldn't be together. "The chemistry we share is enough to contend with, you don't need anything more forcing us together, certainly not a child. What you need is to be free to live the life you're supposed to have."

"But what if you're part of the life I'm supposed to have?"

His heart clenched with a desire to believe that. But he shook his head again, certain she was wrong. He'd let himself get caught up in her beauty and painful brand of gentleness long enough, and his love for her cleaved into his heart with more power than that of a steel axe. Their relationship should have been casual at most, but his feelings had long bolted far from his senses, and now they'd both pay the price. No matter how much he wanted to agree with her, he simply couldn't.

"We had a deal."

"Life isn't a linear plan, Orlando. Isn't that what you've been telling me all along?" Her body went tight within his hold. "Maybe our deal sucks."

He clamped his jaw shut to keep from knee-jerk agreeing with her.

The rise in her voice meant they needed to have this conversation somewhere private. So, he slid his hand down into hers and tugged her along, guiding her through the main exit until they stood to the side of the venue in the fresh night air.

The plan *did* suck, but...

"Our plan will save you, Sophie." She made eye contact, and her frown indicated anger, but he pressed on all the same. The night would be over soon, and he couldn't spare her this cold reality any longer. "This is the only thing I want from you. The only thing I've asked for."

She pushed her chin out, but the hardness in her eyes wavered.

"Why?" She didn't even try to hide the pained tininess in her voice. "Because you think my future is worth more than yours?"

"No." He inched his face closer, his tone now reduced to a strained whisper. "Because you actually have a future and I don't."

"You don't know that. Professor Bandara isn't fin—"

"I won't bring you down with me. Do you understand?"

He wanted Sophie to understand, but her sharp attention surveyed his face, features softening, as if her analytical mind worked to fit a bunch of new and formerly unknown pieces together.

"You could never bring me down. It's not in your nature. The mere fact you so adamantly protect me. I wish you could see yourself through my eyes..." Her voice trailed, and she peered at the ground, hinting she was lost in thought. "You're a good man, Orlando, with an unnerving stare and an uncanny stillness. There are moments where just being beside you brings calm to someone like me. Someone who needs to know the answer to everything at the smallest sign of uncertainty." She gave a heartier grin, her words competing with the rustle of wind through nearby trees. "I don't think I've ever felt as *me* as when I'm with you."

His chest drew tight, like his heart expanded in an attempt to bust out. "It's not enough."

"It is for me." She blinked up at him. "*You* are enough for me."

He stared down at her. Unable to say or do much else. Her eyes held open sincerity, which made his emotions war between pushing her away and holding on to her forever.

As if forever were an option...

He bit down on his burgeoning words, but he couldn't stop now. No matter how messy things got from here on out, he could at least give her this. He didn't want to be without her, but being with her was unworkable. Foolish. The most selfish thing he could do.

The best compromise would be not to let her go without hearing just how much she meant to him.

"If you could see yourself through my eyes, you'd see the woman who saved me." He paused, needing a second to find some stillness. "You'd see the first person to dig deep enough to really notice me. You've forced me to care. You've forced me to see myself and the good that still exists within me and around me. And for the first time in years, I don't completely hate what I see."

The spread of a slow and lazy smile etched small creases over her cheekbones. "What are you trying to say?"

The optimism on her face twisted a knife in his gut. But she had to know.

"Do you think when you first met me, you could have ever imagined we'd get along? That I'd be standing here with you now, immersing myself in your family and life?"

She released a soft laugh. "No, no, and no."

He reached out and stroked his thumb over her cheek, memorizing the velvet softness of her skin and the way the outer corners of her eyes lifted. "Then does that say enough about what I'm thinking? How I feel about you?"

She shook her head, her hand coming to rest over his heart. "Not nearly enough. So, if you've got something to say, say it now. We're at a wedding, right? The timing couldn't be more perfect."

Her glistening eyes, her look of hope, dumped more pain on his heart. She wanted him to say words he'd never said to any woman beside his own mother. Words he *did* want to say, but words that clashed with his need to release her from his life. And damn it. Words he wasn't sure he deserved to utter.

"This isn't easy for me."

"Please." She pressed to him, her small body adding warmth in the night. "Say it anyway."

An amplified voice broke through an outdoor speaker attached to the building's side. The overly loud sound ripped at his attention. Something about the bridal dance starting soon, and could everyone please gather on the dance floor. Next came the muffled scraping of chairs from inside, followed by the stomping of many feet.

He returned his focus to Sophie. To her hopeful stare and her request to hear his declaration of love.

Despite his planned exit from her life, he'd regret missing his one chance to tell her how he felt. To give her something to take with her. Maybe his admission would be as much for her sake, as his. He couldn't leave her wondering.

Her smile dropped, and she tilted her head sideways, her attention on him turning hyper-focused and narrow. Something was off. She looked perplexed.

He pressed his fingertips to his cheek, certain an involuntary tremor reverberated through his jaw.

"Orlando?" Her eyelids flared, and her hand locked around his wrist, hard, unnaturally commanding.

He peered down. His entire hand shook beneath hers.

"Orlando." Her voice rose to a yell. Why did she think he couldn't hear?

A sharp pain sliced through his head. Disorientating. Torturous. He jolted back. Away from her. Swatted at her. As if she'd been the one to hurt him.

"Orlando!"

Her hand beat at his chest. Fierce. Pleading. She wanted to get through to him.

Didn't she know? He could see her. Hear her. Feel her.

But then the world fell around him. Or maybe he fell.

Yes. A fall.

He'd fallen.

The ground was cold.

And then came black.

Twenty~Nine

SOPHIE TURNED to the woman sitting next to her in the hospital waiting room, the one wearing sweat pants and a bedraggled lopsided ponytail. She peered down at her own peach evening gown, with its floor-length hem and glass beads. From her experience, people tended to show up to emergency rooms in all sorts of outfits. At least in that regard, her overdressed state meant she fit right in.

She dropped her head back against the cream-colored wall behind her and let out an exhausted sigh. The white fluorescent lights made her eyes sting and her skull ache. She'd been shut out. Relegated to this waiting room. While the honor of sitting by Orlando's side went to his mother.

Not that she protested Marcella's presence. Sophie had used his phone to call her during the panicked ambulance ride over, after all— moments before he'd woken up in some kind of altered personality state, freaking out at the strange environment, and as a result had been sedated into unconsciousness. He'd since woken up again but banished her from his side. And for the time being, he refused to see her.

She'd tried bargaining with a nurse to gain entry. Had even tried the *but I'm a doctor* card. Only to be told again to stay out. So now she sat here, alone, contemplating what it all meant. What, if any, future existed between her and Orlando.

She leaned forward in the gray plastic seat, elbows pressed to her knees. Too shaken to cry. Too worked up to merely sit and wait. So, she did what most people did when all they could do was begrudgingly cool their heels. She pulled out her phone.

Her social media feed didn't offer much more than videos of friends' babies laughing or various acquaintances holding up drinks at whatever party. None of it steered her thoughts away from the closed double doors ahead of her.

For the briefest moment, she'd thought Orlando had been on the cusp of declaring his love for her. Like maybe she could entertain a reasonable dream of extending her stay another month or two to see if maybe his health stabilized. To support him if it didn't. To perhaps plan an alternate future for her away from London.

Her studies wouldn't start for some time yet. Her professors would potentially let her commence the first few weeks of term online. Despite Orlando's protests, she might have even considered switching to an Australian university. But now...

Now everything lay uncertain.

Still, she had every intention of proving to him they could work through anything. No matter the damage from this latest episode. *They* would be okay.

She scrolled through her phone contacts, contemplating whether to call Hannah, only to decide that would be a bad idea. She still hadn't told Hannah about Orlando. She couldn't do so now. Not in a moment of crisis, with so much to explain, and in light of just how sick she felt at the thought of recounting all that occurred. And if she told Hannah none of it, and called simply to say hi, then Hannah would no doubt go on a verbal tangent about all things Randal Berry. And the last person Sophie cared about right now was *Randal Berry*.

Her insane, illogical crush on that guy might as well have been a million years ago. And in the wake of loving Orlando Piras, Randal Berry was a fresh-faced and bratty schoolboy, with zero substance beyond his last pub crawl and whatever girl he just happened to be dating.

No. She didn't need him. Or any other guy. Or anything else waiting for her back in London. All she wanted was the man she'd watched collapse in front of her some four hours ago. To know he'd be okay and that in spite of him telling her to leave, in spite of her stupid promise to return to the UK, all between them wasn't lost.

Instead of watching him collapse, she wanted to return to the moment just before that. The magical moment where he'd held her, ready to say the words she'd waited to hear her entire life... Even though she'd had no idea she'd been waiting to hear them.

She lifted her gaze to the emergency room doors, the eerie stillness another reminder of all that had been snatched from her. Watching him collapse put her feelings under a microscope. The ordeal changed everything. She was weeks away from leaving, but how could she leave when he needed her?

She simply *had* to be there for him.

Candice's earlier warnings played on her thoughts. Not just about his potentially fragile state of mind, but the sometimes-harsh severity of his episodes. What awaited beyond those doors? Would the Orlando she'd come to know be gone forever?

The air around her hovered at overly cold, and she rubbed her hands over the backs of her exposed arms, her attention dropping to her phone balanced precariously in her lap. A white notification panel at the top of the screen flashed, declaring she had an unopened message. She tapped the panel, and a profile photo of Hector popped up.

HECTOR

Times are tough here in London Town. How much is this photo worth to you?

She tapped the concealed attachment, only to be confronted with a photo of her standing in front of a mirror wearing nothing but her underwear. The same photo she'd sent Orlando weeks ago.

Her mouth dropped open, and her blood ran like ice water through her veins. And just as quickly, she launched into fight mode and typed back.

> You've got to be joking.

> Never contend with a man who has nothing to lose. Right, Sophie? :)

She scowled at her photo, lips pouted in a mock kiss, breasts barely covered in a thin layer of black lace. Not something she was all that ashamed of, but not something she'd want any future employers, colleagues, or patients to see should they run a search of her name.

As amicable as she'd thought the break up with Hector had been, she found herself somehow unsurprised he'd make his presence known in the worse kind of way and at the worst possible time.

He'd always had a buried vindictive streak. Always been somewhat peeved about the good things that entered her life. The few times she and Hannah had hit the town, he'd hounded her with text messages about when she'd be getting home, rather than just wishing her a good night and trusting her to make her own decisions. The fact he'd struggled to find a job in an industry usually falling over itself to hire, only deepened his bitterness. And that bitterness only deepened his dullness.

> So, what's your plan, post the photo to your newsfeed and embarrass me in front of our mutual friends? Why are you doing this?

> Why not?

> Because I haven't done anything to you. This is beneath you.

> What's beneath me is having to pretend it's okay that my girlfriend dumped me so she could jet off across the world. I thought there'd be a chance we'd work things out when you got back. But what's REALLY beneath me is receiving sporadic photos of you with your new boyfriend in our shared photo account.

Oh no. Oh God. Their shared account. She'd forgotten all about that.

Hector had always been the more technical one. He was a programmer after all. At some point in their relationship, he'd insisted on setting up an automatic back up of all photos taken with their phones. She'd forgotten, but Hector clearly hadn't.

> Go for it. You sad-faced little man-baby. You'll just come across as a vindictive ex. Of course, you decided on my behalf that we might get back together. You never did care to actually listen to what I wanted. And by the way, any rational person would have simply reminded me to deactivate my end of the account, not use the opportunity to keep tabs on me.

> Sounds like your new lover boy has turned you into a real bitch, you know that? And no, I won't be sharing anything to my feed. In fact, there'll be nothing linked to me at all. Can't say it won't turn up anywhere a future employer or patient might look though... :)

A ball of heat exploded in her belly. She wanted to scream. Or at least throw her damn phone. But Hector was right about one thing, she was being more brash than usual, and she had Orlando's influence to thank for that.

> What do you even want from me?

> I still need work. Your brother is a power player within the same industry. What do you think?

> So you want a job?

> Bingo. And a good one at that. And a positive introduction to other power players.

She grimaced at her phone. How naïve she must have been to have given this man so many years of her life. As if she'd pull Luke into this mess.

> Have you ever thought that maybe no one will hire you because they see everything you lack? The fact you're trying to blackmail me might be a hot tip on your not-so-charming personality...

> Whatever. I've decided to make my own luck and you're my ticket in. Call it a favor for old time's sake, if that'll make you feel better. You have a month, Sophie. Got it?

> No. I haven't 'got' anything. Why would my brother tarnish his reputation recommending you?

> Everything comes at a cost. Luke's a businessman, he'll know this. Maybe he'll decide your reputation is more valuable than his. Honestly, I don't care.

> You're an ass.

> Screw you. You have one month.

Sophie hissed out an expletive and switched off her phone, before tossing it into her clutch purse on the seat beside her. She didn't have the headspace to think about Hector or his ultimatum, but a new wave of nausea crashed within her. For the second time in her entire life, she felt completely trapped, like a scared rabbit in a cage waiting for whatever terrible thing might happen next. First with Orlando, and now her ex.

She peered up, and a small gasp broke from her at Orlando's mother standing before the emergency doors watching her. Marcella's washed-out blue eyes held no joy; she tilted her head to one side to say Sophie should follow.

The ashen tinge on Marcella's face indicated Sophie would detest what was to come. The nausea didn't abate. It solidified into a hard lump in her gut. Her feet were heavy as lead as they carried her to Marcella's side.

The older woman placed a hand on her shoulder and guided her through the corridors. "This one was bad. Maybe now you take my advice?"

Sophie nodded, her thoughts a soupy fog. *Please don't break my boy's heart. If you feel for him, let him go.*

A twisting maze of cream walls and nurses' desks flicked by, but eventually, she spotted Professor Bandara waiting outside a room, hands crossed over her casual red cardigan as if she'd been called in just for this.

Sophie paused. "How is he?"

"From what I understand…" The professor gave a mild, but telling, cringe. "It's the worst one he's had in over a year."

Sophie nodded and took a step toward the door, but the professor's hand shot out and stopped her. "I need to warn you. He's very unwell, Sophie. I'm talking minor mobility in his limbs, and similar to all his past major episodes, no one knows if or when he'll regain movement. He's not in the best mood, either."

"Is that why you're standing out here and not in there?" Sophie tried to ignore the tremble in her voice, the surge of prickling heat all over her skin.

The professor gave a slow and hopeless nod. She too had been banished.

Sophie envisioned Orlando unleashing his hot temper at Professor Bandara, the one he'd blanketed for weeks under the hope of getting the help he'd dreamed of. That hope and his dreams were now shattered.

She closed her eyes, steeling herself for what awaited through the frosted glass door.

In trying to help him, she'd betrayed him. In trying to know him, she'd knocked down walls built to avoid the same demoralizing blow he dealt with now.

She lifted her chin, as always, hunting for the last sliver of hope. "Does this mean your job is done? The treatment is an official failure?"

"No. Far from it." The professor shook her head. "This episode could be completely separate from my treatment. We're still in the experimental phase, and we may need many months to get his therapy right. But from what I just saw, I don't expect he'll invite me back to do any more experimenting."

Sophie pressed her hand flat to the door.

"There's just one more thing."

She paused and turned to the professor again.

The professor frowned, gaze downcast as she recommenced talking. "Orlando doesn't know this yet, but his lashing out in the ambulance prompted questions from a number of hospital staff. They want to know why he's in an aged care facility without being on behavior modifying drugs." Her expression dimmed, while her lips formed a hard line—perhaps over what she had to say next. "I'm almost certain someone will report this, in which case, there'll be major upheaval at the center. Orlando's might soon not have a home to return to."

Thirty

FOR THE LONGEST TIME, Sophie just stared at Orlando, and he stared right back. A shocked silence ebbed and flowed between them—the moment alive with its own heavy pulse. He lay propped up on the adjustable bed, intravenous lines running from the back of his hand, while a fingertip monitor tracked his oxygen levels. She'd barely made it a meter from the door before she'd had to stop, too shaken at the sight of a usually vital Orlando laid out and vulnerable in this hospital bed.

He rolled his focus off her and sunk his head deeper into the pillow, his resigned gaze redirected to the ceiling. "Say something."

Her mouth hung agape. She opened and closed it a few times before managing a sound. "I...I don't know what to say."

He released a hollow laugh. "That's a first."

"How bad is it?"

"I can't move or feel my legs. Arms are limited. So, bad." Something about his flat delivery worried her more than his inability to move. "I'm thinking the usual months of daily rehab until I regain full function."

"Orlando." She stepped deeper into the room but not quite close enough to take a seat in the chair beside his bed. "I'm so sorry."

"I don't want your sympathy." He pushed out a jagged whisper. "I only asked you here to let you know we need to end what we have. Consider this early permission to move on with your life."

Coldness hit her, and her chest constricted as if fielding an almighty blow. A wild rush of burning tingles overtook her entire body. She said nothing. Just stared.

He spoke again, "You should go."

"I can't." Her tone seemed to come from a place low within, dull and disconnected, so far away someone else might as well have answered for her. "I want to help you. It doesn't have to be like this. Please."

He snapped his head up, his gaze finally rejoining hers, deep brown eyes dilating with palpable fury. "I wasn't suggesting you leave, I was telling you. I want you to go."

The severity of his farewell left her wobbling in place. His old defensive ways had kicked back to life, stronger than ever, a hot iron branding her with rejection.

"Maybe I'll do that, but first, I need to know you won't harm yourself."

He reeled back, as much as any bedridden man *could* reel back— eyes flaring, chin pressing down. "Harm myself? What the hell sort of a question is that?"

"If you're set on removing me from your life, I want to know you'll be okay."

Though her muscles felt weak, she couldn't let him give up. If not for him, then for her. She loved him. Wanted him to love her back. And after months of overcoming seemingly impossible hurdles, surely he could find it in him to fight again. To fight for her. He'd verged on voicing his love just hours before, hadn't he?

His eyes narrowed. "Is that really all it is?"

"Yes."

"How long have you been holding onto the idea I want to harm myself?"

A quiver worked through her muscles, but she forged on. "Just promise me."

"I don't have to promise you anything."

Her shoulders sagged, and the lack of assurance left her feeling sick. But then the silence dragged, and his scowl lost all energy. He turned from her with a sigh.

"Look, let's make one thing clear. I'd be lying if I said harming myself has never crossed my mind, but I'm not suicidal. I'm a realist. I know I'm not expected to get better. I know I'll probably die decades before my time. And in that case, my suffering would be drawn out and my final days difficult. I have no intention of hurting myself anytime soon, nor have I ever. But if I've given you that impression, it's only because I decided long ago that if things got bad enough, I'd go through the proper channels and use the state's assisted dying laws."

Her mind floundered to process what she knew of him against what he'd just said, plus all the various other perspectives given to her from those who knew him.

He turned to her again, seeming to lose patience with her lack of response.

"Do you hear what I'm saying? There'd be doctors and multiple legal hoops to jump through, a well-timed lethal injection, and even that would only happen under very specific circumstances. And if I did go down that path, it'd be with the goal of ending my life humanely, not through whatever gory plan you thought I was hiding." A muscle ticked beneath his now grinding jaw, suggesting the information he offered came under duress.

An iciness expanded in her body, though her cheeks burned with rising shame. Only now did she see just how she'd misjudged him. If things grew bad enough, he wanted control over his end. Not a completely unreasonable desire. She'd seen enough death and frailty to understand his stance. But to her own discredit, in her scramble to organize his life, she'd rushed and dived into a pool of assumptions, blindly accepting Candice's version of this man. She'd been so wrapped up in ensuring he had enough joy and distraction to keep him busy, she'd never once considered that his plans weren't quite as eminent or irrational as she'd decided.

Stupid move.

She cleared the thickness in her throat, her pride still clinging to the logic in her thinking. "But Candice said—"

"Candice doesn't know shit."

She jolted at his searing tone, opening her mouth to respond, but he squeezed his eyes shut and spat out an expletive.

"Candice is the one with the complex. Not me." He snapped his razor-sharp glare back to her. "Her son and I went to school together. We were in the same year level, but we weren't all that close. I know nothing about him except that at some point, years after I'd left Roseford and settled in Melbourne, he fell into a deep depression and decided to park his car on the train tracks ahead of the 6 a.m. express to the city. Me taking up residence at Candice's facility was the best thing to ever happen to her. She's been projecting her baggage over her son onto me ever since, including his issues."

Sophie's hand flew to her chest, and she once again struggled for words. Every time Orlando spoke, a new hole opened up under everything she thought she knew about him and his situation, much less his initial mistrust about her being an aspiring psychiatrist.

"I had no idea."

"Yeah, well. Both you and Candice would look a great deal less unhinged if you'd just bloody asked me. I guess that explains why you both took it upon yourselves to insist on me seeing a psych."

"You know that wasn't the entire reason. Your flashbacks and my unwillingness to carry the total weight of your wellbeing was part of it. I hope you'll continue accepting help, even after today."

His expression grew dark, colder. "Maybe I'll need it, now that I'm left to wonder how much of this whole relationship was one big act of charity for you. How much of my condition is your ticket to fulfilling a constant need to make up for your own regrets?"

The pain of his criticism left her winded, his growing resentment hinting that nothing she said would be enough to convince him this relationship was still worth pursuing. But for all her assumptions and missteps, he didn't get to use her past to hurt her. "This relationship was always more to me than just holding you together."

"I never needed or asked for you to hold me together, Sophie." He settled deeper into his pillow, narrow glare dismissing her in favor of the ceiling again. "I'm starting to think you never really saw me, that maybe I was just a means to make you feel better about yourself."

Her anger rose, bunching and pulling tight within her gut. She wanted to reach out and shake someone—and of all people, a helpless man in his hospital bed. Though even her temper was a sign of just how much he'd changed her. How important he'd become. How much of her true self, good and bad, this man unearthed.

And as much as she wanted to hate him, her better judgment guessed his scornful approach was the only way he could find to say goodbye.

A raw feeling swirled and spluttered within her, but she forced her voice out again, a voice that crackled with a need to do away with regret. "I'm not ready to let you go."

"You don't have a choice."

He still didn't look at her.

"You were ready to declare your love for me just hours ago. Remember that?"

He scoffed out a laugh. "Yeah, and thank fuck I didn't. If you haven't noticed, things have changed."

Her muscles held a dull ache from holding back her true range of emotions. The lights in this room were overly bright and bounced off the pale walls, and neither the lights nor the walls did anything to help with her overwhelming fatigue from an entire evening of great stress and uncertainty.

"You need me." Her tone twisted, loud and pathetic.

"I've lived thirty-six years without knowing you. I'll be fine. Well..." He peered down at his sheet-covered body, wires protruding and drainage bag hooked up to the edge of his bed. His mouth bent in a mocking smirk. "Maybe 'fine' isn't the right word. Let's just settle on me returning to 'business as usual', and you realizing you're not Mary Poppins and that no one asked you to be my nanny."

She'd tried to play calm. Tried to plead. But Orlando was a master at prodding her soft spots. Nothing worked on this man. Nothing. He knew how to hurt her. And maybe he was right. Maybe she was a martyr. Someone too nice for their own good and not so inclined to seize what she wanted. A woman cut off from herself.

But she could change that. Even good people stood up for

themselves at times, and despite what he thought, selflessness didn't always equal manipulation.

She stabbed an accusing finger his way. "I'd ask why you're being so cold right now, but we both know it's because you can't stand to admit you're scared about your future and what my role in that future might be." She ignored his astonished jolt and stepped closer. "It's easier to be a crabby bastard than admit you think vulnerability is weakness. Even though we both know that's not true, and you're really offloading your shit onto everyone else—especially me—just so you don't have to work through any of your messy hang-ups. Stop offloading your shit, Orlando. Just bloody stop it. You're better than this."

His wide glare held hers for the longest time, his expression still and stunned, while the soft murmur of far-off conversations out in the hospital halls filtered in. Her words rung on repeat in her head, like the walls absorbed their impact and bounced those words right back at her.

She sounded like a real monster. She hated being so mean. Especially at such a low point in his life.

But harsh honesty had always been one of the few ways to get through to him, and maybe this was the extreme she needed to resort to for him to see that isolating himself and pushing her away—early and with so little tenderness—wasn't in anyone's best interest.

Soon enough, his stunned stillness morphed into genuine red-faced fury. "We both agreed this ending would happen, so what I'm *better than* doesn't make a lick of difference to you." He jutted his chin toward the door. "Go, Sophie. Go have the life a *crabby bastard* like me could never give you."

Her limbs shook, and she opened and closed her hands in quick, flicking movements. Whatever she said next would not be quiet, and everyone outside this room would hear. But for the first time in her entire life, she didn't care about how she looked or what other people thought.

"I've never asked you for anything but your time, so don't start on what you can't give me. And I care about what you're better than because of *how* you're ending us. You're flaking out on me, Orlando. I never thought I'd see the day Mr. Tough Bravado himself would turn into a fucking coward."

"Look at me." His voice exploded, and the veins in his neck protruded. "Fucking look at me." He gave a sharp nod down at himself. Even the scar on his forehead appeared raised, red, and angry. "Do I give the impression of a man able to take part in a relationship? Christ's sake, I'm involuntarily pissing into a bag. Running through burning buildings used to be nothing to me, but right now, if this building caught fire, I'd be at the mercy of whoever damn-well remembered I exist. So, the last thing I want to think about is how impossible it is for me to be with you. Don't you dare call me a coward. You have no fucking clue."

"You think I've never seen a man in a hospital bed before?"

"Think, Sophie. Think." He released an exasperated breath and clenched his eyes shut. "Think about all the conversations we've had over the last few weeks. How we were never meant to be just friends. How I was meant to be your thrill. That's what we agreed on, remember? Well, there's nothing thrilling about me now."

"If that's your way of pointing out that sex is off the table..." She released a tight and incredulous laugh. Her yelled response about sex had her struggling to believe that she—Miss Neat and Nerdy, Sophie Tindall—was embroiled in a semi-public yelling match. "We're both adults here, Orlando. We can choose to change the course of this relationship."

"Jesus—" He threw his head back and released an explosive growl. "That's only half the point. You're not that scared, sixteen-year-old girl any more, you got it? You need to be the one to dig yourself out of whatever rut you're stuck in. Stop using me and whatever we do together as a crutch to live, and start actually damn-well living. We had sex. Don't get me wrong, lots of great sex. But there's more to life than being holed up in the Australian countryside, getting it on with a man whose life is a complete and utter car wreck. Stop being a doormat, Sophie. A sad, misguided, and eventually threadbare doormat."

"A doormat?" She shook her head at him, mind throbbing from rage-filled offense.

"Yes. You can't do shit unless you look after yourself first."

She'd never once considered herself a doormat, but Orlando's dig, coupled with Hector's earlier ultimatum, cut deep. "What am I supposed to do, Orlando? Set a village on fire? Do a spot of shoplifting? Tell me. Tell me what would make me less of a doormat in your eyes?"

"You know what I mean." His voice tapered and lost steam, his head settling down again. But she wasn't leaving before she either convinced him to take her back or she at least got every last detail on why he pushed her away.

"No, I don't. Spell it out."

"You're too good, Sophie." He turned back to her, the words snapping out. But then his features slackened, as if he came to some final and illuminating conclusion. "And that's our problem. You have no place with me."

The statement sank heavier than a large boulder in a tiny pond. Dramatic. Final. The impact sending ripples that broke the banks in the space lingering between them. A space fast growing wider and pulling them apart. For the longest time, she just stared, her throat tight.

"Don't I get a say on where my place is? Wouldn't that make me less of a doormat?" Her voice lost its volume, her thoughts suddenly clear. She drew a breath, demanding his unbroken, yet reluctant attention. "Because ultimately, this is about self-worth for you, isn't it? About what you think you deserve." She leaned in, so close it was impossible for him to ignore her. "But Orlando, you deserve happiness. You deserve to live. Despite all that's happened, you're still you and there's still so much you can do. You have it in you to fight, but you won't."

He shook his head and turned from her. "Stop it."

"You have so much life in you, can't you see? There are adventures you can still go on, adventures we could share. If only you'd—"

"I said, stop it."

"No. You're pushing me away. You stop it." Her voice hissed, anger creeping back in. "Stop making this about me. Stop blaming me every time things don't go to plan. Do this for yourself. Regardless of what happens with us or however long you have. If you can't give yourself a decent shot, Orlando, then you'll never find peace."

"And maybe giving up is my way of putting myself first, have you ever thought of that?" The sharp edge to his gaze eased, opening a window of fragile intimacy. "Maybe not putting myself through the grinder over and over and over again is my version of self-preservation. And that having you and every other interested person coddle me is one of the most fucking dehumanizing things a person can go through. You have no idea how it feels to lead this life. So yes, I don't want to fight anymore. And when bitterness and vulnerability make up my everyday life, maybe getting by is about as much as I can manage. Maybe I've earned my right to give up. And who the hell are you to tell me I can't?"

His delivery stayed tender, pleading even, despite the cutting choice of words. He was a man truly resigned.

A man saying goodbye.

And that resignation, of all things, cut her deepest.

Tears welled and then spilled down her face—fiery, despondent.

He'd gouged a hole right through her heart, and worst of all, she understood why. She wouldn't ask him again to reconsider his stance on this relationship. Not for himself. Not for her. Not for a man who'd lost everything, multiple times over.

But his rejection still stung, and hopelessness hit her harder than a wayward gust of wind slamming a door shut on her last chance at loving him. Because in outlining his suffering, he'd also outlined that her love wasn't enough.

"You're right." She spoke in a hollow whisper, eyes hot, as she took in her final glimpse of him. "Who the hell am I?"

His brows flexed; a sign he grasped what she'd left out.

Who the hell am I... to you?

The answer to that question had been swept away the moment he'd collapsed at Luke's wedding. The answer lost in the words he'd come close to saying but would never admit to, now.

"Go home, Sophie." His tone fell flat, and he returned to staring at the ceiling.

The answer to whether he loved her was *no*. The answer would *always* be *no*.

"This is the best ending we're going to get."

Thirty-One

SOPHIE STOOD outside the airport's ropes, doing her best to stall the inevitable—not so much because she'd miss Australia, but because she'd be leaving behind one man in particular.

A man she hadn't talked to in weeks.

Luke offered a soft smile, one that recognized her need to delay. "I'm going to miss you."

She returned his smile, at least grateful for the ride and that he'd come to see her off. "I really did enjoy myself."

He tilted his head. "Really?"

"Yeah, really." She patted him on the arm, savoring her last few moments with her brother in what would be an indeterminately long time.

Not everything about Australia had been bad, Orlando included. Despite her broken heart, she'd succeeded in finding pieces of herself. Pieces she'd sought when she first left London. She still had a lot to think over, but already had a few ideas about where she wanted her life to go next.

"Do you think you're about ready?" Luke handed the long handle of her suitcase to her. "Is there anything else I can help with?"

"No. Thanks for dropping me off though, I know how busy you

are. I would have been happy if you'd just spotted me the cash to catch a cab." She gave him a cheeky smile, knowing full well he was the sort of guy to roll up his sleeves rather than just throw money at a problem.

"You really are the best brother, you know that?" A wave of emotion rolled through her, making her voice wobble; she launched forward, flinging her arms around his wide shoulders.

He caught her and laughed. "I'll try not to tell Max you said that." He patted her upper back. "You'll be okay."

She nodded, chin digging into his shoulder, sudden tears soaking into his white t-shirt. She must have looked like a total cliché. An emotional woman clutching desperately to some guy at the airport entrance. But the whole experience with Orlando left her broken wide open. Her old rules of sensible control no longer applied. Barely a day passed where she didn't cry. But even that didn't seem so bad. For the first time in a long time, her emotions ran raw, and something about that left her feeling alive.

He'd given her so much in so short a time. She couldn't be angry at him. Not when she understood why he'd shut her out. Her main source of pain came simply because he *had* shut her out. Much of what remained now was longing and sorrow.

That sorrow gnawed at her, became part of her, and she wondered if its heavy presence would ever leave. Every day, she struggled to let him go. She'd even gone so far as to call Roseford Aged Care Facility. Twice. Attempting to get a surreptitious update on how he was doing. The first call garnered no news, but the second had been a true shock. She'd gotten hold of Shelley, who'd informed her Candice had resigned. Orlando had been moved too, though Shelley didn't know where. But Professor Bandara had been right. Orlando's latest hospital stint had prompted an investigation into his care at Roseford Aged Care.

Candice had taken all the blame, claiming she'd pressured staff and residents into accepting Orlando minus any behavior modifying medication. She'd blamed her decisions on the trauma of her son's death. Anyone close to the situation would know she'd sacrificed herself to spare the facility, as well as everyone else who'd more than willingly complied with having Orlando around.

The center's good track record and lack of internal complaints meant further discipline wasn't likely, though they'd have an increase in surprise checks from industry inspectors for the foreseeable future.

So now Sophie lived in the dark when it came to Orlando, and it had taken all her powers of self-control to rein in her natural compulsion to find out more and track him down. But at least she had something to take away with her. As weird as that logic would have sounded months ago, she now had the stuff that made mature, well-lived, *real* people. Experience. Hurt. A sense of just how convoluted life could be...

And hadn't that been why she'd come to this country?

Well. Yes.

And no.

She'd come to gain. Not lose. To accumulate experience. To take that experience home and become a fully rounded psychiatrist. But now so many former choices about her life no longer fit. Not with what she'd learned of herself. Not with where she wanted to go next.

And she hadn't come to Australia expecting to leave anything behind. Well, besides her naïvety or ideas about people. But not something tangible. Or something so utterly dear and unique. Or should she say, *someone*?

She let go of Luke, unwilling to allow her thoughts to wander any further.

He stroked her arm. "Are you sure you don't need anything more from me?"

"No. No. You've done enough." She dug into her small brown purse for a tissue and then dabbed at her eyes, just as a new thought entered her mind. "Actually. Yes. There's something you could help me with." She peered down at her feet, stomach sinking at thoughts of Hector's nasty ultimatum. "Is there any chance you have an overseas tech buddy that owes you a big favor?"

She cringed, Luke already giving her a sideways glare. "There might be, why?"

She told him about Hector and his plan to blackmail her.

"And you want me to help that slime ball out?" Luke's sea-green eyes blazed with fury. "Not a chance. I'd much rather crush any possibility of him ever working in tech again."

"No. Don't." She checked her phone and saw she'd have to rush if she wanted to board her plane on time. "Hector won't be getting any free rides. I promise. I'll call you when I land at Heathrow and let you know my plan."

"Okay." His scowl didn't abate, but he didn't protest either. He threw his arms around her. "You take care, okay? And remember, there's always a place for you here in Melbourne."

She gave him one final squeeze and held her emotions together. "Thank you. I love you. Goodbye."

She filed into the line of people waiting to get their boarding pass checked. Before long, she'd cleared security and sat aboard her plane. And as the wheels lifted off the tarmac, her heart squeezed and stomach roiled, and the finality of this exit hit her with great force. She was leaving. She'd really and truly given up on a future with Orlando.

She never gave up. Not on anything.

But what more could she do?

This was her farewell to Australia. A farewell to who she'd thought she was. Farewell to the first man she'd ever truly loved.

Her throat constricted, and she buried a sob. Perhaps if she'd known how things would pan out, she would have been more careful with her heart. But even as that thought entered her mind, her heart compressed, confirming it wasn't true.

She loved Orlando.

And even with all the missteps and wrong turns; her multitude of terrible decisions, she wouldn't trade one minute in his presence to be free of her pain now.

He was a broken man. Yes. Full of flaws and full of passion. If only his passion could extend to him crawling out of his all-consuming darkness, so he could find his fight without her help this time. Even if she'd never witness or benefit from his recovery.

She pressed her fingertips to her window's cold glass and closed her eyes, releasing her one silent yet impossible wish. That her heart would mend someday. That Orlando's body would mend, too.

And by some utterly and outrageous miracle, he'd find his way back to her.

Orlando peered down at his feet dangling over the edge of his bed, his blue veins protruding in small mountains and valleys under his skin, the familiar fawn carpet underneath. Four weeks had passed since his episode, two weeks spent relearning how to sit, another two just to shuffle his way into the bathroom alone. *Oh, how the already-not-so-mighty had fallen.*

Still, his recovery had been surprisingly quicker than usual.

If it weren't for the utter boredom or the sheer pain of lying down twenty-four-seven, he wouldn't bother with rehabilitation after each and every episode. He'd just give up. And even in the wake of banishing Sophie from his life, he wondered now why exactly he *did* bother.

"You deserve happiness. You deserve to live."

He spat out a laugh at her proclamation. *Naïve Sophie.* As if everyone in this world got what they deserved. Like some dirtbags didn't lead lives of luxury, and good Samaritans didn't die alone and beaten in gutters. He'd seen enough of both to realize the word *deserve* had no value.

But in the last two days, insomnia hounded him, and a permanent knot had formed in his belly.

Two days since Sophie would have hopped on her plane and returned to the UK.

Far from him.

Where she belonged.

But his more selfish desires hadn't lessened. His heart still ached for her to stay. His mind refused to let her go. And his mouth had lied the day he'd said he wanted her to leave... The same day he'd been seconds from telling her he loved her...

What an asshole.

He scrubbed a hand over his face and released a sigh. Her absence hurt like a bitch. Having met her, only to lose her, he was more alone than ever. Alone to do nothing but ponder her absence. Alone with his thoughts. Dangerous thoughts. Thoughts that reminded him day in and day out how little he mattered.

All I do is take up space.

Sophie would move on. In five years' time, she'd probably not even remember his name. And the knot in his gut grew yet again. The light inside his room dimmed, the sun through his window disappearing behind a cloud, as if to rub salt into the wound of just how much he didn't deserve anything positive.

I should just end things.

Do it now.

He slid his weight forward, feet touching the soft carpet, then lumbered his way toward the shower. A much harder task now that he lived with his mother. The bathroom lay some meters down the hall, a significant trip compared to the tiny ensuite he'd had at Roseford Aged Care. He had a walking frame and caregivers to assist him twice a day; they helped with his rehab, meds, made sure he was clean. But right now, he wanted to see if he could make the distance to the shower on his own.

He stood in the hallway, elbow leaned against a wall. His mother was probably out in the garden or off walking Nero; either way, he refused to bother her. He'd run shit out of luck the day he'd had his episode, not only losing Sophie, but his place at Roseford. His lashing out in the ambulance on the way to the hospital had been his undoing.

He'd been given a choice, ship off to another facility more dedicated to patients his age but farther away—and only *if* a place could be found for him—or stay at Roseford Aged Care. Both options required him to be drugged to the point of docility, rendering him something other than himself. Both were miserable options he didn't want. But then again, so was imposing on his mother.

He drummed his fingers against the wall and growled as he shoved his lump of a body onward. He needed to get away from his thoughts, his mind a murky soup from his already heavy meds and his rising depression.

Maybe he *would* be better to end his pathetic existence, just as Sophie had thought he might. Though maybe he'd wait until his current routine of drugs and fatigue eased and didn't cloud his thoughts so much. Maybe then he'd do things on his terms. Screw the plan. He didn't have much to live for, anyway. No future. No woman. No one cared. Not even him.

"You're flaking out on me, Orlando. I never thought I'd see the day Mr. Tough Bravado himself would turn into a fucking coward."

He got into the shower and turned on the faucet, hoping the gushing water would drown out the sound of her words replaying in his head.

Hot water spread over his shoulders, and he lowered himself into the white plastic chair he used because his legs could only hold him for so long. As he did, he mumbled through gritted teeth at the fatalistic ideas plaguing him. "Not yet, you impatient dickhead. Not today."

Water disappeared down the drain at his feet, and a sense of overwhelming hopelessness ate away at him. Maybe his stalling wasn't really just about wanting control over his end. Would such control even ever come? He sure as shit had been lacking in control from the first day his condition tore through his life.

"You have it in you to fight, but you won't."

Her voice again. He growled, shutting off the water with a sharp snap of his wrist, then leaning over for a towel on the nearby rail. He proceeded to pat himself dry. Maybe being alone in his room was where he'd gone wrong. Maybe if he rehired the psychologist Sophie had made him see, maybe then he'd get some reprieve. Maybe then the voices would stop hounding him.

Or perhaps all he needed was an hour of origami—or whatever the fuck they would be doing at the aged care facility right now. He wouldn't know though, because right now he lived with his mother, like a child... Which in itself was ironic because weeks earlier he'd been living like a geriatric.

Then again, even living as a geriatric trumped putting his mother in the firing line of another of his episodes. So maybe he'd have to go against her wishes after all. Maybe he'd have to pick being a heavily medicated vegetable over putting her through more trauma because of him.

He groaned and urged himself to standing, wrapping the towel around his waist as he did. He was halfway to his room when he paused at a figure standing inside the front door.

"Hello, Orlando."

Professor Bandara stared at him with her midnight eyes, her raven curls acting like some devilish kind of anti-halo.

His mother slunk out from behind the professor and gave him a guilty half-smile, before shutting the front door and then padding away.

He turned for his bedroom door and continued his silent journey back to bed. Unfortunately for him, being a slow cripple and all, meant the professor had no issues keeping up.

Once in his room, she stopped in his doorway behind him, as if waiting for him to acknowledge her. But just to drive home how little he cared for her presence, he turned his back and dropped his towel, showing her his ass.

"Nice view." She held an anticlimactic bored tone. "But I'm a doctor. Your ass cheeks won't make me blush."

He swiped up a pair of gray sweat pants from the end of his bed and tugged them on, followed by a white t-shirt, continuing to deprive her of any direct attention. "Pity."

"Well, I appreciate the effort, but I've spent half my day getting here, and I need just a few minutes of your time."

To his total annoyance, he caught the smile in her voice.

He stifled a need to send the professor an angry glare. He hadn't spoken to her in over a month, and he still didn't want to look at this woman. "Whatever you're selling, I'm not interested. I made that pretty damn clear the last time we spoke. Go knock on someone else's door."

The professor remained silent for a while, as if weighing up whatever hollow thing she planned to say next. "I believe we still have a shot at breaking your condition. I'm here because your mother invited me, and because I want you to reconsider your stance on stopping your treatment. I wasn't joking when I said your case was exceptional to me."

He plonked himself down on his bed, his legs weary and his

stomach queasy from his meds and the novelty of moving around. Frankly, he needed another nap. "No thanks."

She crossed her arms. "I'm offering you a chance to get better."

He nodded down to his less-than-spry body. "Look at me and tell me your last 'chance' was a roaring success."

Professor Bandara didn't reply; she didn't even take up his offer to look him over. She simply scowled. "You gave my treatments mere weeks to work when this stuff needs at least three months to accumulate in your body. Don't pin your failure on me."

His muscles tensed at the word *failure*, but he shuffled back on his pillow and interlaced his fingers behind his head. "Whatever. Unless you can give me a guarantee this time, I'm just going to assume you're dicking me around again."

His last attempt at stirring any sort of hope in his life had only set him up for one cluster fuck of a fall. He wouldn't go there so easily again. Especially now. He didn't have Sophie to motivate him. And as much as he'd despised Roseford Aged Care, he didn't even have that extra support to prop him up either.

Derisive laughter shot from the professor, and she rolled her eyes. "Oh, cut me a break, Orlando. Your demand is a load of total and utter bullshit, and you know it. If anyone should be disappointed here, it would be me. Well, me and Sophie. What happened to your commitment to your recovery? You had one big stumble, and you ran Sophie out of town and derailed your progress. Your choice to quit on both counts was less than what I expected from a former firey like you. So, tell me, why are you so freakin' eager to stick with the life you have now?"

He snapped his gaze at her, and an intense heat burst within the center of his body. "You think I want this life?"

She shrugged, a mocking gesture. "Well, do you? Because I'm offering you a chance—as slim as you think it is—to have a different life. And it seems to me you're set on wasting away at your mum's house."

"You're overestimating your ability to help me."

"Maybe." She stepped closer, her stare boring into him. "But even a slim chance is a chance. And frankly, your recovery isn't about you only."

"What are you talking about?"

"Well, your mother for one. Having spoken to her, it's clear she's been to hell and back for you. Looking after you at her age, watching you languish now, it's slowly undoing her. And then there's Sophie." The professor let out a heavy sigh and uncrossed her arms only to place them on her hips. "Do you think I'd be jumping through these hoops if it weren't for how much that woman campaigned on your behalf in the first place? Can you even see how much she so obviously cares for you?"

"Right, well, you can rid yourself of one guilt. Sophie and I haven't spoken in weeks. I'm certain her life is already improving without me."

And still, shame twisted the knot in his belly.

"You know that for a fact, do you?"

He thought about her initial goal of coming to Australia, in part to gain experience with men. The selfish bastard inside of him still hoped she hadn't resurrected that goal. It hurt too much to think about the alternative, that she'd maybe already moved on.

His throat burned rough and dry on the inside, and the speed in his reply sent a shiver through his body. "Do you know otherwise?"

The professor tilted her chin down like she'd figured she'd got him. "Why do you care?" When he didn't answer, she straightened. "Right, well, Sophie described you as strong-willed. She wasn't completely wrong."

"She said that about me?"

"She called you stubborn-headed, actually, but I padded the wording for you. And anyone with eyes, who'd seen you two together, would know you could call her tomorrow, and she'd fall over herself to get back here again."

He strongly doubted that but didn't contest the bit about him being *stubborn-headed*.

Professor Bandara looked around the room and shook her head, before taking a seat next to him on the bed and placing a hand over his forearm. "Listen, I get that you're as low as any person can get right now. But it's also really not that uncommon for a person to stay sick because they're trapped in a loop of believing their life is what it is. No matter the internal dialogue you've used to survive, Orlando, you don't belong here. Not when there are other options. Not just with regard to your treatment, but your quality of life. Let me do my job."

Her words, her logic, her compassion, sent a shock wave through his body, and some of what she said filtered in. Much of it made sense. It stirred a yearning in him to accept what she offered. Yet a greater part of him didn't want to separate from everything he'd come to know. As illogical as that sounded. Even to him.

So, he lay there, blinking at her, unsure of what to say.

Her brow dipped at the center and her expression implored him to believe her. "I wouldn't have squeezed in appointments to see you, stayed late to work on your case, or traveled out to this Hicksville today if I didn't think you were a good candidate to improve. Imagine, Orlando, if just for the next three months you turned the energy you've used to merely survive, and used it to save yourself instead."

Strain spread across his face, tightening the muscles over his jaw and forehead. Maybe she had a point, but skepticism was hard to let go of.

"How would a change in motivation be different to what I was doing one month ago? Before the last episode wiped me out. And who's to say another episode won't take me out again?"

"There's nothing to say you won't get more episodes, but I hear you're recovering quicker this time. A good indicator that maybe the meds I'd prescribed had some impact. Imagine the results you might have if you stuck with our plan." She offered a light smile, like she saw her encouragement affected him. "And if you do have another episode this time around, you don't stop taking your meds, do you understand? We push through together. We give this a proper go. And if I really, truly, feel the therapy isn't working, I promise to break the news to you early so you don't think I'm 'dicking' you around."

She paused, as if assessing his response. He gave her nothing, though he could already feel himself softening to her idea. If skepticism was hard to let go of, hope was even harder.

"And Orlando, there's more. If you make this commitment, I can secure patient housing for you through the university I conduct my studies through. They'll fund you on compassionate grounds, but also because you'll be a research subject. You'll be close by, so I'll be able to look in on you more. And even if it doesn't work, at least you'll be able to give your mum a break, which I know is important to you."

Her grin grew wide; the spark in her eyes belonged to a woman proud of her scheming. What the doctor offered was riskier than what he'd accepted the first time. She offered immediate escape. A significantly loftier hope to fall from. And more than that, a chance to unburden his mother.

And even though the offer stirred his desire for more than he'd been lumped with all this time, he couldn't fathom a future, much less freedom. Did he dare to grasp for any of it?

His heartbeat surged with a sense that something wasn't right. Risk and faith challenged him to find the *fight* Sophie had been so adamant he didn't possess.

Risk told him he'd been down this road before. That any attempt would only end badly.

But faith.

Faith said to take the chance. To believe in something. Or someone.

Professor Bandara.

Himself.

The meager chance he might have a future with Sophie.

With every niggling doubt, came the memory of her hazel eyes, her soft pink lips, her petite, silken body tucked against his... And then there was her constant determination. The same determination that, for the briefest time, had turned him into a better man.

He had a chance. A chance to recover. To press restart on his life. To piece together a new man and redefine who he was away from his condition. And if recovery didn't happen, he'd need to accept his life as it was.

As Sophie had put it, he needed to find a way to live.

To be happy.

Thirty-Two

Sophie took the few paces across the tiny, but once familiar, cobbled street with its black and white pedestrian crossing. After six months in dreary London, the weather was warming. She turned her face up to the cloudless sky. Her attention caught on a building with bronze-colored bricks, or more precisely, to a second-story window. That window belonged to an apartment she'd been glad not to visit in almost a year.

Still, moving on in life sometimes required doing things she didn't want to do. Though in this case, at least, she wasn't the one struggling to move on.

She traversed a set of stairs and ran through her game plan. By the time she got to her intended door, she found the thing creaking open before she had a chance to knock.

"What the hell are you doing here?" Hector's eyes blazed from the other side of his mesh screen.

An empty pit opened within her stomach, and she eyed the landing from where she'd just come, willing herself to stay put. "Hannah told me your flight leaves today."

He shouldered his way past, a giant black suitcase dragged behind him. "Yeah, and? It's a bit late to pretend you give two shits about me. Besides, I got to get a hurry on, my taxi will be here any minute."

She stepped back, allowing him more space, reacquainting herself with her old *meek-and-mild* act. Six months of careful planning had brought her to this moment. "Oh, okay, sure. Just, with all that's happened between us, I wanted to make sure we're all good now."

"What you mean is, you want to know whether I'll still upload that photo of you?" He pulled his door shut with a loud thud and then patted her on the cheek, his eyes squinting with a mocking grin. "Don't worry, Hun. We're all good."

She followed his hurried steps down the corridor, giving her best impression of a lost puppy, giving him time to relish the power trip. "Oh, that's a relief. And you don't even mind that it took Luke a few extra months to line up the new job? I'm really sorry about the delay."

"Well, I guess an international career in Dubai and a tax-free income will make up for the wait." He marched on, not sparing her a glance, his suitcase bouncing as he pulled it down the rugged old stairwell with its army-green metal banister. He paused at the foot of the stairs, breaths puffing against the effort of lugging his stuff, his gaze sweeping her from top to toe, face crinkling in a show of disgust. "I'm definitely moving onto better things getting out of this shit hole, that's for sure. So why don't you fuck off, and let me get on with it, huh?"

His dismissive glare stung about as much as his rotten language. Maybe she was more sensitive to these things in light of her heart still being nowhere near healed from Orlando's rejection months ago. But even then, time had seen her grow.

She'd paused her studies to figure out what she wanted to do. Traveled to more countries—ones that scared her, ones that opened her eyes to just how lucky she was. Much of her travel had been sponsored in part by her university, in exchange for her providing medical assistance to remote villages in need of care. She'd learned from those people, her views on life challenged. And a single insult from a bitter man like Hector couldn't keep her down.

His cab was indeed idling at the curb outside, and she gave him an easy smile. "I'm glad you're looking forward to the trip. I'm extra glad Luke found a place worthy of you."

The cab driver opened the trunk, and Hector hoisted his suitcase in with a strained grunt. "What's that supposed to mean?"

"Oh." She broadened her smile, making sure her expression showed every bit of the vindictiveness she intended to portray. A cheap emotion, sure, but one that still felt good right about now. "Just that we worked it that way to get you out of my life. You know, for good."

He rolled his eyes, small footsteps trotting him closer to the front passenger door. "Whatever."

He got in, but his scowl dropped as she leaned in front of his window and waited for him to roll it down.

"I want you to know, my brother isn't an idiot. And neither am I. We dragged out your job offer just to make you suffer, and even then, we could have gladly made sure you received every other last punishment you deserved. You only got this job because it will give you something to lose." Cars squeezed past the cab in the narrow side street, but her attention didn't waver from Hector and his narrowed pupils, his face resembling that of a scared weasel. "You're right where we want you. This job will also take you far, far away from me. So just know, I've saved every one of your extortionist messages, and if that photo ever surfaces, if you ever contact me or make any kind of trouble again, Luke and I will make sure *your* employer knows. You *will* get fired. We *will* lawyer up. And good luck finding another tech job with a criminal record after that. You'll never work in IT again."

She straightened and backed away. The cab driver took his cue and rolled the car forward, while Hector pushed his head out the window, rewarding her with a bug-eyed gape.

His uncharacteristic speechlessness made her slow months of stalling worth the wait. She was done with Hector. Done with being anyone's doormat.

Thirty-Three

LESS THAN AN HOUR LATER, Sophie mounted another set of stairs, these belonging to the small, double-story building where she and Hannah lived. She took one slow step at a time, nearing her top-floor apartment, her smile still lingering from her meeting with Hector. But the moment she reached the top of her stairs, her smile sank, and she stopped in her tracks.

A broad, muscular man, in a gray cotton long-sleeve shirt stood at her door. His back stayed to her, while the scent of woodsy-sage cologne wafted across the landing. A small gasp fell from her lips, and she nearly dropped her keys. That scent. She associated it with Luke's wedding, with Orlando holding her, so close to affirming his love.

Her mouth wavered in its open position, but she failed to produce any sound. The thought this man could be him… Surely not.

Orlando lived a literal world away, and she was the last person he wanted to see. This had to be a coincidence. Besides, this guy was slightly broader, his posture a little straighter. He carried himself with a certain confidence Orlando never had. Another stark difference was the sharp clothes he wore compared to Orlando's scruffy t-shirts, sweat pants, or, at best, jeans.

I'm having delusions.

What were the chances a guy that looked a bit like him, and certainly smelled like him, would be standing at her door?

She laughed to herself. *Silly woman.*

Probably just someone wanting to sell me a new electricity plan.

The man spun around. His espresso-colored eyes wide.

Tingles burst through her body in one giant, painful explosion of nerves. "Holy fuck!"

The expletive rushed out—so unlike her. Her muscles turned to metaphorical liquid, and she lashed out a hand to the nearby rail to keep from falling down the stairs.

It *was* him.

Orlando.

His expression eased; a slow exuberance lit his face.

Since when would she ever have described Orlando as exuberant?

Since now… apparently.

Meanwhile, a war of emotions clashed within her mind. She didn't know where to look, much less what to think.

"Holy fuck, indeed." His smile grew, eyes near sparkling. He looked so carefree, but somehow still him. Tidy. Strong. His thick hair was still soft and slightly scruffy, just how she liked it, only perhaps now freshly trimmed. "I want to believe I'm the one who taught you that."

She reeled back a little, face heating at the reference to her colorful language. In truth, yes, because of him, she did swear more these days, out of an expression of her increased confidence *and* her months of frustration.

"I—" Her voice caught in her throat. "What?"

His grin remained, and he took a step toward her. She shuffled back, only to remember she was standing on stairs. Her balance faltered, hand tightening on the cold metal rail, and she righted her stance, just in time.

His smile dropped, her tense reaction seeming to give him all the information he needed. She hadn't forgotten the trauma of their last meeting.

"I think you're trying to say, 'What am I doing here'?"

She gave a quick nod, voice still trapped. She wanted to launch forward. To wrap her arms around him. To congratulate him on looking so amazing and somehow making it all the way across the world to London. Yet, so many sadder memories held her in place.

He outstretched his hands on either side of him, gesturing down to himself. "I took your advice, or rather, Professor Bandara cornered me. It seems I recovered."

For the longest time, she merely stared ahead and blinked.

"You're better?" She gave a tiny, incredulous laugh, sounding manic. Light flutters filled her belly, and her hands shook, the rest of her still struggling to move.

He gave a slow nod, the gesture tentative and controlled, as if he'd decided anything too sudden might shatter her presence before him. "I recovered three months ago, but I waited before coming here, just to make sure. You were right, all I needed was a little more time."

She swallowed and took another look at him, making sure her eyes really weren't defective. "You mean… You mean, you got on a plane all on your own, and you found me here?"

Already her voice quivered, and her eyes stung, but she forced herself to hold her emotions together.

His lips upticked at the corner. The warm expression, the rare coyness of it, made her ache to reach out and touch him. "Luke gave me your address. He said you wouldn't mind."

Her brow grew heavy, and she contemplated that statement. Did she mind?

She didn't hate seeing Orlando, that was for sure. Her heart beat so hard and fast, her emotions clashed between excited, hurt, and confused. But some forewarning from her brother would have been nice.

"I…" She paused, unsure what to say, though she felt she should at least try to fill the silence. "I'm glad for you."

But the silence continued, and she found herself grappling with how much of herself she wanted to throw into this moment. She was happy for him. Genuinely thrilled. She loved him. Still. But she'd learned the hard way to hold on to her emotions, that unchecked love didn't work when it came to this man.

He told me to leave. Even though I wanted to love him regardless of whatever his condition did next.

His focus burned through her, her skin burning right along with it. And with that discomfort came another thought. He was trespassing on her turf. She was the one with the right to scrutinize. To leave him waiting in *her* dust this time.

Another shiver ran up her spine, waking her from whatever dreamland she'd disappeared to. She launched forward and right past him, her hand with the keys finding her front door.

"Sophie?" His deep voice echoed around the stairwell, seeming to find a home way down deep within her rage.

Her attempts to unlock her door weren't going so well, not with her trembling hand. The sound of scuffling shoes against the polished concrete floor behind her meant he intended to follow.

Her heart raced. She kept fumbling with her key, but the damn thing just made a series of sharp metallic tings and refused to fit the lock. "I don't know what you're doing here..."

"Sophie." His voice insisted she turn around, but she continued in her fight with her door, her key finally managing to slide into place. "Sophie. Listen to me."

His hand landed on her shoulder. She froze, her eyes slamming shut while her heart clenched from the pain of the connection.

"Sophie."

"Stop saying my name."

"Why?"

Because it makes me want to turn around. It makes me want to listen. It makes me want to throw my arms around you and forget you ever hurt me.

She took a steadying breath, her body already warming in response to his touch. "Look, I said I'm glad for you, and thanks for the visit, but you should go."

"Because I told you to leave?"

Her eyes flung open. A growl broke from her chest. Something dark and innate burst within her, and she spun around. His hand left her shoulder, while her muscles primed to lash out, even though her better sense stepped in before she managed to actually punch him.

"Yes." She half yelled. "You told me to leave, and I did. I left. And now you're here wanting to… to… what? Tell me I was right? Tell me you're better? Do you want my applause or should I throw a parade? Is that it?" Her voice rose even more. Any minute now her neighbors downstairs would stick out their heads to see what was happening. "I'm happy for you. Okay? I am. I really am. But what else could you possibly have to tell me?"

The echo around the vacant stairwell gave her blistering words a life of their own.

His cheeks fell slack, and his gaze searched her face as if he needed another second to digest her tirade. "Wow. I didn't think Sophie Tindall was capable of being so pissed."

She scowled at him, unsure of what else to do with her rage, so she kicked the brick wall on her left and regretted it instantly.

"Fuck." She stomped her booted foot to the concrete floor, as if that would take away the pain.

"And she really does swear now."

She snapped her gaze to Orlando again, his eyes lit up like a man impressed. Her complete reactivity confirmed that, yes, Sophie Tindall was capable of *being so pissed*. She was also more skilled at *not* psychoanalyzing every tiny decision she made, which was all part of the range of emotions this man pulled from her.

A wide smirk crept over his mouth, and his famous devil's grin made an appearance. "You must really like me."

She clenched her hands at her sides—about all she could do to keep from exploding—which in itself would make for a fascinating medical mystery, though one she'd rather study than be the victim of. His smug ability to bend a conversation made her want to kick the wall again. Though, in this case, she hated his conversation bending because he was right about her still really *liking* him, and she had nowhere to put that *like*.

"Sophie. Please, just listen." His soft tone hinted he was done playing. His close proximity, coupled with his change in tactic, left a small crack in the ice around her heart. This time when his hand connected with her shoulder, she merely stared up at him, less enraged and simply doing as he asked out of a hope she could soon disappear into her apartment. "I'm here because I like you too. I didn't come here just to tell you I'm better, or that you were right, even though both are true. I came here because I want you back."

Time seemed to stop and her heart along with it. "You cast me out. And you never once tried to contact me."

"You knew the deal when we got together."

She shoved at the hard wall of his chest. "And things changed. You *know* things changed."

"They did. And I'm sorry." He grabbed her wrist and rubbed his thumb over her pulse. "But I was in no place to have the relationship I wanted with you, and we needed that break. You have to know that." He smiled down at her, his gaze flitting around her probably red and fury-filled face. "And from the attitude you're giving me, I'd say you benefitted too."

She twisted her hand loose and smacked his chest again, though with a little less intensity now. "You hurt me. If I have an attitude, it's all your fault. I was willing to be there for you. I could have been there through your recovery. I *wanted* to be there. We lost months and months when we could have been together."

Just the thought made her hate him all over again.

He pulled her closer and pressed his palm to the side of her face, his other hand sliding to the small of her back in a gentle possessive gesture that kept her from any escape. With summer gearing up in London, her arms were bare, and already her muscles loosened against his warm touch; that same warmth flooded her body, even though she struggled against him.

"I know. I know I hurt you. I'm sorry. I'm so sorry." His hushed tone coaxed and comforted. He shifted the hand at her face, and his thumb stroked her earlobe. "But let me explain."

"Hey." Randal Berry's voice sailed up the stairwell, a loud TV blasting in the background of his now-open door. Of course, this would be the moment he noticed she existed. "Are you guys okay up there?"

She closed her eyes and drew a slow breath. "Yes, we're fine. Go back inside."

"Okay."

His door clicked shut.

She peered back at Orlando, lowering her volume. "Explain."

His gaze dropped to her chin, and he took a moment before speaking. "I don't want to get to the end of my life and realize I didn't show up, that I took one look at you and chickened out, that you were right about me not feeling worthy of putting up one final fight. But more than any of that…" His beautiful dark stare lifted to hers, and a pained expression pulled at his features. "Sophie, if I didn't try, then the end would have come with the knowledge I'd let you go without fighting to keep you. That, of all things, would be my biggest regret.

"I'm sorry it's taken me this long to front up. I understand if you can't, or don't want to, or if the damage is too great… but I'm sorry. I still want you back. Not an hour has passed in the last six months where I didn't want you. Even as I told you to leave, I wanted you."

No words came to her, though she knew it was her turn to speak. She merely stared at him, body rigid in his arms.

Could she let his honesty get to her? Could she say yes?

Maybe she was better off doing the smart thing and protecting herself from further heartbreak. They didn't exactly have a great track record of getting along for any extended period of time.

His gaze searched her face again. The steady shake of his head seemed an attempt to dowse her rising doubt. "Look, can we just go inside? We can talk about this. Properly. Without bothering your neighbors."

She stepped back and out of his hold, not ready to give in without a clearer explanation. She couldn't open her door for him, didn't want him in her house. Because judging by the sharp need burning through her body, and the way her attention kept flitting over to the scar along his forehead, lighting a deep need to kiss him right there, she still plainly wanted him. She couldn't let arousal get in the way of the biggest decision of her life.

"No." She pressed her hand to the cold brick wall beside her, as if that might stop him from getting past; as if borrowing the wall's strength to hold her up. "What happened to me being too good for you? To me having no place in your life?"

He winced, drawing out a pause, before he offered up an answer. "I lied, Sophie. I lied to myself when I said I wasn't good enough. I allowed others to tell me the same thing. I've been allowing it ever since I was a child, and getting sick only made that worse. I made it okay for others to treat me like I didn't matter, like I didn't fit in, to abandon me, to dictate where my life went. And even if my response was to tell them to fuck off, I still believed them. I still took their words to heart. I let myself be broken because I didn't know how else to be.

"I thought my condition would bring you down, when it was me and who I'd let myself become, who had the power to do that all along. I know that now. I know I screwed up. As a lover, as a friend, as a son... In every relationship, but especially with you. And I screwed myself over too. I told myself, 'this was who I am', and for so long, in the most dysfunctional way possible, it worked. I believed it. That belief helped me survive. Except then you came along, with your prying and bullheadedness, hellbent on adjusting my life—"

"I'll take that as a compliment."

He smiled, and the mere look of that smile provided all the healing warmth of a ray of sunlight to her broken and bruised heart.

"It is. And I wouldn't have come to any of those realizations if you hadn't forced me to get help."

A hard knot formed in her chest, followed by a sinking feeling. Or maybe the feeling was that of melting. It was hard to tell. Except that something had certainly shifted within her.

Here stood Orlando, a man of few words and the epitome of all things brooding, pouring his ever-loving-heart out about the inner workings of his mind, so far removed from his man-of-perpetual-mystery act.

She slumped back, shoulder blades connecting with her door. She wanted to believe him, though maybe the knotted, sinking, melting sensation meant she already did.

He drew closer, crowding her space with his woodsy-sage smell and masculine heat, both of which permeated right through her doubts and reawakened her need.

Her hand itched to reach out and touch the soft weave of his shirt, as if her fingertips remembered his beautiful form hidden underneath. *Which they did.*

"Sophie." His voice redirected her attention. Maybe he'd sensed where her mind wandered, but his furrowed brows said he had serious matters to clear first. "I get that my being here is a shock, and maybe you've moved on. God, I hope that's not the case, but I needed to be here. I needed to see you. To tell you how I feel. I needed it as much for myself as the outcome I'm hoping to get here."

Her throat constricted, and a choked splutter came out instead. "I... ummm..." A light sensation eased the sickness she'd been feeling in her tummy. Maybe she did understand a great deal of what he'd endured and why he'd done the things he'd done. How huge an achievement it was that he even stood before her. "You were right, too."

He tilted his head to one side, confused.

Her thoughts ran to Hector, to her last decade of taking shit she should have walked away from.

"You were right when you said your influence has changed me. I've allowed myself to run through mine fields for people who wouldn't even cross the street for me." And for that she'd misdirected a lot of her anger at him. Because she could. Because a part of her knew he'd take it without truly turning nasty. Because he'd told her to leave, when every other boyfriend had used and depleted her until she had nothing left. "You helped me see who I am, to clarify what wasn't working. You hurt me, but somehow, I'm happier for having known you."

Happier for all his pushing and stonewalling. His resistance had forced her to stand up for herself. His rejection had made her define what she really wanted. To grapple for what seemed worth fighting for. To connect with her aspirations and strike out on her own.

"Having known me?" His jaw tensed. "I'm not sure I like you speaking about me as if I belong in your past."

Despite her struggle to hide her amusement, a small grin managed to escape. "I haven't decided where you belong."

He inched closer, sandwiching her between him and the door. "Is that so?"

"Yeah." The word came out a broken croak, and she gave a quick nod, swallowing hard at her nerves as well as her desire.

Even though anger had seeped in over time, in truth, her feelings for him remained unchanged. But then, she couldn't let their problems lie. She wanted more than what she'd left behind in Melbourne.

"Okay, well." His gaze held hers, direct and certain. "Maybe it's time I told you where I think I belong."

She gave a small nod, wanting promises, wanting *him*.

"You can love me or not, Sophie. God knows, I haven't loved myself, and there are a lot of people who would do anything to never see my face again." He reached for her, pressing his forehead to hers. "But I love you. I love you with my whole heart. And that love still holds even if the next words out of your mouth are to tell me to go to hell. I make no apologies for saying what I'm saying now. I love you, and I don't want to lose you a second time. If I'm correct, then I'm certain I belong right here with you."

Her heart stilled at the ragged edge to his tone, and every muscle in her body turned slack. She would have fallen if not for the door behind her and the man pressed so firmly to her front.

Her mind raced to accept what she'd heard. That Orlando, of all people, could admit to an emotion as soft and fragile, as soul-baring, all-leveling, and ever-lasting, as love.

"You… You love me?"

He gave a small nod, and his molten dark gaze held firm to hers. Despite what he'd said, her first thoughts were far from telling him to go to hell.

"Go ahead." He leaned in, lips close to her ear. "Ask what my dreams are now."

She wanted to sink further. Maybe because his mouth didn't move from the shell of her ear, and she yearned for his kiss. Or maybe because he'd brought up a question she'd asked months ago. A question he'd thrown back in her face and refused to answer.

She cleared her throat, certain her voice would be husky when she spoke. "Tell me about your dreams."

He pressed a feather-light kiss to her ear, then whispered against her lobe. "The answer is simple. My dreams involve you."

She reeled back. "Is that it?"

"You want more?"

She nodded, heart thundering in her chest.

"You sure you can handle it?"

"I'll try."

"I want a family. That means children. But if you don't—"

"No." She swallowed, breath heavy, pulse straining because she too had thought about this and already knew her answer. "I want that too. I just... I want to wait. I want to finish studying and establish a steady career first."

He released a soft chuckle. Her rushed answer seemed to amuse him. "Don't worry, I'll need a good while to get established too. I'm starting my life from scratch, remember?" He paused, his smile dropping. "But, Sophie, there's something else. Before all of that, I want you to be my wife."

She jolted, though not as much as she would have preferred given the door pressing into her back. "You do? But... But we live in different countries. Where will you live, where will I? There's so much to work out."

He laughed again, louder this time, his tone rumbling and rich enough to send butterflies flittering through her tummy. "So, you're happy to have my children, but we need to iron out the details of you being my wife?"

"Well, no." Her cheeks burned, but a smile broke free all the same. "I've got this all a little bit backwards, haven't I?"

He pressed his forehead to hers again, falling just short of their lips joining. "My life is starting over, and I'm free, do you understand? I go where you go. We'll work everything else out from there." He paused, gaze searching hers. "So, what's your answer? Will you take me back?"

She allowed slow seconds to pass, giving the impression she didn't already know her answer. "Go to hell."

Orlando's face paled, before she let loose with a playful laugh. For once she'd had a turn at toying with him. "But if you do, take me with you."

Thirty-Four

SOPHIE'S SMILE dropped as tears gathered in her eyes, the weight of the future she'd just agreed to sinking in. Orlando leaned closer and pressed the lightest kiss to the corner of her mouth. So tender. So intimate. So unlike Orlando. "Invite me in, Sophie."

Every nerve in her body settled to a low thrum, and everything in her world seemed suddenly right. Her heart beat just for this moment, for him. How her life had changed in the brevity of a few minutes. She reached her left hand out to the side and behind her, until her fingers found the door handle and the door sprung open.

She stumbled back, into her apartment; but before she could get too far, Orlando caught her and swept her off her feet. Unrestrained laughter erupted from her, and she pressed her palms on either side of his face. "We should bolt the door. Hannah won't appreciate being locked out, but it's better than her walking in on us."

He planted a strong kiss to her lips and kicked the door shut, his gaze soon sweeping across the tiny living room, with its cluttered arrangement of second-hand furniture, brightly colored cushions on a violet couch, and a stack of textbooks teetering on the coffee table's edge. "Hannah will have to deal. She can always leave again. Now point me to your bedroom."

She jabbed a finger toward an open doorway behind her.

He gave a playful growl, and within a few wide paces, crashed through her door. Before she could take stock of what happened, he pinned her beneath him on her arctic blue, cotton bedspread.

The weight of his body offered welcome comfort and pressure, his lips raining down a firm fall of kisses, like he couldn't believe he got to have her again, like he would never let her go and that he feared at any moment she might disappear.

To be honest, she felt the same.

Her desperation came through on the hard press of her returned kisses, her fingers claiming the thick curls at the nape of his neck.

He pulled his lips from her, breathless, his hands buried in her hair. "Tell me there's been no one else."

The depth of his stare, the clench of his jaw, denoted a man held barely together, as though his next breath depended on her answer.

"No." She shook her head and swallowed back a rise of sadness. "I wanted to, but I couldn't."

She would have loved to have moved on. To pretend he hadn't hurt her. That his absence hadn't existed as a living, breathing thing in her day-to-day life; a dull pain piercing her heart every time another man hit on her, that pain saying she wasn't ready.

She'd loved her six months of freedom and hated it even more.

The muscles across his face relaxed, his broad shoulders easing above her, like he understood why she'd wanted to. "I'm sorry." His voice was a small, sincere whisper, his nose skimming hers. "I need to slow down with you, don't I?"

She gave a hurried shake of her head, the need gathering in her core saying she didn't need *slow* at all. "No. No, you don't."

His deep laughter rumbled through his body and against hers. "I'm going to anyway."

He slid his hand under the hem of her emerald blouse and farther beneath her matching lace bra. His large palm engulfed her breast, and she arched into him, his thumb brushing her nipple with a feather-light touch.

"You're going to kill me." She wriggled against him.

"Shhhh…" His lips landed on the side of her neck. "I've just found you again. I'll make sure you survive. Just let me adore you for a minute."

She bit back her need to shatter the stillness with more words. Bit back the uncertainty that she *would* survive whatever he had planned, especially if that plan meant going slow.

For months, she'd been starved of this man, but now his kiss claimed every one of her breathless moans, while he kneaded her flesh, and the bulge of his excitement dug into her inner thigh. His body overwhelmed hers with sheer size. But she'd never felt so safe. So content. So ready to break from uncharted passion.

He pulled her shirt away, along with her bra. His lips took over where his hand left off, palm grazing over her waist until his long fingers vanished under her white skirt and into her underwear.

She bucked against him, demanding more, but he held her down with the press of his thigh, insisting on patience.

Her nipple puckered under his lips, and she surrendered, sinking deeper into her bedspread, while she vowed to simply enjoy. He was only getting started, but already months of waiting morphed into a splintering need. Never once had she imagined he'd be back in her bed.

A moan broke free. She wanted him and everything he offered. She voiced as much as his finger slid into her, and she clutched around him working at her longing, his thumb drawing slow circles over her bud. Higher and higher her need for him grew, until her breaths turned ragged, and her head thrashed against her burgeoning climax.

He was still a devil of a man, still capable of setting her world on fire, only now he lacked his former bitterness, his wicked edge honed in on bringing her pleasure.

A rushing sensation seared through her body and she released a soft whimper. His hot kisses branded her shoulder, making a meandering journey back to her lips, her excitement rising with each gentle caress; his lips travelling farther, to her brow, and to her cheek, and then her temple. The soft intimacy undid her on a shuddering cry.

He pulled away, tugging at the last of her clothes, taking off his own, while her climax settled; and she watched him roll on a condom, her gaze flicking to the rest of his body to confirm an earlier observation.

"I see you've been hitting the gym since we last met." She quirked a smile, unable to keep from commenting.

He positioned himself between her bent knees, but paused, his eyes glinting, and his devil's grin returning. "Let's just say I'm working with increased energy levels these days. I hope, for your sake, you can say the same."

She wanted to laugh at his challenge and argue back, but he lowered his hips and entered her in one slow, long stroke; his eyes sliding shut, as he released a drawn-out hiss of pleasure.

She allowed her spirit to float with the warm, stretching feel of him; like his body converging with hers made her somehow complete, even though it was his undeniable love that held her most.

His elbows dug into the bed on either side of her shoulders and he watched her, as though invested in her every reaction and detail. His body pressed hot like an engine against hers, his movements building within her, while desire stole at her thoughts, holding her in the moment with this miracle of a man; his strong hands cupping her face, as a tender and completely physical conversation unfolded between them.

A steep avalanche of emotion seemed to roll through him and into her, his entire body claiming her; her breaths bursting with each of his euphoric thrusts, and each thrust growing harder, faster, more desperate to convey how the time apart had hurt him.

She couldn't hold on any longer and an urgent cry broke free from some place deep within. Blasts of light effused from behind her shuttered eyes, similar to sunshine cutting through crystal, bringing with it showers of color, and wonder, and radiant heat settling all around her—just as Orlando swelled and fell along with her.

For the longest time, she surrendered to being right here with him, to the languid sensation of time pausing, his embrace a reality that, for the first time ever, matched her fantasy.

Orlando wasn't leaving.

There would be no bittersweet end.

No fleeting exchange leading to a permanent split.

She could have him again. Have *this* again. And again. Whenever she wanted.

And that thought alone left her heart soaring.

His face hovered just above hers, and his thumbs stroked the edges of her forehead. The dreamy look in his eyes said he'd reached the same conclusion.

Seconds passed, and she sucked in a slow breath, her mind slowly overcoming the adrenaline still lingering in her body.

"Oh!" She smacked her hands over her mouth, almost taking Orlando out with her sudden movement. "I never gave you an answer."

He tipped his head to one side, brow raised.

She yanked his face back down to hers and kissed his lips. "The answer is yes. Yes. Yes. A million times, yes."

When he pulled away, his brows still hadn't lowered. "I love an enthusiastic yes, but Sophie, honey, I need you to elaborate."

A smile took over, and overwhelming joy scattered her thoughts.

Well... all thoughts except one...

"I mean yes to being your wife." A tear rolled down her cheek and she laughed. "Also, I love you too."

Epilogue

THREE YEARS Later

Sophie sat in the airport lounge, her fingers linked with Orlando's, the line of people standing at the boarding gate creeping forward. She never could understand why, the moment a flight was called, people rushed to line-up. She preferred to sit and wait. The line would eventually dwindle, and then she and Orlando would glide through to their plane seats with minimal standing, bumping, and shuffling. But then again, what did she know? This was her first flight in three years, so maybe there was some secret traveler's motivation she didn't understand.

So much had changed in those three years. Not long after Orlando had ambushed her at her apartment, she'd knuckled down on her studies, and now she found herself partway through the core component of her psychiatry training. One of the best parts being that she'd started getting paid for her work.

She and Orlando had been able to afford rent on a small apartment on the outskirts of town. Though she'd planned on specializing in old-age psychiatry, her experience with Orlando had changed her interests.

The transformative effects of his treatments meant she'd befriended Professor Bandara online, and with her encouragement, embarked on studies centered on research and finding new drugs to improve patient outcomes.

The work was fascinating and ever-changing, and she'd come to embrace her bookish tendencies more than ever, rather than run from them.

Meanwhile, the people of Roseford banded together to help Orlando restart his life in the UK. They raised funds and ran social media campaigns. His mother and brother also scraped together what money they could, and he'd gathered enough to live off while he picked up new skills and settled in with Sophie abroad.

In time, he landed a new career he cherished. A job that incorporated his experience and passion in fire risk minimization, as well as land management. A job that kept him outdoors and bouncing between acre upon acre of countryside. One that offered something so completely different to the life he'd endured at the care home.

He worked as a park ranger, a career that suited him to a tee. He'd even made an endless number of friends: from hikers to families, co-workers, and the occasional quirky tourist. So many people knew, loved, and accepted him. And every day he returned home to her, hands a little dirtier, but the rest of him smelling of fresh air and pine trees... along with undertones of sweat and hard work.

His world was a full contrast to her days viewing research papers in air-conditioned rooms. And he'd come to know all the beautiful places to visit on the weekends, and for that, she loved his job too.

Two years had passed since their wedding. A small country ceremony in York, with her mother and everyone they knew from Australia in attendance. Nova, Luke and Agathe's daughter, had only just started walking, but she'd toddled down the aisle, hand in hand with her proud mother, a picture of baby sweetness as Sophie's flower girl.

But the time had come for Sophie and Orlando to jump on a plane. To do the visiting. Her muscles shook with a spike of adrenaline. She half bounced in her boarding lounge seat, itching to have the marathon flight over, so she could see everyone again.

The boarding gate queue dwindled, and Orlando stood, his hand outstretched in an offer to pull her up. She took the offer, only for him to tug a tad harder than expected, causing her body to collide with his.

He engulfed her in a strong embrace, large hands wrapping all the way around her burgundy wool coat, before he gave her a fleeting kiss. "You ready?"

She swallowed at a lump of emotion, overwhelmed with the impending journey, but even more so, the swell of memories flooding back. The state of their lives was unrecognizable to when they'd first met. So many things had needed to go right just for them to be together now.

She nodded, relishing his easy smile, where at one point he'd been neither easy nor the smiling type.

He stepped back and slid his hand into hers, while the other hand dragged their carry-on luggage. They walked over to the now-empty boarding desk, and an attendant checked their tickets, soon waving them through to the plane.

Gusty winds and wild gray skies surrounded the open-air boardwalk. Her fingers clung instinctually tighter around Orlando's, and she allowed her head to lull over to his shoulder. Three years and a different outlook had changed everything forever.

Risks and courage had brought them to a place of harmony.

For her, courage had come in the form of learning to stand up for herself, to risk failure. And with Orlando, she'd failed, big time.

But he'd returned to her life all the same.

For him, courage had meant the will to fight. To believe in his worth and find peace within himself and his condition. To know that, no matter what, his life held value. And regardless of what the future held, he would never be alone. He had love. He had Sophie.

THE END

The Last in Line

LOVE AT LAST, BOOK 3

She's on the run from a horrific past. He's on the verge of a riches to rags nightmare.

Burlesque bar owner Freya Cortez, leads a razzle-dazzle life until she learns her mother has just weeks to live. Now she is forced to juggle a once-in-a-lifetime business opportunity with the torment of her far-from-perfect childhood.

Millionaire party-boy Max Tindall is facing financial ruin, even his most prized possession is at risk—his home. But a casual encounter with Freya gives him one last chance to turn his life around.

Though Freya has vowed to never fall in love, even she can't deny Max is the kindest person she's ever met, the one man to challenge her "no settling" rule. But how can a woman so fiercely independent ignore the fact that there's something gravely amiss with him? Something even he hasn't noticed. Something bound to destroy both their lives.

For fans of slow-burn romance and It Ends With Us.

Turn the page for a peek of *The Last in Line*.

The Last in Line (Sample)

CHAPTER ONE

FREYA CORTEZ BOUNCED on her heels outside The Ruby Room's double doors; her sleeveless, sunny yellow dress, with its nipped-in waistline, doing a piss-poor job of keeping her warm. Late summer in Melbourne, Australia, could be fickle, and lately, the nights held a constant chill.

"How'd things go with the rep?" Crystal loomed to her right, tall, dark, and slender, dwarfing Freya's significantly shorter and rounder physique—probably a good thing, since she'd hired the woman as the bar's bouncer.

"Well enough."

Wednesday nights at the burlesque club weren't usually all that busy, but business had picked up. Freya looked over the small huddle of people still trying to get into her venue, despite the time nearing midnight.

"Just well?" Crystal's voice somehow still held a bored, dull edge, as if very little ever impressed her.

After years of being knocked back, followed by six-months of planning now that they were in, the bar's inclusion in the Live Wire Festival *was* reason for excitement. And that inclusion was what brought Freya to the club on her night off. More planning. More prep.

"Okay, better than well." She shrugged, still downplaying things.

The festival rep she'd met earlier had been impressed with the weeknight atmosphere and the flow of patrons.

Now, four people waited in line, and she whispered for Crystal to admit these last patrons, then lock the doors to anyone new. Her voice held a subtle croakiness from much yelling over bawdy music while talking to that rep. Though with any luck, last drinks would be called in the next hour or so, and then it would be time to go home. She'd rest her voice soon.

A young woman in front of Crystal dug around in her purse for ID, only to drop the hot pink clutch.

Crystal's bored tone returned. "I'm not getting that."

To be fair, Crystal's skin-tight leather pants and five-eleven frame meant Freya was closer to the ground, and therefore the better person to help.

She crouched and began collecting stuff off the pavement, sparing Crystal the long, tight-panted journey down. That said, Freya had her limits too, like collecting the loose tissues floating about; though the rolling pink tube of lipstick and blue pen she could do.

Someone huddled down beside her, the warmth from their hand

crossing hers in the cool night and drawing her gaze to a set of soft blue eyes. Varying shades of stone and sky held her attention for a beat too long; for some reason, she imagined gentle waves atop a wintery sea within those pupils. An irrationally dreamy thought, especially for her.

Her eyes narrowed of their own accord. She knew this guy. One of her regulars. Knew those shaggy, surfer curls kissing his brow, and those broad shoulders paired with his tall physique, a tad on the slender side.

Yes, she knew. Some sort of tech millionaire, or maybe that was his brother, or something along those lines… Unlike his queue of admirers at The Ruby—mostly her own staff—she pretended not to notice.

She gave him a small nod and extracted a case of mints from his long fingers. "First drink's on me. Just tell the bar the door woman sent you."

A smile pulled at his lips and sent a small thrill of electricity through her tummy.

Small, yes, but still enough to compel her back to standing.

She turned away from him, offloading the breath mints on to the bag dropper, catching the jittery movement of her own hand as she did so. *Screw that.* Surfer guy might have had an unintended effect on her, but she wasn't above flirting back out of pure retaliation.

She turned back around, intent on delivering some witty one-liner, only to find someone else standing in his place. Someone who stank of sweat and cigarettes and had a dirty blond buzz cut. *Not the surfer guy at all.* This guy's blue eyes didn't conjure the ocean, unless she counted the turbulent sinking sensation dragging at her belly. No, all she got from this guy was a flat, leering stare.

She offered him a weak smile anyway, and then turned to go back inside the bar, pausing at the low grumble she *thought* she heard, one that sounded something like, "Where's *my* free drink, bitch?"

A distant whisper in the back of her brain warned her, a whisper that saved her life once before. She'd owned The Ruby Room for years now, had worked other bars for years before that. She knew a creeper when she met one. The Leerer positioned himself up against her on purpose. He'd wanted to touch her. Expected she'd shrink away.

Well, he wouldn't get what he wanted. Not from her.

She spun around, ready to ask him to repeat those words, partly so Crystal would hear and keep him out of the bar. But he spared her that trouble, already marching down the street, past the closed stores with their blackened windows, fists clenched at his sides, taking with him his downright *off* energy.

Or at least, so she thought.

She pushed past Crystal and back into the bar. This night was turning out too long and weird for her liking. Time to go home. She crossed the darkened space, with its red-tinged lighting and boisterous patrons, only to catch sight of one of her bar staff clutching his hand.

Blood poured from his enclosed fingers, a glass having shattered in his grasp. She picked up her pace and came at him with a clean wad of paper towels from the counter, ordering him and the bar manager to the back where the first aid kit lived. No way would that employee be returning for his shifts any time soon, so she tended bar till the manager returned, then stayed back even longer to rejig the week's roster.

By the time two a.m. rolled around, and like an idiot who didn't know better, she exited The Ruby Room alone, her attention buried on the stack of fresh messages on her phone. She'd already ambled a few meters from The Ruby's doors, when a sick sensation surged through her tummy, urging her to stop.

No.

The feeling was less *sick,* more *off.*

The feeling offered a premonition, or maybe a warning; she jerked up her chin, but too late. The Creeper from earlier stared at her from across the sidewalk, his back against a banged-up blue van. The super wide pavement meant she stood closer to him than the bar, too far to double back inside, with zero chance of anyone in The Ruby spotting her.

She could scream.

Would anyone inside hear her over the music?

That only left running forward, toward him. Sure as shit not an enticing option, nor was running to her car since she didn't have one. The Creeper didn't even bother to give her a typical, sleazy scowl or an uptick of his lip to spell out his ill intentions. What he offered was worse—a flat stare, soulless and as dead as a long-departed snake.

His hand rested over his crotch, its placement by no means an accident. She darted her gaze to the rusted blue van behind him, his foot pressed against the open door's edge. An aching silence made a sudden coldness rush her body. The sharp night air cut down to her bones.

He would grab her. He would shove her into that van, and no one would see.

A sob broke from her lips. Any second now, the terrified tears would start—a big feat since she pretty much never cried. The Creeper pushed away from the van and took a step toward her, not even giving her the credit of being quick with this attempted kidnapping.

His slow and snake-like movements gave the impression he'd done this before. *Gotten away with this before.* He tipped his head to one side, and the wrinkles over his cheek bones settled, as if he savored the expression on her face. Her open fear.

A loud crash sent more ice through her veins, and she startled as The Ruby Room's doors burst open. The Creeper's expression turned hard, and his stare flicked off her to a point in the background. Modern jazz fused with dance, The Ruby's door always slow to draw shut. Next came the crack of laughter and a jovial male voice calling goodbye to his friends.

Her heart sprung to a wild and racing gallop, the sudden ray of hope twisting another sob through her chest.

Fuck this guy.

He wouldn't get her tears.

She spun around to whoever had just left The Ruby. The millionaire surfer!

The guy already powered away from her, his hands jammed in his pants pockets, his rapid and fading footsteps like claws digging into her heart.

Well, fuck him too.

"Hey, Marcus!" Her voice wobbled, but rang true enough; whether surfer guy liked it or not, she'd make him part of this showdown. "Where are you going?"

Her entire twenties had been spent yelling at people from across noisy bars, so she had friendly yelling down to an art form. Of course, surfer guy's name probably wasn't Marcus, so he didn't turn around, though for the literal life of her, she couldn't remember what his real name was.

"Hey, asshole!" She took a risk and ran after him. "Marcus, are you fucking drunk again?"

This time he did stop, and he spun around, a single brow raised, as if to say, *Who you calling an asshole?*

She caught up to him, plastering on her biggest fake smile and looping her arm through his. "You weren't just about to leave without me, were you?"

She fluttered her eyelashes, hoping the over-dramatic approach would tip him off enough to play along; though her frothy blond curls, Betty Boop dress, and their earlier eyeballing probably only worked to make her look like some kind of psycho-clinger, hoping to nab herself a millionaire pretty-boy.

Maybe when this whole thing was over, and if she got out alive, she would find a moment to puke at that idea.

Surfer guy frowned down at her arm on his. "Who's Marcus? My name's Max. What's wrong with you?"

His cool British accent caught her momentarily off guard, since she'd seen him so many times and never once swapped a single word. But now, she narrowed her eyes, a voice inside her head screaming, *Fucking catch on, you sun-affected doofus!*

But she held onto the charade, because her life depended on it, and gave a bright, air-headed giggle.

"Oh, shut up, you big dope." She gave Max's arm a playful smack, though the space between her shoulders burned with The Creeper's stare.

If Max dropped her, The Creeper would swoop in.

Her leg muscles felt weak, and a pain dug into her gut. Maybe it was time to lose the bimbo act. The man she clung to didn't seem all that quick on the uptake.

So, she rested her head to his bicep, making it seem from the outside that she might be his girlfriend, all while dispensing her situation's harsher truth.

"Please. Just play along, okay?"

Purchase *The Last in Line* to indulge in this journey today!
katerinasimms.com/the-last-in-line *OR* use this QR CODE:

Also by Katerina Simms

The Love at Last Series:

The Last Heartbeat — Love at Last, Book 1

The Last Place You Look — Love at Last, Book 2

The Last in Line — Love at Last, Book 3

The Harlow Series:

Sapphires and Secrets — The Harlow Series, Book 1

Secret Surrender — The Harlow Series, Book 2

Second Hand Secrets – The Harlow Series, Book 3

Small Town Secrets – The Harlow Series, Book 4

For a complete list of releases, go to:

https://katerinasimms.com/books

About the Author

Katerina Simms is a contemporary romance author, RWA Emerald Award finalist, and International North Street Book Prize semi-finalist. She was born on a sunny Mediterranean island, only to move to the weather-challenged suburbs of Melbourne, Australia.

Tea addict, nature lover, and terrible gardener, Katerina's novels feature vivid modern settings and heart-stirring characters, punctuated with the occasional good laugh. Her romances skirt the edges of women's fiction, and her favorite tropes are opposites attract, slow burn, and heat with heart.

www.katerinasimms.com

Acknowledgments

The day Orlando Piras came to my life, he didn't even need to speak a word to convince me he deserved his own book. He entered my mind on a dream, a man with an unwavering, direct stare. He looked at me from across a table, so dark and haunting. That stare put me on a path of unearthing exactly who this man was and what his story would be. Of course, there are always pieces of me in every character, and Orlando and Sophie are no exception. Similar to Orlando, I've had the experience of feeling trapped in an ailing body, convinced I would remain trapped forever. Just like Orlando, I was exceptionally lucky to escape. And still, if only all inspiration came so easily!

I want to start my gratitude list with my thanks to my wonderful friend, Amanda. Her willingness to share her priceless knowledge and experience as a paramedic has shaped the course of my stories on so many occasions. She's delightfully patient with my questions, and doesn't always tell me what I want to hear. Having to accommodate those hard facts always results in a richer tale. That said, I take full ownership of any shaky factoids in this book and bending of truths. Please don't blame poor Amanda. It's all my fault! Either way, thanks million. I'm so lucky to call you a friend (and not just because of the brain picking)!

Special mentions as always go to my editor Chris Hall of The Editing Hall, my proofreader extraordinaire (and fellow author) Jen Katemi, and my cover designer Sarah Paige, of Opium House. I'm so thankful to have such a reliable team behind my work.

And of course, HUGE thank you to my readers, fans, newsletter subscribers, and reviewers. The arts and artists need more people like you. You keep our imaginary worlds turning.

Thank you, Everyone. I mean it.

X Katerina

How About A Review?

Authors love reviews, and good ones help us make a living, and thus write more books! If you've enjoyed this book, please consider leaving a review on Goodreads or your retailer of choice. Just a line or two would make a wonderful difference!

Eternally grateful,

Katerina Simms